Gaston Leroux

French journalist and writer of suspense fiction Gaston Leroux was born in Paris in 1868. His experiences as a crime reporter and war correspondent for a French newspaper gave him the background to create his popular novels. He was one of the originators of the detective story, and his young fictional detective, Joseph Rouletabile, was the forerunner of many reporter-detective characters in modern fiction. Two of Leroux's best-known mysteries are *The Perfume of the Lady in Black* and *The Mystery of the Yellow Room*, which is considered one of the finest "locked room" mysteries ever written. A second series of suspense adventures featured an old rascal named Cheri-Bibi. But Leroux's most enduring work is, of course, *The Phantom of the Opera*, which was first published in 1911. Leroux died in Nice, France, in 1927.

Bantam Classics
Ask your bookseller for these other World Classics

THE BHAGAVAD-GITA (translated by Barbara Stoler Miller)

CHEKHOV: FIVE MAJOR PLAYS, Anton Chekhov
A DOCTOR'S VISIT: SHORT STORIES by Anton Chekhov

THE INFERNO, Dante (translated by Allen Mandelbaum)
PURGATORIO, Dante (translated by Allen Mandelbaum)
PARADISO, Dante (translated by Allen Mandelbaum)

THE BROTHERS KARAMAZOV, Fyodor Dostoevsky
CRIME AND PUNISHMENT, Fyodor Dostoevsky
THE IDIOT, Fyodor Dostoevsky
NOTES FROM UNDERGROUND, Fyodor Dostoevsky

THE COUNT OF MONTE CRISTO, Alexandre Dumas
THE THREE MUSKETEERS, Alexandre Dumas

MADAME BOVARY, Gustave Flaubert

FAUST, Johann Wolfgang von Goethe

THE COMPLETE FAIRY TALES OF THE BROTHERS GRIMM
   (translated by Jack Zipes)

THE HUNCHBACK OF NOTRE DAME, Victor Hugo

FOUR GREAT PLAYS, Henrik Ibsen

THE METAMORPHOSIS, Franz Kafka

LES LIAISONS DANGEREUSES, Pierre Choderlos de Laclos

THE PRINCE, Niccolo Machiavelli

CYRANO DE BERGERAC, Edmond Rostand

THE RED AND THE BLACK, Marie-Henri Beyle de Stendhal

ANNA KARENINA, Leo Tolstoy
THE DEATH OF IVAN ILYICH, Leo Tolstoy

FATHERS AND SONS, Ivan Turgenev

AROUND THE WORLD IN EIGHTY DAYS, Jules Verne
20,000 LEAGUES UNDER THE SEA, Jules Verne

CANDIDE, Voltaire

DEATH IN VENICE, Thomas Mann (translated by David Luke)

The Phantom of the Opera
by Gaston Leroux

Translated by Lowell Bair

BANTAM BOOKS

NEW YORK · TORONTO · LONDON · SYDNEY · AUCKLAND

THE PHANTOM OF THE OPERA

A Bantam Book

PUBLISHING HISTORY

Le Fantome de l'Opera *was first published in Paris in 1910*

Bantam Classic edition / February 1990

ISBN 0-553-21376-8

Published simultaneously in the United States and Canada

Bantam Books are published by Bantam Books, a division of Bantam Doubleday Dell Publishing Group, Inc. Its trademark, consisting of the words "Bantam Books" and the portrayal of a rooster, is Registered in U.S. Patent and Trademark Office and in other countries. Marca Registrada. Bantam Books, 1540 Broadway, New York, New York 10036.

PRINTED IN THE UNITED STATES OF AMERICA

OPM   30 29 28 27 26 25 24 23 22

Contents

Foreword, In Which the Author of This Singular Work Tells the Reader How He Was Led to Become Certain that the Opera Ghost Really Existed   1

1   Was It the Ghost?   6

2   The New Marguerite   16

3   In Which, for the First Time, Debienne and Poligny Secretly Give the New Managers of the Opera, Armand Moncharmin and Firmin Richard, the Real and Mysterious Reason for Their Departure from the National Academy of Music   27

4   Box Five   34

5   Continuation of ''Box Five''   42

6   The Enchanted Violin   49

7   A Visit to Box Five   67

8   In Which Firmin Richard and Armand Moncharmin Dare to Have *Faust* Performed in a ''Cursed'' Opera House, and We See the Frightful Consequences   70

9   The Mysterious Brougham   86

10   At the Masked Ball   95

11   You Must Forget the Name of ''the Man's Voice''   106

12   Above the Trapdoors   111

13   Apollo's Lyre   120

14   A Masterstroke by the Lover of Trapdoors   143

15   The Singular Behavior of a Safety Pin   154

16   ''Christine! Christine!''   160

17   Astonishing Revelations by Madame Giry, Concerning Her Personal Relations with the Opera Ghost   164

18 Continuation of "The Singular Behavior of a Safety Pin" 175

19 The Policeman, the Viscount, and the Persian 181

20 The Viscount and the Persian 187

21 In the Cellars of the Opera 194

22 Interesting and Instructive Tribulations of a Persian in the Cellars of the Opera 210

23 In the Torture Chamber 225

24 The Tortures Begin 232

25 "Barrels! Barrels! Any Barrels to Sell?" 238

26 The Scorpion or the Grasshopper? 248

27 End of the Ghost's Love Story 257

Epilogue 266

The Phantom of
the Opera

FOREWORD
In Which the Author of This Singular Work Tells the Reader How He Was Led to Become Certain that the Opera Ghost Really Existed

THE GHOST IN the Paris Opera existed. He was not, as was long believed, a delusion of the singers, a superstition of the managers, or a ludicrous fantasy concocted by the overheated brains of the dancers in the corps de ballet, their mothers, the ushers, the cloakroom attendants, and the concierge.

Yes, he existed in flesh and blood, even though he gave himself every appearance of a real ghost, a true phantom.

When I first began going through the archives of the National Academy of Music, I was struck by the astonishing correlations between the phenomena attributed to the ghost and the mysterious, fantastic tragedy that occurred at the same time, and I was soon led to the idea that the tragedy could perhaps be rationally explained by the phenomena.

The events in question go back only thirty years, and in the dancers' lounge at the Opera it would still not be hard to find respectable old people of unquestionable honesty who remember, as if it were only yesterday, the mysterious and tragic circumstances surrounding the abduction of Christine Daaé, the disappearance of Viscount Raoul de Chagny, and the death of his older brother, Count Philippe, whose body was found on the shore of the lake that lies beneath the Opera in the direction of the Rue Scribe. But none of those witnesses ever thought that the more or less legendary Opera ghost was involved in that terrible calamity.

I was slow to realize the truth because my mind was troubled by an investigation that kept coming up against seemingly unearthly events. More than once I was on the verge of giving up an endeavor in which I exhausted myself pursuing a vain image without ever grasping it. Finally I had proof that my intuition had not deceived me, and all my efforts were rewarded on the day when I became certain that the Opera ghost had been more than an apparition.

On that day, I had spent long hours poring over *Memoirs of a Manager,* a lightweight book by the overly skeptical Armand Moncharmin, who, during his time at the Opera, understood nothing about the ghost's bewildering actions; he was vigorously making fun of them at the very time when he became the first victim of the curious financial operation that took place inside the "magic envelope."

Feeling disheartened, I had just left the library when I met the charming administrator of our National Academy. He was on the landing, talking with a lively, elegantly dressed little old man to whom he cheerfully introduced me. The administrator was aware of my research and knew how impatiently I had tried, in vain, to discover the whereabouts of Monsieur Faure, the examining magistrate in the famous Chagny case. No one had known what had become of him, or even if he was dead or alive; now he was just back from Canada, where he had spent fifteen years, and the first thing he had done in Paris was to come to the secretariat of the Opera to get a complimentary ticket. That little old man was Monsieur Faure himself.

We spent a good part of the evening together and he told me all about the Chagny case as he had understood it. He had had to conclude, for lack of evidence, that the viscount was insane and that his older brother's death was accidental, but he remained convinced that a terrible tragedy had taken place between the two brothers with regard to Christine Daaé. He was unable to tell me what had become of her or the viscount. And of course he only laughed when I mentioned the ghost. He too had been told about the singular happenings which seemed to indicate that some sort of supernatural being had taken up residence in one of the most obscure parts of the Opera, and he knew the story of the "magic envelope," but in all this, he felt, there was nothing that required the attention of a magistrate investigating the Chagny case. All he had done about it was to listen for a few moments to the testimony of a witness who had come forward of his own accord to say that he had met the ghost. This witness was none other than the man called the Persian in fashionable Paris society. He was well-known to all of the Opera's subscribers. The magistrate decided he was a lunatic.

As you can well imagine, I was prodigiously interested in what Monsieur Faure said about the Persian. I wanted to find that precious original witness, if it was not yet too late. My good luck prevailed and I discovered him in the little apartment on the Rue de Rivoli where he still lived, and where he died five months after my visit.

At first I was skeptical, but I could no longer have any doubts when the Persian told me, with childlike candor, everything he personally knew about the ghost, and when he gave me full possession of proofs of his existence, as well as Christine Daae's strange correspondence, which cast a glaringly bright light on his appalling destiny. No, the ghost was not a myth!

I was told, of course, that some of that correspondence might not be genuine and that all of it might have been fabricated by a man whose imagination had surely been nourished by enchanting tales, but fortunately I was able to find samples of Christine's handwriting outside of the famous packet of letters; I then made a comparative study that removed all uncertainty.

I also found out as much as I could about the Persian and concluded that he was an honest man incapable of contriving a machination that might mislead justice.

And this was also the opinion of the family friends, all prominent people, who were directly or indirectly involved in the Chagny affair. I showed them all my documents and explained all my deductions to them. They gave me generous encouragement. In this connection, I will take the liberty of quoting what General D. wrote to me:

Dear Sir,

I cannot urge you too strongly to make public the results of your investigation. I clearly remember that several weeks before the disappearance of the great singer Christine Daaé and the tragedy that saddened everyone in the Faubourg Saint-Germain, there was a great deal of talk in the dancers' lounge about the "ghost," and I believe that the talk continued until everyone's mind became occupied with the tragedy I have mentioned. But if it is possible, as I believe it is, after having heard you, to explain the tragedy by means of the ghost, I hope you will tell us more about the ghost. However mysterious he may seem at first, he will always be more explainable than that dark affair in which spiteful people tried to create deadly enmity between two brothers who had loved each other all their lives.

I remain, etc.

Finally, with my evidence in hand, I went all over the ghost's vast domain, the majestic building that he had turned into his empire, and the Persian's documents were corroborated by everything my eyes saw and my mind perceived: Then a marvelous discovery decisively completed my work.

It will be recalled that recently, when workmen were digging in the basement of the Opera to bury phonographic recordings of singers' voices, they uncovered a skeleton. As soon as I saw it, I had proof that it was the skeleton of the Opera ghost! I had the administrator of the Opera touch that proof with his own hand, and now it does not matter to me that the newspapers say the skeleton belonged to a victim of the Commune.

The poor people who were slaughtered in the cellars of the Opera at the time of the Commune are not buried on that side; I will later tell where their skeletons can be found, far away from the immense crypt where all sorts of provisions were stored during the siege. I came upon them when I was searching for the remains of the Opera ghost, which I would not have found if it had not been for the highly unlikely circumstance of living voices being buried.

But I will come back to that skeleton and the question of what should be done with it. I must now end this very necessary foreword by thanking those who modestly played secondary roles in the drama but were of great help to me, such as Police

Commissary Mifroid, who made the preliminary investigation after Christine Daae's disappearance; Monsieur Rémy, the former secretary; Monsieur Mercier, the former administrator; Monsieur Gabriel, the former chorus master; and particularly Baroness de Castelot-Barbezac, who was once "little Meg" (and is not ashamed of it), the brightest star in our admirable corps de ballet and the older daughter of the honorable Madame Giry, now deceased, who was the usher of the ghost's box. Because of them, the reader and I will now be able to relive those hours of terror and pure love in all their details.*

*I would be an ingrate if, at the outset of this true and frightful story, I did not also thank the present management of the Opera, who so graciously cooperated with me in all my investigations, and in particular Monsieur Messager; also the very kind administrator, Monsieur Gabion, and the very obliging architect in charge of the building's preservation, who did not hesitate to lend me the works of Charles Garnier even though he was nearly certain that I would not give them back. Finally, I wish to publicly acknowledge the generosity of my friend and former collaborator J.-L. Croze, who allowed me to draw on the resources of his splendid theatrical library and lent me rare editions that he valued very highly.   G.L.

1

Was It the Ghost?

IT WAS THE evening when Monsieur Debienne and Monsieur Poligny, the outgoing managers of the Paris Opera, gave their last gala performance on the occasion of their departure. The dressing room of La Sorelli, one of the leading ballerinas, was suddenly invaded by half a dozen members of the corps de ballet who had just left the stage after "dancing" *Polyeucte*. They rushed into the room in great confusion, some laughing wildly and unnaturally, others uttering cries of terror.

Wanting to be alone for a few minutes to rehearse the speech she would soon give before Debienne and Poligny in the lounge, La Sorelli had been irritated at seeing that throng of overwrought young women come in behind her. She turned to them and asked the reason for their agitation. Little Jammes—a nose of the kind dear to Grévin, eyes the color of blue forget-me-nots, rosy cheeks, a lily-white bosom—explained it in three words, her voice choked and quavering with anxiety:

"It's the ghost!"

And she locked the door.

La Sorelli's dressing room had an official, commonplace elegance. The necessary furniture was composed of a full-length mirror mounted on swivels, a couch, a dressing table, and wardrobes. A few engravings on the walls, souvenirs of her mother, who had known the glorious days of the old Opera House on the Rue Le Peletier. Portraits of Vestris, Gardel, Dupont, and Bigottini. This dressing room seemed like a palace to those girls who were lodged in shared rooms where they spent their time singing, quarreling, pummeling the hairdressers and dressers, and buying each other little glasses of beer or black currant liqueur, or even rum, until the callboy rang his bell.

La Sorelli was very superstitious. When she heard little Jammes mention the ghost, she shuddered and said, "You little fool!"

And since she was the first to believe in ghosts in general, and the Opera ghost in particular, she wanted more information.

"Did you see him?" she asked.

"As plainly as I see you!" little Jammes answered with a moan. Her legs buckled and she let herself fall onto a chair.

And little Giry—dark eyes, jet-black hair, a swarthy complexion, her poor little skin clinging to her bones—immediately said, "If that was the ghost, he's really ugly!"

"Oh, yes!" the other dancers exclaimed in unison.

And they all talked at once. The ghost had appeared to them in the guise of a gentleman in a black swallow-tailed coat who suddenly stood before them in the hall, without anyone's having seen where he came from. He had appeared so abruptly that it was as if he had come out of the wall.

"Oh, you see ghosts everywhere!" said one of the dancers who had more or less kept a cool head.

And it was true that for several months everyone in the Opera had been talking about that ghost in evening dress. He moved all through the building like a shadow, spoke to no one (and no one dared speak to him), and vanished as soon as he was seen, so quickly that no one could say how he did it or where he had gone. As was proper for a real ghost, he made no sound when he walked. At first, everyone had laughed and joked about that phantom dressed as a man about town or an undertaker, but his legend soon took on colossal proportions within the corps de ballet. The dancers all claimed to have met him in one way or another, and to have been victims of his evil spells. And those who laughed the loudest were not the least apprehensive. When he did not let himself be seen, he indicated his presence by comical happenings for which he was held responsible by the superstition that nearly everyone shared. An accident, a lost powder puff, a practical joke played on a dancer by one of her friends—it was all the fault of the ghost, the phantom of the Opera!

Actually, who had seen him? At the Opera there are so many men in black swallow-tailed coats who are not ghosts! But this black swallow-tailed coat differed from others in one respect: it was worn by a skeleton. Or at least that was what the dancers said. And the skeleton, of course, had a death's-head.

Did all this deserve to be taken seriously? The truth is that the idea of a skeleton arose from a description of the ghost given by Joseph Buquet, the chief stagehand, who had really seen him. He had come face to face with him on the little staircase that begins near the footlights and goes down to the "cellars." He had seen him for only a second before the ghost hurried away, but that second had made an indelible impression on him.

And here is what Joseph Buquet said about the ghost to anyone willing to listen:

"He's incredibly thin; his black coat hangs loosely on his bony body. His eyes stare straight ahead, without moving, and they're so deep-set that you can hardly see them. All you really see is two dark holes, like the ones in a skull. His skin is tight as a drum. It's not white, but an ugly yellow. His nose is so small you can't see it when you look at him from the side, and that absence of a nose is something horrible to see. The only hair he has is three or four long, dark locks that hang down over his forehead and behind his ears."

He had vainly tried to catch that strange apparition. It had disappeared as though by magic and he had been unable to find any trace of it.

This chief stagehand was a serious, steady man with a slow imagination, and he was sober. His words were listened to with astonishment and interest. Several other people immediately began saying that they too had encountered an apparition in evening dress, with a face like a death's-head.

At first, sensible people who heard Joseph Buquet's story said he had been the victim of a practical joke by one of his subordinates. Then, one after another, came incidents so curious and inexplicable that even the shrewdest skeptics were shaken.

A fireman is brave. He fears nothing, and certainly not fire!

The fireman in question,* a lieutenant, went to make a tour of inspection in the cellars and, it seems, ventured a little farther than usual. He suddenly reappeared in the auditorium, pale, trembling, and bewildered, with his eyes bulging almost out of

---

*This true story was told to me by Pedro Gailhard, the former manager of the Opera.

their sockets, and he nearly fainted in the arms of little Jammes's noble mother. And why? Because he had seen a head of fire, without a body, coming toward him at eye level. And, I repeat, a fireman is not afraid of fire!

This fireman's name was Papin.

The corps de ballet was in consternation. First of all, that head of fire did not at all match the description of the ghost given by Joseph Buquet. The fireman was carefully questioned, and Joseph Buquet was questioned once again; the dancers were then convinced that the ghost had several heads and changed them at will. They naturally imagined that they were in grave danger. Since a fireman, and a lieutenant at that, had not hesitated to faint, the ballerinas and student dancers found ample excuses for the terror that made them run as fast as their legs could carry them whenever they had to pass by a patch of darkness in a dimly lighted hall.

And so, on the day after the fireman had told his story, La Sorelli decided to give as much protection as possible to the building that had come under such an evil spell. Surrounded by all the dancers, and even followed by the whole body of younger pupils in tights, she went to the doorkeeper's vestibule, near the administration courtyard, and put a horseshoe on the table there. Everyone, other than spectators, who came into the Opera was expected to touch that horseshoe before starting up the stairs. Anyone who failed to do so would risk becoming a victim of the dark power that had taken possession of the building, from the cellars to the attic.

I have not invented that horseshoe—or anything else in this story, unfortunately—and it can still be seen on the table in the vestibule, in front of the doorkeeper's quarters, when one comes into the Opera by way of the administration courtyard.

All this will give some idea of the dancers' state of mind when they went into La Sorelli's dressing room.

"It was the ghost!" little Jammes had exclaimed, and the dancers' anxiety had increased still more.

Now there was an agonizing silence in the room, broken only by the sound of rapid breathing. Finally, showing genuine fear, Jammes ran to the farthest corner and murmured a single word:

"Listen!"

It seemed to everyone that a rustling sound was coming from the other side of the door. No footsteps. It was as if light silk cloth were sliding across the door. Then there was nothing. La Sorelli tried to be less fainthearted than her companions. She went to the door and asked in a toneless voice, "Who's there?"

But no one answered.

Feeling all eyes watching her slightest movements, she forced herself to be brave and asked very loudly, "Is there someone out there in the hall?"

"Oh, yes, of course there is!" said the swarthy little Meg Giry, heroically holding La Sorelli by her gauze skirt. "Don't open the door! My God, don't open it!"

But La Sorelli, armed with a stiletto that was always with her, dared to unlock the door and open it while the dancers retreated into the bathroom and Meg Giry gasped, "Mama! Mama!"

La Sorelli courageously looked out into the hall. It was empty; a gaslight, like a butterfly of fire in a glass prison, cast a grim red glow into the surrounding shadows without succeeding in dissipating them. With a heavy sigh, La Sorelli quickly closed the door again.

"No," she said, "there's no one there."

"But we *saw* him!" Jammes insisted, coming back to La Sorelli with timorous little steps. "He must be prowling around here somewhere. I'm not going back to get dressed. We should all go down to the lounge together right now, for the speech, and come back up together."

She piously touched the little coral finger that was meant to ward off bad luck. And, with the tip of her pink right thumbnail, La Sorelli furtively drew a St. Andrew's cross on the wooden ring that encircled the third finger of her left hand.

A famous newspaper columnist once wrote the following:

La Sorelli is a great dancer, a beautiful woman with a grave, voluptuous face and a body as supple as a willow branch; it is commonly said of her that she is "a lovely creature." Her head sways gently, like an egret plume, on a long, proud, elegant neck. When she dances, her hips have a certain indescribable movement that gives her whole body a quiver of ineffable languor. When she raises her arms and bends to begin a pirouette, thus accentuating the lines of her bust and making her hip stand out, the sight is said to be enough to make a man blow his brains out from unfulfilled desire.

As far as brains are concerned, it seems well established that she had almost none. No one held it against her.

"You must get a grip on yourselves, girls!" she said to the little dancers. "The ghost? Maybe no one has ever seen him!"

"*We* saw him," one of the girls protested, "with his black coat and his death's-head, the way he was when Joseph Buquet saw him!"

"And Gabriel saw him too, only yesterday," said Jammes, "yesterday afternoon, in broad daylight!"

"Gabriel the chorus master?"

"Of course. You mean you didn't know about it?"

"And he was in evening dress, in broad daylight?"

"Who? Gabriel?"

"No, no, the ghost!"

"That's right, he was in evening dress," said Jammes. "Gabriel told me so himself. That's how he recognized him, in fact. Here's how it happened: Gabriel was in the stage manager's office. All at once the door opened and the Persian came in. You know the Persian has the evil eye. . . ."

"Oh, yes!" the little dancers all exclaimed together, and as soon as each of them saw a mental image of the Persian she protected herself from his evil eye by raising her hand and making a pair of horns, extending her forefinger and little finger while her thumb held her other two fingers against her palm.

"And you know how superstitious Gabriel is!" Jammes went on. "He's polite, though, and usually when he sees the Persian he just puts his hand in his pocket and touches his keys. But this time it was different: as soon as he saw the Persian come in, he jumped up from his chair and ran to the lock on the closet door to touch iron. When he did that, he caught his coat on a nail and made a big rip in it. And he was in such a hurry to leave that he banged into a hat peg and gave himself a huge lump on the forehead. Then he quickly stepped backward and scraped his arm on the folding screen by the piano. He tried to lean on the piano but he didn't watch what he was doing and the keyboard cover fell down hard on his fingers. He dashed out of the office like a madman, stumbled on the stairs and slid all the way down on his back. My mother and I were passing by just then. We hurried to help him stand up. We were scared when we saw how he looked: he was battered and bruised, and there was blood all over his face. But he smiled at us and said, 'Thank God I got off with so

little damage!' Then we questioned him and he told us why he'd
been afraid: it was because he'd seen the ghost behind the
Persian, the ghost with the death's-head, the way Joseph Buquet
described him.''

Jammes had spoken so rapidly, as if the ghost were after her,
that she was breathless by the time she came to the end of her
story. It was greeted by a frightened murmur, followed by
another silence, during which La Sorelli feverishly polished her
fingernails.

''Joseph Buquet should keep quiet,'' Meg Giry said in an
undertone.

''Why should he?'' she was asked.

''That's what my mother thinks,'' she replied, lowering her
voice still more and looking around her as if she were afraid of
being heard by ears other than those she could see.

''And why does your mother think so?''

''Not so loud! She says the ghost doesn't like to be bothered.''

''And why does she say that?''

''Because . . . Because . . . Nothing.''

This skillfully expressed reticence goaded the dancers' curiosity. They crowded around Meg and begged her to explain herself. Standing there elbow-to-elbow, leaning forward in a single
entreaty, they transmitted their fear to each other and took keen,
chilling pleasure in it.

''I swore not to tell!'' Meg whispered.

But they continued their urgent pleas and promised secrecy so
convincingly that Meg, who was dying to tell what she knew,
looked intently at the door and began:

''All right. . . . It's because of the box. . . .''

''What box?''

''The ghost's box, here in the Opera.''

''The ghost has a box?''

At this idea that the ghost had his own private box, the
dancers gasped with amazement and a kind of somber joy.

''Oh! Tell us! Tell us about it!''

''Not so loud!'' Meg ordered again. ''It's Box Five. You
know, the one next to the stage box in the first left tier.''

''Really?''

''Yes, really. My mother is the usher in charge of it. But you
swear you won't tell, don't you?''

''Of course!''

"Well, that's the ghost's box. No one has been in it for more than a month—no one but the ghost, that is—and orders have been given that it's never to be rented again."

"And it's true that the ghost comes there?"

"Yes, it is."

"Then *someone* comes into the box."

"The ghost comes into it, but there's no one there."

The little dancers looked at one another. If the ghost came into the box, it should be possible to see him, since he wore a black swallow-tailed coat and had a death's-head.

They said this to Meg, but she answered, "No, it's *not* possible to see him! He doesn't have a black coat or a head. You've heard about his death's-head and his head of fire, but that's all nonsense. He doesn't have anything. . . . He's heard only when he's in the box. My mother has never seen him, but she's heard him. She knows he can't be seen because she's the one who gives him the program!"

La Sorelli felt it was time for her to intervene.

"Meg, you don't really expect us to believe that silly story, do you?"

Meg burst into tears.

"I should have kept my mouth shut! If my mother ever finds out . . . But Joseph Buquet is wrong to stick his nose into things that are none of his business. It will bring him bad luck. My mother said so last night."

Just then they all heard heavy, rapid footsteps in the hall, and a breathless voice shouting, "Cécile! Cécile! Are you there?"

"That's my mother!" said little Jammes. "What can be the matter?"

She opened the door. A respectable-looking lady, built like a Pomeranian grenadier, burst into the dressing room and sank into an armchair with a groan. Her eyes rolled wildly, seeming to illuminate her brick-colored face in an ominous way.

"It's horrible!" she said.

"What's horrible?"

"Joseph Buquet . . . He's . . ."

"He's what?"

"He's dead!"

The room was filled with exclamations, astonished protests, and frightened requests for explanation.

"Yes. . . . He was just found in the third cellar, hanged,"

continued the poor honorable lady, breathing heavily. "But the most terrible part of it is that the stagehands who found his body claim that all around it they heard a sound like the singing of the dead!"

"The ghost did it!" cried Meg Giry. The words seemed to have slipped out against her will. She immediately put her fists in front of her mouth. "No, no, I didn't say anything! I didn't say anything!"

Around her, all her companions were repeating in voices lowered by terror, "Yes! Yes! It was the ghost!"

La Sorelli was pale.

"Now I'll never be able to give my speech," she said.

Little Jammes's mother stated her opinion as she emptied a glass of liqueur that had been left on the table: "The ghost must have had something to do with it."

The fact is that the way Joseph Buquet died never became known. The brief investigation gave no result, except for a conclusion of "natural suicide." In his *Memoirs of a Manager*, Moncharmin, one of the two managers who succeeded Debienne and Poligny, gives this account of Buquet's death:

An unfortunate incident disturbed the little celebration that Debienne and Poligny gave on the occasion of their departure. I was in the managerial office when Mercier, the administrator, suddenly came in. Panic-stricken, he told me that the body of a stagehand had just been found, hanged, in the third cellar, between a flat and a set piece from *Le Roi de Lahore*.

"Let's go and take him down," I said.

By the time I had hurried down the stairs and the ladder, the hanged man had already lost his rope!

Here, then, is a series of events that seems natural to Moncharmin: a man is hanged at the end of a rope, Moncharmin goes to take him down, and the rope has disappeared. He found a simple explanation. Listen to him: "It was during the time of the ballet; the ballerinas and student dancers had quickly taken their precautions against the evil eye." Period, end of explanation. Just imagine the corps de ballet scrambling down the ladder and dividing up the hanged man's rope in less time than it takes to write about it! No, that idea does not deserve to be taken seriously. But when I consider the exact place where the body was found, in the third cellar below the stage, I think that someone might have had an interest in having the rope disappear after it had served its purpose, and we will see later whether or not I am right in thinking so.

The sinister news quickly spread all over the Opera, where Joseph Buquet had been greatly liked. The dressing rooms emptied and the little dancers, grouped around La Sorelli like frightened sheep around their shepherd, headed for the lounge, trotting along dimly lighted halls and staircases as fast as their pink little legs could carry them.

2

The New Marguerite

On the first landing, La Sorelli ran into Count de Chagny as he was coming up. The count, ordinarily so calm, now showed signs of great excitement.

"I was on my way to your dressing room," he said, gallantly bowing to the young woman. "Ah, Sorelli, what a wonderful evening! And for Christine Daaé, what a triumph!"

"Impossible!" protested Meg Giry. "Six months ago, she sang like a rusty hinge! But please let us pass, my dear count," she continued with a pert curtsy, "we're going to try to find out more about a poor man who was found hanged."

Just then the administrator was busily hurrying past. He stopped abruptly when he heard Meg's last words.

"What! You ladies already know about it?" he said rather gruffly. "Well, don't talk about it—and make sure Monsieur Debienne and Monsieur Poligny don't hear about it! It would cause them too much sorrow on their last day."

They all went off to the dancers' lounge, which was already crowded.

Count de Chagny was right: no other gala performance was ever comparable to that one. The privileged people who attended it still tell their children and grandchildren about it with deep emotion. Think of it: Gounod, Reyer, Saint-Saëns, Massenet, Guiraud, and Delibes all went before the orchestra, one after another, and personally conducted some of their works. Faure and Krauss were among the performers, and that was the evening when fashionable Paris society was amazed and enraptured by

16

the discovery of Christine Daaé, whose mysterious destiny I intend to describe in this book.

Gounod conducted *La marche funèbre d'une marionnette;* Reyer, his beautiful overture to *Sigurd;* Saint-Saëns, *La danse macabre* and a *Rêverie orientale;* Massenet, a *Marche hongroise inédite;* Guiraud, his *Carnaval;* Delibes, the *Valse lente* from *Sylvia* and the pizzicati from *Coppélia.* Marie Gabriele Krauss and Denise Bloch sang: the former, the bolero from *Sicilian Vespers;* the latter, the brindisi from *Lucrezia Borgia.*

But it was Christine Daaé who had the greatest triumph. She began by singing a few passages from Gounod's *Roméo et Juliette.* This was the first time she had sung anything from that work. It had not yet been produced at the Opera, and the Opéra-Comique had just revived it long after Madame Carvalho's appearance in its opening performance at the old Théâtre-Lyrique. We must pity those who never heard Christine Daaé in the role of Juliet, who never knew her guileless charm, who never thrilled to the accents of her angelic voice, who never felt their soul soar with hers above the graves of the lovers of Verona: "Lord! Lord! Lord! Forgive us!"

Yet that was nothing compared with the superhuman performance she gave in the prison scene and the final trio in *Faust,* which she sang in place of Carlotta, who was ill. No one had ever heard or seen anything like it! It was "the new Marguerite" that Christine had revealed, a Marguerite with a previously unsuspected splendor and radiance.

The wildly enthusiastic audience paid thunderous tribute to Christine while she sobbed and finally fainted in the arms of her companions. Seemingly lifeless, she had to be carried back to her dressing room.

The great critic P. de St-V. preserved the memory of that marvelous evening in an article that he entitled "The New Marguerite." Being a great artist as well, he was aware that that sweet and beautiful girl had brought more than her art to the stage of the Opera: she had also brought her heart. All friends of the Opera knew that her heart had remained as pure as at the age of fifteen, and P. de St-V. wrote that in order to understand what had happened to her, he had "to assume that she had just fallen in love for the first time." And he continued:

I am perhaps indiscreet, but only love is capable of working such a miracle, of causing such a drastic transformation. Two years ago we heard Christine Daaé in her competition at the conservatory and she gave us a charming hope. What is the origin of the sublime talent she had today? If it did not come down from heaven on the wings of love, I must believe that it came up from hell and that Christine Daaé, like Ofterdingen the mastersinger, has made a pact with the devil! Anyone who has not heard her sing the final trio in *Faust* does not know *Faust:* the exaltation of a voice and the rapture of a pure soul can go no further!

A few subscribers, however, protested. Why had such a treasure been hidden from them so long? Till then, Christine Daaé had played an adequate Siebel to Carlotta's somewhat too splendidly material Marguerite. It was only because of Carlotta's incomprehensible and inexcusable absence from the gala performance that Christine, filling in at a moment's notice, had been able to show her true worth in the part of the program originally reserved for the Spanish diva. But why had Debienne and Poligny chosen Christine when they learned that Carlotta would not appear? Had they known about her hidden genius? If so, why had they kept it hidden? And why had she herself hidden it? Strangely, she was not known to have a teacher. She had said repeatedly that from now on she would work alone. All this was inexplicable.

Standing in his box, Count de Chagny had seen and heard the frenzied ovation given to her, and had joined in it with his own shouts of "Bravo!"

Count Philippe-Georges-Marie de Chagny, forty-one at that time, was a great nobleman and a handsome man. He was taller than average and had a pleasing face despite the hard lines of his forehead and the touch of coldness in his eyes; he treated women with refined courtesy and was a little haughty with men, who did not always forgive him for his social success. He had an excellent heart and an honorable conscience. Through the death of old Count Philibert, he had become the head of one of the most ancient and illustrious families in France, whose nobility went back to the time of Louis X.

The Chagny fortune was substantial. When the old count died a widower, it was no easy task for Philippe to take over the management of such a large estate. His two sisters and his

brother Raoul had never even considered partition; they maintained joint possession and relied on Philippe's judgment in all
matters, as if the law of primogeniture were still in effect. When
his sisters married—on the same day—they took their shares
from him, not as something that belonged to them, but as a
dowry for which they thanked him.

Countess de Chagny—née de Moerogis de la Martynière—had
died in giving birth to Raoul, who was born twenty years after
Philippe. Raoul was twelve when the old count died. Philippe
took an active part in the boy's upbringing, ably assisted first by
his sisters, then by an old aunt who lived in Brest and gave
Raoul a taste for seafaring. The young man took his nautical
training aboard the school ship *Borda*, graduated near the top of
his class, and took the traditional trip around the world. Thanks
to powerful backing, he had just been assigned to the official
mission of the *Requin,* to search the polar ice for survivors of the
D'Artois expedition, which had not been heard from for three
years. In the meantime he was enjoying a long leave that would
not be over for six months, and the dowagers of the elegant
Faubourg Saint-Germain already pitied that handsome youth,
who looked so frail, for the hardships that lay in store for him.

His shyness—I am tempted to call it his innocence—was
remarkable. He gave the impression that he had just left the
women who had brought him up. He had been pampered by his
two sisters and his old aunt, and that purely feminine upbringing
had left him with artless manners that had a charm which nothing
had yet been able to mar. He was now twenty-one and looked
eighteen. He had a little blond mustache, attractive blue eyes,
and a girlish complexion.

Philippe spoiled Raoul a great deal. For one thing, he was
very proud of him and happily looked forward to a glorious
career for him in the navy, where one of their ancestors, the
famous Chagny de La Roche, had held the rank of admiral. He
was taking advantage of the young sailor's leave to show him
Paris. Raoul had known almost nothing of what the city could
offer in the way of luxurious delights and artistic pleasures.

The count felt that at Raoul's age too much goodness was not
good. Philippe had a well-balanced character; he was level-
headed in his pleasures as well as his work, his manners were
always impeccable, and he was incapable of setting a bad example for his brother. He took him with him everywhere. He even

introduced him into the dancers' lounge at the Opera. I know it was said that Philippe was "on the closest of terms" with La Sorelli. But since he was a bachelor and therefore had large amounts of free time, especially now that his sisters were married, it was surely no crime for him to come and spend an hour or two after dinner with a dancer who, though far from being renowned for her sparkling wit, had the prettiest eyes in the world. Furthermore, there are places where a real Parisian of Count de Chagny's rank must show himself, and at that time the dancers' lounge was one of those places.

But Philippe might not have taken his brother into the corridors of the National Academy of Music if Raoul had not repeatedly asked it of him, with a gentle persistence that the count was to remember later.

After applauding Christine Daae that evening, Philippe turned to Raoul and saw him so pale that it alarmed him.

"Don't you see that she's about to faint?" said Raoul.

And it was true that, on the stage, Christine had to be supported by those around her.

"You're the one who's about to faint," said Philippe, leaning toward Raoul. "What's the matter?"

But Raoul stood up.

"Let's go," he said in an unsteady voice.

"Where do you want to go?" asked Philippe, surprised by his brother's intense emotion.

"Let's go and see! This is the first time she's ever sung like that!"

Philippe gave Raoul a curious look and his lips curved into a little smile of amusement.

"Well, why not?" he said, seemingly delighted. "Come, let's go."

They soon reached the subscribers' entrance and found it clogged with people. While he waited till he could get to the stage, Raoul tore his gloves without realizing what he was doing. Philippe was too good-natured to make fun of his impatience. But he had understood: he now knew why Raoul seemed preoccupied when he talked to him, and also why he seemed to take such great pleasure in turning all conversation to the subject of the Opera.

They stepped onto the stage.

A crowd of men in evening dress were hurrying toward the

dancers' lounge or the performers' dressing rooms. The stage-hands' shouts were mingled with vehement outbursts from crew chiefs. The departing supernumeraries from the last tableau, the figurantes who jostle you, the frame of a flat being carried past, a backdrop coming down from the rigging loft, a practicable window being secured with vigorous hammering, the constant warning cries that make you fear that something is about to knock off your top hat or smash into you from behind—such is the usual intermission commotion that never fails to trouble a novice like the young man with a little blond mustache, blue eyes, and a girlish complexion who was crossing, as rapidly as the bustle and congestion would allow, that stage on which Christine Daaé had just triumphed, and under which Joseph Buquet had just died.

That evening, the confusion had never been more complete, but Raoul had never been less timid. He firmly shouldered aside everyone in his way, ignored what was said around him, and did not even try to understand the frantic words of the stagehands. He was concerned only with his desire to see the young woman whose magic voice had captured his heart. Yes, he felt that his poor, inexperienced heart no longer belonged to him. He had tried to defend it since the day when Christine, whom he had known when she was a little girl, had come back into his life. He had decided that he must struggle against the sweet feelings she aroused in him because, true to his respect for himself and his faith, he had sworn to love only the woman who would be his wife, and it was naturally out of the question for him to marry a singer. But the sweet feelings had been succeeded by a terrible sensation. Sensation? Sentiment? It was both physical and emotional. His chest hurt, as if someone had cut it open to take out his heart. He felt a dreadful hollowness in it, a real emptiness that could never be filled except by Christine's heart. Such are the symptoms of a psychological malady that, it seems, can be understood only by those who have had the experience commonly described as "falling head over heels in love."

Count Philippe had difficulty keeping up with him. He was still smiling.

At the back of the stage, past the double door opening onto the steps that lead to the dancers' lounge and those that lead to the ground-floor boxes on the left side, Raoul was stopped by a little troupe of student dancers who had just come down from their attic and were now blocking the passageway he wanted to enter. Mocking words were spoken to him by little painted lips, but he did not answer. Finally he was able to get past and started along a corridor filled with the sound of exclamations from enthusiastic admirers. One name rose above the hubbub: "Daae! Daae!"

Behind Raoul, Philippe said to himself, "He knows the way, the rascal!" and wondered how he had learned it. He had never taken him to Christine's dressing room. Raoul must have gone there by himself while Philippe went to the lounge, as usual, to talk with La Sorelli. She often asked him to stay with her till she went onstage, and she sometimes carried her tyranny so far as to ask him to keep the little gaiters she wore when she came down from her dressing room, to preserve the luster of her satin slippers and the cleanness of her flesh-colored tights. She had an excuse: she had lost her mother.

Postponing for a few minutes the visit he owed to La Sorelli, Philippe followed Raoul along the corridor that led to Christine's dressing room. He had never before seen that corridor so crowded as it was now, when everyone in the Opera seemed to be excited by Christine's success and upset by the fact that she had fainted. She had not yet come to, and the house doctor had been sent for. He was now heading for her dressing room, pushing his way through groups of people. Raoul followed so closely behind him that he almost stepped on his heels.

So the doctor and Raoul reached Christine at the same time; she was given first aid by the former and opened her eyes in the latter's arms. Philippe was part of the tightly packed throng in front of the doorway.

"Don't you think, doctor, that those gentlemen ought to clear out of the room?" Raoul asked with incredible boldness. "It's terribly stuffy in here."

"You're quite right," said the doctor, and made everyone leave the room except Raoul and the maid.

The maid stared at Raoul in wide-eyed bewilderment. She had never seen him before. But she did not dare to question him.

The doctor assumed that since this young man had acted that way, he had a right to. So Raoul remained in the dressing room, watching Christine regain her senses, while even the two managers, Debienne and Poligny, who had come to express their admiration of her, were pushed into the hall, along with the men in evening dress.

Count Philippe de Chagny, expelled like the others, laughed aloud and exclaimed, "Oh, the rascal! The rascal!" Then he thought, "It shows you can't trust those young fellows with girlish faces!" He grinned and concluded, "He's a real Chagny!"

He started toward La Sorelli's dressing room, but she was already going down to the lounge with her frightened little flock and she met him on the way, as we saw at the beginning of this chapter.

In her dressing room, Christine heaved a deep sigh that was answered by a groan. She turned her head, saw Raoul, and started. She looked at the doctor and smiled at him, then looked at her maid, and finally at Raoul again.

"Who are you, sir?" she asked him in a voice that was not yet much louder than a whisper.

He knelt on one knee and ardently kissed her hand.

"Mademoiselle," he said, "I'm the little boy who went into the sea to get your scarf."

Christine again looked at the doctor and the maid, and the three of them laughed. Raoul stood up, red-faced.

"Mademoiselle, since it pleases you not to recognize me, I'd like to tell you something in private, something very important."

"Would you mind waiting till I'm feeling better?" she said, her voice quavering. "You're very kind. . . ."

"But you must leave," the doctor said to Raoul with his most gracious smile. "Let me take care of Mademoiselle Daae."

"I'm not sick," Christine said abruptly, with a vigor as strange as it was unexpected. She stood up and rapidly passed her hand over her eyes. "I thank you, doctor, but I need to be alone now. Please leave, all of you. I'm very nervous this evening."

The doctor tried to protest but, seeing her agitation, he decided that the best remedy for such a state would be to let her have her way. He left with Raoul, who found himself standing in the hall, disconcerted.

"I don't recognize her this evening," the doctor said to him. "She's usually so calm and gentle. . . ."

And he walked away.

Raoul was alone: that whole part of the Opera was now deserted. The farewell ceremony had evidently begun in the dancers' lounge. Thinking that Christine might go there, Raoul waited in solitude and silence. He even hid in the welcome darkness of a doorway. He still had that terrible pain in the empty place where his heart had been. And that was what he wanted to tell Christine about, without delay.

Suddenly the door of the dressing room opened and he saw the maid leave alone, carrying several packages. He stopped her and asked her how her mistress was feeling. She laughed and answered that her mistress was feeling quite well now, but that he should not disturb her, because she wanted to be alone. Then she hurried away.

An idea flashed into Raoul's overheated mind: Christine obviously wanted to be alone *for him!* He had told her he wanted to talk to her in private, and that was why she had told everyone to leave. Scarcely breathing, he went back to the door of her dressing room, put his ear close to it to hear what she would answer, and raised his hand to knock. But then he lowered it. He had just heard a man's voice coming from the dressing room, saying in a singularly authoritarian tone, "Christine, you must love me!"

And Christine's voice, quavering and tearful, answered, "How can you say that to me, when I sing only for you?"

Raoul's suffering weakened him to the point where he had to lean against the door. His heart, which had seemed to be gone forever, had now come back into his chest and was pounding loudly. The whole corridor resounded with the noise and his ears felt deafened by it. If his heart went on making such a din, it would be heard, the door would open, and he would be ignominiously sent away. What a position for a Chagny to be in: eavesdropping at a door! He put both hands over his heart to quiet it. But a heart is not a dog's mouth, and even if you hold a dog's mouth shut with both hands to stop his unbearable barking, you still hear him growl.

The man's voice spoke again:

"You must be tired."

"Oh, yes! Tonight I gave you my soul, and I'm dead."

"Your soul is very beautiful, my child," said the man's deep voice, "and I thank you. No emperor ever received such a gift! The angels wept tonight."

After those words, "The angels wept tonight," Raoul heard nothing more. He did not leave, but since he was afraid of being seen he went back into his dark doorway, determined to wait there till the man left the dressing room. He had just learned love and hatred in the same evening. He knew that he loved; he wanted to discover whom he hated.

To his surprise, the door opened and Christine, wrapped in furs, with her face hidden by a lace veil, came out alone. She closed the door, but Raoul observed that she did not lock it. She walked past him. He did not even follow her with his eyes, because his eyes were on the door. It did not open. When the corridor was empty again, he crossed it, opened the door of the dressing room, went in, and closed it behind him. He found himself in total darkness. The gaslights had been turned off.

"There's someone here!" he said in a vibrant voice. "Why is he hiding?"

He stood with his back against the closed door. Darkness and silence. He heard only the sound of his own breathing. He did not realize that his conduct was unbelievably indiscreet.

"You won't leave here till I let you!" he said. "If you don't answer, you're a coward! But I'll unmask you!"

He struck a match. The flame lighted the room. He saw no one! After taking the precaution of locking the door, he lit the gaslights, went into the bathroom, opened the closets, searched, felt the walls with moist hands. Nothing!

"Am I losing my mind?" he said aloud.

He stood there for ten minutes, listening to the hiss of the gas in the peace of that abandoned dressing room; although he was in love, he did not even think of taking a ribbon that would have brought him the perfume of the woman he loved. He left, not knowing what he was doing or where he was going.

At one point in his aimless wandering, he felt cold air on his face and saw that he was at the bottom of a narrow staircase. Coming down it, behind him, were a group of workmen carrying a makeshift stretcher covered with a white cloth.

"Will you please tell me the way out?" he asked.

"It's right in front of you," one of the men replied. "As you can see, the door is open. But let me pass."

Raoul pointed to the stretcher and asked, with no real interest, "What's that?"

"That's Joseph Buquet. He was found hanged in the third cellar, between a flat and a set piece from *Le Roi de Lahore*."

Raoul stepped aside to let them pass, then bowed and went out.

3

In Which, for the First Time, Debienne and Poligny Secretly Give the New Managers of the Opera, Armand Moncharmin and Firmin Richard, the Real and Mysterious Reason for Their Departure from the National Academy of Music

MEANWHILE, THE FAREWELL ceremony was taking place. As I have said, that magnificent celebration was given by Debienne and Poligny on the occasion of their departure from the Opera; to use a common expression, they wanted to go out in a blaze of glory. Everyone who mattered in Parisian society and the arts had helped them to organize that ideal program with melancholy overtones.

They all gathered in the dancers' lounge, where La Sorelli was waiting for the two outgoing managers with a glass of champagne in her hand and a prepared speech on the tip of her tongue. Her young and old companions in the corps de ballet were crowded around her, some talking quietly about the day's events, others discreetly gesturing to their friends, who had already formed a chattering throng around the buffet that stood on the sloping floor between two paintings by Boulenger: *La Danse guerrière* and *La Danse champêtre*.

A few of the dancers had already changed into their ordinary clothes, but most of them still wore their light gauze skirts. They all had the serious look that they considered proper for the occasion—all, that is, except little Jammes, who, being at the happy, carefree age of fifteen, seemed to have already forgotten the ghost and Joseph Buquet's death and was constantly bab- bling, hopping around, and playing tricks on her friends. La Sorelli, exasperated, sternly called her to order when Debienne and Poligny appeared on the steps of the lounge.

Everyone noticed that the two outgoing managers seemed cheerful. In the provinces, this would not have appeared natural to anyone, but in Paris it was regarded as being in very good taste. No one will ever be a Parisian without learning to put a mask of joy over his sorrows and a mask of sadness, boredom, or indifference over his inner joy. If you know that one of your friends is in distress, do not try to comfort him: he will tell you that things are already looking up for him; and if he has had a stroke of good luck, do not congratulate him on it: he will consider it so natural that he will be surprised that anyone should mention it. Parisians are always at a masked ball, and two men as sophisticated as Debienne and Poligny would not have made the mistake of coming into the dancers' lounge and showing the genuine sorrow they were feeling.

They smiled a little too much at La Sorelli when she began her speech. Then an exclamation from that scatterbrained little Jammes made their smiles vanish so suddenly that everyone saw the distress and fear they had been hiding.

"The Opera ghost!"

Jammes spoke these words in a tone of agonizing terror, and among the men in evening dress she pointed to a face so pale, mournful, and ugly, with such deep, dark eye sockets, that it looked like a death's-head and was enthusiastically acclaimed.

"The Opera ghost! The Opera ghost!"

The delighted onlookers laughed, jostled each other, and tried to approach the Opera ghost to offer him a drink, but a moment later he was gone, apparently having slipped away in the crowd. They looked for him in vain while two old gentlemen tried to calm little Jammes and little Giry screeched like a peacock.

La Sorelli was furious: she had not been able to finish her speech. Debienne and Poligny had kissed her, thanked her, and gone away as quickly as the ghost himself. No one was surprised by this, because everyone knew that they had to go through the same ceremony in the singers' lounge on the floor above, and that finally they would entertain their close friends one last time in the large vestibule of the managerial office, where a real supper awaited them.

And that is where we now find them, with the new managers, Armand Moncharmin and Firmin Richard. The two pairs of men scarcely knew each other, but they exchanged resounding compliments and great declarations of friendship, with the result that those guests who had been dreading a rather gloomy evening smiled brightly. During supper there was almost an atmosphere of gaiety. There were several occasions for toasts, and the government representative showed such special ability in proposing them, mingling the glory of the past with the success of the future, that great cordiality soon reigned among the guests.

The transfer of managerial powers had taken place the day before, in an informal way, and the questions that needed to be settled between the new management and the old one had been resolved, under the moderating authority of the government representative, with such a great desire for agreement on both sides that no one could now be surprised, during that memorable evening, to see warm smiles on the four managerial faces.

Debienne and Poligny gave Moncharmin and Richard the two little master keys that could unlock all of the several thousand doors in the National Academy of Music. Everyone was curious to see those keys. They were being passed from hand to hand when the attention of some of the guests was diverted by the sight of that strange figure with the pale, fantastic, hollow-eyed face who had already appeared in the dancers' lounge and been greeted by little Jammes's exclamation: "The Opera ghost!"

He sat at the end of the table, acting as if his presence there were perfectly natural, except that he was not eating or drinking.

Those who had smiled when they first saw him soon looked away because the sight of him aroused morbid thoughts. No one treated his appearance as a joke, as had been done in the lounge; no one cried, "There's the Opera ghost!"

He had so far said nothing. Not even those beside him could have said exactly when he had come in and sat down there, but everyone thought that if the dead sometimes returned and sat at the table of the living, they could not show a more macabre face than this one. The friends of Moncharmin and Richard thought the cadaverous guest was a friend of Debienne and Poligny, while the friends of Debienne and Poligny thought he was a friend of Moncharmin and Richard, and so no one asked for an explanation and there were no unpleasant remarks or jokes in bad taste that might have offended him.

A few of the guests who knew about the legend of the ghost and the description of him given by the chief stagehand—they had not yet learned of Joseph Buquet's death—felt that the man at the end of the table could very well pass for a materialization of what they considered to be a fictitious character created by the incorrigible superstition of the Opera personnel. According to the legend, however, the ghost had no nose, whereas this man had one; but Moncharmin says in his memoirs that it was transparent— his exact words are "His nose was long, thin, and transparent" —and I will add that it may have been a false nose. Moncharmin may have mistaken shininess for transparence. Everyone knows that science can make excellent false noses for people who have been deprived of a nose by nature or some sort of operation.

Did the ghost really come and sit down at the managers' banquet that night without being invited? And can we be sure that the face in question was that of the Opera ghost himself? Who would venture to say so? I have mentioned the incident not because I want to convince my readers that the ghost actually did show such splendid audacity, but only because I think that, all things considered, it is quite possible that he did.

Here, it seems to me, is a sufficient reason for thinking so. Moncharmin writes in the eleventh chapter of his memoirs: "When I recall that first evening, I cannot separate the presence at our supper of that ghostly individual, whom none of us knew, from what Debienne and Poligny confided to us in their office." What happened is as follows.

Debienne and Poligny, sitting at the middle of the table, had not yet seen the man with the death's-head when he suddenly began to speak.

"The dancers are right," he said. "Poor Buquet's death may not be as natural as people think."

Debienne and Poligny started, and both cried out at once, "Buquet is dead?"

"Yes," replied the man, or the specter of a man. "This evening he was found hanging in the third cellar, between a flat and a set piece from *Le Roi de Lahore*."

The two managers, or rather ex-managers, stood up and stared at him strangely. They were more agitated than one would have expected them to be upon learning that a stagehand had hanged himself. They looked at each other. They had both turned as white as the tablecloth. Finally Debienne motioned to Moncharmin and Richard, Poligny said a few words of apology to the guests, and the four men went into the managerial office. I will now quote from Moncharmin's memoirs:

Debienne and Poligny seemed more and more agitated, and it appeared to us that they had something to tell us but found it difficult to say. First they asked us if we knew the man at the end of the table who had told them about Joseph Buquet's death, and when we answered in the negative their agitation increased still more. Poligny took the master keys from us, looked at them for a moment, shook his head, and advised us to have new locks made, in secret, for all rooms, closets, and objects that we wanted to keep securely closed. As he said this, he and Debienne looked so funny that Richard and I laughed, and I asked if there were thieves in the Opera. Poligny answered that there was something worse than thieves: the ghost. We laughed again, thinking they were playing some sort of joke on us that was meant to crown the evening's festivities.

But finally, at their request, we became "serious" again; we were willing to humor them by taking part in their little game. They told us they would never have spoken to us about the ghost if they had not been ordered by the ghost himself to urge us to treat him courteously and grant him whatever he asked of us. Glad that they were about to rid themselves of the ghost by leaving the domain where he exercised his tyrannical rule, they had hesitated till the last moment to tell us about that strange situation, for which our skeptical minds were surely not prepared. But then the announcement of Joseph Buquet's death had forcefully reminded them that whenever they had failed to comply with the ghost's wishes, some fantastic or appalling occurrence had quickly brought them back to an awareness of their dependence.

While these unexpected things were being told to us in a

solemn and confidential tone, I looked at Richard. In his student days he had been known as an accomplished practical joker, one familiar with all the many tricks and pranks devised by students, and the concierges of the Boulevard Saint-. Michel could testify that he deserved his reputation. He seemed to relish the dish that was now being served to him. He did not miss a single mouthful of it, even though its seasoning was a little macabre because of Buquet's death. He sadly nodded his head and, as Debienne and Poligny spoke, his face took on a look of dismay which seemed to say that he bitterly regretted becoming a manager of the Opera now that he knew there was a ghost in it. I could do no better than to faithfully imitate his attitude of despair. But finally, despite all our efforts, we could not help laughing in the faces of Debienne and Poligny. Seeing us pass without transition from deep gloom to insolent gaiety, they acted as if they thought we had gone mad.

Richard felt that the joke had gone on a little too long.

"But what does that ghost want?" he asked half seriously.

Poligny went to his desk and came back with a copy of the instruction book for the management of the Opera.

It begins with these words: "The management of the Opera must give to performances of the National Academy of Music the splendor that befits the foremost French opera house," and ends with Article 98: "The manager may be removed from his position: 1. If he acts contrary to the provisions set forth in the book of instructions," followed by the provisions in question.

Poligny's copy of the instruction book was in black ink and seemed to be exactly like the one we had, except that at the end a paragraph had been added in red ink, in strange, jagged handwriting that looked as if it might have been made with inked matchsticks; it suggested a child who was still learning to write and had not yet reached the point of joining the letters. That paragraph was a fifth provision added to the four in Article 98: "5. If the manager is more than two weeks late in making one of the monthly payments owed to the Opera ghost, payments to be made until further notice at the rate of 20,000 francs each, totaling 240,000 francs per year."

Poligny hesitantly pointed to this last clause, which certainly came as a surprise to us.

"Is that all? Does he want anything else?" Richard asked with perfect composure.

"Yes, he does," replied Poligny.

He leafed through the instruction book and read aloud:

"Article 63. Stage Box One, in the first right tier, will be reserved at all performances for the head of state.

"Ground-floor Box Twenty on Mondays, and First-Tier Box Thirty on Wednesdays and Fridays, will be placed at the minister's disposal.

"Second-Tier Box Twenty-seven will be reserved every day for the use of the Prefect of the Seine and the Chief Commissioner of the Paris Police."

He then showed us another paragraph that had been added in red ink:

"First-Tier Box Five will be placed at the disposal of the Opera ghost for all performances."

At this, Richard and I could only stand up, warmly shake hands with our two predecessors and congratulate them on that charming joke that showed that the old French sense of humor was as lively as ever. Richard even added that he now understood why Debienne and Poligny were leaving their positions: it was impossible to conduct the affairs of the Opera and contend with such a demanding ghost.

"Of course," Poligny replied without batting an eye. "You don't find two hundred and forty thousand francs growing on every tree. And do you realize how much it cost us to keep First-Tier Box Five reserved for the ghost at all performances? We couldn't rent it and we had to give back the money that a subscriber had paid for it. It's appalling! We don't want to work to support ghosts! We prefer to leave."

"Yes, we prefer to leave," echoed Debienne. "And let's do it now."

He stood up.

"But it seems to me that you're very kind to that ghost," said Richard. "If I had such a bothersome ghost, I wouldn't hesitate to have him arrested."

"Where? How?" cried Poligny. "We've never seen him!"

"Not even when he comes to his box?"

"We've never seen him in his box."

"Then why not rent it?"

"Rent the Opera ghost's box? Try it, gentlemen, just try it!"

The four of us left the office. Richard and I had enjoyed ourselves immensely.

4

Box Five

ARMAND MONCHARMIN WROTE such voluminous memoirs that one may wonder if during the rather long period of his comanagement he ever found time to concern himself with the Opera other than by describing what went on there. He did not know one note of music, but he was on close terms with the Minister of Public Education and the Fine Arts, he had done a little newspaper reporting on the variety theater, and he had a rather large fortune. He had considerable charm, and no lack of intelligence, since, having decided to become a silent partner in the Opera, he had chosen the man who would be the most effective manager: he had gone straight to Firmin Richard.

Firmin Richard was a distinguished composer and a man of honor. Here is the description of him published in the *Revue des théâtres* at the time when he became a comanager of the Opera:

> Firmin Richard is about fifty. He is tall and broad, without an ounce of fat. He has distinction and an imposing presence. His complexion is florid; his thick hair comes down rather low on his forehead and is cut short; his beard matches his hair; his face has a slight look of sadness that is tempered by his forthright gaze and charming smile.
>
> Firmin Richard is a very distinguished composer, highly proficient in harmony and counterpoint. The principal characteristic of his compositions is grandeur. He has published some highly regarded chamber music, piano music—sonatas and minor pieces—full of originality, and a collection of

melodies. Finally, his *Death of Hercules*, performed at the concerts of the conservatory, has an epic inspiration reminiscent of Gluck, one of his venerated masters. Though he adores Gluck, however, he loves Piccinni none the less; he takes his pleasure where he finds it. Full of admiration for Piccinni, he pays homage to Meyerbeer, he delights in Cimarosa, and no one has a better appreciation of Weber's inimitable genius. Finally, as to Wagner, Monsieur Richard is not far from claiming to be the first person in France, and perhaps the only one, to have understood him.

I will stop my quotation here. It clearly implies, I believe, that while Firmin Richard liked nearly all music and all composers, it was the duty of all composers to like Firmin Richard. To end this quick sketch of him, I will say that his character was of the kind known as dictatorial; that is, he was very bad-tempered.

During the first days that the two partners spent in the Opera, they were absorbed in the pleasure of feeling themselves the masters of such a vast and splendid enterprise, and they had no doubt forgotten about the curious, outlandish story of the ghost. Then there was an incident that proved to them that the joke—if that was what it was—had not yet ended.

Richard arrived in his office at eleven that morning. His secretary, Monsieur Rémy, showed him half a dozen letters that he had not opened because they were marked "Personal." One of them immediately caught Richard's attention, not only because the envelope was addressed in red ink, but also because it seemed to him that he had seen that handwriting before. He quickly realized that it was the red writing in which the book of instructions had been so strangely completed. He recognized its clumsy, childish appearance. He opened the envelope and read:

My Dear Manager,
     Please excuse me for disturbing you during this precious time when you are deciding on the fate of the best performers in the Opera, renewing important engagements and concluding new ones, and doing all that with a firmness of purpose, an understanding of the theater, a knowledge of the public and its tastes, and an authority that I, with my long experience, have found simply astounding. I know what you have done for Carlotta, La Sorelli, and little Jammes, and several others whose admirable qualities, talent, or genius you have

discerned. (You know to whom I am referring by those last words: it is obviously not to Carlotta, who sings like a yowling cat and should never have left the Ambassadeurs or the Café Jacquin; or to La Sorelli, whose success is primarily corporeal; or to little Jammes, who dances like a calf in a meadow. Nor is it Christine Daaé; her genius is unquestionable, but you have carefully excluded her from any important creation.)

.. You are, of course, free to manage your operatic affairs as you see fit. However, I would like to take advantage of the fact that you have not yet thrown out Christine Daaé by hearing her tonight in the role of Siebel, since the role of Marguerite is now forbidden to her, after her triumph the other day. I ask you not to dispose of my box tonight or any other night, for I cannot end this letter without admitting to you how unpleasantly surprised I was recently when I came to the Opera and learned that my box had been rented, at the box office, *by your order*.

I did not protest, first because I dislike making a scene, and also because I thought that your predecessors, Debienne and Poligny, who were always very gracious to me, must have neglected to tell you about my little idiosyncrasies before they left. But in response to my request for an explanation, they have just given me an answer that proves you are acquainted with my book of instructions, and therefore that you are showing intolerable disrespect for me. *If you want us to live in peace, you must not begin by taking my box away from me!*

Having made these little remarks, I ask you to consider me your humble servant,

                                                            Opera Ghost

This letter was accompanied by a clipping from the personal column of the *Revue théâtrale,* which contained the following: "O. G.: R. and M. are inexcusable. We told them, and left your book of instructions in their hands. Best regards."

Firmin Richard had scarcely finished reading the letter when the door of his office opened and Armand Moncharmin came in, holding a letter exactly like the one his colleague had received. They looked at each other and laughed.

"The joke is still going on," said Richard, "and it's not funny."

"What does this mean?" asked Moncharmin. "Do they think

we're going to let them have a box forever because they used to be managers of the Opera?''

"I'm in no mood to let them keep up their hoax much longer," declared Richard.

"It's harmless," remarked Moncharmin. "Actually, what is it they want? A box for tonight?"

Richard told his secretary to send Debienne and Poligny tickets for First-Tier Box Five, if it was not already rented.

It was not. The tickets were sent immediately. Debienne lived at the corner of the Rue Scribe and the Boulevard des Capucines; Poligny, on the Rue Auber. The two letters signed Opera Ghost had been mailed from the post office on the Boulevard des Capucines. Moncharmin noticed this as he was examining the envelopes.

"You see!" said Richard.

They shrugged and expressed regret that men as old as Debienne and Poligny should still be amusing themselves with such childish pranks.

"At least they could have been polite!" said Moncharmin. "Did you notice what they said about us with regard to Carlotta, La Sorelli, and little Jammes?"

"My friend, those men are sick with jealousy! Think of it: they even went so far as to pay for an advertisement in the personal column of the *Revue théâtrale!* Do they really have nothing better to do?"

"By the way, they seem to have a great interest in little Christine Daae. . . ."

"You know as well as I do that she has the reputation of being virtuous!"

"Reputations are often undeserved," said Moncharmin. "I have the reputation of knowing all about music, but I don't know the difference between the treble clef and the bass clef."

"Don't worry, you've never had that reputation," Richard assured him.

He then ordered the doorkeeper to show in the singers and dancers who had been pacing back and forth in the hall for the past two hours, waiting for the managerial door to open, the door behind which they would find glory and money—or dismissal.

The whole day was spent in carrying on discussions and negotiations, in signing and breaking contracts. You may therefore be certain that that night—the night of January 25—our two managers, tired from a hard day of anger, scheming, urging, threats, protestations of love or hatred, went to bed early without even having the curiosity to glance into Box Five to see if Debienne and Poligny were enjoying the evening's performance. The Opera had not come to a standstill after the former managers' departure and Richard had had some necessary work done on the building without disrupting the schedule of performances.

The next morning, he and Moncharmin found a card from the ghost in their mail:

My Dear Manager,
    Thank you. Delightful evening. Daae exquisite. Choruses need work. Carlotta a magnificent and commonplace instrument. Will soon write to you about the 240,000 francs or, to be exact, 233,424.70: Debienne and Poligny sent me 6575.30 francs for the first ten days of this year's allotment, since they ceased to be managers on the evening of the tenth.

Kind regards,
O. G.

They also received a letter from Debienne and Poligny:

Gentlemen,
    We thank you for your kindness, but you will readily understand that the prospect of hearing *Faust* again, no matter how pleasant it may be to former managers of the Opera, cannot make us forget that we have no right to occupy First-Tier Box Five. You know to whom that box belongs exclusively, for we had occasion to speak of him to you when we reread the book of instructions with you one last time. We refer you to the last paragraph of Article 63.
    We remain, etc.

"They're beginning to get on my nerves!" Richard said violently, snatching the letter from Moncharmin's hands.

That night, First-Tier Box Five was rented.

When Richard and Moncharmin came to their office the next day, they found a report from the supervisor of the Opera, written the night before, concerning events that had taken place that same night in First-Tier Box Five. Here is the essential passage of that brief report:

Twice this evening, at the beginning and in the middle of the second act, I had to call in a policeman to eject the occupants of First-Tier Box Five, who had arrived at the beginning of the second act. They made a scandalous disturbance with their loud laughter and inane remarks. There were cries of "Quiet!" all around them, and the audience was beginning to protest when an usher came to me. I went into the box and said what was necessary. The occupants talked stupidly to me and seemed not to be in their right mind. I warned them that if the disturbance was repeated, I would be forced to make them leave. As soon as I was gone, I again heard their laughter, and protests from the audience. I went back with a policeman who made them leave the box. Still laughing, they said they would stay in the hall until their money was refunded. Finally they became calm and I let them go back into the box. The laughter immediately began again, and this time I had them permanently ejected.

"Send for the supervisor," Richard said to his secretary, who had been the first to read the report, and had already written notes on it in blue pencil.

The secretary, Monsieur Rémy, was always shy in front of the managers. He was an intelligent, elegant, distinguished young man of twenty-four who had a thin mustache, dressed impeccably—which at that time meant that he wore a frock coat during the day—and received a salary of twenty-four hundred francs a year, paid by the managers. He examined the newspapers for useful information, answered letters, distributed box reservations and complimentary tickets, scheduled appointments, talked with people waiting to see the managers, went to see sick performers, looked for understudies, and corresponded with department heads, but his main duty was to act as a lock on the managers' door. He could be discharged at a moment's notice without compensation, because he was not recognized by the administration.

Rémy had already sent for the supervisor. He told him to come in.

The supervisor stepped into Richard's office, looking a little uneasy.

"Tell us what happened," Richard said brusquely.

The supervisor stammered something and referred to his report.

"Why were those people laughing?" asked Moncharmin.

"They must have had a good dinner with plenty of wine, sir, and they seemed to be more in a mood for horseplay than for listening to good music. As soon as they went into the box, they came out again and called the usher. She asked them what they wanted. One of the men said, 'Look in the box—there's no one in it, is there?' The usher said, 'No,' and the man said, 'Well, when we went in, we heard a voice saying someone was there.' "

Moncharmin could not look at Richard without smiling, but Richard did not smile back. He himself had too much experience in that sort of thing not to recognize, in the story that the supervisor was innocently telling him, all the marks of one of those malicious practical jokes that first amuse their victims, then finally enrage them.

To curry favor with Moncharmin, who was still smiling, the supervisor felt that he should smile also. It was an unfortunate smile! Richard gave him a withering look. The supervisor instantly tried to take on a suitably dismayed expression.

"But when those people arrived," asked the formidable Richard, "was there anyone in the box?"

"No one, sir, no one at all! And there was no one in the boxes on either side of it, no one! I swear the box was empty, I'd stake my life on it! That's why I'm sure the whole thing was only a joke."

"And what did the usher say?"

"Oh, as far as she's concerned, it's simple: she says it was the Opera ghost. What else can you expect?"

The supervisor laughed, but again he realized he had made a mistake, because as soon as Richard heard "she says it was the Opera ghost," his face, already somber, became furious.

"I want to see that usher!" he said. "Immediately! Have her brought here! And send all those people away!"

The supervisor tried to protest but Richard closed his mouth with a menacing "Quiet!" Then, when his unfortunate subordinate's lips seemed closed forever, Richard demanded that he open them again.

"What is this 'Opera ghost'?" he finally brought himself to ask, with a grunt of displeasure.

But the supervisor was now unable to say a word. By desperate gestures, he gave Richard to understand that he did not know, or rather that he did not want to know.

"Have you seen the ghost yourself?"

The supervisor vigorously shook his head.

"So much the worse for you," Richard said coldly.

The supervisor's eyes opened so wide that they seemed ready to pop out of their sockets and, regaining his power of speech, he asked the manager why he had spoken those sinister words.

"Because I'm going to settle accounts with everyone who hasn't seen him!" Richard answered. "Since he's everywhere, it's intolerable that he's not seen anywhere. I want my employees to do their work and do it right!"

5

Continuation of "Box Five"

HAVING SAID THIS, Richard paid no further attention to the supervisor and began discussing various matters with his administrator, who had just come in. The supervisor thought he could leave. He was backing slowly, ever so slowly, toward the door when Richard saw what he was doing and nailed his feet to the floor with a thunderous "Don't move!"

Rémy had sent for the usher, who also worked as a concierge on the Rue de Provence, near the Opera. She soon came in.

"What's your name?" asked Richard.

"Madame Giry. You know me, sir: I'm the mother of little Giry, or little Meg, she's also called."

She said this in a gruff, serious tone that briefly gave him pause. He looked at her (faded shawl, worn-out shoes, old taffeta dress, soot-colored hat) and it was obvious from his expression that he had never met her before, or had forgotten meeting her, and that he did not know her daughter either. But that famous usher's pride was so great that she imagined everyone knew her. (I believe that *giries,* a familiar word in backstage slang at the Opera, came from her name. An example of its use: If one singer wants to accuse another of repeating idle gossip, she will say to her, "All that is nothing but *giries.*")

"No, I don't know you," Richard finally declared. "But I'd still like you to tell me what happened last night to make you and the supervisor call in a policeman."

"Yes, I wanted to talk to you about that, sir, so we won't have the same unpleasantness as Monsieur Debienne and Monsieur Poligny. At first, they wouldn't listen to me either, and . . ."

"I'm not asking you about all that," Richard interrupted. "I'm asking you to tell me what happened last night."

Madame Giry turned red with indignation. No one had ever spoken to her in such a tone before. She stood up as though to leave, gathering the folds of her skirt and shaking the feathers of her soot-colored hat with dignity; but then she changed her mind, sat down again, and said haughtily, "What happened was that someone annoyed the ghost again!"

At this point, seeing that Richard was on the verge of an angry outburst, Moncharmin intervened and took charge of the questioning. It soon revealed that to Madame Giry it was perfectly natural for people to hear a voice proclaiming that there was someone in a box where there was no one. She could explain that phenomenon, which was not new to her, only as an act of the ghost. No one ever saw the ghost in his box, but everyone could hear him. She had heard him often, and they could take her word for it, because she never lied. They could ask Monsieur Debienne and Monsieur Poligny, and everyone else who knew her, including Isidore Saack, whose leg had been broken by the ghost.

"Is that so?" asked Moncharmin. "The ghost broke poor Isidore Saack's leg?"

Madame Giry's eyes showed her amazement at such ignorance. Finally she consented to enlighten those two unfortunate simpletons. The incident had happened in the time of Debienne and Poligny, and, like the one of the night before, it had happened in Box Five during a performance of *Faust*.

Madame Giry coughed and cleared her throat, acting as if she were preparing to sing all of Gounod's score.

"Here's how it was, sir," she began. "That night, Monsieur Maniera and his wife—they're gem dealers on the Rue Mogador—were sitting in the front of the box. Behind Madame Maniera was their close friend, Isidore Saack. Mephistopheles was singing." And Madame Giry sang: " 'Thou, who here art soundly sleeping.' Then, in his right ear (his wife was sitting to his left), Monsieur Maniera heard a voice saying, 'Ha, ha! Julie isn't soundly sleeping!' (His wife's name is Julie.) He turned his

head to the right to see who had said that. No one! He rubbed his
ear and said to himself, 'Did I dream it?' Mephistopheles was
still singing. . . . But maybe I'm boring you gentlemen.''

"No, no, go on.''

"You're very kind,'' she said with a grimace. "As I said,
Mephistopheles was still singing.'' She sang: " 'You whom I
adore, refuse not, I implore, a sweet kiss . . .' And again
Monsieur Maniera heard the voice in his right ear: 'Ha, ha!
Julie won't refuse a sweet kiss to Isidore!' He turned his head
again, but this time in the direction of his wife and Isidore.
And what did he see? Isidore had taken Madame Maniera's
hand from behind and was kissing it through the little opening
in her glove, like this, gentlemen.'' She kissed the patch of
skin left bare by her silk glove. "Well, you can be sure the
three of them didn't just sit there quietly after that! Bang!
Bang! Monsieur Maniera, who was big and strong like you,
Monsieur Richard, gave a pair of healthy slaps to Isidore
Saack, who was thin and weak like you, Monsieur Moncharmin,
with all due respect. There was a big commotion. People in
the audience were shouting, 'He's going to kill him!' Finally
Isidore Saack was able to get away.''

"Then the ghost didn't break his leg?'' asked Moncharmin,
a little miffed at the poor impression his physique had made
on Madame Giry.

"He did break it, sir,'' she replied a little scornfully, for
she had sensed his offensive intention. "He broke it on the
big staircase, which Isidore Saack was going down too fast,
and he broke it so badly that it will be quite a while before the
poor man can go up those stairs again!''

"Was it the ghost himself who told you what he whispered
in Monsieur Maniera's right ear?'' Moncharmin asked with
the seriousness of a judge, feeling that he was being very
comical.

"No, sir, it was Monsieur Maniera who told me. So . . .''

"But you *have* talked with the ghost, haven't you, my
good lady?''

"Yes, just as sure as I'm talking with you, my good
gentleman.''

"And when the ghost talks to you, what does he say?''

"He tells me to bring him a footstool.''

As she solemnly spoke these words, Madame Giry's face

became as cold as the red-veined yellow marble, known as Sarrancolin marble, in the pillars supporting the great staircase.

Richard, Moncharmin, and Rémy, the secretary, all laughed at once; but the supervisor, having learned from experience, did not join in their laughter. Leaning against the wall and nervously toying with the keys in his pocket, he wondered how all this was going to turn out. The haughtier Madame Giry became, the more he was afraid that Richard's anger would return. And now, facing the managers' laughter, she dared to become threatening, positively threatening!

"Instead of laughing at the ghost," she said indignantly, "you should do like Monsieur Poligny—he found out for himself."

"Found out about what?" asked Moncharmin, who had never been so amused before.

"The ghost! I'm trying to tell you . . . Listen." Madame Giry suddenly became calm, feeling that this was a crucial time. "I remember it as if it were yesterday. They were performing *La Juive* that night. Monsieur Poligny had decided to watch it, alone, in the ghost's box. Mademoiselle Krauss was a huge success. She'd just sung, you know, that thing in the second act." She began singing softly: " 'I want to live and die with the man I love, and death itself cannot . . .' "

"Yes, I know the part you mean," Moncharmin said with a discouraging smile.

But she went on singing, swaying the feathers of her soot-colored hat: " 'Let us away! Here below, the same fate awaits us . . .' "

"Yes, yes, we know the part you mean!" Richard interrupted impatiently. "What of it?"

"Well, it was just when Léopold says, 'Let us flee!' and Eléazar stops them by asking, 'Where are you going?' It was just then that Monsieur Poligny—I was watching him from the back of the next box, which was unrented—it was just then that he stood up straight and walked out, stiff as a statue. I barely had time to ask him, like Eléazar, 'Where are you going?' But he didn't answer me and he was pale as a corpse! I watched him go down the stairs. He didn't break a leg, but he walked as if he were in a dream, a nightmare. He couldn't even find his way—and he was paid to know the Opera from top to bottom!''

Having expressed herself in this way, Madame Giry paused to judge the effect she had produced.

Her story about Poligny had made Moncharmin shake his head.

''All that still doesn't tell me how, and in what circumstances, the Opera ghost asked you for a footstool,'' he insisted, looking her straight in the eyes.

''Well, after that night, the ghost was left alone and nobody tried to take his box away from him. Monsieur Debienne and Monsieur Poligny gave orders that it was to be left free for him at all performances. And every time he came, he asked me for his footstool.''

''So here we have a ghost who asks for a footstool. . . . Your ghost is a woman, then?''

''No, the ghost is a man.''

''How do you know?''

''He has a man's voice, a beautiful man's voice. I'll tell you what happens. When he comes to the Opera, he usually arrives in the middle of the first act. He knocks three times on the door of Box Five. The first time I heard those three knocks, when I knew very well there was nobody in the box, you can imagine how puzzled I was! I opened the door, I listened, I looked—nobody! Then I heard a voice say to me, 'Madame Jules'—my late husband's name was Jules—'will you please bring me a footstool?' It knocked me flat, if you know what I mean, sir. Then the voice said, 'Don't be afraid, Madame Jules, I'm the Opera ghost.' It was such a kind, friendly voice that I almost did stop being afraid. I looked in the direction it came from. The voice, sir, was in the first seat on the right in the first row. Except that I didn't see anyone there, it was exactly as if someone were sitting in that seat and talking to me, someone very polite too.''

''Was the box to the right of Box Five occupied?'' asked Moncharmin.

''No. Box Seven, and Box Three on the left, were still empty. The performance had just started.''

''And what did you do?''

''I brought the footstool, what else? He didn't want it for

himself, of course. It was for his lady. But I never heard or saw her.''

What! The ghost had a wife now? Moncharmin and Richard raised their eyes from Madame Giry to the supervisor, who was standing behind her and waving his arms to catch their attention. He sadly tapped his forehead with his finger to indicate that Madame Giry was crazy, which made Richard decide to dismiss a supervisor who kept a lunatic in his service. She was still talking, totally absorbed in her ghost; now she was praising his generosity.

''At the end of the performance he usually gives me at least two francs, sometimes five, sometimes even ten, when it's been several days since the last time he came. But now that they've started annoying him again, he hasn't been giving me anything.''

''Excuse me, my good woman''—Madame Giry angrily shook the feathers of her soot-colored hat at this persistent familiarity—''but how does the ghost go about giving you that money?'' asked Moncharmin, who was born curious.

''He just leaves it on the railing of the box. I find it there, along with the program I always bring him. Sometimes I also find flowers in the box, a rose that must have fallen from his lady's bodice. He must come there sometimes with a lady, since they once left a fan behind.''

''Ha, ha! The ghost left a fan? And what did you do with it?''

''I brought it back to him the next time, of course.''

At this point the supervisor's voice was heard:

''You didn't follow the rules, Madame Giry. I'm going to fine you.''

Then Richard's deep voice:

''Shut up, you fool!''

''So you brought back the fan. Then what happened?''

''They took it away, sir. I didn't find it after the performance, and in its place they left a box of the tart candy I like so much. That's another way the ghost shows his kindness.''

''Thank you, Madame Giry. You may leave now.''

When she had left, after bowing to the two managers respectfully, though with the dignity that never abandoned her, Richard told the supervisor he had decided to dispense with that old lunatic's services. Then he told him that he could also leave.

The supervisor declared his devotion to the Opera and left. The two managers sent word to the administrator that he was to give the supervisor what was owed to him and remove him from the payroll. Then, when the secretary had left and they were alone together, they each expressed a thought that had come to both of them at the same time: they should go and have a look at Box Five.

We will soon follow them there.

6

The Enchanted Violin

BECAUSE OF INTRIGUES that will be examined later, Christine Daae did not immediately repeat, at the Opera, the triumph she had won at the famous gala performance. She did, however, have an opportunity to appear at the Duchess of Zurich's house, where she sang the best pieces in her repertory. And here is what the great critic X.Y.Z., who was among the distinguished guests, wrote about her:

> When one hears her in Ambroise Thomas's *Hamlet*, one wonders if Shakespeare came from the Elysian Fields to rehearse her in the role of Ophelia. It is true that when she dons the starry diadem of the Queen of the Night, Mozart must leave his eternal abode to come and hear her. But no, there is no need for him to leave, because the strong, vibrant voice of the magic interpreter of his *Magic Flute* comes to him, easily rising up to heaven, just as she herself went effortlessly from her thatched cottage in the village of Skotelof to the gold and marble palace built by Monsieur Garnier.*

But after the evening at the Duchess of Zurich's house, Christine did not sing again in society. She rejected all invitations and all offers of paid appearances. Without giving a plausible explanation, she refused to appear at a charity concert in which she had previously promised to take part. She acted as if she were no

---

*Jean-Louis-Charles Garnier, known as Charles Garnier, was the architect of the Paris Opera. (Translator's note.)

longer in control of her life, as if she were afraid of a new triumph.

She learned that, to please his brother, Count Philippe de Chagny had made very active efforts on her behalf with Monsieur Richard. She wrote to thank him and also to ask him to say nothing more about her to the managers of the Opera. What reason could she have for such strange behavior? Some attributed it to boundless pride, others to divine modesty. But theatrical people are not overburdened with modesty. Actually, the most likely explanation may have been fear. Yes, I believe that Christine Daae was frightened by what had just happened to her, and that she was as much surprised by it as everyone around her. Surprised? On second thought, no. I have one of her letters (from the Persian's collection) relating to the events of that time, and having reread it, I will not write that she was surprised or even frightened by her triumph, but that she was terrified. Yes, terrified! "I don't recognize myself anymore when I sing," she said. Poor, sweet, pure child!

She showed herself nowhere, and Viscount Raoul de Chagny tried in vain to meet her. He wrote to her, asking permission to come and see her. He was beginning to lose hope of receiving an answer when one morning she sent him the following note:

I have not forgotten the little boy who went into the sea to get my scarf. I cannot restrain myself from writing that to you, now that I am about to go to Perros-Guirec to carry out a sacred duty. Tomorrow is the anniversary of my father's death. You knew him, and he liked you. He is buried there with his violin, in the graveyard that surrounds the little church, at the foot of the hill where we played so often when we were children, and at the edge of the road where, a little older, we told each other good-bye for the last time.

When he had read this note from Christine Daae, Raoul consulted a railroad timetable, quickly got dressed, wrote a few lines for his valet to take to his brother, and jumped into a cab, which brought him to the Montparnasse station too late for the morning train he had hoped to catch.

He spent a dreary day. His good spirits did not return until evening, when he boarded a train. All during the trip he reread Christine's note, smelled its fragrance, and revived sweet images of his younger days. He spent that whole abominable night on the train in a feverish dream that began and ended with Christine.

Dawn was breaking when he got off the train at Lannion and took the coach to Perros-Guirec. He was the only passenger. He questioned the driver and learned that on the evening of the day before a young woman who seemed to be a Parisian had gone to Perros and taken a room at the Inn of the Setting Sun. It could only have been Christine. She had come alone. Raoul sighed deeply. He would be able to talk with her undisturbed in that solitude. He loved her so much that it almost took his breath away. That tall young man who had traveled around the world was as pure as a virgin who has never left her mother's house.

As he came closer to her, he devoutly recalled the story of the little Swedish singer. Many of its details are still unknown to the public.

Once upon a time, in a small town near Uppsala, Sweden, a peasant who lived there with his family cultivated his land during the week and sang bass in the choir on Sunday. This peasant had a little daughter to whom he taught the musical alphabet before she knew how to read. Perhaps without realizing it, Christine Daae's father was a great musician. He played the violin and was regarded as the best fiddler in all of Scandinavia. His reputation spread far and wide, and he was always called on to play for the dancing at weddings and feasts.

Mrs. Daae, an invalid, died when Christine had just begun her sixth year. Her father, who loved only his daughter and his music, immediately sold his land and went off to seek glory in Uppsala. He found only poverty there.

He then returned to the country and began going from fair to fair, playing his Scandinavian melodies while his daughter, who never left him, listened enraptured or sang to the accompaniment of his violin. After hearing them both at the Limby fair one day, Professor Valerius took them to Göteborg. He maintained that the father was the world's best fiddler and that the daughter had the makings of a great singer. He provided for her education and training. Wherever she went, everyone who met her was captivated by her beauty, her charm, and her eagerness to speak and behave well. Her progress was rapid.

When Professor Valerius and his wife had to go and live in France, they took Daae and Christine with them. Mama Valerius treated Christine as her daughter. As for Daae, he began wasting away from homesickness. In Paris he never went out. He lived in a kind of dream that he kept alive with his violin. He spent hours at a time in his room with Christine, playing his violin and singing softly. Sometimes Mama Valerius came to listen to them through the door, sighed heavily, wiped tears from her eyes, and tiptoed away. She too longed to see her Scandinavian skies again.

Daae seemed to regain his vigor only in summer, when the whole family went to stay at Perros-Guirec, in a part of Brittany that was then all but unknown to Parisians. He liked the sea there because, he said, it had the same color as the sea at home. He often played his most plaintive melodies on the beach, and he claimed that the sea fell silent to listen to them.

After much pleading with Mama Valerius, he persuaded her to indulge a whim of his: at the time of religious processions, village festivals, and dances, he went off with his violin as he had done in the past, and he was allowed to take Christine with him for a week. The villagers never tired of listening to them. They would pour a year's worth of harmony into some little hamlet, refuse a bed at the inn that night and sleep in a barn, lying close to each other on the straw, as they had done when they were so poor in Sweden.

They were properly dressed, refused the money that was offered to them, and took up no collections. The people around them did not understand the conduct of that fiddler who roamed the countryside with that beautiful child who sang like an angel in heaven. They were followed from village to village.

One day a boy from Paris, on an outing with his governess, made her walk a long way because he could not bring himself to leave the girl whose sweet, pure voice seemed to have chained him to her. They came to the edge of a cove that is still called Trestraou. In those days, nothing was there but the sky, the sea, and the golden shore. And on this particular day there was a high wind that blew away Christine's scarf and dropped it into the sea. She reached out for it, with a cry, but it was already floating on the waves. Then she heard a voice say, "Don't worry, I'll go and get it for you."

She saw a boy running as fast as he could, despite the shouts and indignant protests of a worthy lady dressed in black. He plunged into the sea fully dressed and brought Christine's scarf back to her. He and the scarf were, of course, sopping wet. The lady in black seemed unable to calm herself but Christine laughed heartily and kissed the boy. He was Viscount Raoul de Chagny, staying for the moment with his aunt at Lannion.

During the summer he and Christine saw each other nearly every day and played together. At his aunt's request, conveyed by Professor Valerius, Daaé began giving the young viscount violin lessons. And so Raoul learned to love the melodies that had enchanted Christine's childhood.

They both had the same kind of calm, dreamy soul. They loved stories, old Breton tales, and their main pastime was to go and ask for them from door to door, like beggars. "Do you have a little story to tell us, please?" they would ask, and it was very seldom that they were not "given" one. Where is the old Breton grandmother who, at least once in her life, has not seen goblins dancing on the moor in moonlight?

But their greatest delight came when, after the sun had sunk into the sea and the great peace of twilight had settled over the countryside, Christine's father sat down with them on the roadside and in a quiet voice, as if to avoid frightening the ghosts he evoked, told them the beautiful, gentle, or terrible legends of the Northland. They were sometimes as charming as Andersen's fairy tales, sometimes as sad as the lyrics of the great poet Runeberg. When he stopped, the two children would say, "More!"

There was one story that began this way: "A king was sitting in a little boat on one of those calm, deep lakes that open like shining eyes among the mountains of Norway." And another that began: "Little Lotte was thinking of everything and nothing. She floated in the golden sunlight like a summer bird, wearing a crown of flowers on her blond curls. Her soul was as clear and blue as her eyes. She was affectionate to her mother and faithful to her doll, she took good care of her dress, her red shoes, and her violin, but what she liked most of all was to listen to the Angel of Music as she was falling asleep."

While Daaé was saying these things, Raoul looked at Christine's blue eyes and golden hair. And Christine thought that little Lotte was lucky to hear the Angel of Music as she was falling asleep. There were few of Daaé's stories in which the Angel of Music did not appear, and the two children questioned him endlessly about that angel. He claimed that all great composers and performers were visited by the Angel of Music at least once in their lives. Sometimes they were visited in the cradle, as little

Lotte was, and that was why there were child prodigies who at the age of six played the violin better than men of fifty, which was extraordinary, as anyone would admit. Sometimes the angel came much later, to children who were disobedient and would not learn their lessons or practice their scales. And to children who did not have a pure heart and a clear conscience, he never came at all. No one ever saw him, but he made himself heard to those predestined to hear him. It often happened when they least expected it, when they were sad and disheartened. Then they suddenly heard heavenly harmonies and a divine voice, and they would remember it all their lives. People visited by the angel were left with a kind of flame burning inside them. They felt a pulsation unknown to other mortals. And they had the privilege of not being able to touch an instrument or open their mouths to sing without making sounds so beautiful that they shamed all other human sounds. Those who did not know that these people had been visited by the Angel of Music said that they had genius.

Little Christine asked her father if he had heard the angel. He sadly shook his head, then looked at her with his eyes shining and said, "You'll hear him some day, my child. When I'm in heaven, I'll send him to you, I promise."

It was during this time that he began coughing.

Autumn came and separated Raoul and Christine.

They saw each other again three years later; by then, they were no longer children. Again it happened in Perros, and the impression it made on Raoul was so strong that it stayed with him ever after. Professor Valerius was dead, but Mama Valerius had remained in France to take care of her financial interests. Christine and her father had also stayed. They still sang and played the violin, sharing their harmonious dream with their beloved benefactress, who now seemed to live only on music. Raoul returned to Perros on the chance of finding them there, and went into the house where they had lived.

He first saw old Daaé, who stood up from his chair with tears in his eyes and embraced him, saying that he and Christine had never forgotten him. And in fact hardly a day had gone by when she did not mention Raoul to him. The old man was still talking when the door opened and Christine briskly walked into the room, looking exquisite and carrying steaming tea on a tray. She recognized Raoul and put down the tray. A light blush spread over her charming face. She stood hesitantly and said nothing. Her father looked at the two young people. Raoul stepped toward her and kissed her, and she did not avoid his kiss. She asked him a few questions, graciously did her duty as a hostess, picked up the tray, and took it away.

She then went out to take refuge on a bench, in the solitude of the garden. Feelings that she had never known before were stirring in her adolescent heart. Raoul came to join her and they talked till evening, ill at ease. They had both changed so much that they scarcely knew each other now, and each felt that the other had acquired a weightier personality. They were as cautious as diplomats and talked about things that had nothing to do with their budding feelings.

As they were taking leave of each other, at the edge of the road, he politely kissed her trembling hand and said, "I'll never forget you!" Then he left, regretting those impulsive words, because he knew that Christine Daaé could not be the wife of Viscount Raoul de Chagny.

As for Christine, she went back to her father and said, "Doesn't it seem to you that Raoul isn't as nice as he used to be? I don't like him anymore!"

She tried to stop thinking about him. Finding it hard to do, she fell back on her art, which took up all her time. Her progress was amazing. Those who listened to her predicted that she would become the world's greatest singer.

But then her father died and it seemed that in losing him she had also lost her voice, her soul, and her genius. She still had enough of all that to enable her to enter the conservatory, but only just enough. She did not distinguish herself in any way; she took her classes without enthusiasm and won a prize to please old Mama Valerius, with whom she continued to live.

The first time Raoul saw Christine at the Opera, he was charmed by her beauty and by his recollection of sweet images from the past, but he was rather surprised by the negative side of her art. She seemed detached from everything. He returned to listen to her. He went backstage, waited for her behind a flat, and tried in vain to attract her attention. More than once he accompanied her to the door of her dressing room, but she did not see him. She seemed, in fact, to see no one. She was indifference personified. Raoul suffered from it, because she was beautiful; he was shy and did not admit to himself that he loved her. Then came the overwhelming revelation on the night of the gala performance, when the heavens opened and an angelic voice was heard on earth, enrapturing everyone who heard it and enthralling Raoul's heart.

And then there was that man's voice heard through the door—"Christine, you must love me!"—and no one in the dressing room. . . .

Why had she laughed when he said to her, just as she was opening her eyes, "I'm the little boy who went into the sea to get your scarf"? Why had she not recognized him? And why had she written to him?

That hill was so long, so long. . . . Here was the crucifix at the crossroads, then the deserted moor, the frozen heath, the motionless landscape under the white sky. The windowpanes rattled and seemed about to break. The coach made so much noise, yet moved so slowly! He recognized the cottages, the farmyards, the slopes, the trees along the way. Here was the last bend in the road; after it, the coach would dash down to the sea, the broad Bay of Perros.

So she was staying at the Inn of the Setting Sun—not surprising, since it was the only inn. Besides, it was very comfortable. He remembered listening to good stories there, long ago. How his heart was pounding! What was she going to say when she saw him?

The first person he saw when he walked into the smoke-darkened dining room of the inn was Mama Tricard. She recognized him, greeted him, and asked what had brought him there. He blushed and said that, having come to Lannion on business, he had decided to go to the inn and tell her hello. She wanted to serve him lunch, but he said, "In a little while." He seemed to be waiting for something or someone.

The door opened and he leapt to his feet. He was not mistaken: it was Christine! She stood before him, smiling, evidently not at all surprised to see him. Her face was as fresh and pink as a shade-grown strawberry. Her breathing was a little hurried, no doubt because she had been walking rapidly. Her bosom, which contained an honest heart, heaved gently. Her eyes—clear, light-blue mirrors, the color of the still lakes that lie dreaming in the far north—calmly showed him a reflection of her guileless soul.

Her fur coat was open, revealing her slender waist and the harmonious lines of her graceful young body.

Raoul and Christine looked at each other a long time. Mama Tricard smiled and discreetly slipped away. Finally Christine spoke:

"You've come and it doesn't surprise me. I had a feeling that I'd find you here when I came back from mass. Someone told me so, at the church. Yes, I was told that you'd come."

"Who told you?" asked Raoul, taking her little hand in both of his own. She did not draw it back.

"My father, my poor dead father."

There was a silence, then he asked, "Did your father also tell you that I love you, Christine, and that I can't live without you?"

She blushed to the roots of her hair and looked away from him.

"You love *me?*" she said in an uncertain voice. "You must be out of your mind, my friend!"

And she laughed, to put up a bold front.

"Don't laugh, Christine, this is very serious."

"I didn't make you come here to tell me such things," she replied gravely.

"But you did make me come here. You knew your letter wouldn't leave me indifferent, and that I'd hurry to Perros. How could you know that without also knowing that I love you?"

"I thought you'd remember our childhood games, which my father joined in so often. . . . Actually, I'm not really sure what I thought. Maybe I shouldn't have written to you. Your sudden appearance in my dressing room the other night took me far back into the past, and I wrote to you like the little girl I was then, a little girl who should be glad to have her little friend with her at a time when she was sad and lonely."

For a few moments, neither of them spoke. There was something in her attitude that seemed unnatural to him, though he could not have said exactly what it was. However, he did not feel that she was hostile to him. Far from it. The sad fondness he saw in her eyes removed any doubt he might have had on that subject. But why was her fondness sad? Maybe that was what puzzled him and had already begun to irritate him.

"When you saw me in your dressing room, Christine, was it the first time you'd seen me?"

She did not know how to lie.

"No," she said, "I'd already seen you several times in your brother's box, and also on the stage."

"I thought so!" Raoul said, pursing his lips. "But then, when you saw me in your dressing room, at your knees, reminding you of the time when I brought your scarf back from the sea, why did you answer as if you didn't know me, and why did you laugh?"

The tone of this question was so harsh that she looked at him in astonishment and made no reply. He too was astonished, to find himself suddenly acting as if he wanted to quarrel with her when he had intended to speak to her gently of love and devotion. Instead, he had sounded like a husband or lover with recognized rights, speaking to a wife or mistress who had offended him. But knowing he was in the wrong only angered him still more. Judging himself to be stupid, he could find no other way out of that ridiculous situation than to persist in his fierce determination to behave odiously.

"You haven't answered me," he said, incensed and miserable. "All right, then, I'll answer for you! It was because there was someone in your dressing room whose presence bothered you, someone you didn't want to show that you could be interested in anyone but him!"

"If someone bothered me," Christine said in an icy tone, "it must have been you, since you're the one I asked to leave."

"Yes, so that you could be alone with the other man!"

"What are you saying?" she asked, breathing rapidly. "What other man are you talking about?"

"The one to whom you said, 'I sing only for you! Tonight I gave you my soul, and I'm dead!' "

She seized his arm and gripped it with a strength that one would not have suspected in such a frail-looking young woman.

"So you were listening at the door?"

"Yes, because I love you. And I heard everything."

"What did you hear?"

Becoming strangely calm, she let go of his arm.

"I heard, 'You must love me.' "

At these words, a deathly pallor spread over Christine's face and dark rings formed around her eyes. She staggered and seemed about to fall. Raoul rushed toward her with his arms outstretched, but she overcame her passing faintness and said in a low, barely audible voice, "Go on, tell me everything you heard."

He looked at her hesitantly, puzzled by her reaction.

"Go on!" she repeated. "Can't you see I'm dying to know?"

"When you told him you'd given him your soul, I heard him answer, 'Your soul is very beautiful, my child, and I thank you. No emperor ever received such a gift! The angels wept tonight.' "

Christine put her hand over her heart and looked at Raoul with indescribable emotion. Her gaze was so intense and unwavering that she almost seemed mad. He was alarmed. But then her eyes became moist and two pearls, two heavy tears, rolled down her ivory cheeks.

"Christine!"

"Raoul!"

He tried to take her in his arms but she slipped away from him and ran off in disarray.

While she remained locked in her room, he bitterly reproached himself for his brutality; but, at the same time, jealousy was still throbbing in his overheated veins. Since she had shown such emotion at learning that he had discovered her secret, it must be a very important secret! In spite of what he had overheard, however, he did not doubt her purity. He knew she had a great reputation for virtue and he was not so unsophisticated as to be unaware that a beautiful young singer sometimes had to listen to words of love. She had answered by saying that she had given her soul, but she had obviously been referring only to her singing. Obviously? Then why did she become so upset just now? Poor Raoul was so unhappy! And if he could have gotten his hands on that man, the man he knew only from his voice, he would have demanded a very precise explanation from him.

Why had Christine run away? Why was she staying in her room?

He refused to have lunch. He was deeply grieved at having to be without Christine during the time that he had hoped to spend so delightfully with her. Why didn't she come downstairs and go with him to wander over that countryside where they had so many shared memories? And since she seemed to have nothing more to do in Perros, and was in fact doing nothing there, why hadn't she already gone back to Paris? He had learned that she had had a mass said for the repose of her father's soul that morning, and that she had spent long hours praying in the little church and at his grave.

Sad and disheartened, Raoul went to the graveyard that surrounded the church. He opened its gate and walked alone among the graves, reading the inscriptions, until he was behind the apse. There, the location of the grave he had been seeking was indicated to him by the brightly colored flowers that covered the granite tombstone and overflowed to the snow-whitened ground. Their fragrance filled the icy air of the Breton winter. Those miraculous red roses, which seemed to have bloomed that morning in the snow, were a little life among the dead, for death was everywhere there. It, too, overflowed, from the ground that had rejected some of its corpses: hundreds of skeletons and skulls were piled up against the wall of the church, held only by a network of thin wire that left the whole macabre edifice in plain view. The skulls, placed in superposed rows like bricks, with whitened bones between them, seemed to form the foundation on which the walls of the vestry had been built, and the door of the vestry opened in the middle of that bone pile. Many old Breton churches still have such piles beside them.

Raoul prayed for Christine's father. Then, unnerved by the eternal smiles of the skulls, he left the graveyard, climbed the slope, and sat down at the edge of the moor overlooking the sea. The wind raced mischievously across the beach, chasing after the scanty remnants of daylight, which finally gave up, fled, and became only a wan streak on the horizon. Then the wind died down. It was evening.

Raoul was enveloped in frigid shadows but he did not feel the cold. All his thoughts and memories were wandering over the deserted, desolate moor. He and little Christine had often come there at nightfall to see the goblins dance when the moon began to rise. He had never seen any goblins, even though he had good eyes, but Christine, who was a little nearsighted, claimed to have seen many of them. He smiled at that recollection, then suddenly started. A well-defined form was standing beside him, having somehow come there without making a sound, and he heard a voice:

"Do you think the goblins will come tonight?"

It was Christine. He opened his mouth to speak but she closed it with her gloved hand.

"Listen to me, Raoul. I've made up my mind to tell you

something serious, very serious." Her voice quavered. He waited. She continued, seeming to have difficulty breathing: "Do you remember the legend of the Angel of Music?"

"Of course I do!" he said. "And I think it was here that your father told us about him for the first time."

"Yes, and it was also here that he said to me, 'When I'm in heaven, I'll send him to you, I promise.' Well, Raoul, my father is in heaven and I've been visited by the Angel of Music."

"I'm sure you have," the young man said gravely, assuming that she was piously associating the memory of her father with her latest triumph.

She seemed a little surprised by the calm with which he took the news that she had been visited by the Angel of Music.

"How do you interpret that?" she asked, moving her pale face so close to his that he thought she was going to kiss him. But she was only trying to read his eyes, in spite of the darkness.

"I interpret it to mean that a human being can't sing as you did the other night unless there's some sort of miracle, unless heaven is involved in some way. No teacher on earth could have taught you such tones. You've heard the Angel of Music, Christine."

"Yes," she said solemnly, "*in my dressing room.* That's where he comes to give me a lesson every day."

She spoke with such singular intensity that he looked at her apprehensively, as if she had just said something shocking, or as if she were a lunatic describing a wild vision in which she believed with all the strength of her poor sick brain. But she had taken a few steps away from him and was now only a motionless shadow in the night.

"In your dressing room?" he repeated like a mindless echo.

"Yes, that's where I've heard him, and I'm not the only one who's heard him."

"Who else?"

"You, Raoul."

"I've heard the Angel of Music?"

"Yes. The other night, he was the one talking to me while you listened at the door of my dressing room. He was the one who said to me, 'You must love me.' I thought no one but me could hear his voice, so you can imagine how surprised I was this morning when I learned that you could hear it too."

Raoul laughed. Just then the darkness over the deserted moor was dispelled and the two young people were enveloped in the first rays of the rising moon. She turned to him with a hostile expression. Her eyes, ordinarily so gentle, flashed lightning.

"Why are you laughing? Do you think you heard a man's voice?"

"Well . . . yes, of course," said Raoul, whose thoughts were becoming confused as a result of Christine's belligerent attitude.

"How can *you* say that to me, Raoul? You, my childhood playmate, my father's friend! You seem to have changed into someone else! What do you believe? I'm an honorable woman, Viscount de Chagny, and I don't shut myself up in my dressing room with men's voices. If you'd opened the door, you'd have seen there was no one there!"

"I know. After you left, I did open the door and I found no one in your dressing room."

"You see? Well, then?"

Raoul summoned up all his courage.

"Christine, I think someone is playing a joke on you."

She uttered a cry and ran away. He ran after her, but she said to him with fierce anger, "Leave me alone! Leave me alone!"

And she disappeared. He went back to the inn overwhelmed with weariness, discouragement, and sadness.

He learned that Christine had just gone up to her room after saying she would not come down for dinner. He asked if she was ill. The good-natured innkeeper answered ambiguously that if she was ill, her sickness must not be very serious. Then, thinking there had been a lovers' quarrel, she walked away, shrugging her shoulders and muttering about what a pity it was for young people to waste time on silly bickering when God had given them only a certain number of days to spend on earth.

Raoul ate dinner by the fireside, alone and, as you may well suppose, plunged in gloom. In his room, he tried to read; then, in bed, he tried to sleep. No sound came from the room next door. What was Christine doing? Was she asleep? If not, what was she thinking about? And what was *he* thinking about? It would have been hard for him to say. His strange conversation with Christine had thoroughly confused him. He thought not so much *of* her as *around* her, and that "around" was so diffuse, so nebulous, so elusive, that it made him feel an odd, distressing kind of uneasiness.

So the hours went by, very slowly. It was about eleven-thirty at night when he distinctly heard light, furtive footsteps from the next room. Was Christine still up? Without reasoning about what he was doing, he quickly got dressed, being careful not to make a sound. Then, ready for anything, he waited. Ready for what? He did not know. His heart pounded when he heard Christine's door turn on its hinges. Where was she going at that time of night when the whole town of Perros was asleep?

He gently pushed his door ajar and, in a ray of moonlight, saw Christine's white form cautiously moving along the hall. She reached the stairs and went down. Above her, he leaned over the banister. Suddenly he heard two voices conversing rapidly. He was able to make out only one sentence: "Don't lose the key." It was the innkeeper's voice. Downstairs, the door facing the waterfront was opened and closed, and then there was silence. Raoul went back into his room, hurried to his window, and opened it. Christine's white form was standing on the deserted wharf.

The second floor of the Inn of the Setting Sun was not very high. A tree growing against the wall held out its branches to Raoul's impatient arms and enabled him to climb down, unknown to the innkeeper. The good woman was therefore astounded the next morning when he was brought to her half frozen, more dead than alive, and she learned that he had been found lying on the steps of the high altar of the little church in Perros. She immediately went to give the news to Christine, who ran downstairs and, with the innkeeper's help, anxiously tried to bring Raoul back to his senses. He soon opened his eyes and completely regained consciousness when he saw Christine's charming face above him.

What had happened? A few weeks later, when tragic events at the Opera required action by the Department of the Public Prosecutor, Police Commissary Mifroid had occasion to question Viscount de Chagny about that night in Perros. Here is how his testimony was transcribed in the records of the investigation (Document no. 150):

Question. Did Mademoiselle Daaé see you come down from your room in the unusual way you chose?

Answer. No, sir, no. But I went after her without making any effort to muffle the sound of my footsteps. All I wanted was for her to turn around, see me, and recognize me, because I'd just realized that the way I was following her and spying on her was unworthy of me. But she seemed not to hear me and acted as if I weren't there. She calmly left the wharf and began walking rapidly up the road. The church clock had just struck a quarter to midnight, and it seemed to me that hearing it was what had made her go faster. She was almost running. Before long she came to the gate of the graveyard.

Q. Was the gate open?

A. Yes, and that surprised me, though it didn't seem to surprise Mademoiselle Daae at all.

Q. Was there anyone in the cemetery?

A. I saw no one. If someone had been there, I would have seen him. The moon was shining, and the snow on the ground reflected its light and made it even brighter.

Q. Couldn't someone have been hiding behind a gravestone?

A. No. The gravestones are small there. They were covered by the snow, except for their crosses. The only shadows were the ones cast by the crosses and by Mademoiselle Daae and me. The church was dazzling in the moonlight. I've never seen such a bright night. It was very beautiful, very clear and very cold. It was the first time I'd ever been in a graveyard at night, and I hadn't known that such light could be found there, "a light that weighs nothing."

Q. Are you superstitious?

A. No. I'm a believing Christian.

Q. What was your state of mind at that time?

A. I was clearheaded and relaxed. At first I'd been deeply troubled to see Mademoiselle Daae go out like that, in the middle of the night, but when I saw her go into the grave-yard, I thought she intended to fulfill a vow at her father's grave, and it seemed so natural to me that I regained all my calm. I was simply surprised that she hadn't yet heard me walking behind her, because the snow was crunching under my feet. But she must have been completely absorbed in her pious thoughts. I decided not to disturb her, and when she stopped at her father's grave I stood a few steps behind her. She knelt in the snow, crossed herself, and began praying.

Just then the clock struck midnight. The twelfth stroke was still ringing in my ears when I saw her look up at the sky and raise her arms toward the moon. She seemed to be in some sort of rapture and I wondered what could have caused it. Then I also raised my head; I looked all around in bewilderment and my whole being was drawn toward the invisible, which was playing music! And what music! Christine and I already knew it, we had heard it in our childhood. But on her father's violin it had never been played with such divine art. I couldn't help remembering what Christine had said about the Angel of Music and I didn't quite know what to think of those unforgettable sounds: although they weren't coming down from heaven, it was easy to believe they didn't have an earthly origin, since there was no violin, bow, or violinist in sight.

I clearly recalled that marvelous melody. It was *The Resurrection of Lazarus,* which Christine's father used to play for us when he was feeling sad and pious. If Christine's angel had existed, he couldn't have played better on her father's violin. The invocation of Jesus lifted us above the earth, and I almost expected to see her father's gravestone rise into the air. I also had the idea that his violin had been buried with him, but I can't say how far my imagination took me during those melancholy yet radiant moments, in that isolated little provincial graveyard, beside those skulls grinning at us with their motionless jaws. Then the music stopped and I came back to my senses. I seemed to hear sounds from the direction of the skulls in the pile of bones.

Q. Ah, you heard sounds from the pile of bones?

A. Yes, it seemed to me that the skulls were laughing at us now. I couldn't help shuddering.

Q. Didn't it immediately occur to you that the heavenly musician who had just captivated you so strongly might be hiding behind the pile of bones?

A. Yes, it did occur to me, and it was so much on my mind that I didn't think to follow Christine when she stood up and calmly walked out of the graveyard. As for her, she was so deeply absorbed in her thoughts that it's not surprising she didn't see me. I stayed still, looking at the pile of bones, determined to carry that incredible adventure through to the end and find out what was behind it.

Q. How did it come about that in the morning you were found lying half dead on the steps of the high altar?

A. It happened quickly. . . . A skull rolled toward me, then another, and another. It was as if I were the target in a gruesome game of bowls. And I thought that the musician hiding behind the pile of bones must have accidentally bumped against it and destroyed its balance. That idea seemed all the more plausible to me when I saw a shadow suddenly move along the brightly lit wall of the vestry.

I rushed forward. The shadow had already opened the door of the church and gone inside. I ran as fast as I could and was able to take hold of the cloak that the shadow was wearing. At that moment the two of us were just in front of the high altar, and the moonlight coming through the stained-glass window of the apse fell directly onto us. I was still clutching the cloak. The shadow turned around, the cloak opened a little and I saw, as clearly as I see you, sir, a horrible death's-head glaring at me with eyes in which the fires of hell burned. I thought it was Satan himself. At the sight of that unearthly apparition, my heart failed me in spite of all its courage and I don't remember anything from then until the time when I woke up in my little room at the Inn of the Setting Sun.

7

A Visit to Box Five

WE LEFT FIRMIN Richard and Armand Moncharmin just as they had decided to pay a little visit to First-Tier Box Five.

They walked away from the broad staircase that leads from the vestibule of the administration to the stage and its dependencies. They crossed the stage, went into the auditorium through the subscribers' entrance, and took the first corridor on the left. Then they walked past the first rows of orchestra seats, stopped, and looked at First-Tier Box Five. They could not see it clearly because it was in semidarkness and protective covers had been put over the red velvet railings.

They were almost alone in the vast, shadowy auditorium and great silence surrounded them. It was the quiet hour when the stagehands went to have a drink. They had temporarily deserted the stage, leaving a flat only partly secured. A few rays of light (a wan, dreary light that seemed to have been stolen from a dying star) had slipped in through some opening or other and were shining on an old tower, topped by cardboard battlements, that stood on the stage. In that artificial night, or rather in that deceptive daylight, things took on strange forms. The cloth that covered the orchestra seats looked like an angry sea whose bluish green waves had been instantaneously immobilized by secret order of the storm giant, whose name, as everyone knows, is Adamastor.

Moncharmin and Richard were like shipwrecked sailors at the edge of that motionlessly agitated cloth sea. As if they had abandoned their boat and were trying to swim to shore, they made their way toward the left-side boxes. The eight big pillars of polished stone rose in the shadows like prodigious pilings intended to support the menacing, tottering, bulging cliffs whose foundation was represented by the curved, parallel, sagging lines of the railings in the first, second, and third tiers of boxes.

At the very top of the cliff, lost in Lenepveu's* copper sky, figures grimaced, laughed, jeered, and made fun of Moncharmin and Richard's apprehension, though ordinarily they were very serious figures. Their names were Isis, Amphitrite, Hebe, Flora, Pandora, Psyche, Thetis, Pomona, Daphne, Clytie, Galatea, and Arethusa. Yes, Arethusa herself, and Pandora, known to everyone because of her box, looked down at the two new managers of the Opera, who had finally clutched some piece of wreckage and were now silently contemplating First-Tier Box Five.

I have said that they were apprehensive. At least I presume they were. In any case, Moncharmin admitted that he was perturbed. He wrote in his memoirs:

> The claptrap about the Opera ghost that we had been fed [What an elegant stylist Moncharmin was!] ever since we succeeded Poligny and Debienne as managers must have impaired the balance of my imaginative faculties and, all things considered, of my visual faculties as well. Perhaps it was the extraordinary setting in which we found ourselves, in the midst of an incredible silence, that perturbed us so much; perhaps we were victims of a kind of hallucination made possible by the semidarkness in the auditorium and the even deeper shadows in Box Five. At the same moment, Richard and I both saw a shape in Box Five. Neither of us said anything, but we gripped each other's hand. Then we waited a few minutes like that, without moving, always staring at the same point. But the shape had disappeared.
>
> We went out, and in the hall we told each other about our impressions and talked about the shape. Unfortunately, my shape was not the same as Richard's. I had seen what seemed to be a skull on the railing of the box, whereas Richard had seen the shape of an old woman who looked like Madame Giry. We realized that we had been victims of an illusion.

*Jules-Eugène Lenepveu was a French painter who decorated the ceiling of the Paris Opera. (Translator's note.)

Laughing wildly, we immediately hurried to Box Five, went into it, and found no shape there.

And now we are in Box Five. It is a box like all the other first-tier boxes. Nothing distinguishes it from its neighbors.

Obviously amused, laughing at each other, Moncharmin and Richard moved the furniture in the box, lifted the covers and the chairs, and carefully examined the chair in which "the voice" usually "sat." But they saw that it was an honest chair, with nothing magic about it. The box was thoroughly ordinary in every way, with its red hangings, its chairs, its carpet, and its railing covered with red velvet. After feeling the carpet with perfect seriousness and discovering nothing more there than anywhere else in the box, they went down to the ground-floor box directly below. In Ground-Floor Box Five, which is just at the corner of the first left-hand exit from the orchestra seats, they also failed to find anything noteworthy.

"Those people are all trying to make fools of us!" Firmin Richard finally said angrily. "*Faust* is being performed on Saturday—we'll both watch it from First-Tier Box Five!"

8

In Which Firmin Richard and Armand Moncharmin Dare to Have *Faust* Performed in a "Cursed" Opera House, and We See the Frightful Consequences

WHEN THE TWO managers came to their office on Saturday morning, they found a double letter from O. G.:

My Dear Managers,
   Are we at war, then? If you still want peace, here is my ultimatum. It has four conditions:
   1. You will give me back my box—and I want it placed at my disposal immediately.
   2. The role of Marguerite will be sung tonight by Christine Daae. Do not worry about Carlotta; she will be ill.
   3. I insist on having the good and loyal services of Madame Giry, my usher. You will restore her to her position without delay.
   4. In a letter to be delivered by Madame Giry, you, like your predecessors, will accept the provisions in my book of instructions concerning my monthly allowance. I will later let you know in what form you will pay it to me.

If you do not meet these conditions, tonight you will present *Faust* in a cursed house.

A word to the wise is sufficient.

O. G.

"I've had enough of him!" shouted Richard, vigorously pounding his desk with both fists.

Mercier, the administrator, came in.

"Lachenal would like to see one of you gentlemen," he said. "He says it's urgent, and he seems upset."

"Who's Lachenal?" asked Richard.

"He's your head stableman."

"What? My head stableman?"

"Yes, sir," replied Mercier. "There are several stablemen at the Opera, and Lachenal is their leader."

"And what does he do?"

"He's in charge of the stable."

"What stable?"

"Yours, sir. The stable of the Opera."

"There's a stable in the Opera? I had no idea! Where is it?"

"In the cellars, in the direction of the rotunda. It's an important department. We have twelve horses."

"Twelve horses! What for, in God's name?"

"For the processions in *La Juive, Le Prophète*, and so on, we need trained horses that 'know the stage.' The stablemen have the duty of teaching it to them. Lachenal is a highly skilled trainer. He used to manage the Franconi stables."

"Very well. . . . But what does he want with me?"

"I don't know. I only know I've never seen him in such a state."

"Bring him in."

Lachenal came in and impatiently struck one of his boots with the riding crop he had in his hand.

"Good morning, Monsieur Lachenal," said Richard, a little intimidated. "To what do I owe the honor of your visit?"

"Sir, I've come to ask you to get rid of the whole stable."

"What! You want to get rid of our horses?"

"Not the horses: the stablemen."

"How many stablemen do you have, Monsieur Lachenal?"

"Six."

"Six stablemen! That's at least two too many!"

"Those positions," Mercier explained, "were created and imposed on us by the undersecretary of the Fine Arts Administration. They're occupied by protégés of the government, and if I may venture to . . ."

"I don't care about the government!" Richard declared emphatically. "We don't need more than four stablemen for twelve horses."

"Eleven," Lachenal corrected.

"Twelve!" Richard repeated.

"Eleven!" Lachenal repeated.

"Monsieur Mercier told me you had twelve horses!"

"I did have twelve, but I only have eleven now that César has been stolen!"

And Lachenal gave himself a mighty blow on the boot with his riding crop.

"César has been stolen?" asked Mercier. "César, the big white horse in *Le Prophète?*"

"There aren't two Césars!" Lachenal said curtly. "I was with the Franconi stables for ten years, and I saw many, many horses, and I can tell you that there aren't two Césars! And he's been stolen!"

"How did it happen?"

"I don't know. Nobody knows. That's why I've come to ask you to get rid of everybody in the stable."

"What do your stablemen say about the theft?"

"Foolish things. Some of them accuse the supernumeraries, others claim it was the administration's bookkeeper."

"The administration's bookkeeper? I'm as sure of him as I am of myself!" Mercier protested.

"But, Monsieur Lachenal," said Richard, "you must have some idea . . ."

"Yes, I have an idea," Lachenal said abruptly, "and I'll tell you what it is. As far as I'm concerned, there's no doubt." He stepped closer to the managers and said in an undertone, "It was the ghost who did it."

Richard started.

"Ah! You too! You too!"

"What do you mean, me too? It's perfectly natural . . ."

"Perfectly natural, Monsieur Lachenal? What's perfectly natural?"

"For me to tell you what I think, after what I saw."

"And what did you see, Monsieur Lachenal?"

"I saw, as plainly as I see you, a dark figure riding a white horse that looked exactly like César."

"And you didn't run after the white horse and the dark figure?"

"Yes, I did, and I shouted too, but they kept going at great speed and disappeared into the darkness of the gallery."

Richard stood up.

"Very well, Monsieur Lachenal, you may go now. We'll lodge a complaint against the ghost."

"And you'll fire everyone in my stable?"

"Yes, yes, of course. Good-bye."

Lachenal bowed and left.

Richard was fuming with anger.

"Take that idiot off the payroll immediately!" he ordered Mercier.

"He's a friend of the government representative," Mercier dared to point out.

"And he has a drink every day at the Café Tortoni with Lagréné, Scholl, and Pertruiset, the lion killer," Moncharmin added. "We'll have the whole press on our back! He'll tell about the ghost and everyone will laugh at us. If we're ridiculous, we're dead!"

"All right, let's not talk about it anymore," Richard conceded, and he was already thinking about something else.

Just then the door opened. It was evidently not being guarded by its usual defender, because Madame Giry burst into the room with a letter in her hand and said hurriedly, "Excuse me, gentlemen, but this morning I got a letter from the Opera ghost telling me to come and see you because you had something to . . ."

She did not finish her sentence. She saw Firmin Richard's face and it was a terrifying sight. He seemed ready to explode. So far, the only outer signs of the anger boiling inside him were the color of his furious face and the lightning flashing in his eyes. He said nothing. He was unable to speak. But suddenly he went into action. First his left hand seized the drab Madame Giry and turned her in such a rapid, unexpected semicircle that she uttered a desperate cry, and then his right foot imprinted its sole on the black taffeta of a skirt that had surely never before been subjected to such an outrage at such a place.

It was all over so quickly that when Madame Giry found herself in the hall, she was still dazed and seemed not to realize what had happened to her. Then all at once she did realize it, and the Opera resounded with her indignant shrieks, fierce protests, and threats of death. It took three boys to get her downstairs and two policemen to carry her into the street.

At about this same time, Carlotta, who lived in a small house on the Rue du Faubourg-Saint-Honoré, rang for her maid and had her mail brought to her in bed. In it she found an anonymous letter:

> If you sing tonight, you must expect a great misfortune to strike you just when you begin to sing, a misfortune worse than death.

This threat was clumsily written in red ink. After reading it, Carlotta had no appetite for breakfast. She pushed away the tray on which the maid had brought her hot chocolate. She sat up in bed and became lost in thought. That letter was not the first of its kind that she had received, but it was more threatening than any of the others.

She believed that all sorts of jealous scheming was directed against her, and she often said that she had a secret enemy determined to ruin her. She claimed to be the target of a vicious plot that would eventually come to light, but, she added, she was not the kind of woman who would let herself be intimidated.

The truth is, however, that the only plot was the one that Carlotta herself directed against poor Christine, who was unaware of it. Carlotta had not forgiven Christine for achieving a great triumph when she replaced her at a moment's notice.

When she learned of the extraordinary reception that had been given to her replacement, Carlotta had felt instantly cured of an incipient case of bronchitis and a fit of sulking against the administration, and she had no longer shown the slightest desire to give up her position at the Opera. Since then, she had been working with all her might to "smother" her rival, having her powerful friends exert pressure on the managers to prevent them from giving Christine a chance for another triumph. Certain newspapers that had begun praising Christine's talent were now exclusively devoted to Carlotta's glory. At the Opera itself, the famous diva said outrageously offensive things about Christine and tried to cause her endless annoyances.

Carlotta had neither heart nor soul. She was only an instrument, though undeniably a marvelous one. Her repertory included everything that might tempt the ambition of a great singer, from German, Italian, and French composers. She had never been known to sing off-key or lack the vocal volume required for any part of her vast repertory. In short, the instrument was powerful and admirably precise, and had a broad range. But no one could have said to Carlotta what Rossini said to Marie Gabriele Krauss when she had sung *Dark Forests* for him in German: "You sing with your soul, my child, and your soul is beautiful."

Where was your soul, Carlotta, when you danced in disreputable taverns in Barcelona? Where was it later, in Paris, when you sang coarse, cynical songs in dingy music halls? Where was your soul when, in front of the masters gathered in the house of one of your lovers, you drew music from that docile instrument remarkable for its ability to sing about sublime love or sordid debauchery with the same indifferent perfection? Carlotta, if you once had a soul and then lost it, you would have regained it when you became Juliet, Elvira, Ophelia, and Marguerite, for others have risen from greater depths than you, and been purified by art, with the help of love.

When Carlotta had finished thinking about the threat in the strange letter she had just received, she stood up from her bed.

"We'll see," she said, and swore a few oaths in Spanish, with a very determined expression.

The first thing she saw when she went to the window was a hearse. The hearse and the letter convinced her that she would be in great danger that night. She summoned all her friends to her house, announced that a plot organized by Christine Daae threatened to harm her during that evening's performance, and said she wanted to foil it by filling the house with her own admirers. And she had plenty of admirers, didn't she? She was counting on them to be ready for anything and to silence her enemies if, as she feared, they tried to create a disturbance.

Having come for news of Carlotta's health, Firmin Richard's secretary went back to report that she was perfectly well and would sing the role of Marguerite that night "even if she is dying."

Since the secretary had, on Richard's behalf, urged her to be careful, stay at home all day, and avoid drafts, after his departure she could not help comparing those unusual and unexpected recommendations with the threat conveyed by the letter.

At five o'clock she received another anonymous letter in the same handwriting as the first one. It was brief; it said simply:

> You have a cold; if you are sensible, you will realize that it would be madness to try to sing tonight.

Carlotta laughed disdainfully, shrugged her magnificent shoulders, and sang two or three notes, which reassured her.

Her friends kept their promise: they were all at the Opera that evening. But they vainly looked around for the ferocious conspirators they were supposed to battle against. Except for a few outsiders—respectable middle-class citizens whose placid faces reflected no other intention than to listen once again to music that had long since won their favor—the audience was composed of regular operagoers whose elegant appearance and peaceful, proper manners ruled out any suspicion that they might be planning to create a disturbance. The only thing that seemed abnormal was the presence of Richard and Moncharmin in Box Five. Carlotta's friends thought that perhaps the managers had gotten wind of the planned disturbance and had wanted to be in the auditorium so that they could stop it as soon as it began, but that was a baseless hypothesis, as you know: Richard and Moncharmin were now thinking only of their ghost.

> *Vain! In vain do I call*
> *Throughout my vigil weary*
> *On Creation and its Lord!*
> *Never reply will break the silence dreary,*
> *No sign! no single word!*

Carolus Fonta, the famous baritone, had scarcely begun Dr. Faust's first appeal to the powers of hell when Richard, who was sitting on the ghost's own chair—the first chair on the right in the first row—leaned toward his colleague and said jovially, "What about you? Has a voice said something in your ear yet?"

"Wait, let's not be in too much of a hurry," Moncharmin replied in the same joking tone. "The performance has just begun, and you know that the ghost usually doesn't arrive till the middle of the first act.''

The first act went by without incident, which did not surprise Carlotta's friends, since Marguerite does not sing in that act.

When the curtain fell, the two managers looked at each other and smiled.

"One down!" said Moncharmin.

"Yes, the ghost is late," Richard answered.

"It's a fairly distinguished audience," Moncharmin remarked, still joking, "for a 'cursed house.' ''

Richard deigned to smile again and pointed out to his colleague a fat, rather vulgar-looking woman dressed in black, sitting in an orchestra seat in the middle of the auditorium and flanked by two men of coarse appearance wearing broadcloth frock coats.

"What's that?" asked Moncharmin.

" 'That,' my friend, is my concierge, her brother, and her husband.''

"You gave them tickets?"

"Yes, I did. My concierge had never been to the Opera. This is her first time. And since she'll be coming here every night from now on, I wanted her to have a good seat at least once, before she begins showing other people to theirs.''

Moncharmin asked for an explanation and Richard told him that he had decided to have his concierge, in whom he had great confidence, come and take Madame Giry's place for a time.

"Speaking of Madame Giry," said Moncharmin, "do you know she's going to lodge a complaint against you?"

"With whom? The ghost?"

The ghost! Moncharmin had almost forgotten him, and so far the mysterious being had done nothing to remind the managers of his existence.

Suddenly the door of their box opened and the stage manager came in, looking flustered.

"What's wrong?" they both asked at once, astonished to see him come there at such a time.

"What's wrong," he replied, "is that Christine Daae's friends have hatched a plot against Carlotta! Carlotta is furious!"

"What are you talking about?" said Richard, frowning.

But then, seeing that the curtain was rising for the second act, he motioned the stage manager to leave.

When the stage manager was gone, Moncharmin leaned close to Richard's ear and asked, "So Daae has friends?"

"Yes."

"Who are they?"

Richard nodded toward a first-tier box in which there were only two men.

"Count de Chagny?"

"Yes. He spoke to me in her favor so warmly that if I hadn't known he was La Sorelli's friend . . ."

"Well, well . . ." Moncharmin murmured. "And who's the pale young man sitting beside him?"

"His brother, the viscount."

"He ought to be in bed. He looks sick."

The stage resounded with joyous singing. Intoxication in music. The triumph of the goblet.

> *Red or white liquor,*
> *Coarse or fine!*
> *What can it matter,*
> *So we have wine?*

Lighthearted students, burghers, soldiers, young women, and matrons where whirling in front of a tavern with the god Bacchus on its sign. Siebel entered.

Christine Daae was appealing in her masculine attire. Her fresh youth and melancholy charm made her captivating at first sight. Carlotta's partisans assumed that Christine was going to be greeted with an ovation that would inform them of her friends' intentions. Such an indiscreet ovation would have been a glaring blunder. It did not take place.

But Carlotta, in the role of Marguerite, was loudly cheered when she had crossed the stage and sung her only lines in that second act:

> *No, my lord, not a lady am I,*
> *Nor yet a beauty, not a lady, not a beauty;*
> *And do not need an arm*
> *To help me on my way!*

The cheering was so unexpected and inappropriate that those who knew nothing about the supposed plans for a disturbance looked at each other and wondered what was going on.

This act also ended without incident. Carlotta's supporters assumed that the disturbance would surely occur during the next act. Some of them, apparently better informed than the others, said it would begin with "the King of Thule's gold cup," and they hurried off toward the subscribers' entrance to go and warn Carlotta.

Richard and Moncharmin left their box during the intermission to see if they could find out something about the plot that the stage manager had mentioned to them, but they soon came back, shrugging their shoulders and saying that the whole affair was nothing but foolishness.

When they went into the box, the first thing they noticed was a box of hard candy on the railing. Who had put it there? They questioned the ushers but none of them knew anything. Turning toward the railing again, this time they saw a pair of opera glasses beside the box of candy. They looked at each other; neither of them felt like laughing now. They remembered everything Madame Giry had told them. And then they seemed to feel a strange kind of draft around them. . . . They sat down in silence, extremely ill at ease.

The scene represented Marguerite's garden.

And assure her my love is strong and pure,
Tell my hopes and fears. . . .

As Christine sang these opening lines, holding a bouquet of roses and lilacs, she looked up and saw Viscount Raoul de Chagny in his box. From then on it seemed to everyone that her voice was less firm, less pure, less crystalline than usual, as if something were dulling and muffling it. It gave an impression of fear and trembling.

"She's a strange girl," remarked one of Carlotta's friends in the orchestra seats, speaking almost loudly. "The other night she was divine, and now she's bleating like a goat. No experience, no training!"

Tell her, sweet flowers, I love her.

Raoul buried his head in his hands. He was weeping. Behind him, Count Philippe chewed the tip of his mustache, shrugged his shoulders, and frowned. To be showing his inner feelings by so many outer signs, the count, ordinarily so proper and cold, must have been furious. He was. He had seen his brother come back from a rapid and mysterious journey in an alarming state of ill health. The explanations that followed had failed to put Philippe's mind at rest. Wanting to know more about what had happened, he had asked Christine Daaé for an appointment. She had had the audacity to answer that she could not receive him or his brother. He had thought she was engaging in some sort of contemptible maneuver. He considered that she was unforgivable for making Raoul suffer, but that Raoul was even more so for suffering because of her. How wrong he had been to take a brief interest in that girl whose one-night triumph was now incomprehensible to everyone!

> *Thus speak, sweet flowers, for me;*
> *Thus plead, sweet flowers, for me.*

"The crafty little wench!" Philippe muttered.

And he wondered what she wanted, what she could be hoping for. She was pure, she was said to have no gentleman friend, no protector of any kind. That Scandinavian angel must be sly as a fox!

Still sitting with his hands in front of his face like a curtain hiding his childish tears, Raoul thought only of the letter he had received when he returned to Paris, where Christine had arrived before him, having fled from Perros like a thief:

> *My dear former little friend,*
>   *You must have the courage never to see or speak to me again. If you love me a little, do that for me. I will never forget you, my dear Raoul. Most important of all, never come into my dressing room again. My life depends on it. So does yours.*
>   *Your little Christine*

A thunder of applause: Carlotta was making her entrance.

The garden act unfolded with its usual plot developments. When Carlotta had finished singing the King of Thule aria, she was cheered and applauded, and the same thing happened when she had finished the gem aria:

> *No! 'tis a princess I view,*
> *'Tis a princess before me!*

Sure of herself, her friends in the audience, her voice, and her success, no longer fearing anything, Carlotta gave herself entirely, with ardor and enthusiasm, ecstatically. Her acting was now without restraint or modesty. She was no longer Marguerite, she was Carmen. She was applauded all the more, and it seemed that her duet with Faust was about to bring her a new triumph. But all at once something terrible happened.

Faust had knelt:

> *Let me gaze on the form before me,*
> *While from yonder ether blue,*
> *Look how the star of eve,*
> *Bright and tender, lingers o'er me*
> *To love, to love thy beauty too!*

And Marguerite replied:

> *O how strange, like a spell*
> *Does the evening bind me!*
> *And a deep languid charm*
> *I feel without alarm*
> *With its melody enwind me.*

Just then, at that very moment, something . . . something terrible, as I have said, happened.

The whole audience stood up at once. In their box, the two managers could not hold back an exclamation of horror. The spectators exchanged puzzled looks, as though to ask each other for an explanation of that startling occurrence. Carlotta's face expressed agonizing pain and her eyes seemed haunted by madness. The poor woman stood with her mouth half open, having just sung ". . . with its melody enwind me."

But her mouth was not singing now. She was afraid to utter a word or make a sound, because that mouth created for harmony, that deft instrument which had never faltered, that magnificent organ which generated the most enchanting sounds, the most difficult chords, the subtlest modulations, the most ardent rhythms, that sublime human mechanism which, to be divine, lacked only the fire of heaven that alone gives true emotion and uplifts souls—that mouth had . . . From that mouth had come . . . a toad! A hideous, ghastly, scaly, venomous, foaming, croaking toad!

Where had it come from? How had it crouched on her tongue? With its hind legs bent so that it could jump higher and farther, it had waited, then treacherously come out of her larynx and croaked. Croak! Croak! Ah, that terrible croak!

As you must have realized, we are not talking about an actual, flesh-and-blood toad, but about the sound of one. That toad could not be seen but, by the devil, it could be heard! Croak!

The people in the audience felt as if they had been spattered. No real toad at the edge of a clamorous pond ever rent the night with an uglier croak!

And, of course, it was completely unexpected to everyone. Carlotta could not believe her throat or her ears. Lightning striking the stage in front of her would have surprised her less than the croaking toad that had just come from her mouth. And lightning would not have dishonored her, whereas it is well known that a toad on a singer's tongue always dishonors her. Some singers have even died of it.

Who would have believed it? She had been singing serenely, ". . . with its melody enwind me," she had been singing effortlessly, as easily as you say, "Hello, how are you?"

It cannot be denied that there are presumptuous singers who make the grave mistake of overestimating their strength and, in their arrogance, try to use the weak voice given to them by heaven to produce extraordinary effects and sing notes that are simply beyond the reach of the vocal equipment they were born with. Then, to punish them, heaven unexpectedly afflicts them with a croaking toad in the mouth. Everyone knows that. But no one could accept the idea that a singer like Carlotta, who had at least two octaves in her voice, also had a toad in it.

The members of the audience could not have forgotten her powerful high notes and incredible staccati in *The Magic Flute*. They remembered her resounding triumph one night when, as Elvira in *Don Giovanni*, she sang the B flat that her comrade Doña Anna was unable to sing. Really, then, what was the meaning of that croak at the end of the tranquil ". . . with its melody enwind me"?

It was not natural. There was sorcery in it. Dark powers were behind that toad. Poor, wretched, despairing, overwhelmed Carlotta!

The tumult in the audience was growing. If such a thing had happened to another singer, they would have booed her, but with Carlotta, knowing her perfect voice, they showed consternation and alarm, rather than anger. It was the kind of consternation they would have felt if they had witnessed the catastrophe that broke off the arms of the Venus de Milo. In that case, however, they would have been able to see what happened, and understand it, whereas now . . . That toad was incomprehensible!

For a few seconds Carlotta wondered if she had really heard that note come out of her mouth. But could that sound be called a note? Could it even be called a sound? A sound was still music. . . . She tried to convince herself that she had not really heard that infernal noise, that she had been deceived by her ears, and not criminally betrayed by her voice.

She desperately looked around as though seeking protection, a refuge, or rather a spontaneous assurance of her voice's innocence. She put her stiffened fingers to her throat in a gesture of self-defense and protest. No, no, that croak had not come from her! And it seemed that Carolus Fonta agreed with her: he was looking at her with an indescribable expression of boundless, childish amazement. For he was still with her, he had not left her—maybe he could tell her how such a thing could have happened. No, he could not. He was staring at her mouth in bewilderment, like a child staring at a conjurer's inexhaustible hat. How could such a little mouth have contained such a big croak?

Everything that I have been describing in detail—toad, croak, consternation, terror, tumult in the audience, confusion on the stage and in the wings, where several supernumeraries showed frightened faces—lasted a few seconds.

A few horrible seconds that seemed endless to the two managers in Box Five. Moncharmin and Richard were very pale. That incredible, inexplicable incident had filled them with an anguish that was all the more mysterious because for several moments now they had been under the direct influence of the ghost.

They had felt his breath. A few of Moncharmin's hairs had stood on end beneath that breath. Richard had taken out his handkerchief to wipe the sweat off his forehead. Yes, the ghost was there, around them, behind them, beside them. They sensed him without seeing him. They heard him breathing—so close to them, so close! Somehow one *knows* when someone is present, and now they knew! They were certain that they were not alone in the box. They trembled, they wanted to run away but were afraid to try. They were afraid to make a move or say a word that might tell the ghost they knew he was there. What was going to happen?

The croak happened. Their double exclamation of horror was heard above all the other sounds in the auditorium. They felt that they were under attack by the ghost. Leaning over the railing of their box, they looked at Carlotta as if they did not recognize her. With her croak, that devilish woman must have given the signal for some sort of disaster. And they had been expecting a disaster! The ghost had promised it to them! The house was cursed! Their double managerial chest was already heaving beneath the weight of the disaster.

Everyone heard Richard's choked voice cry out to Carlotta: "Go on! Go on!"

But Carlotta did not go on from the point where she had stopped. Bravely, heroically, she resumed the lines at the end of which the toad had appeared.

> *O how strange, like a spell*
> *Does the evening bind me.*

The audience also seemed spellbound.

> *And a deep languid charm* [Croak!]
> *I feel without* [Croak!] *alarm*
> *With its melody* [Croak!] . . .

The toad too had resumed.

The audience burst into a prodigious uproar. Slumped back in their seats, the two managers lacked both the courage and the strength to turn around. The ghost was laughing close behind them! And finally, in their right ears, they distinctly heard his voice, his impossible, mouthless voice:

"The way she's singing tonight, she'll bring down the chandelier!"

They both looked up and uttered a terrible cry. The chandelier, the enormous mass of the chandelier, was falling, answering the call of that satanic voice. It plunged from the ceiling and crashed into the middle of the orchestra seats in the midst of countless screams and shouts. A moment later there was panic and a wild stampede. It is not my purpose here to make that historic event come alive again. Those who are curious about it can read the newspapers of the time.

There were many injuries and one death. The chandelier fell on the head of the poor woman who had come to the Opera that night for the first time in her life, the one Richard had chosen to replace Madame Giry, the ghost's usher! She died instantly and the next day one of the newspapers had this headline: "Two Hundred Thousand Kilos on a Concierge's Head!" That was her only funeral oration.

9

The Mysterious Brougham

THAT TRAGIC EVENING was bad for everyone. Carlotta fell ill. Christine Daaé disappeared after the performance, and two weeks later she still had not been seen at the Opera or anywhere else.

This first disappearance, which took place without commotion, must not be confused with the famous abduction that occurred some time later under such dramatic and inexplicable circumstances.

Raoul was the first, of course, to be concerned about Christine's absence. He wrote to her at Mama Valerius's address and received no answer. At first he was not particularly surprised, since he knew her frame of mind and her determination to break off all relations with him, though he had not yet been able to guess the reason for it.

His sorrow continued to grow and he finally became worried at not seeing her name on any program. *Faust* was performed without her. One afternoon at about five o'clock he went to the Opera to ask for an explanation of her disappearance. He found the managers greatly preoccupied. Their friends no longer recognized them: they had lost all gaiety and enthusiasm. They were sometimes seen walking across the stage, frowning, with their heads bowed and their cheeks pale, as if they were being pursued by some abominable thought, or had fallen prey to a prank of fate that would not leave them in peace.

The fall of the chandelier had involved many responsibilities, but it was hard to make the managers talk about it.

The official investigation had concluded that it was an accident caused by deterioration of the means of suspension, but either the former managers or the present ones should have detected that deterioration and remedied it before it reached the point of disaster.

And I must say that during this time Richard and Moncharmin seemed so different and remote, so mysterious and incomprehensible, that many subscribers believed that something even worse than the fall of the chandelier must have altered their state of mind.

In their everyday relations they showed great impatience, except with Madame Giry, who had been restored to her position. It is therefore easy to imagine how they received Viscount Raoul de Chagny when he came to ask them about Christine. They simply replied that she was on a leave of absence. When he asked how long it would last, he was curtly told that it was unlimited, since she had requested it for reasons of health.

"She's sick!" he exclaimed. "What's the matter with her?"

"We don't know."

"You didn't send the Opera doctor to her?"

"No. She didn't ask for him, and since we trust her, we took her word for her illness."

Christine's absence did not seem natural to Raoul. He left the Opera, absorbed in somber thoughts, and decided that, come what might, he would go to Mama Valerius and ask for news of Christine. He remembered how strongly Christine's letter had forbidden him to make any attempt to see her, but what he had seen at Perros, what he had heard through the door of her dressing room, and his conversation with her at the edge of the moor made him suspect some sort of machination that, though perhaps a little diabolical, was still human. Her excitable imagination, her affectionate and credulous soul, the primitive upbringing that had surrounded her childhood with a circle of legends, her constant thoughts of her dead father, and especially the sublimely ecstatic state into which music plunged her when she heard it in certain exceptional circumstances, as he had seen for himself during the scene in the graveyard—all this, it seemed to him, had made her particularly vulnerable to the pernicious enterprises of some mysterious, unscrupulous person.

Whose victim had she become? That was the sensible question he asked himself as he hurried on his way to see Mama Valerius.

For Raoul had a very sound mind. He was a poet and loved music in its most ethereal aspects, he was very fond of old Breton tales in which goblins danced, and above all he was in love with a Scandinavian nymph named Christine Daae, but it was still true that he believed in the supernatural only in matters of religion and that the most fantastic story in the world could not make him forget that two plus two is four.

What was Mama Valerius going to tell him? He trembled as he rang the doorbell of the little apartment on the Rue Notre-Dame-des-Victoires.

The door was opened by the maid he had seen coming out of Christine's dressing room one evening. He asked if he could see Madame Valerius. He was told that she was ill, in bed, and unable to receive visitors.

"Please take her my card," he said.

He did not wait long. The maid returned and led him into a dimly lighted and sparsely furnished living room in which portraits of Professor Valerius and Christine's father faced each other.

"Madame asks you to excuse her, sir," said the maid, "but she can receive you only in her bedroom, because her poor legs will no longer support her."

Five minutes later, Raoul was taken into an almost dark bedroom where the first thing he saw, in the shadows of an alcove, was Mama Valerius's kindly face. Her hair was white now, but her eyes had not aged; never before, in fact, had they been so clear, pure, and childlike.

"Monsieur de Chagny!" she said joyfully, holding out both hands to him. "Ah, you must have been sent by heaven! Now we can talk about Christine."

To Raoul, this last sentence had an ominous ring.

"Where is she?" he quickly asked.

And the old lady answered calmly, "She's with her guiding spirit."

"What guiding spirit?" cried poor Raoul.

"Why, the Angel of Music."

Overcome with dismay, Raoul sank into a chair. Christine was with the Angel of Music, and Mama Valerius lay there in her bed, smiling at him and putting her finger to her lips to urge him to be silent.

"You musn't tell anyone," she said.

"You can count on me," he answered, hardly knowing what he was saying, because his ideas about Christine, already highly uncertain, were becoming more and more confused and it seemed to him that everything was beginning to whirl around him, around the room, and around that extraordinary white-haired lady with pale sky-blue eyes, with empty sky-blue eyes. . . .

"Yes, I know I can count on you!" she said with a happy laugh. "But come close to me, the way you used to do when you were a little boy. Give me your hands, as you did when you came to tell me the story of little Lotte, after hearing it from Christine's father. I like you, you know, Monsieur Raoul. And Christine likes you too."

"She likes me. . . ." He said with a sigh.

He was finding it difficult to collect his thoughts and focus them on Mama Valerius's "guiding spirit," the Angel of Music about whom Christine had spoken to him so strangely, the death's-head he had glimpsed in a kind of nightmare on the steps of the high altar in Perros, and the Opera ghost, whose renown had come to his ears one evening when he lingered on the stage near a group of stagehands who were recalling the cadaverous description of him that Joseph Buquet had given shortly before his mysterious death by hanging.

"What makes you think Christine likes me?" he asked in a low voice.

"She used to talk to me about you every day!"

"Really? What did she say?"

"She said you'd made a declaration of love to her."

And the good-natured old lady laughed loudly, showing her well-preserved teeth. Raoul stood up with his face flushed, suffering terribly.

"What are you doing? Please sit down," she said. "You can't just walk out like that. You're angry because I laughed, and I apologize. After all, what happened isn't your fault. You didn't know. You're young, and you thought Christine was free."

"Is she engaged?" Raoul asked miserably, in a choked voice.

"No, of course not! You know Christine couldn't get married even if she wanted to!"

"What? No, I don't know that! Why can't she get married?"

"Because of the Spirit of Music."

"Again . . ."

"Yes, he forbids it."

"He forbids it? The Spirit of Music forbids her to get married?"

Raoul leaned toward Mama Valerius with his jaw thrust forward, as though to bite her. If he had wanted to devour her, he could not have looked at her more fiercely. There are times when excessive innocence seems so monstrous that it becomes hateful. He felt that she was too innocent.

Unaware of the savage gaze fixed on her, she said with a perfectly natural expression, "Oh, he forbids her without forbidding her. . . . He just says that if she married, she'd never see him again. That's all. He also says he'd go away forever. So, you understand, she doesn't want to make the Spirit of Music go away forever. It's only natural."

"Yes, yes," he agreed, almost in a whisper, "it's only natural."

"Besides, I thought she'd told you all that in Perros, when she went there with her guiding spirit."

"Oh? She went to Perros with her guiding spirit?"

"Well, not exactly: he told her to meet him in the graveyard there, at her father's grave. He promised to play *The Resurrection of Lazarus* on her father's violin."

Raoul stood up again, and this time he spoke with great authority:

"Madame, you will tell me where that spirit lives."

The old lady did not seem particularly surprised by that indiscreet demand. She raised her eyes and answered, "In heaven."

Such guilelessness baffled him. He felt dazed by her simple, perfect faith in a spirit who came down from heaven every evening to visit singers' dressing rooms at the Opera.

He now realized the state of mind that might be produced in a girl brought up by a superstitious fiddler and a deranged old lady, and he shuddered at the thought of the consequences it might have.

"Is Christine still an honorable girl?" he could not help asking abruptly.

"Yes, I swear it by my place in heaven!" exclaimed the old lady, seemingly outraged. "And if you doubt it, I don't know why you've come here."

He tugged at his gloves.

"How long ago did she meet that spirit?"

"About three months. Yes, it's been a good three months since he began giving her lessons."

He raised his arms in a broad gesture of despair, then wearily let them fall.

"The spirit gives her lessons? Where?"

"Now that she's gone off with him, I can't tell you, but up until two weeks ago he gave them to her in her dressing room. Here, in this little apartment, it would be impossible. Everyone would hear. But at the Opera, at eight in the morning, there's no one. They weren't disturbed. You understand?"

"Yes, yes, I understand," he said, and took leave of her so hurriedly that she wondered if he might be not quite right in the head.

As he was walking through the living room he found himself face-to-face with the maid. For a moment he was about to question her, but then he thought he saw a faint smile on her lips and felt that she was inwardly laughing at him. He fled. He already knew enough. He had wanted information—what more could he ask? He walked to his brother's house in a pitiful state.

He felt like punishing himself, banging his head against a wall! How could he have believed in her innocence and purity? How could he have tried, even for an instant, to explain everything by her naïveté, simplicity, and immaculate candor? The Spirit of Music! He knew him now! He could see him! He was undoubtedly some idiotic tenor who sang with a silly, affected smile. Raoul felt thoroughly ridiculous and miserable. "What a wretched, little, insignificant, asinine young man you are, Viscount de Chagny!" he furiously told himself. As for Christine, she was a brazen, satanically deceitful creature.

Even so, his swift walk through the streets had done him good and cooled his overheated brain a little. When he went into his room he thought only of throwing himself on his bed and stifling his sobs. But his brother Philippe was there and Raoul let himself fall into his arms, like a baby. Philippe comforted him paternally, without asking for any explanations; and the fact is that Raoul would have been reluctant to tell him about the Spirit of Music. There are some things that one does not boast of, and others for which it is too humiliating to be pitied.

Count Philippe offered to take him to dinner at a cabaret. With such a fresh despair, Raoul would probably have declined the invitation if the count had not changed his mind by telling him that the lady of his dreams had been seen with a man the night before, on an avenue in the Bois de Boulogne. At first Raoul refused to believe it, but then he was given such precise details that he stopped protesting. And, after all, it was a commonplace occurrence. She had been seen in a brougham with the window open, apparently taking deep breaths of the cold night air. There was bright moonlight and she had been clearly recognized. The man with her, however, was visible only as a vague figure in the shadows. The carriage was moving at a leisurely pace along a deserted avenue behind the grandstand of the Longchamps racecourse.

Raoul changed clothes with frenzied haste, ready to throw himself into "the whirlwind of pleasure," as the expression goes, to forget his distress. Unfortunately he was a gloomy companion. He left Philippe early, and by ten o'clock he was in a hired carriage behind the grandstand of the Longchamps racecourse.

It was a bitterly cold night. The road seemed deserted and was brightly lighted by the moon. He told the driver to wait for him patiently at the corner of a little side road, got out, and, hiding himself as much as possible, began stamping his feet to keep them warm.

He had been engaged in that hygienic exercise less than half an hour when a carriage coming from Paris turned the corner and slowly came toward him, with its horses at a walking pace.

He immediately thought, "It's Christine!" and his heart began pounding violently, as it had done when he listened to the man's voice through the door of her dressing room. Dear God, how he loved her!

The carriage was still coming toward him. He had not moved. He was waiting. If it was Christine, he would stop the carriage by seizing the horses' heads! He was determined to call the Angel of Music to account.

A few more steps and the brougham would be in front of him. He had no doubt that she was in it. He could see a woman leaning her head out the window.

Suddenly the moon illuminated her with a pale halo.

"Christine!"

The sacred name of his love burst from his lips and his heart. He had to hold her back! He dashed forward, because that name hurled into the night had seemed to be an expected signal for the horses to break into a gallop. The carriage was past him before he could carry out his plan to stop it. The window was closed now. The young woman's face had disappeared. He ran after the brougham, but soon it was only a black dot on the white road.

He called out again: "Christine!" Nothing answered him. He stopped, in the midst of silence.

He looked up in despair at the starry sky, he struck his burning chest with his fist; he loved and he was not loved!

He stared dully at the desolate, cold road and the pale, dead night. Nothing was colder or more dead than his heart. He had loved an angel and now he despised a woman!

How his little Scandinavian sprite had pulled the wool over his eyes! Was there really any need to have such fresh cheeks and such a shy forehead, always ready to cover itself with the pink veil of modesty, in order to pass by in the solitary night, in a luxurious brougham, with a mysterious lover? Shouldn't there be sacred limits to hypocrisy and deceit? And shouldn't a woman be forbidden to have the clear eyes of childhood when she had the soul of a courtesan?

She had passed without answering his call. . . . Why had he placed himself in her path? By what right had he suddenly confronted her with the reproach of his presence when all she asked was to forget him?

"Go away! Disappear! You don't count!"

He thought of dying and he was twenty-one years old!

The next morning, his valet found him sitting on his bed. He had not undressed and his face was so haggard that the servant was afraid something disastrous might have happened. Raoul saw the mail he was bringing and snatched it from his hand. He had recognized a letter, a paper, a handwriting. Christine said to him:

My friend, go to the masked ball at the Opera, night after next. At midnight, be in the little drawing room behind the fireplace of the main lobby. Stand near the doorway that leads to the rotunda. Don't tell anyone in the world about this appointment. Wear a white domino and be well masked. For the sake of my life, don't let anyone recognize you. Christine.

10

At the Masked Ball

THE MUDSTAINED, UNSTAMPED envelope bore the words "To be delivered to Viscount Raoul de Chagny" and the address, written in pencil. It had evidently been thrown out in the hope that a passerby would pick it up and take it to Raoul, which had happened. It had been found on a sidewalk of the Place de l'Opéra.

Raoul reread it with feverish excitement. It was enough to make hope revive in him. The dark image he had briefly formed, of a Christine who had forgotten her duty to herself, gave way to his first image: an unfortunate, innocent child who was a victim of imprudence and oversensitivity. To what extent was she now really a victim? Whose prisoner was she? Into what abyss had she been dragged? He wondered about all this with cruel anguish, but that pain seemed bearable to him, compared with the frenzy into which he had been thrown by the idea of a hypocritical and deceitful Christine. What had happened? What influence had been exercised on her? What monster had abducted her, and with what weapons?

With what weapons, if not those of music? Yes, the more he thought about it, the more he became convinced that he would find the truth in that direction. The recent course of her life would help him to dispel the darkness in which he was struggling. He knew the despair that had overcome her after her father's death, and the aversion she had then had to everything, even her art. She had gone through the conservatory like a soulless singing machine. Then all at once she had awakened, as

though by the effect of a divine intervention. The Angel of
Music had come! She sang Marguerite in *Faust* and triumphed.
The Angel of Music . . . Who was making her believe he was
that wondrous spirit? Who, knowing about the legend that had
been dear to her father, was using it to make her into a helpless
instrument from which he could draw whatever sounds he pleased?

And Raoul told himself that such a situation was not unprece-
dented. He remembered what had happened to Princess Belmonte
when she had just lost her husband and her despair had turned
into apathy. For a month she could neither speak nor weep. Her
physical and mental inertia worsened every day, and the weaken-
ing of her reason was gradually leading toward the annihilation
of her life. Every evening she was carried into her garden, but
she did not seem to realize where she was. When Raff, the
greatest German singer, was passing through Naples he wanted
to see that garden because it was renowned for its beauty. One of
the princess's attendants asked him to sing, without letting himself be seen, near the clump of trees in which she was lying. He
consented, and sang a simple yet expressive and touching song
that she had heard her husband sing in the early days of their
marriage. The melody, the words, and Raff's magnificent voice
combined to stir her soul deeply. Tears welled up in her eyes;
she wept and was saved, and from then on she was always
convinced that her husband had come down from heaven that
evening to sing her that song from their past.

Yes, that evening . . . An evening, Raoul thought, a single
evening . . . But that figment of the grieving princess's imagination would not have stood up against repeated experience. She
would eventually have discovered Raff behind the clump of trees
if she had gone back to her garden every evening for three
months. The Angel of Music had given Christine lessons for
three months! He was an assiduous teacher. And now he was
taking her out for rides in the Bois de Boulogne!

Raoul dug his fingernails into the flesh of his chest, over his
jealous heart. Inexperienced, he wondered what game Christine
was summoning him to play at that masked ball. How far could a
girl of the Opera go in making fun of a tenderhearted young man
who was new to love? What misery!

And so Raoul's thoughts went to extremes. Not knowing whether
he should pity Christine or curse her, he alternately pitied and
cursed her. Even so, he bought a white domino.

Finally the time of his appointment came. Wearing a mask trimmed with long, thick lace and feeling like a clown in his white costume, he judged that he had made himself ridiculous by getting all decked out like that, as though for a romantic masquerade. A man of the world did not disguise himself to go to a ball at the Opera; it would make others smile disdainfully. One thought consoled Raoul: He would certainly not be recognized. And his costume and mask had another advantage: He could walk around in them as if he were at home, alone with the distress of his soul and the sadness of his heart. He would have no need to pretend, or turn his face into an expressionless mask: it was already covered by one.

This ball was a special celebration given just before Shrovetide to honor the birthday of a famous artist who did drawings of festivities in bygone times, an emulator of Gavarni, whose pencil had immortalized fantastically costumed revelers and the traditional cavalcade of merrymakers that left the Courtille public garden in the early hours of Ash Wednesday. It was therefore meant to be gayer, noisier, and more bohemian than an ordinary masked ball. Many artists had gathered there, along with a retinue of models and art students who began making a mighty uproar as midnight approached.

Raoul climbed the great staircase at five minutes to midnight, without pausing to look at the spectacle around him: the multicolored costumes moving up and down the marble steps, in one of the world's most sumptuous settings. He did not allow any masked merrymakers to engage him in conversation, responded to no jokes, and rebuffed the brash familiarity of several couples whose gaiety was already a little frenetic.

After crossing the main lobby and escaping from a round dance that captured him for a moment, he finally went into the room that Christine's letter had indicated. Its small space was packed with people because it was the crossroads where those on their way to have supper at the rotunda met those returning from having a glass of champagne. Here the tumult was high-spirited and joyous. Raoul thought that Christine must have decided to have their mysterious meeting in that congested room because, wearing their masks, they would be less noticeable than in some more isolated place. He leaned against the door and waited. He did not wait long. Someone in a black domino passed by and quickly squeezed his fingertips. He realized it was Christine.

He followed her.

"Is that you, Christine?" he asked, almost without moving his lips.

She abruptly turned around and put her finger to her lips, evidently to tell him not to say her name again.

He went on following her in silence. He was afraid of losing her, after having found her again in such a strange way. He no longer felt any hatred of her. He was even sure that she had done nothing wrong, however odd and inexplicable her conduct might appear. He was ready to show any amount of indulgence, forgiveness, or baseness. He was in love. And she was surely about to give him a perfectly natural explanation of her singular absence.

The black domino turned around from time to time to see if the white domino was still following.

As Raoul was crossing the main lobby again, this time behind his guide, he could not help noticing that there was a larger throng among the other throngs, that among all the groups of people throwing themselves into the wildest kind of revelry there was a group crowding around a man whose costume and bizarre, macabre appearance were creating a sensation. He was dressed in scarlet, with a big plumed hat on a death's-head. Ah, what a clever imitation of a death's-head it was! The art students around him acclaimed and congratulated him, asked him by what master, in what studio frequented by Pluto, such a magnificent death's-head had been designed, made, and painted. The Grim Reaper himself must have posed for it!

The man in scarlet, with the death's-head and the plumed hat, dragged behind him an immense red velvet cloak that spread across the floor like a sheet of fire; and on that cloak, embroidered in gold letters, were words that everyone read and repeated aloud: "Do not touch me. I am the Red Death passing by."

And someone tried to touch him. A skeletal hand came out of a scarlet sleeve and brutally seized the foolhardy man's wrist. In the bony, relentless grip of death, with the feeling that it would never let him go, the man cried out in pain and terror. When the Red Death finally released him, he ran away like a madman, pursued by the jeering of the onlookers.

That was when Raoul came near the gruesome masquerader, who had just turned toward him. He nearly exclaimed, "The death's-head at Perros!" He had recognized him! He was about to rush toward him, forgetting Christine. But she too seemed to have been seized with some kind of strange agitation; she took him by the arm and pulled him out of the lobby, away from that demoniacal crowd through which the Red Death was passing.

She looked back every few moments, and twice she seemed to see something that frightened her, because she quickened her pace and Raoul's still more, as if they were being pursued.

They went up two floors, to a part of the building where the stairs and halls were nearly deserted. She opened the door of a box and gestured to Raoul to follow her into it. She closed the door behind them. His certainty of her identity was confirmed when he recognized her voice as she quietly told him to stay at the rear of the box and not let anyone see him. He took off his mask. She kept hers on. And just as he was about to ask her to take it off, he was surprised to see her lean against the wall and listen attentively to what was taking place on the other side. Then he pushed the door ajar, looked into the hall, and said in a low voice, "He must have gone up to the Box of the Blind." Suddenly she cried out, "He's coming back down!"

She tried to close the door but Raoul stopped her because he had just seen a red foot, followed by another, appear on the top step of the staircase that led to the floor above. And slowly, majestically, the scarlet garment of the Red Death came down the stairs. Once again he saw the death's-head that he had first seen at Perros.

"There he is!" he exclaimed. "This time he won't get away from me!"

But just as he rushed forward, Christine closed the door. He tried to push her aside.

"Who is 'he'?" she asked in a changed voice. "Who is it who won't get away from you?"

Raoul suddenly tried again to overcome her resistance, but she shoved him back with unexpected strength. He understood, or thought he did, and immediately became furious.

"Who is it?" he said angrily. "It's the man who hides behind that hideous deathly disguise, the evil spirit in the Perros grave-yard, the Red Death! Your friend, your Angel of Music! But I'll unmask him, as I've unmasked myself, and this time we'll look at each other face-to-face, with no veils or deception, and I'll know whom you love and who loves you!"

He burst into mad laughter while Christine moaned plaintively behind her mask.

In a tragic gesture, she raised her arms to form a barrier of white flesh on the door.

"In the name of our love, Raoul, you mustn't go out there!"

He stopped. What had she said? In the name of their love? Never before had she said she loved him. Yet there had been many times when she could have said it! She had seen him unhappy, in tears before her, begging for a kind word of hope that did not come. She had seen him ill, half dead from terror and cold after that night in the Perros graveyard. Had she at least stayed with him at the time when he most needed her care? No, she had run away! And now she said she loved him! She spoke "in the name of their love." What hypocrisy! All she wanted was to delay him for a few seconds, to give the Red Death time to escape. Their love? She was lying!

And he said to her in a tone of childish hatred, "You're lying! You don't love me, you've never loved me! Only a poor, unhappy young man like me would let himself be deluded and ridiculed as I've been. During our first meeting in Perros, why did you give me reason for hope by your attitude, the joy in your eyes, even your silence? I mean honorable hope, because I'm an honorable man. And I thought you were an honorable woman, when your only intention was to deceive me! You've deceived everyone! You've even shamefully taken advantage of your benefactress's innocent heart: she still believes in your sincerity, when you go to an Opera ball with the Red Death! I despise you!"

And he wept. She had let him insult her, thinking only of one thing: to keep him from leaving the box.

"Some day, Raoul, you'll ask me to forgive you for all those ugly words, and I will."

He shook his head.

"No, no! You'd driven me mad! When I think that I had only one goal in life: to give my name to a common girl from the Opera!"

"Raoul! Stop!"

"I'll die of shame!"

"Live, my friend, and good-bye," Christine said gravely, in a faltering voice. "Good-bye forever, Raoul."

He stepped toward her, unsteady on his feet, and ventured one more piece of sarcasm:

"Why forever? You'll let me come and applaud you now and then, won't you?"

"I'll never sing again."

"Really?" he said with even heavier sarcasm. "So he's going to let you become a lady of leisure? Congratulations! But we'll see each other in the Bois one of these nights."

"Not there or anywhere else, Raoul. You'll never see me again."

"May I at least know into what shadows you're going to return? For what hell are you leaving, mysterious lady—or what heaven?"

"I came here to tell you that, but I can't tell you anything more. You wouldn't believe me. You've lost your faith in me, Raoul. It's all over!"

She said that "It's all over!" with such despair that he started, and remorse for his cruelty began to trouble his soul.

"But won't you tell me what all this means?" he cried. "You're free, unfettered. You ride in a carriage, you go to a ball, wearing a domino. Why don't you go home? What have you been doing the last two weeks? What was that story about the Angel of Music you told to Mama Valerius? Maybe someone deceived you, took advantage of your credulity. In Perros, I myself saw . . . But now you know what the truth is! You're very sensible, Christine. You know what you're doing. And yet Mama Valerius is still waiting for you, and invoking your 'guiding spirit'! Explain yourself, Christine, please! Anyone would have been misled, as I was! What's the purpose of this farce?"

Christine took off her mask.

"It's a tragedy, Raoul," she said simply.

Seeing her face, he could not hold back an exclamation of surprise and alarm. Her complexion had lost its fresh coloring. Deathly pallor had spread over that face he had known so gentle and charming, reflecting peaceful grace and a conscience without conflict. How tormented it was now! Sorrow had mercilessly furrowed it, and her beautiful blue eyes, once as clear as the lakes that served as eyes for little Lotte, now appeared to have dark, mysterious, and unfathomable depths and were ringed by distressingly sad shadows.

"Oh, my darling!" he moaned, holding out his arms to her.
"You promised to forgive me. . . ."

"Maybe. Maybe some day. . . ."

She put on her mask again and left, with a gesture that forbade
him to follow her. He tried to come after her anyway, but she
turned around and repeated her farewell gesture with such sovereign authority that he did not dare to take another step.

He watched her walk away. Then he went downstairs, into the
crowd, not knowing exactly what he was doing. His temples
throbbed and his heart ached. As he crossed the ballroom he
asked people if they had seen the Red Death go by. When they
asked who the Red Death was, he answered, "He's a disguised
man with a death's-head and a big red cloak." He was told
everywhere that the Red Death had just passed, trailing his royal
cloak, but he found him nowhere. At two in the morning he
headed down the backstage hall that led to Christine's dressing
room.

His footsteps took him to that place where he had begun to
suffer. He knocked on the door. There was no answer. He went
in as he had done when he was looking everywhere for "the
man's voice." The dressing room was empty. A gaslight was
burning, turned down low. There was some stationery on a little
desk. He thought of writing to Christine, but just then he heard
footsteps in the hall. He barely had time to hide in the boudoir,
which was separated from the dressing room only by a curtain. A
hand pushed open the door. It was Christine!

He held his breath. He wanted to see! He wanted to know!
Something told him that he was about to witness part of the
mystery and that perhaps he would soon begin to understand. . . .

Christine came in, wearily took off her mask, and tossed
it onto the table. She sat down at the table, sighed, bowed
her beautiful head, and took it between her hands. What was
on her mind? Was she thinking about Raoul? No, because he
heard her murmur, "Poor Erik!"

He thought he must have misunderstood. First of all, he was
convinced that if anyone deserved pity, it was he, Raoul. After
what had just happened between them, it would have been
perfectly natural for her to say with a sigh, "Poor Raoul!" But
she repeated, shaking her head, "Poor Erik!" What did that Erik
have to do with her sighs, and why was she feeling sorry for Erik
when Raoul was so miserable?

She began writing, so calmly and deliberately that it made a disagreeable impression on Raoul, who was still trembling from the dramatic scene that had separated them. "What a cool head!" he thought. She went on writing, filling two, three, four pages. Suddenly she raised her head and hid the sheets of paper in her bodice. She seemed to be listening. Raoul listened too. Where was that strange sound coming from, that faraway rhythm? Muffled singing seemed to come from the walls. Yes, it was as if the walls were singing!

The singing became clearer, until words were intelligible. Raoul distinguished a voice, a very beautiful, soft, and captivating voice. But its softness had a masculine quality and he judged that it could not belong to a woman. It kept coming closer and finally went through the wall; now it was *in the room,* in front of Christine. She stood up and spoke to the voice as if she were speaking to someone near her.

"Here I am, Erik," she said. "I'm ready. You're the one who's late, my friend."

Cautiously watching from behind the curtain, Raoul could not believe his eyes: they showed him nothing.

Christine's face lit up. Her bloodless lips formed a happy smile, the kind of smile that convalescents have when they begin to hope that the illness that attacked them is not going to kill them.

The bodiless voice began singing again. It was a voice that united all extremes at once, in a single surge of inspiration. Raoul had never heard anything so amply and heroically sweet, so victoriously insidious, so delicate in strength, so strong in delicacy, so irresistibly triumphant. It had consummate, masterly accents whose example must have been enough to inspire lofty accents in anyone who felt, loved, and performed music. It was a serene, pure wellspring of harmony at which the faithful could safely and devoutly drink, certain that they were drinking in musical grace. And their art, having touched the divine, would be transfigured.

Raoul listened to that voice with excitement, beginning to understand how Christine had been able to appear before an audience one evening and hold them spellbound with singing that displayed superhuman exaltation and a previously unknown beauty—she must have been still under the influence of her mysterious, unknown teacher! And he understood the transformation even better as he listened to the extraordinary voice, precisely because it was not singing anything extraordinary: it was making gems from mud. Because the words were commonplace and the melody was facile, almost vulgar, they seemed all the more radically changed into beauty by a creative force that lifted them and carried them off into the sky on the wings of passion. For that angelic voice was glorifying a pagan hymn. It was singing the wedding-night song from *Roméo et Juliette*.

Raoul saw Christine put out her arms toward the voice, as she had done in the Perros graveyard toward the invisible violin playing *The Resurrection of Lazarus*.

Nothing could describe the passion with which the voice sang:

> *Destiny has chained you to me forever!*

Raoul felt as if he had been stabbed in the heart. Struggling against the spell that seemed to deprive him of all will and energy, and almost all rationality, just when he needed them most, he succeeded in pushing aside the curtain that had hidden him and walking toward Christine. She was moving toward the wall at the back of the room, which was entirely covered by a mirror. She saw her own image but not his, because he was directly behind her and concealed by her.

> *Destiny has chained you to me forever!*

Christine and her image continued coming toward each other. The two Christines—the body and the image—finally touched and merged into each other, and Raoul reached out to seize them both.

But, by a kind of dazzling miracle that staggered him, he was suddenly thrown backward while an icy wind swept across his face. He saw not two, but four, eight, twenty Christines. They nimbly whirled around him, laughed at him, and moved away from him so quickly that he could not touch any of them. Finally everything became still again and he saw himself in the mirror. But Christine had disappeared.

He ran to the mirror. He collided with the walls. No one! And meanwhile a faraway, passionate voice still resounded in the room:

Destiny has chained you to me forever!

He wiped the sweat from his forehead, felt his awakened body, groped in the semidarkness, and turned the gaslight up to its full brightness. He was sure he was not dreaming. He was at the center of a formidable physical and mental game which he did not understand, and which was perhaps going to crush him. He felt a little like an adventurous prince in a fairy tale who had gone beyond a forbidden boundary and could expect to be a victim of the magical forces he had rashly defied and unleashed, out of love.

How had Christine gone? How would she come back?

Would she come back? Alas, she had told him it was all over! And the walls kept repeating, *"Destiny has chained you to me forever!"* To me? To whom?

Exhausted, overwhelmed, his thoughts in disarray, he sat down where Christine had sat a short time before. Like her, he took his head between his hands. When he raised it, tears were flowing abundantly down his young face, real, heavy tears, like those shed by jealous children, tears lamenting a sorrow that was not at all imaginary, but was common to all lovers on earth. He expressed it aloud:

"Who is that Erik?"

11

You Must Forget the Name of "the Man's Voice"

THE DAY AFTER Christine vanished before his eyes in a kind of dazzlement that still made him doubt his senses, Viscount Raoul de Chagny went to Mama Valerius's apartment to ask about her. He came upon a charming picture.

The old lady was sitting up in bed, knitting. At her bedside, Christine was making lace. Never had a lovelier oval face, a purer forehead, or gentler eyes leaned over maidenly needle-work. Fresh colors had returned to Christine's cheeks. The bluish rings around her eyes had disappeared. Raoul no longer saw the tragic face of the day before. If the veil of melancholy spread over her adorable features had not seemed to him the last vestige of the incredible drama in which the mysterious young woman had been struggling, he might have thought that she was not its incomprehensible heroine.

When she saw him approaching, she stood up without apparent emotion and held out her hand to him. But he was so astounded that he stopped in his tracks and stared at her without a word or a gesture.

"Well, Monsieur de Chagny, don't you recognize our Christine anymore?" asked Mama Valerius. "Her guiding spirit has brought her back to us!"

"Mama!" Christine exclaimed, her face turning bright red. "I thought we weren't ever going to mention that again! You know very well that there's no Angel of Music!"

"Yet he gave you lessons for three months, my child!"

"Mama, I promised to explain everything soon. I hope I can. . . . But you promised me to be silent till then, and not to ask me any more questions!"

"Why don't you promise never to leave me? But have you promised me that, Christine?"

"Mama, all this doesn't interest Monsieur de Chagny."

"That's not true," Raoul said; he tried to make his voice firm and brave, but could not prevent it from quavering. "Everything concerning you interests me to a degree that you may eventually come to realize. I'm both surprised and delighted to find you with your adoptive mother. What happened between us yesterday, what you said to me, what I was able to guess—nothing made me expect that you'd be back so soon. I'd be overjoyed at seeing you again if you didn't stubbornly persist in maintaining a secrecy that may be harmful to you. And I've been your friend too long not to worry, with Madame Valerius, about a sinister adventure that will be dangerous as long as we haven't untangled it. You may finally be its victim, Christine."

At these words, Mama Valerius moved convulsively on her bed.

"What do you mean?" she cried. "Christine is in danger?"

"Yes," Raoul answered courageously, in spite of the signs that Christine was making to him.

"My God!" the good, naive old lady exclaimed, gasping. "You must tell me everything, Christine! Why did you try to reassure me? What danger is she in, Monsieur de Chagny?"

"An impostor is taking advantage of her good faith!"

"The Angel of Music is an impostor?"

"She told you herself that there is no Angel of Music!"

"What's wrong, then, in heaven's name? Tell me before you make me die of suspense!"

"What's wrong is that around us—around you, around Christine—there's an earthly mystery much more to be feared than all ghosts and spirits put together."

Mama Valerius turned to Christine with a terrified expression. Christine quickly went to her and took her in her arms.

"Don't believe him, dear mama, don't believe him!" she said. And she tried to comfort her with caresses, because the old lady was heaving heartrending sighs.

"Then tell me you'll never leave me again!" Mama Valerius begged her.

Christine remained silent. It was Raoul who spoke:

"You must promise that, Christine. It's the only thing that can reassure your mother and me. We'll agree not to ask you a single question about the past if you'll promise to stay in our safekeeping from now on."

"I won't ask you for that agreement and I won't give you that promise!" Christine said haughtily. "I'm free to do as I please, Monsieur de Chagny. You have no right to keep watch over my behavior and I ask you to stop doing it. As for what I've done in the past two weeks, only one man in the world would have a right to demand that I tell him about it: my husband. But I have no husband, and I'll never marry!"

As she said this emphatically, she put out her hand toward Raoul, as though to make her words more solemn. He turned pale, not only because of what he had just heard, but also because he saw a gold ring on her finger.

"You have no husband, and yet you're wearing a wedding ring."

He tried to take hold of her hand but she quickly drew it back.

"It's a gift," she said, blushing again and vainly trying to hide her embarrassment.

"Christine! Since you have no husband, that ring can only have been given to you by the man who hopes to become your husband! Why go on deceiving us? Why torture me still more? That ring is a promise, and the promise has been accepted!"

"That's what I told her!" exclaimed the old lady.

"And what did she answer?"

"I answered what I wanted to!" said Christine, exasperated. "Don't you think this interrogation has gone on long enough? As for me . . ."

Deeply perturbed, and afraid she was about to announce a permanent break between them, Raoul interrupted her:

"Please forgive me for speaking to you as I did. You know the honorable feeling that now makes me meddle in things I probably have no right to be concerned with. But let me tell you what I saw—and I saw more than you think I did—or rather what I thought I saw, because anyone having such an experience will naturally find it hard to believe his eyes.''

"What did you see, or think you saw?''

"I saw your rapture at the sound of the voice coming from the wall, or from a dressing room next to yours. Yes, your *rapture!* And that's what makes me so afraid for you! You're under a dangerous spell! Yet it seems you've become aware of the deception, since you now say there is no Angel of Music. But then why did you follow him once again? Why did you stand up with your face radiant, as if you really were hearing an angel? That voice is very dangerous, because I was so entranced while I listened to it that you disappeared before my eyes and I didn't know how you had left. Christine! Christine! In the name of heaven, in the name of your father, who's now in heaven and who loved you so much, and loved me too, tell your benefactress and me to whom that voice belongs! We'll save you in spite of yourself! Come, tell me that man's name, Christine. Tell me the name of the man who had the audacity to put a gold ring on your finger!''

"Monsieur de Chagny,'' she said coldly, "you will never know his name.''

Seeing the hostility with which Christine had spoken to Raoul, Mama Valerius suddenly sided with her.

"If she loves that man, viscount,'' she said harshly, "it's not your concern!''

"Unfortunately, madame,'' he replied humbly, unable to hold back his tears, "I think she does love him. Everything seems to prove it. But that's not the only reason for my despair. I'm not sure that the man she loves is worthy of her love.''

"That's for me alone to judge,'' said Christine, looking him straight in the eyes with an angry expression.

"When a man,'' he continued, feeling his strength abandoning him, "uses such romantic means to seduce a girl . . .''

"Then either the man is a scoundrel or the girl is a fool? Is that what you mean?''

"Christine!''

"Why do you condemn a man you've never seen, a man no one knows, a man you know nothing about?''

"Not quite nothing, Christine. I at least know the name you thought you could hide from me forever. Your Angel of Music is named Erik!''

Christine betrayed herself immediately. She turned white as an altar cloth and stammered, "Who . . . who told you?"

"You did!"

"How?"

"By pitying him the other night, the night of the masked ball. When you came into your dressing room, you said, 'Poor Erik!' Well, Christine, there was a poor Raoul who overheard you."

"That was the second time you listened outside my door!"

"I wasn't outside your door. I was in your dressing room—in your boudoir, to be more precise."

"Oh, no!" she cried, showing every sign of great fear. "Did you want to be killed?"

"Maybe."

He spoke that word with so much love and despair that she could not hold back a sob.

She took his hands and looked at him with all the pure fondness of which she was capable, and beneath her gaze he felt that his sorrow was already diminished.

"Raoul," she said, "you must forget 'the man's voice' and not even remember the the name you overheard. And you must never again try to penetrate the mystery of 'the man's voice.' "

"Is it really such a terrible mystery?"

"There's none more terrible on earth!"

A silence separated the two young people. Raoul was overwhelmed.

"Swear to me that you'll make no effort to find out," she insisted. "And swear that you'll never again come into my dressing room unless I ask you to."

"Will you promise to ask me to come there sometimes?"

"I promise."

"When?"

"Tomorrow."

"Then I swear what you want."

Those were the last words they exchanged that day.

He kissed her hands and left, cursing Erik and telling himself that he must be patient.

12

Above the Trapdoors

THE NEXT DAY, he saw her again at the Opera. She still had the gold ring on her finger. She was gentle and kind to him, and talked with him about his plans, his future, his career.

He told her that the departure of the polar expedition had been moved forward and that he would leave France in three weeks, or a month at the most.

She urged him, almost gaily, to look forward to that voyage as a step toward his future glory. And when he answered that glory without love did not appeal to him, she called him a child whose sorrows would not last long.

"How can you talk so lightly about such serious things?" he said. "Maybe we'll never see each other again! I may die during that expedition!"

"So may I," she said quietly.

She was no longer smiling, no longer joking. She seemed to be thinking of something that had just occurred to her for the first time, something that had set her eyes aglow.

"What are you thinking of, Christine?"

"I'm thinking that we'll never see each other again."

"Is that what makes your face so radiant?"

"And that in a month we'll have to tell each other good-bye—forever."

"Unless we become engaged and wait for each other forever."

She put her hand over his mouth.

"Quiet, Raoul! You know that's out of the question! And we'll never be married. That's understood!"

She suddenly seemed to feel joy that she could scarcely contain. She clapped her hands with childish delight. He looked at her, worried and perplexed.

She held out her hands to him, or rather she gave them to him, as if she had decided to make him a present of them.

"But although we can't be married," she went on, "we *can* be engaged! No one but us will know, Raoul! There have been secret marriages, and there can be a secret engagement! We're engaged for a month, my dearest. In a month you'll leave, and I'll be happy with the memory of that month for the rest of my life."

She was overjoyed with her idea. Then she became serious again.

"This," she said, "is a happiness that will harm no one."

Raoul had understood. He leapt at that idea and wanted to make it a reality immediately. He bowed to her with great humility and said, "Mademoiselle, I have the honor of asking you for your hand."

"But you already have both my hands, my dear fiancé! Oh, Raoul, we're going to be so happy! We'll play at being a future husband and a future wife!"

Raoul thought, "She's being rash! In a month I'll have time to make her forget 'the mystery of the man's voice,' or to clear it up and destroy it, and in a month she'll consent to be my wife. In the meantime, we'll play!"

It was the prettiest game in the world and they enjoyed it like the pure children they were. They said such marvelous things to each other, and exchanged so many eternal vows! The idea that at the end of a month there might be no one to keep those vows threw them into an agitation that they experienced with fearful delight, between laughter and tears. They "played hearts" as others "play ball"; but since it was really their hearts that they tossed back and forth, they had to be very skillful to catch them without hurting them.

One day—it was the eighth day of their game—Raoul's heart was badly hurt and he stopped playing, with these foolish words: "I won't go to the North Pole!"

In her innocence, Christine had not thought of that possibility; she suddenly realized the danger of the game and bitterly reproached herself for it. She made no reply and Raoul went home.

This happened in the afternoon, in Christine's dressing room, where their meetings always took place and where they amused themselves by having "dinners" consisting of three cookies and two glasses of port, with a bouquet of violets on the table.

That evening she did not sing. And he did not receive the usual letter from her, even though they had given themselves permission to write to each other every day during that month.

The next morning he hurried to Mama Valerius, who told him that Christine would be gone for two days. She had left the day before at five o'clock, saying she would come back two days later. Raoul was thunderstruck. He hated Mama Valerius for giving him news like that with such astounding calm. He tried to get more information out of her but she obviously knew nothing. To his overwrought questions she merely answered, "That's Christine's secret." And she raised her finger as she said this with touching gentleness, intending to urge discretion and reassure him at the same time.

When he had left her and was racing down the stairs, he thought maliciously, "A girl is well guarded by an old woman like that!"

Where could Christine be? Two days . . . Two days taken away from their already short happiness! And it was his own fault! It had been understood between them that he would leave with the polar expedition. He had changed his mind, but he should not have told her about it so soon. He accused himself of having stupidly blundered, and for forty-eight hours he was the unhappiest of men. Then Christine reappeared.

She reappeared in triumph. She finally renewed her extraordinary success of the gala performance. Since the misadventure of the "toad," Carlotta had not been able to return to the stage. Fear of another croak filled her heart and made her incapable of singing, and the scene of her incomprehensible disaster had become odious to her. She found a way to break her contract. Christine was asked to replace her temporarily. Her performance in *La Juive* was received with wild enthusiasm.

Raoul was present that night, of course, and he was the only one who suffered as he listened to the countless echoes of her new triumph, because he saw that she was still wearing her gold ring. A faraway voice murmured in his ear, "Tonight she's still wearing the gold ring, and you're not the one who gave it to her. Tonight she gave her soul again, but not to you." And the voice continued: "If she won't tell you what she did during the last two days, or where she was, you must go and ask Erik!"

He hurried backstage and stood where he knew she would pass by. She saw him, because her eyes were looking for him. She said to him, "Come, quickly!" and led him to her dressing room with no concern for all the courtiers of her young glory who looked at her closed door and murmured, "It's scandalous!"

Raoul fell to his knees as soon as he was in the dressing room. He swore he would leave with the polar expedition and begged her not to take away one more hour from the ideal happiness she had promised him. She let her tears flow. They hugged each other like a grieving brother and sister who had just suffered a common loss and had come together to mourn it.

Suddenly she pulled herself away from his gentle, timid embrace and seemed to listen to something he could not hear. Then she abruptly pointed to the door. When he was on the threshold she said to him, so softly that he guessed her words more than he heard them, "Till tomorrow, my dear fiancé. And be happy—I sang for you tonight!"

He came back, but unfortunately those two days of absence had broken the spell of their charming make-believe. In her dressing room they looked at each other with their sad eyes and said nothing. He restrained himself from shouting, "I'm jealous! I'm jealous! I'm jealous!" But she heard him anyway.

Finally she said, "Let's get away from here, Raoul. The change of air will do us good."

He thought she wanted them to go on an outing in the country, far away from that building he hated as if it were a jail; he angrily felt the jailer moving within its walls, the jailer named Erik. . . . But she took him to the stage and asked him to sit down with her on the wooden rim of a fountain in the peace and dubious freshness of a first-scene set for the next performance.

Another day, she held his hand and wandered with him along the deserted paths of a garden whose climbing plants had been cut out by the skilled hands of a property man, as if real skies, real flowers, and the real earth were forbidden to her forever and she had been condemned to breathe no other atmosphere than that of the theater.

It was obvious to him that she could not answer most of the questions he asked her, and so, not wanting to make her suffer needlessly, he had become reluctant to question her at all. Now and then a fireman passed, watching over their melancholy idyll from a distance. Sometimes she bravely tried to deceive him and herself about the spurious beauty of that setting invented to produce illusions. Her lively imagination would adorn it with elegant colors that, she said, were totally unlike any colors found in nature. She would grow excited while he pressed her feverish hand.

"Look, Raoul," she said to him once, "at those walls, those woods, those arbors, those images made of painted cloth—all that has witnessed love scenes more sublime than any others, because they were invented by poets who tower far above ordinary people. So tell me that our love is at home here, my Raoul, since it too was invented, and it too, sad to say, is only an illusion."

Disconsolate, he made no reply.

"Our love is too sad on earth," she went on, "so let's take it into the sky! You'll see how easy that is to do, here!"

And she led him higher than the clouds, into the magnificent disorder of the upper flies, where she enjoyed making him dizzy by running in front of him on the fragile bridges of the rigging loft, among the thousands of ropes attached to pulleys and winches in the midst of a veritable aerial forest of masts and yardarms. If he hesitated, she said to him with an adorable pout, "You, a sailor!"

Then they came down to terra firma; that is, to a solid corridor that led them to laughter, dancing, and youth scolded by a stern voice: "Limber up, girls! Watch your pointes!" It was the class for girls seven to nine years old. They already wore low-cut bodices, light tutus, and pink stockings, and they worked and worked, with their little feet aching, in the hope of becoming ballerinas, or even prima ballerinas, and being covered with diamonds. In the meantime, Christine gave them candy.

On still another day, she took Raoul into a vast room of her palace, full of gaudy finery, knights' costumes, lances, shields, and plumes, and inspected all the motionless, dusty ghosts of warriors. She spoke to them kindly, promising them that they would again see brilliantly illuminated evenings and parades with music before the glaring footlights.

And so she took him all over her empire, which was artificial but immense, covering seventeen stories, from the ground floor to the roof, and inhabited by an army of subjects. She passed among them like a popular queen, encouraging their work, sitting down in storerooms, giving good advice to the seamstresses whose hands hesitated to cut into the rich cloth that was to be turned into costumes for heroes. The inhabitants of that country plied all trades. There were shoemakers and goldsmiths. They had all come to like her because she took an interest in their troubles and their little quirks.

She knew out-of-the-way parts of the building secretly inhabited by old couples. She would knock on their door and introduce Raoul to them as a Prince Charming who had asked for her hand in marriage. She and Raoul would sit on some dilapidated prop and listen to legends of the Opera, as they had listened to old Breton tales in their childhood. Those old couples remembered nothing but the Opera. They had lived there for countless years. Past managements had forgotten them there; palace revolutions had overlooked them; outside, French history had passed by without their realizing it, and no one remembered them.

Thus, precious days flowed past. By seeming to take great interest in outside matters, Raoul and Christine awkwardly tried to hide the sole thought of their hearts from each other. One thing is certain: Christine, who till then had proved to be the stronger of the two, suddenly became intensely nervous. During their expeditions she would begin running for no reason, or else she would stop abruptly and her hand, having instantly turned cold, would hold Raoul back. Her eyes sometimes seemed to be following imaginary shadows. She would cry out, "This way," and then "This way," and then "This way," with a gasping laugh that often ended in tears. Raoul would try to talk, to question her in spite of his promises, but before he had even asked a question she would answer feverishly, "Nothing! I swear there's nothing!"

Once when they were on the stage and came to a partly open trapdoor, he leaned over the dark abyss and said, "You've shown me the upper part of your empire, Christine, but strange stories are told about the lower part. . . . Shall we go down to it?"

Hearing this, she clasped him in her arms as if she were afraid of seeing him disappear into the black hole and said to him in a low voice, trembling, "Never! You mustn't go there! And it doesn't belong to me. Everything underground belongs to *him!*"

Raoul looked her straight in the eyes and said harshly, "So he lives down there?"

"I didn't say that! Who could have told you such a thing? Come, let's go away from here. There are times, Raoul, when I wonder if you're not insane—you always hear impossible things! Come! Come!"

She tried to pull him away but he stubbornly insisted on staying by the trapdoor; that hole seemed to draw him toward it.

All at once the trapdoor was closed, so suddenly that they did not see the hand that did it, and they were both left feeling dazed.

"Maybe *he* was there," Raoul finally said.

Christine shrugged, but did not seem at all reassured.

"No, no, it was the trapdoor-closers. They have to do something, so they open and close the trapdoors for no special reason. They're like the door-closers: they have to kill time."

"What if he really was there, Christine?"

"No, he couldn't have been! He's shut himself in, he's working!"

"Oh, really? He's working?"

"Yes. He can't work and open and close trapdoors at the same time. There's no need for us to worry."

She shuddered as she said this.

"What is he working on?" Raoul asked.

"Something terrible! That's why I say there's no need for us to worry: when he works on that, he sees nothing, he doesn't eat or drink, he hardly breathes. He goes on like that for whole days and nights. He's a living dead man and he doesn't have time to play with trapdoors."

She shuddered again and leaned toward the trapdoor, listening. Raoul said nothing. He was now afraid that the sound of his voice might make her stop and think, putting an end to her still tentative willingness to confide in him.

She had not left him. She was still holding him in her arms. She sighed, and this time it was she who said, "What if he really was there?"

"Are you afraid of him?" Raoul asked timidly.

"No, of course not!"

Unintentionally, he took a pitying attitude toward her, as one does toward an impressionable person still in the grip of a recent nightmare. He seemed to say, "Don't be afraid: I'm here."

And, almost unintentionally, he made a threatening gesture toward some unspecified enemy. She looked at him in astonishment, as if he were a wonder of courage and virtue, and she appeared to be assessing the worth of his bold and futile chivalry. She kissed him like a sister rewarding him, by that show of affection, for having clenched his brotherly little fist to defend her against the dangers that were always possible in life.

He understood and blushed with shame. He felt he was as weak as she was. "She claims she's not afraid," he thought, "but she trembles and wants us to get away from the trapdoor."

It was true. In the following days they carried on their chaste and curious love affair almost at the top of the building, far away from the trapdoors. Christine's agitation grew as time passed. Finally one afternoon she arrived very late, with her face so pale and her eyes so reddened by despair that Raoul resolved to take extreme measures if necessary, including the one he told her about as soon as he saw her: He would not go on the expedition to the North Pole, he said, unless she told him the secret of the man's voice.

"Quiet!" she exclaimed. "You mustn't talk like that! What if he heard you, poor Raoul?"

And she looked all around them, wild-eyed.

"I'll take you out of his power, I swear I will! And you'll stop thinking about him. You must."

"Is it possible?"

She expressed this doubt, which was an encouragement, as she led him toward the upper floors of the building, where they would be far away from the trapdoors.

"I'll hide you in an unknown part of the world," he said, "where he won't come looking for you. You'll be saved, and then I'll leave, since you've sworn never to marry."

She took his hands and squeezed them with intense emotion. But then her anxiety returned. She turned away from him, said, "Higher, still higher!" and began leading him upward again.

He had difficulty following her. Soon they were just below the roof, in the labyrinth of timberwork. They slipped between struts, rafters, and braces; they ran from beam to beam as if they were in a forest, running from one massive tree to another.

And despite her precaution of looking behind her every few

moments, she did not see a shadow following her as if it were her own, stopping with her, starting again with her, and making no more noise than a shadow should. Raoul saw nothing, for with Christine in front of him, he had no interest in anything happening behind him.

13

Apollo's Lyre

AND SO THEY reached the roof. She glided over it, light and familiar, like a swallow. Looking between the three domes and the triangular pediment, they scanned the empty space before them. She breathed deeply, standing over the whole valley of Paris that could be seen in labor far below. She looked at Raoul with confidence. She called him to her and they walked side by side, high above the earth, along zinc streets and iron avenues. Their twin shapes were reflected in big open tanks of motionless water in which, during the summer months, the score of little boys in the ballet dived and learned to swim.

The shadow had come out behind them and continued following them, flattening itself on the roof, stretching itself out with movements of black wings at intersections of metal streets, silently moving around tanks and domes; and the two unfortunate young people did not suspect its presence when they finally sat down, untroubled, under the protection of Apollo, who, with a bronze gesture, raised his prodigious lyre into the heart of a blazing sky.

They were surrounded by a radiant summer evening. Clouds slowly drifted by, trailing the gold and crimson robes they had just received from the setting sun.

"Soon we'll go farther and faster than the clouds, to the end of the world," Christine said, "and then you'll leave me, Raoul. But if I refuse to go with you when the time comes for you to take me away, you must *make* me go!"

Vigorously pressing herself against him, she spoke these words with a forcefulness that seemed to be directed against herself. He was struck by her tone.

"Are you afraid you may change your mind, Christine?"

"I don't know," she said, shaking her head in a strange way. "He's a demon!" She shivered and huddled in his arms with a moan. "Now I'm afraid to go back and live with him underground."

"Why do you have to go back?"

"If I don't go back to him, terrible things may happen. But I can't stand it any more! I know we should feel sorry for people who live 'under the earth,' but he's too horrible! And it's almost time: I have only one more day, and if I don't come to him, he'll come for me with his voice. He'll take me with him, to his underground home, and he'll kneel in front of me, with his death's-head. And he'll tell me he loves me! And he'll weep! Oh, those tears, Raoul! Those tears·in the two black holes of the death's-head! I can't bear to see those tears flow again!"

She wrung her hands in torment while Raoul, gripped by her contagious despair, pressed her to his heart.

"No, no, you'll never again hear him tell you he loves you! You'll never again see his tears! We'll run away, Christine! Now! Let's go!"

He tried to lead her away but she stopped him.

"No," she said, sorrowfully shaking her head, "not now. It would be too cruel. . . . Let him hear me sing tomorrow night, one last time, and then we'll go. At midnight you'll come for me in my dressing room—at exactly midnight. He'll then be waiting for me in the dining room by the lake. We'll be free and you'll take me away, even if I refuse. You must promise me that, Raoul, because I feel that if I go back to him this time, I may never leave him again." And she added, "You can't understand!"

She sighed, and it seemed to her that her sigh was answered by another one behind her.

"Did you hear something?" she asked.

Her teeth were chattering.

"No, nothing," he assured her.

"It's too terrible," she said, "to be always trembling like this! But we're in no danger here. We're at home, in my home, in the sky, in the open air, in daylight. The sun is flaming, and nightbirds don't like to look at the sun. I've never seen him in daylight. It . . . it must be horrible!" she stammered, turning her

distraught eyes toward Raoul. "Oh, the first time I saw him . . .
I thought he was going to die!"

"Why?" asked Raoul, now truly frightened by the tone her
strange and alarming confession was taking. "Why did you think
he was going to die?"

"Why? *Because I'd seen him!*" she answered.

A moment later, she and Raoul both turned around at the same
time.

"There's someone here in pain," he said, "maybe someone
who's been injured. Did you hear?"

"I can't really say, because even when I'm not with him, my
ears are full of his sighs. . . . But if you heard . . ."

They stood up and looked around them. They were alone on
the immense metal roof. They sat down again.

"How did you see him for the first time?" asked Raoul.

"For three months I'd heard him without seeing him. The first
time I heard his marvelous voice begin singing all at once,
seemingly close beside me, I thought, as you did, that it must be
coming from another room. I went out and looked everywhere,
but my dressing room is isolated, as you know. I couldn't find
the voice outside it, and it went on singing inside. Then it not
only sang, but talked to me. It answered my questions like a real
man's voice, except that it was as beautiful as the voice of an
angel. How was I to explain something so incredible? I'd never
forgotten about the 'Angel of Music' that my poor father had
promised to send me as soon as he died.

"I'm not afraid to talk to you about such childishness, Raoul,
because you knew my father and he liked you, and you believed
in the Angel of Music at the same time I did, when you were a
little boy, and because I'm sure you won't smile or make fun of
me. I still had the same kind of loving, gullible soul as little
Lotte, and being with Mama Valerius did nothing to make me
lose it. I held that innocent little soul in my naive hands and
naively offered it to the man's voice, thinking I was offering it to
the Angel. It was partly Mama Valerius's fault. I told her about
the inexplicable incident and she said, 'It must be the Angel;
anyway, you can always ask him.'

"I did, and the Voice answered that it really was the angelic
voice I'd been waiting for, the one my father had promised he
would send me after he died. From then on, the Voice and I
were on very close terms and I trusted it completely. It told me it

had come down to earth to help me experience the supreme joy of eternal art, and it asked me to let it give me singing lessons every day. I eagerly consented and I always kept the appointments it gave me in my dressing room at times when that part of the Opera was deserted. How can I tell you about those lessons? You can't have any idea of what they were like, even though you've heard the Voice yourself."

"Of course I can't have any idea of what they were like!" said Raoul. "What was your accompaniment?"

"A kind of music that was unknown to me. It came from the other side of the wall and was wonderfully accurate. The Voice seemed to know exactly at what point my father had stopped teaching me when he died, and what a simple method he had used. I—or rather my voice—remembered all my past lessons. Benefiting from them as well as from the ones I was now taking, I made prodigious progress that would have taken years under different conditions! I'm rather delicate, as you know, and at first my voice didn't have much character: its lower register was undeveloped, its upper register was a little harsh, and its middle register lacked clarity. My father struggled against those faults and triumphed over them for a short time; the Voice overcame them permanently.

"I gradually increased the volume of my voice to an extent that my past weakness wouldn't have even let me hope for; I learned to give my breathing its greatest possible amplitude. But mainly the Voice taught me the secret of developing chest sounds in a soprano voice. And it enveloped all that in the sacred fire of inspiration, it awakened an ardent, voracious, sublime life in me. It had the ability to raise me to its level when I heard it. It put me in unison with its magnificent, soaring sounds. Its soul lived in my mouth and breathed harmony there.

"After a few weeks, I no longer recognized myself when I sang! It even frightened me; for a time, I was afraid there might be some kind of sorcery behind it. But Mama Valerius reassured me. She said she knew I was such a simple girl that the devil couldn't get a hold on me.

"By the Voice's order, my progress was a secret known only to me, Mama Valerius, and the Voice. For some reason, when I wasn't in my dressing room I sang with my ordinary voice and no one noticed any change. I did everything the Voice wanted. It said to me, 'You must wait; you'll see, we'll amaze Paris!' And

I waited. I lived in a kind of ecstatic dream where the Voice was in command.

"Then I saw you in the audience one night, Raoul. I was overjoyed, and had no thought of hiding it when I went back to my dressing room. Unfortunately for both of us, the Voice was already there, and it saw from my face that something new had happened. When it asked me what it was, I saw no reason not to tell it about us and the place you still held in my heart. When I had finished, the Voice said nothing. I called it; it didn't answer. I begged it, in vain. I was terrified at the thought that it might have gone away forever. I wish to God that it had, Raoul. . . .

"I went home that night in a desperate state. I threw my arms around Mama Valerius and said, 'The Voice is gone! Maybe it will never come back!' She was as frightened as I was, and asked me to explain. I told her everything. She said, 'Of course: the Voice is jealous!' And that, Raoul, made me realize that I loved you. . . .''

At this point Christine stopped short. She leaned her head against Raoul's chest and for a time they remained silent, in each other's arms. Absorbed in their feelings, they did not see, or sense, that only a few paces away from them the shadow of two great black wings was moving across the roof, coming so near to them that it could have smothered them by closing over them.

"The next day," Christine continued with a deep sigh, "I was thoughtful when I went to my dressing room. The Voice was there. Oh, Raoul, it talked to me so sadly! It told me plainly that if I gave my heart to someone on earth, it, the Voice, would have to go back to heaven. And it said that in such a tone of *human* sorrow that I should have immediately become suspicious and begun to realize I'd been misled by my deluded senses. But I still had complete faith in that apparition, in the Voice, which was so closely mingled with the thought of my father. I was more afraid of never hearing it again than of anything else. Furthermore, I'd thought of my feelings for you and realized their useless danger; I didn't even know if you still remembered me. And no matter what might happen, your social position would always mean that marriage between us was out of the question. I swore to the Voice that you were only like a brother to me, that you would never be anything else, and that my heart was empty of all earthly love.

"And that, Raoul, is when I looked away from you whenever

you tried to catch my attention on the stage or in the halls; it's why I didn't seem to recognize you, or even see you. Meanwhile, my hours of lessons with the Voice went by in divine rapture. Never before had I been so possessed by the beauty of sound. One day the Voice said to me, 'Go now, Christine Daaé: you can give human beings a little of heaven's music!'

"That night was the night of the gala performance. Why didn't Carlotta come to the Opera then? I don't know; but I sang—I sang with an elation I'd never known before. I was as light as if I'd been given wings. My soul was aflame, and for a moment I thought it had left my body!"

"Oh, Christine, my heart quivered with every note you sang that night!" said Raoul, whose eyes were moist at that memory. "I saw tears run down your pale cheeks, and I wept with you. How could you sing while you wept?"

"I felt faint," said Christine, "and closed my eyes. . . . When I opened them, you were beside me. But the Voice was there too, Raoul! I was afraid for you, and again I didn't want to act as if I recognized you. I laughed when you reminded me that you'd saved my scarf from the sea.

"But unfortunately no one can deceive the Voice. It had recognized you, and it was jealous. During the next two days it made terrible scenes with me.

" 'You love him!' it said to me angrily. 'If you didn't love him, you wouldn't avoid him. If he were simply an old friend, you'd shake hands with him as you would with any other friend. If you didn't love him, you wouldn't be afraid to be alone with him and me in your dressing room! If you didn't love him, you wouldn't send him away!'

" 'Enough!' I said. 'Tomorrow I'm going to Perros to visit my father's grave. I'll ask Monsieur Raoul de Chagny to go with me.'

" 'Do as you please,' the Voice answered, 'but I'll be in Perros too, because I'm wherever you are, Christine, and if you're still worthy of me, if you haven't lied to me, at exactly midnight I'll play *The Resurrection of Lazarus* on your father's violin, beside his grave.'

"And that's how I came to write you the letter that brought you to Perros, Raoul. How could I have let myself be taken in so completely? When I saw how personal the Voice's concerns were, I should have suspected some sort of deceit. But I was no

longer able to think for myself: the Voice had total control of
me. And with the means it had at its disposal, it could easily
deceive a child like me!''

"But you soon found out the truth!" Raoul exclaimed at this
point in her story where she seemed to be tearfully sorrowing
over the excessive innocence of an unsophisticated mind. "Why
didn't you get out of that abominable nightmare immediately?"

"The truth, Raoul? Get out of that nightmare? You don't
understand! The nightmare didn't begin for me till I found out
the truth! Quiet! Quiet! I've told you nothing. . . . And now that
we're about to leave heaven and come back to earth, pity me,
Raoul, pity me! One night, one fateful night, the night when
Carlotta must have felt that she'd been turned into a hideous toad
onstage, and began croaking as if she'd spent all her life in a
marsh, the night when the chandelier came crashing down and
the house was plunged into darkness—people were killed and
injured that night, and the whole auditorium was filled with
heartrending screams.

"My first thought when the disaster struck, Raoul, was for
both you and the Voice, because at that time the two of you were
the two equal halves of my heart. I was immediately reassured as
far as you were concerned, since I'd seen you in your brother's
box and I knew you were in no danger. As for the Voice, it had
told me it would attend the performance and I was afraid for it;
yes, really afraid, as if it were an ordinary living person, capable
of dying. I said to myself, 'My God! The chandelier may have
crushed the Voice!' I was on the stage then, and so panic-
stricken that I was about to run into the auditorium to look for
the Voice among the dead and injured. But then it occurred to
me that if nothing had happened to the Voice, it must already be
in my dressing room and would quickly reassure me there. I
hurried to my dressing room and, with tears in my eyes, begged
the Voice to make its presence known to me if it was still alive.

"There was no answer, but suddenly I heard a long, soul-
stirring moan that I knew well. It was Lazarus's moan when, at
the sound of Jesus's voice, he begins to open his eyes and see
the light of day again. I heard the plaintive notes of my father's
violin. I recognized his style of playing, the same style that used
to hold us spellbound on the roads of Perros, Raoul, and captivated us that night in the graveyard. Then the joyful, triumphant
cry of life came from the invisible violin and the Voice finally

made itself heard, singing the supreme, dominant words, 'Come, and believe in me! Those who believe in me will live again. Walk! Those who have believed in me cannot die.'

"I can't tell you the effect that music had on me as it sang of eternal life at a time when, under the same roof, people crushed by the fallen chandelier were dying. I felt that it was also commanding me to come, to stand up, to walk toward it. It moved away and I followed it. 'Come, and believe in me!' I believed in it, I came. . . . I came and, to my amazement, my dressing room seemed to grow longer and longer as I walked. It must have been a mirror effect, of course—I had the mirror in front of me. Then all at once I found myself outside my dressing room, without knowing how I'd come to be there, and . . ."

"What?" Raoul interrupted brusquely. "Without knowing how? Christine, Christine! You must try to stop dreaming!"

"I wasn't dreaming. I found myself outside my dressing room without knowing how it happened. Since you saw me disappear from my dressing room one night, maybe you can explain it, but I can't. All I can tell you is that I was in front of my mirror, then suddenly I didn't see it and I looked for it behind me, but it and my dressing room were gone. I was in a dark hall. I was afraid and I screamed.

"Everything around me was dark. In the distance, a dim red glow lighted a corner of a wall where two halls crossed. I screamed again. My own voice was the only sound I heard, because the singing and the violin had stopped. All at once, in the darkness, a hand, or rather something cold and bony, closed over my wrist and held it firmly. Once again I screamed. An arm imprisoned my waist and I was lifted off the ground. For a few moments I struggled in horror. My fingers slipped over damp stones, unable to hold onto them. Then I stopped moving, feeling as if I were going to die of terror.

"I was carried toward the little red glow. When we came close to it, I saw that I was being held by a man wearing a big black cloak and a mask that hid his whole face. I made one last effort: my arms and legs stiffened and my mouth opened to cry out my fear, but a hand closed it, a hand that I felt on my lips, on my flesh—and it smelled of death! I fainted.

"I don't know how long I was unconscious. When I opened my eyes again, the man in black and I were still in darkness, except that a shaded lantern, on the floor, now shone on a gushing fountain set into a wall. Its water splashed down the wall and disappeared under the floor on which I was lying. My head was resting on the knee of the man in the black cloak and mask. He was putting cool water on my temples with an attentive care and gentleness that seemed to me more horrible to bear than the brutality he had shown when he carried me away. His hands touched me lightly, but they still smelled of death. I made a feeble attempt to push them away and asked weakly, 'Who are you? Where's the Voice?' His only answer was a sigh.

"Suddenly a warm breath passed over my face and in the darkness I vaguely saw a white shape beside the black shape of the man. I was startled to hear a joyful neighing and I murmured, 'César!' The horse quivered. The man lifted me onto the saddle. I'd recognized César, the white horse from *Le Prophète*. I used to pamper him by feeding him delicacies. One night there was a rumor backstage that he'd disappeared and been stolen by the Opera ghost. I believed in the Voice; I'd never believed in the ghost, but now I shuddered and wondered if I was his prisoner. I inwardly called on the Voice to help me, because I would never have imagined that the Voice and the ghost were the same! You've heard of the Opera ghost, haven't you?"

"Yes," Raoul answered. "But tell me what happened to you while you were on the white horse from *Le Prophète*."

"I let myself be carried on his back, without making a movement. A strange torpor gradually replaced the anxiety and terror that my hellish adventure had aroused in me. The man in black held me and I didn't try to escape from him. The inner peace I felt made me think that I must be under the influence of some sort of potion, though I had full command of my senses. My eyes were becoming used to the darkness and it was broken here and there by brief gleams. I judged that we were in a narrow circular gallery and I imagined that it went all around the building, whose underground part is immense.

"Once, only once, I'd gone down into those prodigious cellars and I'd stopped at the third level, afraid to go any farther. I'd seen two more levels below me, big enough to hold a town, but the figures that appeared had made me run away. There are black demons in front of boilers down there. They work with shovels and pitchforks, and stir up fires, and light them, and if you come close to them they threaten you by suddenly opening the red mouths of their furnaces.

"While César calmly carried me on his back through that nightmarish darkness, far off in the distance I saw the black demons in front of the red fires of their furnaces, looking very small, as if I were seeing them through the wrong end of a telescope. They appeared, disappeared, and reappeared, depending on the twists and turns of the course we were following. Finally they disappeared for good. The man was still holding me and César went on walking, unguided and surefooted.

"I couldn't tell you even approximately how long that journey into darkness lasted. My only thought was that we were circling around and around, going down in an inflexible spiral toward the farthest depths of the earth. Maybe I thought so because my head was spinning, but I don't believe that. No, I was incredibly lucid.

"César raised his nostrils, sniffed the air for a moment, and quickened his pace a little. I felt damp air and then he stopped. The night had brightened. We were surrounded by a bluish glow. I looked and saw that we were on the shore of a lake. Its gray water merged with the darkness in the distance, but the glow lighted the shore and I saw a little boat tied to an iron ring on a wharf.

"I knew all that existed, and there was nothing supernatural about the sight of that underground lake with a boat floating on it, but think of the fantastic situation I was in when I came to that shore! The souls of the dead couldn't have felt more anxiety when they came to the River Styx, and Charon couldn't have been gloomier or more silent than the man who lifted me into the boat. Maybe the effects of the potion had worn off, or maybe the coolness of that place had been enough to revive me; in any case, my torpor was nearly gone. I made a few movements which showed that my terror was returning. My grim companion must have noticed it, because he made a quick gesture to send César away. I saw César vanish into the darkness of the gallery and heard his hooves loudly stamping on the steps of a staircase.

"The man jumped into the boat, unfastened it from the iron ring, took the oars, and began rowing fast and powerfully. Looking through the holes in his mask, his eyes never left me and I felt the weight of their motionless pupils on me. The water around us made no sound. We glided along in the bluish glow I told you about, and then we were in total darkness again. Finally the boat bumped into something hard and came to a stop. The

man picked me up. By now I'd recovered enough of my strength
to scream again, and I did. But then I stopped, dazed by the
light— yes, the man had put me down in dazzlingly bright light.

"I leapt to my feet. All my strength had returned. I was in the
middle of a drawing room. It seemed to be decorated and
furnished only with magnificent flowers that looked absurd because of the silk ribbons with which they were tied to baskets of
the kind sold in shops on the boulevards; they were overcivilized
flowers like the ones I always found in my dressing room after
an opening performance. In the midst of those typically Parisian
flowers, the masked man in black stood with his arms folded. And
he spoke: 'Don't be afraid, Christine,' he said, 'you're in no
danger.'

"*It was the Voice!*

"I was dumbfounded and furious. I reached for his mask and
tried to pull it off, so I could see the Voice's face. He gently
gripped my wrists, pushed me into a chair, and said, 'You're in
no danger if you don't touch my mask!'

"Then he knelt in front of me and said nothing more. His
humility gave me back some of my courage. By clearly showing
me all the things around me, the light made me regain my
awareness of life's reality. No matter how extraordinary it might
seem, my adventure was now surrounded by earthly things that I
could see and touch. The tapestries on the walls, the furniture,
the candlesticks, the vases, and even the flowers—I could almost
have said where they had come from, in their gilded baskets, and
how much they had cost—inevitably enclosed my imagination
within the limits of a drawing room as commonplace as many
others, which at least had the excuse of not being in the cellars
of the Opera. I decided that I was probably dealing with an
outlandish eccentric who had somehow begun living in the cellars, just as others, out of need, and with the silent complicity of
the administration, had found permanent shelter in the attics of
that modern Tower of Babel where people schemed, sang in all
languages, and loved each other in all dialects.

"And the Voice, the Voice I had recognized behind the mask
that hadn't been able to hide it from me, was what now knelt in
front of me: *a man!*

"I didn't think of the horrible situation I was in, I didn't
wonder what would happen to me, or what dark, coldly tyrannical
destiny had led me to be enclosed in that drawing room like a

prisoner in a cell or a slave girl in a harem. No, I said to myself, 'This is what the Voice is: a man!' and I began crying.

"The man, still on his knees, evidently understood the reason for my tears, because he said, 'It's true, Christine: I'm not an angel, a spirit, or a ghost. I'm Erik.' "

At this point Christine's story was again interrupted. It seemed to her and Raoul that an echo behind them had repeated, "Erik." What echo? They looked around and saw that night had fallen. Raoul made a movement as though to stand up, but she held him back.

"Stay," she said, "I want to tell you everything *here*."

"Why here? I'm afraid the night may be too chilly for you."

"We have nothing to fear but trapdoors, and here we're at the other end of the world from them. And I'm not allowed to see you away from the Opera. This is no time to make him angry. We mustn't arouse his suspicion."

"Christine! Christine! Something tells me that we're wrong to wait till tomorrow night, that we ought to run away right now!"

"If Erik doesn't hear me sing tomorrow night, it will give him great pain."

"It will be hard to escape from him forever without giving him any pain."

"You're right, Raoul: I'm sure my escape will kill him." She added in a muffled voice, "But at least it's an even match, because there's a chance that he'll kill us."

"Then he really loves you?"

"Yes, enough to make him stop at nothing, not even murder!"

"But it's possible to find the place where he lives and go to him there. Since he's not a ghost, it's possible to talk to him and even force him to answer!"

Christine shook her head.

"No, nothing can be done against Erik. You can only run away from him!"

"Then why, since you could have run away from him, did you go back to him?"

"Because I had to. You'll understand that when you know how I left his house."

"Oh, I hate him!" cried Raoul. "And you, Christine, tell me . . . I need you to tell me this so that I can listen more calmly to the rest of that incredible story. Do you hate him too?"

"No," she said simply.

"Then why have you wasted all those words? You obviously love him, and your fear, your terror—all that is still love, of the most exciting kind! The kind you don't admit to yourself," Raoul explained bitterly, "the kind that thrills you when you think of it. Just imagine—a man who lives in an underground palace!"

And he laughed scornfully.

"Do you want me to go back there?" she asked harshly. "Be careful, Raoul: I've already told you that if I go there again, I'll never come back!"

There was a tense silence among the three of them: the two who had been talking and the shadow listening behind them.

"Before I answer you," Raoul finally said slowly, "I'd like to know what feeling you have for him, since you don't hate him."

"Horror!" she said, and she spoke the word so loudly that it drowned out the sigh of the night. "That's the worst of it:" she went on with growing intensity, "he horrifies me but I don't hate him. How could I hate him, Raoul? Imagine him as he was, kneeling in front of me, in the underground house by the lake. He accused himself, he cursed himself, he begged me to forgive him! He admitted his deceit. He said he loved me! He laid an immense, tragic love at my feet. He had abducted me out of love, but he respected me, he cringed before me, he moaned, he wept! And when I stood up and told him that I could only despise him if he didn't immediately give me back the freedom he had taken from me, I was amazed to hear him offer it to me: I could go whenever I pleased, and he was willing to show me the mysterious path. But . . . but he stood up too, and then I had to realize that although he wasn't an angel, a spirit, or a ghost, he was still the Voice, because he sang! And I listened . . . and I stayed.

"We said nothing more to each other for the rest of the evening. He took a harp, and he, the man's voice, the angel's voice, began singing Desdemona's love song to me. My memory of having sung it myself made me feel ashamed. Music has the power to abolish everything in the outside world except its sounds, which go straight to the heart. My bizarre adventure was forgotten. The Voice had come to life again and I followed it, enraptured, on its harmonious journey; I belonged to Orpheus's flock! It took me into sorrow, joy, martyrdom, despair, bliss, death, and triumphant nuptials. I listened, it sang; it sang unknown pieces to me, and new music that gave me a strange impression of gentleness, languor, and peace, music that stirred my soul, then gradually soothed it and led it to the threshold of a dream. I fell asleep.

"When I woke up I was alone, on a chaise lounge in a simple little bedroom with an ordinary mahogany bed. There were cretonne hangings on its walls and it was lighted by a lamp standing on the marble top of an old Louis-Philippe chest of drawers. Where was I now? I passed my hand over my forehead, as though to drive away a bad dream. Unfortunately it didn't take me long to realize that I wasn't dreaming. I was a prisoner: I could leave my bedroom only to go into a very comfortable bathroom with hot and cold running water. When I came back into the bedroom I saw on the chest of drawers a note written in red ink that clearly informed me of my sad situation. If I had had any doubts about the reality of what had happened, that note would have taken them away.

" 'My dear Christine,' it said, 'there is no need for you to worry about your fate. You have no better or more respectful friend in the world than I. For the time being you are alone in this house, which belongs to you. I have gone out to do some shopping and will bring back all the linen and other personal effects that you may need.'

" 'I've obviously fallen into the hands of a madman!' I said to myself. 'What's going to become of me? And how long does that scoundrel intend to keep me in his underground prison?'

"I ran wildly around my little apartment, looking for a way out. I found none. I bitterly reproached myself for my stupid superstition and took perverse pleasure in making fun of the perfect innocence with which I'd accepted the Voice of the Angel of Music when I heard it through the walls of my dressing room. Anyone as foolish as I had been could expect enormous catastrophes, and know they were fully deserved! I felt like hitting myself, and I began laughing and crying over myself at the same time. I was in that state when Erik came back.

"After tapping three times on the wall, he calmly came in through a door that I hadn't been able to discover. He left it open. He was holding an armload of boxes and packages. He unhurriedly put them down on the bed while I angrily berated him and demanded that he take off his mask if he claimed that it hid the face of an honorable man. He answered with great composure, 'You will never see Erik's face.'

"He then rebuked me for not yet having washed and groomed myself at that time of day, and deigned to inform me that it was two o'clock in the afternoon. He would give me half an hour, he said, winding my watch and setting it at the right time, and then we would go to the dining room, where an excellent lunch was waiting for us. I was very hungry. I slammed the door in his face, went into the bathroom, and took a bath after putting a magnificent pair of scissors beside me, determined to kill myself with them if, after behaving like a madman, he stopped behaving like an honorable man.

"The cool water of the bath made me feel much better. By the time I was with Erik again, I'd wisely decided not to offend him in any way, and even to flatter him if need be, in the hope of making him free me quickly. He said he wanted to reassure me by telling me about his plans for me. He enjoyed my company too much to deprive himself of it immediately, as he had done the day before when he saw my expression of fear and indignation. By now, he said, I should realize that there was no reason to be afraid of having him with me. He loved me, but he would tell me so only when I allowed it, and the rest of the time would be spent on music.

" 'What do you mean by the rest of the time?' I asked him.

" 'Five days,' he answered firmly.

" 'And after that, I'll be free?'

" 'You'll be free, Christine, because by the time those five days are over you'll have learned not to be afraid of me, and then you'll come back to see poor Erik now and then.'

"He said these last words in a tone that deeply moved me. I seemed to hear such real and pitiful despair in it that I looked up at his masked face with compassion. I couldn't see his eyes behind the mask, and that increased the strange feeling of uneasiness I had when I questioned that mysterious piece of black silk, but I saw one, two, three, four tears run down from its edge.

"With a gesture, he invited me to sit facing him at a pedestal table in the middle of the room where he had played the harp for me the night before. I sat down feeling greatly troubled but I ate with a good appetite: several crayfish and a chicken wing, with Tokay wine he said he had personally brought from the cellars in Königsberg that Falstaff had frequented. He, however, neither ate nor drank. I asked him what his nationality was, and whether the name Erik meant that he was of Scandinavian origin. He answered that he had neither a name nor a country and that he had taken the name Erik 'by chance.' I asked him why, since he loved me, he hadn't found some other way of letting me know it than by taking me away and imprisoning me underground.

" 'It's hard to make yourself loved in a grave,'' I said.

" 'One takes whatever rendezvous one can get,' he answered in a strange tone.

"Then he stood up and held out his hand to me because he wanted, he said, to show me his apartment. But I quickly drew back my hand from his, with a cry. What I had touched was both clammy and bony, and I remembered that his hands smelled of death.

" 'Oh, forgive me!' he moaned. He opened a door in front of me. 'This is my bedroom. It's rather curious. . . . Would you care to see it?'

"I didn't hesitate. His manner, his words—everything about him told me to trust him. And I sensed that I shouldn't be afraid.

"I went in. It seemed to me that I'd just stepped into a funeral room. The walls were hung with black, but instead of the white tears that usually appear on such funereal hangings, there was an enormous musical staff and the repeated notes of the *Dies Irae*. In the middle of the room was a canopy with red brocade curtains, and under the canopy was an open coffin. I shrank back at the sight of it.

" 'I sleep in it,' Erik said. 'We should get used to everything in life, even eternity.'

"The coffin made such a sinister impression on me that I looked away from it. I then saw the keyboard of an organ that took up one whole wall. On the music stand was a notebook covered with red notes. I asked permission to look at it and read the title on the first page: *Don Juan Triumphant*.

" 'Yes, I compose sometimes,' he said. 'I began that work twenty years ago. When it's finished, I'll take it with me into that coffin and I won't wake up.'

" 'You should work on it as seldom as possible,' I said.

" 'I sometimes work on it for two weeks at a time, day and night, and during that time I live only on music. Then I rest for several years.'

" 'Will you play me something from your *Don Juan Trium-*

phant?' I asked, thinking I would please him by overcoming my aversion to staying in that deathly room.

" 'Don't ever ask me that,' he said grimly. 'That *Don Juan* wasn't written to the words of Mozart's Lorenzo Da Ponte, inspired by wine, love affairs, and vice, and finally punished by God. I'll play Mozart for you if you like; it will bring tears to your eyes and edifying thoughts to your mind. But my *Don Juan* burns, Christine, and yet he's not struck down by the fire of heaven!'

"We went back into the drawing room that we'd just left. I noticed that there were no mirrors anywhere in the apartment. I was about to remark on it when Erik sat down at the piano and said, 'You see, Christine, some music is so formidable that it consumes everyone who approaches it. But you haven't yet come to that kind of music—luckily, because you'd lose your fresh colors and no one would recognize you when you went back to Paris. Let's sing music from the Opera, Christine Daaé.'

"He said 'music from the Opera' as if he were hurling an insult at me. But I didn't have time to think about what he meant by those words. We immediately began singing the duet from *Otello,* and we were already heading for disaster. I sang the part of Desdemona with a genuine despair and fear that I'd never achieved before. Rather than being disheartened by singing with such a partner, I was filled with magnificent terror. My recent experiences brought me very close to the poet's thoughts, and I sang in a way that would have dazzled the composer. As for Erik, his voice was thunderous; his vengeful soul weighed on each sound and awesomely increased its power. Love, jealousy, and hatred burst out around us in piercing cries. Erik's black mask made me think of the natural face of the Moor of Venice. He was Othello himself. I thought he was going to strike me, batter me till I fell, yet I made no move to get away from him, to avoid his fury like the timid Desdemona. No, I stepped closer to him, attracted and fascinated, enticed by the idea of dying at the center of such passion. But before dying I wanted to see his face—which, I thought, must be transfigured by the fire of eternal art—and take that sublime image with me into death. I wanted to see *the face of the Voice.* Unthinkingly, with a quick movement beyond my control, I pulled off his mask. . . . Oh, horror, horror, horror!"

Christine stopped at this vision, which she seemed to be still pushing away with trembling hands, while the echo of the night, just as it had repeated Erik's name, now repeated her exclamation: "Horror, horror, horror!" United still more by the terror of her story, Raoul and Christine looked up at the stars shining in the clear, peaceful sky.

"It's strange," he said, "how this soft, calm night is full of moans. It seems to be lamenting with us!"

"Now that you're about to learn the secret," she replied, "your ears will soon be full of lamentations, as mine are." She imprisoned his protecting hands in hers and was shaken by a long tremor. "Oh, if I live to be a hundred I'll always hear the superhuman cry that came from him, the cry of his pain and infernal rage, when that sight appeared to me. My eyes opened wide in horror, and so did my mouth, though I didn't make a sound.

"Oh, Raoul, that sight! How can I ever stop seeing it? My ears will always be filled with his cries, and my eyes will always be haunted by his face. What an image! How can I stop seeing it, and how can I make you see it? You've seen skulls that have dried for centuries, and maybe, if you weren't the victim of a terrible nightmare, you saw his death's-head that night in Perros. And you saw the Red Death at the masked ball. But all those skulls were motionless and their mute horror wasn't alive. Imagine, if you can, the mask of death suddenly coming to life and, with its four dark holes—for the eyes, nose, and mouth—expressing anger carried to its ultimate degree, the supreme fury of a demon, with no eyes showing in the sockets, because, as I later learned, his glowing eyes can be seen only in darkness. . . . As I stood with my back against the wall, I must have looked like terror personified, just as he was the very image of hideousness.

"Then he came toward me, grinding his teeth in his lipless mouth. I fell to my knees. In a tone of fierce hatred, he said insane things to me, incoherent words, curses, frenzied raving, and I don't know what else, I don't know. . . .

"Finally he leaned over me and shouted, 'Look! You wanted to see! Now see! Feast your eyes, sate your soul with my cursed ugliness! Look at Erik's face! Now you know the face of the Voice! It wasn't enough for you to hear me, was it? You wanted to know what I looked like. You women are so curious!'

"He burst into harsh, rumbling, powerful laughter and re-

peated, 'You women are so curious!' He said things like this:
'Are you satisfied? You must admit I'm handsome. When a
woman has seen me as you have, she belongs to me. She loves
me forever! I'm the same kind of man as Don Juan.'

"He drew himself up to his full height, put his hand on his
hip, tilted the hideous thing that was his head and thundered,
'Look at me! *I'm Don Juan triumphant!*'

"And when I turned away from him, begging him to spare
me, he grabbed me by the hair with his dead fingers and brutally
turned my head back toward him."

"Enough, enough!" Raoul interrupted. "I'll kill him! In heaven's name, Christine, tell me where that 'dining room by the
lake' is! I must kill him!"

"Be quiet, Raoul, if you want to know!"

"Yes, I want to know how and why you went back there!
That's the secret! But in any case I'll kill him!"

"Listen to me, since you want to know. Listen! He dragged
me by the hair, and then . . . and then . . . Oh, it was even more
horrible!"

"Tell me, now!" Raoul exclaimed fiercely. "Quickly!"

"Then he said to me, 'What? You're afraid of me? It's
possible that . . . Do you think I'm still wearing a mask? Well,
then,' he bellowed, 'pull it off, the way you did the other one!
Come, pull it off! I want you to! Your hands, give me your
hands! If they can't do it themselves, I'll lend you mine and
we'll pull off the mask together.'

"I tried to roll away from him on the floor but he took hold of
my hands and plunged them into the horror of his face. With my
fingernails he lacerated his flesh, his ghastly dead flesh!

" 'You must know,' he said, speaking from the back of his
throat and roaring like a furnace, 'that I'm made entirely of
death, from head to foot, and that it's a corpse that loves you,
adores you, and will never leave you, never! I'm going to have
the coffin enlarged, Christine, for later, when we've come to the
end of our love. Look: I'm not laughing anymore, I'm crying
. . . I'm crying for you; you pulled off my mask and, because of
that, you can never leave me. As long as you could think I was
handsome, you could come back. I know you'd have come back.
But now that you know how hideous I am, you'd run away
forever. I'm keeping you! Why did you want to see me? It was
insanely foolish of you to want to see me, when even my father

never saw me, and my weeping mother gave me my first mask so she wouldn't have to see me anymore!'

"He had finally let go of me and was writhing on the floor, sobbing. Then he crawled out of the room like a snake. When he had gone into his bedroom and closed the door, I was left alone with my thoughts, still horrified but now rid of the revolting sight of his face. A prodigious silence, the silence of the grave, had followed that storm and I was able to reflect on the terrible consequences of my having pulled off that mask. The monster had told me what to expect. I was imprisoned forever and my curiosity would be the cause of all my misery. He had given me fair warning: he had told me that I was in no danger as long as I didn't touch his mask, and I had touched it anyway.

"I cursed my rashness but I realized with a shudder that the monster's reasoning was logical. Yes, I would have come back if I hadn't seen his face. He had already touched and interested me enough, and aroused my pity enough by his masked tears, to make it impossible for me to resist his plea. And finally, I wasn't ungrateful: his repulsiveness couldn't make me forget that he was the Voice and that he had animated me with his genius. I would have come back! But now, if I ever got out of those catacombs, I certainly would *not* come back! You don't go back into a grave with a corpse that loves you!

"During our last scene, I'd been able to judge the savageness of his passion from his frenzied way of looking at me, or rather his frenzied way of moving the two black holes of his invisible eyes toward me. Since he hadn't taken me in his arms when I couldn't have put up any resistance, that monster must also have been an angel; maybe, after all, he really was the Angel of Music to some small extent, and maybe he would have been the Angel of Music to the fullest extent if God had clothed his soul in beauty rather than loathsome decay.

"Frantic at the thought of what lay in store for me, and terrified that at any moment the door of the bedroom with the coffin in it might open and reveal the monster's unmasked face, I slipped back into my apartment and picked up the scissors that could put an end to my appalling fate. . . . Then I heard the sound of the organ.

"That was when I began to understand what Erik had felt when he referred to 'music from the Opera' with a contempt that had surprised me. What I was hearing had nothing in common with what had delighted me till then. His *Don Juan Triumphant*—I was sure he had thrown himself into his masterpiece to forget the horror of the present moment—seemed to me at first only a long, terrible, magnificent sob in which poor Erik had placed all his cursed misery.

"I remembered the notebook with red notes in it, and easily imagined that this music had been written in blood. It took me into all the details of martyrdom and into every part of the abyss inhabited by *the ugly man;* it showed me Erik banging his poor, hideous head against the grim walls of that hell, and avoiding being seen by people, so as not to frighten them. Gasping, overwhelmed, and compassionate, I listened to the swelling of gigantic chords in which sorrow was made divine. Then the sounds from the abyss suddenly came together in a prodigious, threatening flight, a swirling flock that seemed to rise into the sky like an eagle soaring toward the sun, and I heard such a triumphal symphony, seemingly setting the world ablaze, that I realized the work was ending and that ugliness, lifted on the wings of love, had dared to look beauty in the face.

"I felt as if I were drunk. I pushed open the door that separated me from Erik. He stood up when he heard me, but he was afraid to turn around.

" 'Erik,' I said, 'show me your face without fear. I swear that you're the most heartrending and sublime man in the world, and if I ever quiver again when I look at you, it will be because I'm thinking about the splendor of your genius!'

"He turned around, because he believed me, and I too, unfortunately, had faith in myself. He raised his fleshless hands toward destiny and fell at my knees with words of love. . . . With words of love from his dead mouth, and the music had stopped. . . . He kissed the hem of my dress and didn't see that I'd closed my eyes.

"What else can I tell you, Raoul? Now you know the tragedy. . . . It went on for two weeks, two weeks during which I lied to him. My lies were as hideous as the monster who inspired them, and at that price I was able to gain my freedom. I burned his mask, and I behaved so convincingly that even when he wasn't singing he dared to try to make me look at him, like a timid dog staying close to its master. He acted like my faithful slave and lavished all sorts of care on me.

"He gradually came to trust me so much that he took me for

walks along the shore of Lake Averne, and for rides across its gray water in his boat. Toward the end of my captivity he took me, at night, through the gate that closes the underground passage of the Rue Scribe. There a carriage was waiting for us and it took us into the lonely parts of the Bois de Boulogne. The night we met you was nearly disastrous for me, because he's terribly jealous of you. I was able to calm him by telling him that you were about to leave the country.

"Finally, after two weeks of that abominable captivity in which I was filled with pity at some times, and with enthusiasm, despair, or horror at others, he believed me when I told him, 'I'll come back.' "

"And you did come back," Raoul said dejectedly.

"Yes, I did, and I must say it wasn't the frightening threats he made when he set me free that helped me to keep my word: it was the way he sobbed on the threshold of his tomb." She sadly shook her head. "Those sobs attached me to him more strongly than I thought when I said good-bye to him. Poor Erik! Poor Erik. . . ."

"Christine," said Raoul, standing up, "you say you love me, yet you went back to Erik only a few hours after he freed you! Remember the masked ball!"

"That was our agreement. . . . And you, Raoul, remember that I spent those few hours with you—and put us both in great danger."

"During those hours I doubted that you loved me."

"Do you still doubt it? If so, let me tell you that each of my visits to Erik increased my horror of him, because each of them, instead of calming him as I hoped, made him even more madly in love with me. And I'm afraid! I'm afraid!"

"You're afraid, but do you love me? If Erik were handsome, would you love me?"

"Why tempt fate, Raoul? Why ask about things that I keep hidden at the back of my mind, like sins?" She stood up also, and put her beautiful trembling arms around his neck. "Oh, my fiancé of a day, if I didn't love you I wouldn't give you my lips. For the first and last time, take them."

He took them, but the surrounding night was torn apart so violently that he and Christine ran away, as though from an approaching storm, and before they disappeared into the forest of roof timbers, their eyes, filled with terror of Erik, showed them an immense nightbird high above them, glaring at them with its glowing eyes and seeming to cling to the strings of Apollo's lyre.

14

A Masterstroke by the Lover
of Trapdoors

RAOUL AND CHRISTINE ran and ran, away from the roof where there were glowing eyes that could be seen only in the dark, and they did not stop until they came to the eighth floor on the way down. There was no performance that night and the halls were deserted.

Suddenly a strange figure appeared in front of them, blocking their path.

"No! Not this way!"

And the figure pointed to another hall that would take them to the wings.

Raoul wanted to stop and ask for an explanation.

"Go! Hurry!" ordered the vague shape, hidden beneath a kind of greatcoat and wearing a pointed hat.

Christine pulled Raoul along, forcing him to go on running.

"Who is he?" he asked. "Who is that man?"

"He's the Persian."

"What's he doing here?"

"No one knows. He's always in the Opera."

"You're making me do something cowardly, Christine," said Raoul, deeply perturbed. "You're making me run away, for the first time in my life."

"I think we've run away from the shadow of our imagination," replied Christine, who was becoming calmer.

"If we really saw Erik, I should have nailed him to Apollo's

143

lyre, as owls are nailed to farmhouse walls in Brittany, and then we'd have been finished with him.''

"First you'd have had to climb up to Apollo's lyre, and that's not easy.''

"The glowing eyes were up there.''

"Now you're becoming like me: ready to see him everywhere! But you'll think it over and then say to yourself, 'What I saw as glowing eyes was probably only the gold dots of two stars looking down at the city through the strings of the lyre.' ''

Christine went down one more floor and Raoul followed.

"Since you've made up your mind to leave,'' he said, ''it's better to do it now, believe me. Why wait till tomorrow? He may have heard us tonight!''

"No, he didn't. I've already told you that he's working on his *Don Juan Triumphant*. He's not concerned with us.''

"You're so uncertain of it that you keep looking behind you.''

"Let's go to my dressing room.''

"Let's meet somewhere outside the Opera instead.''

"No, not till we actually go away together. It would bring us bad luck if I didn't keep my word: I promised him that I wouldn't see you anywhere but here.''

"It's lucky for me that he allowed you even that. Do you know,'' he said bitterly, ''that it was daring of you to let us play at being engaged?''

"But he knows about it, Raoul. He said to me, 'I trust you. Viscount Raoul de Chagny is in love with you and he'll soon leave the country. Before he goes, I want him to be as unhappy as I am!' ''

"Will you please tell me what that means?''

"You're the one who should tell me. Are people unhappy when they're in love?''

"Yes, when they're in love and aren't sure of being loved.''

"Are you saying that for Erik?''

"For Erik and for myself,'' answered Raoul, shaking his head with a thoughtful, forlorn expression.

They came to Christine's dressing room.

"Why do you think you're safer in this room than in the rest of the building?'' he asked. ''Since you hear him through the walls, he can hear us through them too.''

"No, he gave me his word that he wouldn't be behind the walls of my dressing room anymore, and I believe in his word.

My dressing room, and my bedroom in the house by the lake, belong exclusively to me and he respects my privacy when I'm in them.''

"How could you have left this room and been taken into the dark hall? Shall we try to reconstruct your movements?"

"It would be dangerous, because the mirror might take me away again. Then, instead of running away with you, I'd have to go to the end of the secret passage that leads to the lake, and call Erik there.''

"Would he hear you?"

"No matter where I call him, he'll hear me. He told me so himself; he's a very curious genius. You mustn't think that he's a man who finds it amusing to live underground. He does things that no other man could do, and he knows things that are unknown to the world of the living."

"Be careful, or you'll turn him back into a ghost."

"No, he's not a ghost. He's a man of heaven and earth, that's all.''

" 'A man of heaven and earth, that's all!' How you talk about him! Are you still determined to go away with me?"

"Yes, tomorrow."

"Shall I tell you why I'd like us to go away tonight?"

"Tell me, Raoul."

"Because by tomorrow you won't be determined to do anything!''

"Then you must make me go in spite of myself! That's agreed, isn't it?"

"Yes. I'll be here in your dressing room tomorrow night, at midnight," Raoul said, his face somber. "No matter what happens, I'll keep my promise. You say that after attending the performance he's to go and wait for you in the dining room of his house?''

"Yes, that's where he told me to meet him."

"And how are you supposed to go there if you don't know how to leave your dressing room 'through the mirror'?"

"By going directly to the lake."

"Through all the cellars? Down staircases and along halls where stagehands and other workers are passing by? How could you have gone there in secret? Everyone would have followed Christine Daaé and she'd have arrived at the lake with a crowd around her.''

She took a big key from a box and showed it to him.

"This is the key to the underground passage of the Rue Scribe."

"I understand. The passage leads directly to the lake. Please give me that key."

"Never!" she replied firmly. "That would be a betrayal!"

He suddenly saw her change color. Deathly pallor spread over her face.

"Oh, my God!" she exclaimed. "Erik! Erik! Have mercy on me!"

"Quiet!" Raoul ordered. "You told me he could hear you!"

But Christine's behavior became more and more inexplicable. She slid her fingers along each other and repeated with a distraught expression, "Oh, my God! Oh, my God!"

"What's wrong? Tell me," he pleaded.

"The ring."

"What do you mean? Get a grip on yourself, Christine!"

"The gold ring he gave me . . ."

"Ah, so it was Erik who gave you that gold ring!"

"You knew that, Raoul! But what you didn't know is that when he gave it to me he said, 'I'm setting you free, but on condition that this ring will always be on your finger. As long as you have it on, you'll be protected from all danger and Erik will be your friend. But if you ever part with it, you'll wish you hadn't, because Erik will take revenge!' Oh, Raoul, Raoul, the ring is gone from my finger! This is terrible for both of us!"

They looked all around them for the ring but did not find it. He could not calm her.

"It must have happened when I gave you that kiss, up on the roof, under Apollo's lyre," she tried to explain, trembling. "The ring must have slipped off my finger and fallen into the street! How can we find it now? Something awful will happen to us! Oh, if only we could escape!"

"We'll run away, now," he insisted once again.

She hesitated. He thought she was going to consent. But then fear showed in her eyes and she said, "No! Tomorrow!"

And she hurried away in great distress, still sliding her fingers along each other, no doubt in the hope that it might make the ring reappear.

As for Raoul, he went home, preoccupied with everything he had heard.

"If I don't save her from that fraud," he said aloud in his bedroom, as he was going to bed, "she's lost. But I'll save her!"

He put out his lamp and, lying in the darkness, felt a need to insult Erik. He shouted three times: "Fraud! Fraud! Fraud!"

But suddenly he raised himself on one elbow and cold sweat trickled down his temples. Two eyes, glowing like hot coals, had just appeared at the foot of his bed. They stared at him menacingly in the darkness.

Brave though he was, Raoul was trembling. He reached out his hand to the bedside table and groped hesitantly. When he found the box of matches, he lighted the lamp. The eyes vanished.

He thought uneasily, "She told me that his eyes could be seen only in the dark. His eyes disappeared when the light came, but maybe he himself is still there."

He got up and cautiously searched the room. He looked under the bed, like a child. Then he felt ridiculous.

"What should I believe?" he said aloud. "What should I *not* believe, with such a fairy tale? Where does reality end and the fantastic begin? What did she see? What did she think she saw?" He added, quivering, "And what did *I* see? Did I really see two glowing eyes just now? Did they shine only in my imagination? Now I'm not sure of anything! I wouldn't want to swear I saw those eyes."

He got back into bed and again put out his lamp.

The eyes reappeared.

"Oh!" he gasped.

He sat up and stared back at the eyes as bravely as he could. After a silence during which he summoned up his courage, he cried out, "Is that you, Erik? Man, spirit, or ghost, is it you?"

And he thought, "If it *is* Erik, he's on the balcony."

He ran, in his nightshirt, to a little chest of drawers and took a pistol from it in the dark. With the pistol in his hand, he opened the glazed door to the balcony. The night was chilly. He took time only to glance over the deserted balcony, then he came back inside and closed the door. He went to bed again, shivering, with the pistol within reach on the bedside table.

Once again he put out the lamp.

The eyes were still there, at the foot of the bed. Were they between the bed and the glass of the door, or behind the glass, on the balcony? That was what he wanted to know. He also wanted to know if those eyes belonged to a human being. He wanted to know everything. . . .

Patiently, calmly, without disturbing the night around him, he picked up his pistol and aimed it at the two golden stars that were still looking at him with a strange motionless glow. He aimed a long time. If those stars were eyes, and if there was a forehead above them, and if he was not too clumsy . . .

The shot shattered the peace of the sleeping house. And while footsteps hurried along the halls, Raoul sat looking into the darkness, holding out his pistol, ready to shoot again.

This time the two stars had disappeared.

Light, people, Count Philippe, terribly anxious.

"What happened, Raoul?"

"I think I was dreaming. I shot at two stars that kept me from sleeping."

"You're delirious! You're sick! Please tell me what happened!" And Philippe picked up the pistol.

"No, I'm not delirious," said Raoul. "And we'll soon find out . . ."

He got up, put on his robe and slippers, took a candle from a servant, opened the glazed door, and stepped onto the balcony.

Philippe saw that a bullet had gone through the glass at the height of a man's head. Raoul was leaning over the floor of the balcony with his candle.

"Oh!" he exclaimed. "Blood! Blood . . . here . . . there. More blood! Good! A ghost that bleeds is less dangerous!" he said with a grim laugh.

"Raoul! Raoul! Raoul!"

Philippe shook him as if trying to rouse a sleepwalker from his dangerous sleep.

"I'm not asleep, my dear brother!" Raoul protested impatiently. "You can see the blood, anyone can see it. I thought I was dreaming and had shot at two stars. They were Erik's eyes—and this is his blood!" He added with sudden anxiety, "But maybe I was wrong to shoot, and Christine may not forgive me for it! All this wouldn't have happened if I'd taken the precaution of closing the balcony curtains before going to bed."

"Raoul! Have you lost your mind? Wake up!"

"Again! You'd do better to help me look for Erik. After all, it should be possible to find a bleeding ghost."

"It's true, sir," said Philippe's valet, "there's blood on the balcony."

A servant brought a lamp and they were able to examine everything in its light. The trail of blood followed the railing of the balcony, then went to a drainpipe and continued along it.

"You shot at a cat, my boy," said Philippe.

"Unfortunately," Raoul said with another laugh that resounded sorrowfully in Philippe's ears, "it's quite possible. With Erik, you never know! Was it Erik? Was it a cat? Was it the ghost? Was it flesh or shadow? No, no, with Erik you never know!"

Raoul went on in that vein, making bizarre remarks that were closely and logically related to his concerns and the strange things, seemingly both real and supernatural, that Christine had told him; and those remarks helped to convince many people that his mind was deranged. Even Philippe was swayed by them, and later the examining magistrate had no difficulty in reaching a conclusion on the basis of the police commissary's report.

"Who is Erik?" asked Philippe, squeezing Raoul's hand.

"He's my rival! And if he's not dead, I wish he were!"

Raoul made a gesture telling the servants to leave. The door of the bedroom closed on the two brothers. But the servants did not leave quickly enough to prevent Philippe's valet from hearing Raoul say distinctly and emphatically, "Tomorrow night I'm going to elope with Christine Daaé."

This sentence was later repeated to Monsieur Faure, the examining magistrate, but exactly what the brothers said to each other that night never became known. The servants said it was not their first quarrel behind closed doors. Shouting was heard through the walls, and it always concerned a singer named Christine Daaé.

The next morning at breakfast, which Philippe always took in his study, he sent word asking his brother to join him. Raoul arrived, gloomy and silent. The scene was short.

Philippe: "Read this!"

He holds out a newspaper, *L'Epoque*, and points to an item in a gossip column.

Raoul, reading aloud in a stilted manner: " 'The great news in aristocratic circles is the engagement between Mademoiselle Christine Daaé, an operatic singer, and Viscount Raoul de Chagny. If we are to believe backstage gossip,

Count Philippe de Chagny has sworn that for the first time a member of his family will fail to keep a promise. Since love, especially in the Opera, is all-powerful, one may well wonder what means Count Philippe can use to prevent his brother, the viscount, from leading "the new Marguerite" to the altar. The two brothers are said to adore each other, but the count is greatly mistaken if he expects brotherly love to win out over romantic love.' "

Philippe, sadly: "You see, Raoul, you're making us ridiculous! That girl has completely turned your head with her ghost stories."

(This shows that Raoul has repeated Christine's story to his brother.)

Raoul: "Good-bye, Philippe."

Philippe: "Your mind is made up? You're leaving tonight?" No answer. "You're leaving . . . with her? You won't do anything foolish, will you?" Still no answer. "No, you won't! I'll stop you!"

Raoul: "Good-bye, Philippe."

He walks away.

This scene was described to the examining magistrate by Philippe himself, who did not see Raoul again till that evening at the Opera, a few minutes before Christine's disappearance.

Raoul spent the whole day making preparations for the elopement.

The horses, the carriage, the coachman, provisions, baggage, the necessary money, the itinerary (to throw the ghost off their trail, they would not travel by train)—all this kept him busy till nine o'clock in the evening.

At nine o'clock a kind of berlin with curtains drawn over its tightly closed windows joined the line of carriages on the rotunda side. It was drawn by two vigorous horses and driven by a coachman whose face was largely hidden by the long scarf he wore. In front of this berlin were three other carriages: broughams belonging, as was later established during the preliminary investigation, to Carlotta, who had abruptly returned to Paris; to La Sorelli; and, at the head of the line, to Count Philippe de Chagny. No one got out of the berlin. The coachman remained on the seat. The three other coachmen did the same.

A figure wrapped in a big black cloak, and wearing a black felt hat, passed along the sidewalk between the rotunda and the carriages. It seemed to look at the berlin with special attention. It approached the horses, then the coachman, and then it went away without having said a word.

The investigation concluded that the figure was Viscount Raoul de Chagny. I, however, do not believe it, since Raoul wore a top hat that evening, as he did every other evening, and that hat was later found. I believe, rather, that the figure was the Opera ghost, who knew about everything, as will soon become apparent.

It happened that the opera being performed that evening was *Faust*. The audience was highly distinguished. Aristocratic society was magnificently represented. In those days, subscribers did not lend or rent their boxes, or share them with financiers, businessmen, or foreigners. Nowadays, in the box of Marquis So-and-So—which is still called the box of Marquis So-and-So because the marquis has a contract giving him possession of it—we may see a pork merchant sitting at ease with his family, as he has a perfect right to do, since he has paid for the marquis's box. In the past, such practices were all but unknown. Boxes at the Opera were drawing rooms where one was almost certain to meet or see members of fashionable society, who used to love music.

Those people were all acquainted with each other. Though they did not necessarily frequent each other socially, they knew everyone's name and face, and Count Philippe de Chagny's face was known to them all.

The item published in the gossip column of *L'Epoque* that morning had evidently produced its effect, because all eyes were turned toward the box where Count Philippe sat alone, apparently carefree and unconcerned. The women in that splendid gathering seemed greatly intrigued, and the absence of the count's brother gave rise to endless whispering behind fans.

When Christine appeared on the stage, she was given a rather cold reception. Those exalted members of the audience could not forgive her for having aspired to marry a man from a social class so far above her own. She sensed their hostility and was upset by it.

The regular operagoers, who claimed to know about the viscount's love affair, smiled openly at certain passages in Marguerite's part. And they conspicuously turned toward Philippe de Chagny's box when Christine sang these words:

I wish I could but know, who is he that address'd me?
If he is noble, or, at least, what his name is?

With his chin resting on his hand, Philippe seemed unaware of the attention given to him. His eyes were fixed on the stage; but was he looking at it? He appeared to be far away from everything.

Christine was rapidly losing all her self-assurance. She was trembling. She was heading for a catastrophe. . . . Carolus Fonta wondered if she was sick, and if she could hold out till the end of the act, which was the garden act. The audience remembered what had happened to Carlotta at the end of that act: the historic croak that had temporarily ended her career in Paris.

And just then Carlotta made her entrance into one of the boxes facing the stage. It was a sensational entrance. Poor Christine looked up at that new cause for commotion and recognized her rival. She thought she saw Carlotta sneer at her. That saved her. She forgot everything so that she could triumph again.

From then on, she sang with all her soul. She tried to surpass everything she had done before, and she succeeded. In the last act, when she began to invoke the angels and rise into the air, she took the whole quivering audience with her, and they all felt that they had wings.

At that superhuman call a man in the middle of the amphitheater stood up facing Christine, as if he were leaving the earth with her. It was Raoul.

Angel, in Heaven bless'd . . .

And, with her arms outstretched and her bosom heaving ardently, enveloped in the glory of her hair hanging loosely over her bare shoulders, Christine uttered the divine cry:

My spirit longs with thee to rest!

It was then that the stage was suddenly plunged into darkness. It was over so quickly that the spectators barely had time to exclaim in surprise before the stage was lighted again.

But Christine was no longer there! What had become of her? What kind of miracle had taken place? The spectators exchanged looks of perplexity. Agitation rapidly rose to a peak, on the stage as well as among the audience. People rushed from the wings to the place where Christine had been singing only a few moments before. The performance was interrupted in great disorder.

Where had Christine gone? What sorcery had snatched her away from thousands of enthusiastic spectators, and from Carolus Fonta's arms? It was enough to make one wonder if an angel might have answered her fervent plea by taking her away, body and soul, to rest in heaven.

Still standing in the amphitheater, Raoul had cried out. Count Philippe had stood up in his box. People looked at the stage, at the count, and at Raoul, and wondered if that singular occurrence might have some connection with the item of gossip reported in that morning's newspaper.

Raoul quickly left his place, Philippe disappeared from his box, and, while the curtain was being lowered, the subscribers hurried toward the backstage entrance. The audience waited for an announcement in an indescribable hubbub, all talking at once. Everyone had an explanation of how things had happened:

"She fell through a trapdoor."

"She was pulled up into the rigging loft. The poor girl may have been the victim of some stage effect that the new management was trying for the first time."

"It was an abduction, planned in advance. That's proved by the fact that the stage went dark just when she disappeared."

Finally the curtain rose slowly. Carolus Fonta stepped up to the orchestra conductor's podium and announced gravely and sadly, "Ladies and gentlemen, something incredible and deeply disquieting has just happened. Our colleague Christine Daae has vanished before our eyes, and no one knows how!"

15

The Singular Behavior of a Safety Pin

A CHAOTIC THRONG had invaded the stage. Singers, stagehands, dancers, supernumeraries, chorus members, subscribers—they were all questioning, shouting, jostling each other.

"What happened to her?"

"She was abducted!"

"Viscount de Chagny did it!"

"No, it was his brother!"

"Ah, there's Carlotta! She's the one who did it!"

"No, it was the ghost!"

Some were laughing, especially since examination of the floor and the trapdoors had ruled out the idea of an accident.

In that tumultuous crowd, three men were talking in low voices, with despairing gestures: Gabriel, the chorus master; Mercier, the administrator; and Rémy, the secretary. They had withdrawn to one corner of a passage between the stage and the broad corridor leading to the dancers' lounge. There, behind some enormous properties, they carried on their conversation.

"I knocked, but they didn't answer. Maybe they've left the office. But there's no way to find out, because they took the keys."

So spoke Rémy, and he was undoubtedly referring to the two managers. During the last intermission they had given orders that they were not to be disturbed for any reason; as far as everyone else was concerned, they were gone.

"But a singer disappearing from the stage isn't something that happens every day!" said Gabriel.

"Did you tell them about it, through the door?" Mercier asked Rémy.

"I'll go back there," said Rémy, and ran away.

Then the stage manager arrived.

"Well, Monsieur Mercier, are you coming? What are you two doing here? You're needed, Monsieur Mercier."

"I don't want to do or hear anything till Commissary Mifroid comes," Mercier declared. "I've sent for him. When he's here, we'll see!"

"And I say you must go down to the pipe organ immediately!"

"Not till Mifroid gets here."

"I've already gone down there."

"Oh? And what did you see?"

"I saw nobody! Do you understand? Nobody!"

"There's nothing I can do about that, is there?"

"Of course not," replied the stage manager, frenziedly pushing his hands through his unruly hair. "But maybe if somebody was at the pipe organ, that somebody could tell us how the stage went dark all at once. And Mauclair can't be found anywhere, you understand?"

Mauclair was the lighting-crew chief, who dispensed day and night at will on the stage of the Opera.

"Mauclair can't be found anywhere," Mercier repeated, shaken, "but what about his helpers?"

"Neither Mauclair nor his helpers! No one from the lighting crew, I'm telling you!" the stage manager shouted. "You know that girl didn't disappear all by herself! It was planned and organized, and we have to find out about it. And the managers aren't here. . . . I gave orders no one is to go down to the lighting controls and I posted a fireman in front of the recess of the pipe organ. Was I wrong to do that?"

"No, no, you were quite right. And now, let's wait for the commissary."

The stage manager walked away with an angry shrug, muttering against those "milksops" who calmly huddled in a corner while the whole Opera was "turned upside down."

Gabriel and Mercier could scarcely be accused of being calm. But they had received an order that paralyzed them: The manag-

ers were not to be disturbed for any reason in the world. Rémy
had tried to violate that order, with no success.

And now he came back from his new expedition. His face had
a look of bewilderment.

"Well, did you talk to them?" asked Mercier.

"Moncharmin finally opened the door," Rémy answered.
"His eyes were bulging out of his head. I thought he was going
to hit me. I couldn't get a word in, and do you know what he
yelled at me? 'Do you have a safety pin?' 'No,' I said. 'Then
leave me alone!' I tried to tell him that something unbelievable
had happened on the stage, but he said, 'A safety pin! Get me a
safety pin, right now!' An office boy who heard him—he was
roaring at the top of his lungs—came running up with a safety
pin and gave it to him, and Moncharmin slammed the door in my
face! And there you have it!"

"Why couldn't you have said, 'Christine Daaé . . .' "

"I'd like to have seen you try it! He was foaming at the
mouth. He wasn't thinking about anything but his safety pin. I
think that if he hadn't been given one on the spot, he'd have died
of apoplexy! The whole thing is unnatural. Our managers are
going crazy." Rémy was not pleased, and he expressed his
displeasure: "It can't go on like that! I'm not used to being
treated that way!"

Suddenly Gabriel whispered, "It's another trick played by
the O. G."

Rémy laughed disdainfully.

Mercier sighed and seemed about to unburden himself of a
secret, but, having seen Gabriel motioning him to be silent, he
said nothing. He felt his responsibility growing as the minutes
passed and the managers still had not appeared. Finally he could
restrain himself no longer.

"I'm going after them myself!" he decided.

Gabriel, suddenly very serious and stern, stopped him.

"Think of what you're doing, Mercier! Maybe they're staying
in their office because it's necessary! The O. G. has more than
one trick up his sleeve!"

But Mercier shook his head.

"I'm going anyway! If anyone had listened to me, the police
would have been told about everything long ago!"

And he left.

"What does he mean by 'everything'?" Rémy asked. "What

it that would have been told to the police? You don't answer, Gabriel—that means you're in on it too! Well, you'd better tell me about it if you don't want me to shout that you're all going crazy! Yes, crazy!"

Gabriel gave Rémy a blank stare, pretending to be puzzled by his unseemly outburst.

"Tell you about what? I don't know what you mean."

"During the intermission tonight, right here," said Rémy, exasperated, "Richard and Moncharmin were acting like lunatics!"

"I didn't notice," Gabriel said with annoyance.

"Then you're the only one who didn't! Do you think I didn't see them? And that Monsieur Parabise, the manager of the Crédit Central, didn't see anything? And that Ambassador de La Borderie kept his eyes closed? The chorus master and all the subscribers were pointing at our managers!"

"What's the matter with our managers?" Gabriel asked with his most simpleminded expression.

"What's the matter with them? You know better than anyone else what they did! You and Mercier were there! and you were the only ones who didn't laugh."

"I don't understand."

With his face impassive, Gabriel raised his arms and let them fall, a gesture obviously meant to convey the idea that he had no interest in the matter. Rémy continued:

"What's this new mania of theirs? Now they won't let anyone come near them."

"What? They won't let anyone come near them?"

"They won't let anyone touch them."

"Really? You noticed that they wouldn't let anyone touch them? That's certainly odd!"

"I'm glad you admit it. It's about time. And they walk backward!"

"Backward? You noticed that our managers were walking backward? I thought only crayfish did that!"

"Don't joke about it, Gabriel!"

"I'm not joking," Gabriel protested, looking serious as a judge.

"You're a close friend of the managers, Gabriel, so maybe you can explain this to me: Outside the lounge, during the intermission after the garden act, when I was walking toward

Richard, holding out my hand to shake his, Moncharmin quickly whispered to me, 'Go away! Go away! Whatever you do, don' touch him!' Do they think I have the plague?''

"Incredible!"

"And a little later, when Ambassador de La Borderie also walked toward Richard, you must have seen Moncharmin step between them, and you must have heard him say loudly, 'Please sir, please don't touch Monsieur Richard!' ''

"Astounding! And what did Richard do?"

"What did he do? You saw him yourself! He turned around bowed even though there was no one in front of him, and walked away backward.''

"Backward?"

"And Moncharmin quickly turned around behind Richard, and he walked away backward too! And they both went to the administration staircase like that, backward—backward! If they're not crazy, can you tell me what all that means?''

"Maybe they were rehearsing a ballet figure," Gabriel suggested without conviction.

Rémy was outraged to hear such a silly joke at such a serious time. He scowled, tightened his lips, and leaned close to Gabriel's ear.

"Don't try to be smart, Gabriel. Things are happening here that you and Mercier are partly responsible for.''

"What things?"

"Christine Daae isn't the only one who's suddenly disappeared tonight.''

"Really?"

"Yes, really! Can you tell me why, when Madame Giry came down to the lounge a little while ago, Mercier took her by the hand and led her away in a great hurry?''

"I didn't notice that," said Gabriel.

"You noticed it so well that you followed Mercier and Madame Giry to Mercier's office. Since then, you and Mercier have been seen, but no one has seen Madame Giry.''

"Do you think we ate her?"

"No, but you locked her in the office, and do you know what people hear when they go past the door of that office? They hear these words: 'Oh, the scoundrels! The scoundrels!' ''

At this point in that singular conversation, Mercier arrived out of breath.

"Now it's worse than ever," he said gloomily. "I shouted to them, 'It's very serious! Open the door! It's me, Mercier!' I heard footsteps. The door opened and I saw Moncharmin. He was very pale. He asked me, 'What do you want?' I said, 'Christine Daae has been abducted.' Do you know what he answered? 'Good for her!' Then he closed the door, after putting this in my hand."

Mercier opened his hand. Rémy and Gabriel looked at what he was holding.

"The safety pin!" cried Rémy.

"Strange! Strange!" murmured Gabriel, who could not help shuddering.

Suddenly a voice made the three of them turn their heads.

"Excuse me, gentlemen, can you tell me where Christine Daae is?"

Despite the gravity of the situation, this question would probably have made them laugh if they had not seen a young man with such a sorrowful face that they immediately felt sorry for him. He was Viscount Raoul de Chagny.

16

"Christine! Christine!"

AFTER CHRISTINE'S FANTASTIC disappearance, Raoul's first thought was to accuse Erik. He no longer had any doubt about the almost supernatural power of the Angel of Music in that realm of the Opera where he had diabolically established his dominion.

And Raoul rushed to the stage, in a frenzy of despair and love.

"Christine! Christine!" he moaned, distraught, calling her as she must have been calling out to him from the dark abyss into which the monster had carried her like a wild animal carrying its prey, while she was still quivering from her divine exaltation, wearing the white shroud in which she had offered herself to the angels of heaven.

"Christine! Christine!" he repeated. And he seemed to hear her cries through the fragile boards that separated her from him. He leaned down and listened. He wandered over the stage like a madman. If only he could go down, down, down, into that pit of darkness whose entrances were all closed to him!

The fragile obstacle that ordinarily slid aside so easily to let him see the abyss toward which all his desire now drew him, the boards that creaked beneath his footsteps and sent their sounds echoing into the prodigious void of the cellars—those boards were more than motionless tonight: they seemed immutable. They had taken on such a look of solidity that they seemed never to have been moved. And now the stairs that led below the stage were forbidden to everyone!

"Christine! Christine!"

160

People pushed him aside, laughing, making fun of him. They thought the poor fiancé's sanity had deserted him.

In a wild dash along dark, mysterious passages known only to him, Erik must have dragged poor, innocent Christine to his abominable den, to the Louis-Philippe bedroom overlooking the hellish underground lake.

"Christine! Christine! You don't answer! Have you died in a moment of overwhelming horror beneath the monster's hot breath?"

Hideous thoughts flashed like lightning through Raoul's congested brain.

Erik had obviously discovered their secret and learned that Christine had betrayed him. And now he was taking revenge! After that blow to his lofty pride, he would stop at nothing. In his powerful hands, Christine was doomed!

Raoul thought again of the golden stars that had appeared on his balcony. If only his pistol had been able to destroy them!

There are, of course, extraordinary human eyes that dilate in darkness and shine like stars or cat's eyes. (And, as everyone knows, some albinos appear to have rabbit's eyes in daylight but have cat's eyes at night.)

Yes, he really had shot at Erik! If only he had killed him! The monster had escaped by means of the drainpipe, like cats or convicts, who—again, as everyone knows—could climb a drainpipe all the way up to the sky. He had probably intended to take decisive action against Raoul, but, having been wounded, he had fled and turned against Christine instead.

Such were poor Raoul's cruel thoughts as he ran to Christine's dressing room.

"Christine! Christine!"

Bitter tears burned his eyelids when he saw, scattered over the furniture, the clothes that his beautiful fiancée had intended to wear when she eloped with him. If only she had been willing to leave sooner! Why had she delayed so long? Why had she toyed with the threatening catastrophe, and with the monster's heart? Why, in a final act of mercy, had she given that demonic soul the spiritual nourishment of her divine song:

Angel, in Heaven bless'd,
My spirit longs with thee to rest!

With his throat full of sobs, oaths, and insults, Raoul clumsily moved his hands over the big mirror that had opened one night to let Christine go down into Erik's shadowy domain. He pushed and groped in vain; evidently the mirror obeyed only Erik. Maybe actions were useless with that kind of mirror, maybe what was needed was to speak certain words. In his childhood he had been told stories about objects that obeyed words. . . .

Suddenly he remembered: a gate opening onto the Rue Scribe, an underground passage leading directly from the lake to the Rue Scribe. Yes, Christine had told him about that! To his dismay, he found that the big key was no longer in the box, but he decided to go to the Rue Scribe anyway.

When he was outside, he felt the gigantic stones with trembling hands, searching for openings. He found iron bars. Were they the ones he wanted? Or was it those others? Or was it that barred window? He looked helplessly between the bars. How dark it was in there! He listened. What silence! He went around the building. Ah, there were huge bars, and a colossal gate! But it was only the gate to the administration courtyard. . . .

He went to the concierge.

"Excuse me, madame, can you tell me how to find a gate, a gate made of bars, iron bars, that faces the Rue Scribe and leads to the lake? You know: the lake, the underground lake, under the Opera."

"I know there's a lake under the Opera, sir, but I don't know which gate leads to it—I've never been there."

"And what about the Rue Scribe, madame? The Rue Scribe! Have you ever been to the Rue Scribe?"

She laughed! She burst out laughing! Raoul hurried away, bellowing with rage. He ran up and down stairs, went through the whole administrative part of the building and found himself back in the bright light of the stage.

He stopped, panting, with his heart pounding violently. Maybe Christine had been found. He approached a group of men.

"Excuse me, gentlemen, have you seen Christine Daaé?" he asked.

And they laughed.

Just then a new hubbub was heard on the stage and Raoul saw

a man who showed every sign of calm despite the excited gesticulations of the crowd of men in black swallow-tailed coats surrounding him. He had a pink, chubby, friendly face framed by curly hair and brightened by two wonderfully serene blue eyes.

Mercier nodded toward the newcomer and said to Raoul, "This is the man to whom you should address your question, sir."

And he introduced him to Police Commissary Mifroid.

"Ah, Viscount de Chagny!" said Mifroid. "I'm delighted to see you, sir. If you'll be so kind as to come with me . . . And now, where are the managers? Where are the managers?"

Since Mercier remained silent, Rémy took it upon himself to tell Mifroid that the managers had locked themselves in their office and still knew nothing about Christine Daaé's disappearance.

"How odd! Let's go to their office."

And Mifroid, followed by a crowd that continued to grow, headed for the office. Mercier took advantage of the disorder to slip a key into Gabriel's hand.

"Things are going badly," he said to him in an undertone. "Go and let Madame Giry get some fresh air."

Gabriel walked away.

They soon came to the door of the managers' office. Mercier fulminated in vain; the door did not open.

"Open in the name of the law!" ordered Mifroid's clear and somewhat anxious voice.

Finally the door opened. They all rushed into the office behind Mifroid.

Raoul was the last to go in. As he was about to follow the group, a hand came down on his shoulder and he heard these words spoken close to his ear: "Erik's secrets concern no one but him."

He turned around and stifled an exclamation. The hand that had come down on his shoulder was now in front of the lips of a swarthy man with jade-green eyes, wearing an astrakhan hat—the Persian!

He prolonged his gesture recommending discretion, and then, just as the astonished Raoul was about to ask him the reason for his mysterious intervention, he bowed, walked away, and disappeared.

17

Astonishing Revelations by Madame Giry, Concerning Her Personal Relations with the Opera Ghost

BEFORE WE FOLLOW Police Commissary Mifroid into the managers' office, which Mercier and Rémy had vainly tried to enter earlier, the reader must allow me to present certain extraordinary events that had just taken place there. Richard and Moncharmin had locked themselves in for a purpose that is still unknown to the reader. It is my historical duty—that is, my duty as a historian—to reveal that purpose without further delay.

I have had occasion to remark on the disagreeable change that had recently taken place in the managers' mood, and I have given the reader to understand that this change was not caused entirely by the fall of the chandelier in the circumstances that we have seen.

Even though the managers would prefer that it remain forever unknown, I will now tell the reader that the Opera ghost had succeeded in collecting his first payment of twenty thousand francs. There had been weeping and gnashing of teeth, but the thing had happened quite simply.

One morning they found an envelope on their desk, addressed to "O. G. (personal)." With it was a note from O. G. himself:

164

The time has come for you to meet an obligation stipulated in the book of instructions. You will put twenty thousand-franc bills in this envelope, seal it with your own seal, and give it to Madame Giry, who will do what is necessary.

The managers did not wait to be told twice. Without wasting time wondering once again how those diabolical notes could get into a room that they had very carefully locked, they decided that this was a good chance to get their hands on the mysterious blackmailer. They told Gabriel and Mercier everything, under a promise of strict secrecy, then placed the twenty thousand francs in the envelope and, without asking for any explanation, gave it to Madame Giry, who had been reinstated in her position. She showed no surprise. It goes without saying that she was closely watched.

She went straight to the ghost's box and put the precious envelope on the railing. Gabriel, Mercier, and the two managers were hidden in such a way that the envelope was never out of their sight during the whole performance that evening, or even afterward, because, seeing that the envelope had not moved, they did not move either. They were still there when the auditorium had emptied and Madame Giry had gone home. Finally they became tired of waiting and opened the envelope, after making sure that the seals had not been broken.

At first sight, Richard and Moncharmin judged that the money was still there, but then they saw that it was not the same: the twenty genuine bills had been replaced with "play money"! The managers were furious—and frightened as well.

"That's better than anything Robert Houdin* could do!" said Gabriel.

"Yes," replied Richard, "and it's more expensive too!"

Moncharmin wanted to send for the police commissary immediately. Richard was opposed to it, no doubt because he had a plan of his own.

"Let's not make ourselves ridiculous," he said. "Everyone in Paris would laugh at us. O. G. has won the first round, but we'll win the second."

He was obviously thinking of the next monthly payment.

Even so, they had been so thoroughly outwitted that for weeks

*An eminent nineteenth-century French stage magician. (Translator's note.)

they could not help feeling a bit dejected. And it was quite understandable. They did not call in the police because in the back of their minds they still had the idea that the strange incident might have been a detestable practical joke, probably played on them by their predecessors, and that nothing should be divulged about it until they had gotten to the bottom of it. Moncharmin's suspicion, however, occasionally shifted away from their predecessors and toward Richard, whose imagination sometimes took a farcical turn.

And so, ready for all contingencies, they awaited further events, having Madame Giry watched and keeping an eye on her themselves. Richard did not want her to be told anything.

"If she's an accomplice," he said, "the money was taken away long ago. But I think she's only an idiot."

"There are several idiots in this business," Moncharmin replied thoughtfully.

"How could we have known?" Richard groaned. "But don't worry: next time, I'll have taken all my precautions."

And that next time came—on the day when Christine disappeared.

In the morning, a gracious note from the ghost reminded them that another payment was due:

Do as you did last time. It went very well. Put the twenty thousand francs in an envelope and give it to that excellent Madame Giry.

The note was accompanied by the customary envelope. It had only to be filled.

The operation was to be carried out that evening, half an hour before the performance. And so we will now look into the managerial lair half an hour before the curtain rose on that too-famous performance of *Faust*.

Richard showed Moncharmin the envelope, then counted the twenty thousand-franc bills in front of him and put them in the envelope, but did not close it.

"And now," he said, "let's have a talk with Madame Giry."

The old woman was sent for. She made a graceful curtsy when she came in, still wearing her black taffeta dress, whose color was turning to rust and lilac, and her soot-colored plumed hat. She seemed in a good mood.

"Good evening, gentlemen," she said. "I suppose you wanted me to come here for the envelope?"

"That's right, Madame Giry, for the envelope," Richard said amiably. "And for something else too."

"I'm at your service, sir, at your service! And what is that something else?"

"First of all, Madame Giry, I'd like to ask you a little question."

"Ask it, sir, I'm here to answer you."

"Are you still on good terms with the ghost?"

"Very good terms, sir. Couldn't be better."

"We're delighted to hear that. Now, just between ourselves," Richard said in the tone of someone about to reveal an important secret, "there's no reason why we can't tell you. . . . After all, you're not stupid."

"Of course not, sir!" she exclaimed, stopping the gentle swaying of the two black feathers on her soot-colored hat. "No one has ever doubted it, believe me!"

"I do believe you, and I'm sure we're going to understand each other very well. That story about the ghost is only a joke, isn't it? And, still just between ourselves, it's gone on long enough."

Madame Giry looked at the directors as if they had spoken Chinese to her. She stepped closer to Richard's desk and said rather uneasily, "What do you mean? I don't understand."

"You understand perfectly. In any case, you *must* understand. First, you're going to tell us what his name is."

"Whose name?"

"The man whose accomplice you are, Madame Giry!"

"I'm the ghost's accomplice? You think I'm . . . His accomplice in what?"

"You do whatever he wants."

"Oh, he's not very bothersome, you know."

"And he always gives you a tip!"

"I have no complaint about that."

"How much does he give you to bring that envelope to him?"

"Ten francs."

"That's all? It's not much!"

"Why do you say that?"

"I'll tell you in a little while. Right now, we'd like to know for what extraordinary reason you've given yourself body and soul to that ghost rather than another. Five or ten francs won't buy Madame Giry's friendship and devotion.''

''That's true! And I can tell you the reason, sir. There's certainly nothing dishonorable about it, nothing at all.''

''We have no doubt of it, Madame Giry.''

''All right, then. . . . The ghost doesn't like me to talk about him.''

''Oh?'' Richard said with a sarcastic laugh.

''But this concerns only me,'' the old woman went on. ''One night in Box Five I found a letter for me, or rather a note, written in red ink. I don't have to read that note to you, sir, because I know it by heart and I'll never forget it, even if I live to be a hundred!''

And, sitting erect, she began reciting the note with touching eloquence: '' 'Madame, In 1825, Mademoiselle Ménétrier, a ballerina, became Marquise de Cussy. In 1832, Marie Taglioni, a dancer, married Count Gilbert des Voisins. In 1846, La Sora, a dancer, married the brother of the King of Spain. In 1847, Lola Montez, a dancer, morganatically married King Louis of Bavaria and became Countess Lansfeld. In 1848, Mademoiselle Maria, a dancer, became Baroness d'Hermeville. In 1870, Therese Hessler, a dancer, married Don Fernando, brother of the King of Portugal. . . .' ''

Richard and Moncharmin listened to her recite that curious list of glorious marriages. She had stood up, and the longer she talked, the bolder and more animated she became. Finally, inspired like a sibyl on her tripod, she spoke the last sentence of the prophetic note in a voice bursting with pride: '' *'In 1885, Meg Giry: empress!'* ''

Exhausted by that supreme effort, she let herself fall back onto her chair and said, ''Gentlemen, it was signed 'The Opera Ghost.' I'd heard of the ghost, but I'd only half believed in him. From then on, after he told me that my little Meg, the flesh of my flesh, the fruit of my womb, was going to be an empress, I believed in him completely.''

And there was no need to make a long study of Madame Giry's excited face to realize what it had been possible to obtain from that fine mind with the two words ''ghost'' and ''empress.'' But who was pulling the strings of that absurd puppet? Who?

"You've never seen him, he talks to you, and you believe everything he says?" asked Moncharmin.

"Yes. First of all, I have him to thank for the fact that my little Meg became a ballerina. I said to him, 'If she's going to be an empress in 1885, you don't have any time to lose: she has to become a ballerina right away.' He answered, 'I'll take care of it.' He just said a few words to Monsieur Poligny and it was done."

"So Monsieur Poligny saw him!"

"No, he didn't see him any more than I did, but he heard him! The ghost said something in his ear—you know, the night he came out of Box Five looking so pale."

"What an incredible business this is!" Moncharmin said with a sigh.

"I always thought there were secrets between the ghost and Monsieur Poligny," said Madame Giry. "Monsieur Poligny did everything the ghost asked of him. He couldn't refuse the ghost anything."

"You hear, Richard? Poligny couldn't refuse the ghost anything."

"Yes, yes, I heard!" Richard declared. "Poligny is a friend of the ghost, and Madame Giry is a friend of Poligny, and there we are!" he added harshly. "But I don't care about Poligny. I don't mind saying that the only person whose fate really interests me is Madame Giry. Madame Giry, do you know what's in this envelope?"

"No, of course not," she replied.

"Well, then, look!"

She looked into the envelope with uneasy eyes that quickly brightened.

"Thousand-franc bills!" she exclaimed.

"Yes, Madame Giry, thousand-franc bills. And you knew it very well!"

"Oh, no, sir! I swear . . ."

"Don't swear, Madame Giry. And now I'll tell you the other reason I sent for you: I'm going to have you arrested."

The two black feathers on the soot-colored hat, which ordinarily had the shape of two question marks, instantly turned into exclamation points; as for the hat itself, it swayed threateningly above Madame Giry's agitated coil of hair. Her surprise, indig-

nation, protest, alarm, and offended virtue were expressed in a
turning, leaping, sliding movement that brought her nose to nose
with Richard, who could not help pushing back his chair.

"Have me arrested?"

The mouth that said this seemed about to spit its three remaining teeth into Richard's face.

He was heroic. He moved back no farther. His menacing
forefinger was already pointing out the usher of Box Five to the
absent magistrates.

"I'm going to have you arrested, Madame Giry, as a thief!"

"Say that again!"

She dealt Richard a mighty avenging blow before Moncharmin
could intervene. But it was not the irascible old woman's bony
hand that struck the managerial cheek: it was the envelope itself,
the magic envelope, the cause of all the trouble. The impact
made it burst open. The banknotes flew through the air, swirling
and fluttering like giant butterflies.

The two managers uttered a cry, then the same thought made
them both fall to their knees and begin feverishly picking up and
hastily examining the precious pieces of paper.

"Are they still genuine, Moncharmin?"

"Are they still genuine, Richard?"

"They're still genuine!"

Above them, Madame Giry's three teeth were clashing in a
noisy melee filled with hideous interjections, but only this leit-
motif could be clearly distinguished:

"A thief? *I'm* a thief?"

Suddenly she cried out in a choked voice, "It's more than I
can stand!" and again confronted Richard nose to nose. "Anyway, Monsieur Richard," she said, "you should know better
than I do where the twenty thousand francs went!"

"*I* ought to?" he asked, taken aback. "How would I know?"

Looking stern and concerned, Moncharmin asked the old woman
to explain herself.

"What do you mean? Why do you claim Monsieur Richard
should know better than you where the twenty thousand francs
went?"

Richard felt his face turning red beneath Moncharmin's gaze.
He took hold of Madame Giry's hand and shook it violently. His
voice imitated thunder. It growled, it rumbled, it boomed.

"Why should I know better than you do where the twenty thousand francs went? Why?"

"Because it went into your pocket!" she said breathily, now looking at him as if he were the devil.

It was Richard's turn to be thunderstruck, first by that unexpected reply, and then by Moncharmin's increasingly suspicious look. He lost the strength he would have needed at that difficult moment to reject such a contemptible accusation.

And so it is that when perfectly innocent people are attacked by surprise with their conscience at peace, they suddenly seem guilty because the blow they have received makes them turn pale, or blush, or stagger, or draw themselves erect, or slump forward, or protest, or say nothing when they ought to speak, or speak when they ought to say nothing, or remain dry when they ought to sweat, or sweat when they ought to remain dry.

Having chilled the fury with which Richard, who was quite innocent, had been about to assail Madame Giry, Moncharmin hastened to question her, gently and encouragingly.

"How could you suspect my colleague Monsieur Richard of putting the twenty thousand francs in his pocket?"

"I never said that," she declared, "since *I* was the one who put the twenty thousand francs in his pocket." And she added in an undertone, "There, I've told you. I hope the ghost will forgive me."

Richard began shouting again, but Moncharmin firmly ordered him to stop.

"Quiet! Quiet! Let her explain herself. Let me question her. I don't understand why you behave like that when we're about to clear up this whole thing. You're furious, but you shouldn't be. I'm enjoying myself."

Madame Giry took on a martyred expression, her face radiant with faith in her own innocence.

"You say there was twenty thousand francs in the envelope I put in Monsieur Richard's pocket, but I'm telling you again that I didn't know. And neither did Monsieur Richard."

"Aha!" said Richard, suddenly taking on a swaggering air that displeased Moncharmin. "So I didn't know either! You put twenty thousand francs in my pocket and I didn't know anything about it! I'm very glad to hear that, Madame Giry."

"Yes, it's true," the implacable old woman agreed, "neither of us knew. But you must have finally found out."

Richard would surely have demolished her if Moncharmin had not been there. But Moncharmin protected her. He went back to his interrogation.

"What kind of envelope did you put in Monsieur Richard's pocket? It wasn't the one we gave you, the one we watched you take to Box Five, and yet only that one contained the twenty thousand francs."

"Excuse me, but it *was* the one you gave me that I put in Monsieur Richard's pocket. The one I put in the ghost's box was another envelope exactly like the first one. I had it up my sleeve, all ready, and it was given to me by the ghost."

Saying this, Madame Giry took from her sleeve an envelope exactly like the one containing the twenty thousand francs, addressed in the same way. The managers snatched it from her, examined it, and saw that it was closed with wax stamped by their own managerial seals. They opened it. It contained twenty bills of "play money" like the ones that had so astounded them a month earlier.

"It's so simple!" said Richard.

"It's so simple!" repeated Moncharmin, more solemn than ever.

"The best tricks are always the simplest. All it takes is an accomplice."

"Like the one we have before us," Moncharmin said in a toneless voice. And he continued, with his eyes fixed on Madame Giry as if he were trying to hypnotize her: "It was the ghost who gave you this envelope, told you to substitute it for the one we gave you and put that one in Monsieur Richard's pocket?"

"Yes, it was the ghost."

"Then will you give us a demonstration of your skill? Here's the envelope. Act as though we knew nothing."

"I'll be glad to, gentlemen."

She took the envelope containing the twenty bills and headed for the door. Just as she was about to leave, the two managers made a rush for her.

"Oh, no! No! You're not going to pull the same trick on us again! We've had enough! No more!"

"Excuse me, gentlemen," she said apologetically, "but you told me to act as if you knew nothing, and if you didn't know anything I'd walk away with your envelope."

"But how did you slip it into my pocket?" asked Richard.

Moncharmin kept his left eye on him while his right one was busy watching Madame Giry; it was a difficult visual feat, but he was willing to do anything to discover the truth.

"I was supposed to slip it into your pocket when you least expected it," said Madame Giry. "As you know, during the evening I always come backstage, and I often go to the dancers' lounge with my daughter, which I have a right to do, since I'm her mother. I bring her ballet shoes to her when it's time for the divertissement. In other words, I come and go as I please. The subscribers come backstage too. So do you, Monsieur Richard. There are plenty of people around. I went behind you and slipped the envelope into your coattail pocket. There was nothing magic about it!"

"No, there was nothing magic about it," growled Richard, glaring at her with the sternness of Thundering Jove, "but I've caught you in a lie, you old witch!"

This epithet stung Madame Giry less than the accusation of dishonesty. She bristled and drew herself erect, with her three teeth bared.

"Why do you claim I lied?"

"Because I spent that evening in the auditorium, watching Box Five and the false envelope you'd put there. I didn't go to the dancers' lounge for one second!"

"And that wasn't the evening when I put the envelope in your pocket! It was during the next evening, the one when the Undersecretary of the Fine Arts Administration . . ."

At these words, Richard abruptly stopped her.

"It's true," he said thoughtfully, "I remember. . . . I remember now! The undersecretary came backstage and asked for me. I went to the dancers' lounge for a little while. I was on the steps of the lounge, the undersecretary and his private secretary were in the lounge itself. All at once I turned around. You were walking past me, Madame Giry, and it seemed to me that you'd brushed against me. There was no one else behind me. Yes, I remember. I can still see you!"

"That's right, sir, I'd just finished my little business with your pocket. That pocket is very handy."

She showed how she had done her "little business." She stepped behind Richard and placed the envelope in one of his coattail pockets so quickly and deftly that Moncharmin, who was watching her closely, was impressed by her dexterity.

"Of course!" exclaimed Richard, a little pale. "It's very clever of O. G. The problem for him was to eliminate any dangerous intermediary between the person who gave the twenty thousand francs and the person who took it. He found the best solution: to take the money from my pocket, confident that I wouldn't notice it because I didn't know it was there! It's admirable."

"It may be admirable," said Moncharmin, "but you're forgetting that I gave ten thousand of those twenty thousand francs, and no one put anything in *my* pocket!"

18

Continuation of "The Singular Behavior of a Safety Pin"

WHAT MONCHARMIN HAD just said so clearly expressed the suspicion he now had of his colleague that it touched off a stormy argument, at the end of which it was agreed that Richard would do whatever Moncharmin asked of him, to help him discover the scoundrel who was fleecing them.

This brings us to the "intermission after the garden act" during which Rémy, who never let anything slip past him, curiously observed the managers' strange conduct, and it will now be quite easy for us to find a reason for those exceptionally odd actions, so inconsistent with accepted ideas of managerial dignity.

The conduct of Richard and Moncharmin was determined by what had just been revealed to them. First, that evening Richard would exactly repeat the movements he had made when the first twenty thousand francs disappeared; second, Moncharmin would not for one second lose sight of Richard's coattail pocket, into which Madame Giry would have slipped the second twenty thousand francs.

With Moncharmin several paces behind him, Richard stood in exactly the same place where he had been when he had greeted the Undersecretary of the Fine Arts Administration. Madame Giry passed by, brushed against Richard, put the twenty thousand francs in his coattail pocket, and disappeared.

Or, rather, she was made to disappear. Carrying out the order that Moncharmin had given him a few moments before the reenactment of the scene, Mercier locked Madame Giry in the administration office. That way she would be unable to communicate with her ghost. And she put up no resistance, because she was now only a poor, shabby, frightened figure with the eyes of a bewildered chicken open wide beneath a disorderly crest, already hearing in the resonant hall the footsteps of the police commissary with whom she had been threatened, and heaving sighs pitiful enough to rend the pillars of the great staircase.

Meanwhile Richard bowed and walked backward as if he had that high and powerful official, the Undersecretary of the Fine Arts Administration, in front of him. This show of politeness would not have been surprising if the undersecretary had actually been in front of him, but, since there was no one in front of him, the spectators of that natural but seemingly inexplicable scene were understandably dumbfounded. Richard was bowing to empty space, bending at the waist before no one, and walking backward in front of nothing.

A short distance away, Moncharmin was also bowing and walking backward. As he did so, he told Rémy to go away and asked Ambassador de La Borderie and the manager of the Crédit Central not to touch Richard. Moncharmin had his own idea and did not want Richard to come to him later, when the twenty thousand francs had disappeared, and say, "Maybe it was the ambassador, or the manager of the Crédit Central, or maybe even Rémy." Especially since, by Richard's own account, during the original scene he had met no one in that part of the Opera after Madame Giry brushed against him. Why, then, I ask you, should he meet someone this time, since he was supposed to be doing exactly as he had done before?

Having first walked backward to bow, Richard continued walking that way out of caution, until he came to the administration hallway. Thus he was always watched from behind by Moncharmin, and he himself could see anyone approaching him from in front.

Once again this new way of walking backstage that had been adopted by the managers of the National Academy of Music did not pass unnoticed. It attracted attention. Nearly all the student dancers were in the attic during the curious scene—luckily for Richard and Moncharmin, because they would have caused a sensation among the girls. But they were thinking only of their twenty thousand francs.

When they came to the half-dark administration hallway, Richard said quietly to Moncharmin, "I'm sure no one touched me. Now I want you to stay rather far away from me and watch me in the shadows till I get to the door of the office. We mustn't make anyone suspicious, and we'll see what happens."

But Moncharmin replied, "No: walk in front of me and I'll stay close behind you."

"But in that case it won't be possible to steal our twenty thousand francs!"

"That's precisely what I'm hoping."

"Then what we're doing is absurd!"

"We're doing exactly what we did the last time: I joined you at the corner of this hall, just after you'd left the stage, and I followed *close behind you.*"

"That's true," Richard admitted with a sigh, shaking his head.

He did as Moncharmin wanted.

Two minutes later they went into their office and closed the door behind them. It was Moncharmin himself who put the key in his pocket.

"We both stayed in the office like this the last time," he said, "until you left to go home."

"Yes, so we did. And no one came to disturb us?"

"No one."

"Then," said Richard, trying to collect his memories, "I must have been robbed on my way home."

"No, that's impossible," Moncharmin said sharply. "I took you home in my carriage. The twenty thousand francs disappeared *from your home.* I don't have the slightest doubt of it."

This was the view that Moncharmin had now adopted.

"It's unbelievable!" Richard protested. "I'm sure of my servants—and if one of them had done it, he would have disappeared by now."

Moncharmin shrugged, seeming to say that he would not go into such details, whereupon Richard began to feel that Moncharmin was taking an intolerable attitude toward him.

"Moncharmin, I've had enough of this!"

"Richard, I've had too much of it!"

"You dare to suspect me?"

"Yes. I suspect you of a deplorable practical joke."

"One doesn't joke with twenty thousand francs!"

"I thoroughly agree!" said Moncharmin.

He unfolded a newspaper and made a pointed display of reading it.

"What are you doing?" asked Richard. "Are you really going to read the paper now?"

"Yes, until it's time for me to take you home."

"Like last time?"

"Like last time."

Richard snatched the newspaper from Moncharmin's hands. Moncharmin angrily stood up.

He found himself facing an exasperated Richard who folded his arms over his chest—an insolent gesture of defiance since the world began—and said to him, "Here's what I'm thinking of: I'm thinking of what I might think if, like last time, we spent the evening alone together and you took me home, and if, as we were about to leave each other, I found that the twenty thousand francs had disappeared from my coat pocket . . . like last time."

"And what might you think?" asked Moncharmin, his face turning crimson.

"I might think that since you'd been with me every second, and since, by your own wish, you'd been the only one to come near me, like last time—I might think that if the twenty thousand francs was no longer in my pocket, it had a good chance of being in yours!"

Moncharmin was infuriated by this suggestion.

"Oh, for a safety pin!" he cried.

"What do you want to do with a safety pin?"

"Attach you! A safety pin! A safety pin!"

"You want to attach me with a safety pin?"

"Yes, attach you to the twenty thousand francs! Then, whether it's here, or on your way home, or at home, you'll feel the hand that tries to take the money from your pocket—and you'll see whether it's *my* hand! Oh, *you* suspect *me* now! A safety pin!"

And that was when Moncharmin opened the door of the office and shouted into the hall, "A safety pin! Who can give me a safety pin?" And we know how at that same time he received Rémy, who had no safety pin, and how an office boy gave him the safety pin he wanted so much.

Here is what happened next:

After closing the door, Moncharmin knelt behind Richard.

"I hope the twenty thousand francs is still there," he said.

"So do I," said Richard.

"Are they the genuine bills?" asked Moncharmin, determined not to let himself be taken in this time.

"Look for yourself. I don't want to touch them."

Moncharmin took the envelope from Richard's pocket and drew out the money, trembling. This time, so that he could often verify the presence of the bills, he had not sealed the envelope or even glued it shut. He reassured himself by seeing that they were all there, and genuine, put them in Richard's coattail pocket, and carefully pinned them to it. Then he sat down behind the coattail and kept his eyes on it while Richard sat motionlessly at his desk.

"Be patient, Richard, we have only a few more minutes to wait. The clock will soon strike midnight, and it was on the stroke of midnight that we left last time."

"I'll have all the patience I need!"

Time went by, slow, heavy, mysterious, and oppressive. Richard tried to laugh.

"I may end up believing that the ghost is all-powerful," he said. "Right now, especially, don't you feel that there's something disturbing, upsetting, and frightening about the atmosphere in this room?"

"Yes, I do," confessed Moncharmin, who really was beginning to feel deeply affected.

"The ghost!" Richard said in a low voice, as if he were afraid of being heard by invisible ears. "Suppose it actually was a ghost who knocked three times on this table, as we clearly heard, and who put magic envelopes on it, and talked in Box Five, and killed Joseph Buquet, and made the chandelier fall—and robbed us! Because after all, there's no one here but you and me, and if the money disappears and neither of us has anything to do with it, we'll have to believe in the ghost. . . ."

Just then the clock on the mantelpiece whirred briefly and the first stroke of midnight sounded.

The two managers shuddered. Anxiety gripped them and they vainly struggled against it without knowing its cause. Sweat trickled down their foreheads. And the twelfth stroke resounded strangely in their ears.

When the clock had fallen silent, they sighed and stood up.

"I think we can go now," said Moncharmin.

"So do I," Richard agreed.

"Before we leave, will you let me look in your pocket?"

"Of course! You *must* do it!" said Richard. "Well?" he asked while Moncharmin was making his inspection.

"I can still feel the safety pin."

"Naturally. As you pointed out, I'll be sure to notice it if anyone tries to rob us."

But Moncharmin, whose hands were still busy around the pocket, shouted, *"I can feel the safety pin but not the money!"*

"Don't joke about it, Moncharmin. This isn't the time for it."

"Feel for yourself!"

Richard quickly took off his coat. He and Moncharmin both made a grab for the pocket. It was empty. And the strangest part of it was that the safety pin was still fastened in the same place.

The two men turned pale. They were dealing with something supernatural, there could no longer be any doubt of it.

"The ghost," Moncharmin murmured.

But Richard suddenly rushed at him.

"You're the only one who touched my pocket! Give me back my twenty thousand francs! Give it back to me!"

"I swear on my soul that I don't have it," Moncharmin said weakly, evidently on the verge of fainting.

There was a knock on the door. He went to open it, walking almost like an automaton, and exchanged a few words with Mercier, seemingly without recognizing him or understanding what he said. Then, in an unconscious movement, he handed the totally bewildered Mercier a safety pin that was no longer of any use to him.

19

The Policeman, the Viscount, and the Persian

WHEN POLICE COMMISSARY Mifroid came into the managers' office, he immediately asked about the singer.

"Christine Daae isn't here?"

He was surrounded by a crowd, as I have said earlier.

"Christine Daae? No," replied Richard. "Why?"

As for Moncharmin, he no longer had the strength to say anything. He was in a much worse frame of mind than Richard, because Richard could still suspect Moncharmin, but Moncharmin found himself facing the great mystery, the one that had made the human race shiver since its beginning: the Unknown.

"Why do you ask if Christine Daae is here?" Richard continued in the impressive silence maintained by the surrounding crowd.

"Because she must be found," Mifroid answered solemnly.

"What do you mean, she must be found? Has she disappeared?"

"Yes. In the middle of a performance."

"In the middle of a performance? That's incredible!"

"It is, isn't it? And what's equally incredible is that you've first heard about it from me."

"Yes," Richard agreed. He took his head between his hands and murmured, "One more problem! It's enough to make me resign!" He pulled several whiskers from his mustache without realizing it. "So she disappeared in the middle of a performance," he said as though in a dream.

"Yes, she was abducted during the prison act, just when she was calling on heaven for help, but I doubt that she was abducted by angels."

"And I'm sure she was!"

A young man, pale and trembling with emotion, repeated, "I'm sure she was!"

"What do you mean?" asked Mifroid.

"Christine Daae was abducted by an angel, and I can tell you his name."

"Ah, Viscount de Chagny, you claim that Christine Daae was abducted by an angel, no doubt an angel of the Opera?"

Raoul looked around him, obviously hoping to see someone. At that moment when it seemed to him so necessary to call on the police for help in finding his fiancée, he would have been glad if he could again see the mysterious stranger who only a short time earlier had urged him to be discreet.

"Yes, by an angel of the Opera," he replied to Mifroid, "and I'll tell you where he lives, when we're alone."

"You're right to wait," said Mifroid.

He asked Raoul to sit down beside him, then made everyone else leave the room, except, of course, for the two managers, though they seemed so far removed from everything that they probably would not have protested if they too had been asked to leave.

Raoul had made up his mind.

"The angel's name is Erik," he said, "he lives in the Opera, and he's the Angel of Music."

"The Angel of Music! You don't say! How odd. . . . The Angel of Music!" Mifroid turned to the managers. "Gentlemen, do you have such an angel here?"

Richard and Moncharmin shook their heads without even smiling.

"These gentlemen have certainly heard of the Opera ghost," said Raoul, "and I can assure them that the Opera ghost and the Angel of Music are the same. And his real name is Erik."

Mifroid had stood up and was looking at Raoul intently.

"Excuse me, sir, but are you trying to make fun of the law?"

"Not at all!" Raoul protested, and he thought sorrowfully, "Here's one more person who won't listen to me."

"Then what *are* you trying to do with your talk about an Opera ghost?"

"These gentlemen have heard of him, as I've told you."

"Gentlemen, is it true that you know the Opera ghost?"

Richard stood up, with the last whiskers from his mustache in his hand.

"No, we don't know him, but we'd very much like to, because only this evening he stole twenty thousand francs from us!"

And Richard turned to Moncharmin with a stern look that seemed to say, "Give me back the twenty thousand francs or I'll tell everything."

Moncharmin understood him so well that he made a desperate gesture and said, "Go ahead, tell everything!"

Mifroid looked at the managers and Raoul, one by one, and wondered if he had somehow strayed into a lunatic asylum.

"A ghost," he said, passing his hand through his hair, "who abducts a singer and steals twenty thousand francs, all in one evening, is a very busy ghost! If you don't mind, we'll take the questions one at a time. First the singer, then the twenty thousand francs. Come, Monsieur de Chagny, let's try to talk seriously. You believe that Christine Daaé was abducted by someone named Erik. Do you know him? Have you seen him?"

"Yes."

"Where?"

"In a graveyard."

Mifroid started, gave Raoul another intent look, and said, "Of course: that's usually where one meets ghosts. And what were you doing in that graveyard?"

"I realize how strange my answers are," said Raoul, "and the effect they must be having on you. But please believe me when I tell you that I'm sane. The safety of the person dearest to me in the world, along with my beloved brother Philippe, is at stake. I wish I could convince you with a few words, because time is pressing and each minute is precious; unfortunately, though, if I don't tell you my whole strange story, from the beginning, you won't believe me. I'll tell you everything I know about the Opera ghost, but I'm afraid it's not much."

"Tell it anyway!" Richard and Moncharmin both exclaimed at once, suddenly greatly interested.

Unfortunately for their hope of learning some detail that might put them on the trail of their swindler, they soon had to accept the sad and obvious fact that Viscount Raoul de Chagny had completely lost his reason. That whole story—Perros-Guirec, the skulls, the enchanted violin—could only have been spawned in the unhinged mind of a lover.

It was clear that Police Commissary Mifroid increasingly shared this view. He would surely have put an end to Raoul's chaotic narrative, of which I have given some idea at the beginning of this account, if circumstances had not taken it upon themselves to interrupt it.

The door opened and a man came in, singularly dressed in a vast black frock coat and a shiny, worn-out top hat that came down to his ears. He hurried to Mifroid and talked to him in an undertone. He was no doubt some detective who had come to report on an urgent assignment.

During this conversation, Mifroid kept his eyes on Raoul. Finally he said to him, "We've talked enough about the ghost. Let's talk a little about you, if you don't mind. You planned to elope with Christine Daaé tonight, didn't you?"

"Yes."

"When she left the Opera after the performance?"

"Yes."

"You'd made all your arrangements?"

"Yes."

"The carriage that brought you was to take you both away. The coachman knew about your plan. His route had been decided in advance—and, even better, he would find fresh horses waiting at every stage."

"That's true."

"Yet your carriage is still there, beside the rotunda, awaiting your orders, isn't it?"

"Yes."

"Did you know there were three other carriages there?"

"I didn't pay any attention."

"They belonged to La Sorelli, who hadn't found a place in the administration courtyard; to Carlotta; and to your brother, Count de Chagny."

"It's possible."

"And it's certain that while your carriage, La Sorelli's, and Carlotta's are still lined up along the sidewalk next to the rotunda, Count de Chagny's is no longer there."

"That has nothing to do with . . ."

"Excuse me: wasn't the count opposed to your marrying Mademoiselle Daae?"

"That concerns only my family."

"You've answered my question: he was opposed to it. And that's why you were going to elope with Christine Daae, or take her beyond the range of anything your brother might try to do. Well, Monsieur de Chagny, allow me to tell you that your brother was quicker than you: *he's* the one who took Christine Daae away!"

"Oh!" Raoul moaned, putting his hand over his heart. "It can't be. . . . Are you sure?"

"Immediately after Mademoiselle Daae's disappearance, which was arranged with the complicity of people whose identities we still have to establish, he jumped into his carriage and dashed wildly across Paris."

"Across Paris?" asked poor Raoul. "What do you mean by that?"

"He not only crossed the city, he left it."

"He left Paris. . . . By what road?"

"The road to Brussels."

A hoarse cry escaped from Raoul.

"Oh! I swear I'll catch them!"

And he ran out of the office.

"And bring her back to us!" Mifroid gaily called after him. "That tip is worth at least as much as the one about the Angel of Music, isn't it?"

He then turned to his astonished audience and gave them this honest but not at all naive little lecture on police work:

"I have no idea if it really was Count de Chagny who abducted Christine Daae. But I need to know, and at this moment I don't believe anyone is more eager to inform me than his brother, the viscount. He's now running, flying! He's my main assistant! Such is the art of the police, gentlemen. It's thought to be complicated, but its simplicity becomes apparent as soon as you realize that it consists in having police work done by people who don't belong to the police."

But Mifroid might not have been so satisfied with himself if he had known that his swift messenger had been stopped as soon as he entered the first corridor, even though it was no longer filled with the crowd of curious onlookers, who had been dispersed. It now seemed deserted, but a tall man suddenly stepped in front of Raoul, blocking his way.

"Where are you going so fast, Monsieur de Chagny?" the man asked.

Raoul impatiently looked up and recognized the astrakhan hat he had seen a short time earlier. He stopped.

"You again!" he cried feverishly. "You're the man who knows Erik's secrets and doesn't want me to talk about them. Who are you?"

"You know very well. I'm the Persian."

20

The Viscount and the Persian

RAOUL REMEMBERED THAT once, during a performance at the Opera, his brother had pointed out that mysterious man about whom nothing was known except that he was a Persian and lived in a little old apartment on the Rue de Rivoli.

The swarthy man with jade-green eyes, wearing an astrakhan hat, leaned toward Raoul.

"I hope, Monsieur de Chagny, that you haven't betrayed Erik's secret."

"And why should I have hesitated to betray that monster?" Raoul retorted haughtily, unsuccessfully trying to push his way past that irritating obstacle. "Is he your friend?"

"I hope you haven't said anything about Erik, because his secret is Christine Daae's. To speak of one is to speak of the other."

"You seem to know about many things that concern me," said Raoul, becoming more and more impatient, "but I don't have time to listen to you."

"Once again, Monsieur de Chagny, where are you going so fast?"

"Can't you guess? I'm going to help Christine Daae."

"Then stay here, because she's here!"

"With Erik?"

"With Erik."

"How do you know?"

"I was at the performance," said the Persian, "and no one but Erik could have planned and carried out an abduction like that!'' He sighed deeply. ''I recognized the monster's touch.''

''Then you know him?''

The Persian sighed again, without answering.

''I don't know what your intentions are,'' Raoul went on, ''but can you do anything for me? I mean, for Christine?''

''I think so, Monsieur de Chagny. That's why I stopped you.''

''What can you do?''

''Try to take you to her—and to him.''

''I've already tried to find her tonight, and failed. If you can take me to her, my life will belong to you! One more thing: The police commissary just told me that Christine was abducted by my brother, Count Philippe.''

''I don't believe that, Monsieur de Chagny.''

''It's not possible, is it?''

''I don't know if it's possible, but there are different ways of abducting and, as far as I know, your brother had no experience in spectacular stage effects.''

''Your arguments are convincing, sir. I've been a fool! Let's go! I trust you completely! Why shouldn't I believe you when no one but you believes me, when you're the only one who doesn't smile when I say Erik's name?''

Raoul spontaneously took the Persian's hands in his. His were hot with fever; the Persian's were ice-cold.

''Quiet!'' said the Persian, stopping to listen to the distant sounds of the theater and the faint crackings that came from the walls and the nearby halls. ''Let's not say that name here. Let's just say 'he'; we'll have less chance of attracting his attention.''

''You think he's near us now?''

''Anything is possible. Assuming he's not with his victim in the house by the lake . . .''

''Ah, so you know that house too?''

''If he's not there, he may be in this wall, in this floor, in this ceiling! There's no telling where he may be. His eyes may be in that lock, his ears in that beam!''

The Persian asked Raoul to soften the sound of his footsteps and led him along halls that he had never seen before, even in the days when Christine had guided him through that labyrinth.

''I only hope Darius has come!'' said the Persian.

''Who's Darius?'' Raoul asked as he ran.

''My servant.''

They were now in the middle of a vast empty room, almost as big as a public square, dimly lighted by a small lamp. The Persian stopped Raoul and asked him, so softly that he could hardly hear, "What did you tell the police commissary?"

"I told him that Christine's abductor was the Angel of Music, known as the Opera ghost, and that his real name was . . ."

"Sh! And did he believe you?"

"No."

"He didn't attach any importance to what you said?"

"None."

"He thought you were a lunatic?"

"Yes."

"Good," the Persian said with a sigh.

And they continued on their way.

After going up and down several staircases unknown to Raoul, they found themselves facing a door. The Persian unlocked it with a little skeleton key that he took from his vest pocket.

Raoul and the Persian both wore swallow-tailed coats, of course. But while Raoul wore a top hat, the Persian wore an astrakhan hat, as I have already mentioned. This was a violation of the backstage code of elegance, which requires a top hat, but it is well-known that France allows everything to foreigners: the traveling cap to Englishmen, the astrakhan hat to Persians.

"Your top hat," said the Persian, "would bother you in the expedition we're about to undertake, so I suggest that you leave it in the dressing room."

"Which dressing room?" asked Raoul.

"Christine Daae's, of course!"

Having invited Raoul to go through the door he had just opened, the Persian pointed to Christine's dressing room in front of them.

Raoul had not known that he could come there by a route different from the one he had always taken. He was now at the end of the hall whose whole length he usually covered before knocking on the door of the dressing room.

"You know the Opera very well!"

"Not as well as *he* does," the Persian said modestly.

And he pushed Raoul into Christine's dressing room. It was still as it had been when Raoul left it a short time earlier.

After closing the door, the Persian went to the thin partition that separated the dressing room from the large storeroom next to it. He listened, then coughed loudly. Sounds of movement immediately came from the storeroom, and a few seconds later there was a knock on the door of the dressing room.

"Come in," said the Persian.

A man entered, wearing a long cloak and, like the Persian, an astrakhan hat. He bowed, took a richly carved box from under his coat, put it down on the dressing table, bowed again, and stepped toward the door.

"No one saw you come in, Darius?"

"No, master."

"Don't let anyone see you go out."

The servant ventured a glance into the hall and quickly disappeared.

"It occurs to me," said Raoul, "that someone may very well come in and find us here. That, of course, would be a hindrance to us. The police commissary will soon come to search this room."

"It doesn't matter. He's not the one we have to fear."

The Persian opened the box. In it was a pair of long pistols, superbly designed and decorated.

"Immediately after Christine Daae's abduction," he said, "I sent word to my servant to bring me these pistols. I've had them a long time and I know they're completely reliable."

"Do you intend to fight a duel?" asked Raoul, surprised by the arrival of that arsenal.

"Fighting a duel is just what we're about to do," replied the Persian, examining the percussion caps of his pistols. "And what a duel!" He handed one of the weapons to Raoul. "In that duel we'll be two against one, but be ready for anything: I won't hide the fact that we'll be dealing with the most terrible adversary imaginable. But you love Christine Daae, don't you?"

"Yes, with all my heart! But you don't love her, so I don't understand why you're willing to risk your life for her. You must hate Erik."

"No, I don't hate him," the Persian said sadly. "If I did, he'd have stopped doing harm long ago."

"Has he harmed you?"

"I've forgiven him for the harm he's done to me."

"It's puzzling to hear you talk about that man! You call him a monster, you talk about his crimes, you say he's harmed you—

yet I find in you the same incredible pity that drove me to despair when I found it in Christine!''

The Persian made no reply. He went to get a stool and put it next to the wall opposite the big mirror that took up the whole facing wall. Then he stood on the stool and, with his nose against the wallpaper, seemed to be looking for something.

''I'm waiting for you!'' said Raoul, seething with impatience. ''Let's go!''

''Go where?'' the Persian asked without turning his head.

''To the monster! Let's go down after him. Didn't you say you had a way of doing that?''

''I'm looking for it.''

And the Persian's nose went on moving across the wall.

''Ah!'' he exclaimed. ''Here it is!'' With his hand above his head, he pushed on one corner of the pattern in the wallpaper. Then he turned around and jumped down from the stool. ''Within half a minute, we'll be on his trail!'' He walked across the room and touched the big mirror. ''No, it's not yielding yet.''

''Oh! Are we going out through the mirror, like Christine?'' asked Raoul.

''So you knew she left through this mirror?''

''She did it in front of me! I was hiding there, behind the curtain of the boudoir, and I saw her: she didn't go through the mirror, she disappeared into it!''

''And what did you do?''

''I thought my senses were playing tricks on me, I thought I must be going mad, or dreaming!''

''Or maybe you thought it was some new whim of the ghost's,'' the Persian said with an ironic laugh. ''Ah, Monsieur de Chagny,'' he went on, still holding his hand against the mirror, ''would to God that we *were* dealing with a ghost! We could leave our pistols in their box. . . . Please put down your hat . . . there. And now, close your coat over your shirt front as much as you can, as I've done. Turn up the collar and fold over the lapels. We must make ourselves as invisible as possible.''

After a short silence he added, still pressing on the mirror, ''When you push on the spring inside the room, the release of the counterweight takes time to produce its effect, but it's different when you're on the other side of the wall and can act directly on the counterweight. Then the mirror begins turning instantly and moves with amazing speed.''

"What counterweight?" asked Raoul.

"Why, the one that raises this whole section of wall, of course," the Persian replied. "You didn't think it moved by itself, by magic, did you?" He pulled Raoul close to him with one hand and continued pressing on the mirror with the other, the one that held a pistol. "If you watch carefully, in a little while you'll see the mirror rise a few millimeters, then move a few more millimeters to the right. It will then be on a pivot, and it will turn. It's incredible what can be done with a counterweight! A child can make a whole house turn with one, using only his little finger. When a section of wall, no matter how heavy, is balanced by a counterweight on a pivot, it weighs no more than a spinning top on its point."

"It's not turning!" Raoul said impatiently.

"Wait! You have time enough to be impatient! It's obvious that the mechanism is rusty, or the spring no longer works." The Persian's forehead wrinkled into a worried frown. "Or it may be something else. . . ."

"What do you mean?"

"He may have simply cut the rope of the counterweight and blocked the whole system."

"Why? He didn't know we'd try to come down this way, did he?"

"He may have suspected it, because he knows I'm familiar with the system."

"Did he show it to you?"

"No. I looked beyond him, and beyond his mysterious disappearances, and I found what I was looking for. It's the simplest secret-door system, a mechanism as old as the sacred palaces of Thebes, each with a hundred doors, and the tripod room at Delphi."

"It's not turning! And Christine, sir, Christine . . ."

"We'll do everything that's humanly possible," the Persian said coldly, "but he may stop us as soon as we begin."

"Then he's in control of the walls?"

"He's in control of the walls, the doors, and the trapdoors. In my country, he was called by a name that means 'the lover of trapdoors.' "

"That's how Christine talked to me about him—with the same mystery, and attributing the same formidable power to him. . . .

But I don't understand all this. Why do the walls obey only him? He didn't build them, did he?"

"Yes, he did."

And as Raoul looked at him, disconcerted, the Persian motioned him to be silent and pointed to the mirror. Their reflection seemed to quiver and was blurred as if it were on the rippled surface of a pond; then it became still again.

"You see: it's not turning! Let's go down in some other way."

"Tonight, there is no other way," the Persian said in a singularly mournful tone. "And now, be careful, and be ready to shoot!"

Standing in front of the mirror, he raised his pistol. Raoul did the same. With his free hand, the Persian drew Raoul to his chest. Suddenly the mirror turned, in a dazzling glare of crosslights; it turned like one of the revolving doors that have now been placed in public buildings; it turned, carrying the two men along in its irresistible movement and taking them abruptly from bright light to deep darkness.

21

In the Cellars of the Opera

"HOLD YOUR PISTOL up, ready to shoot!" the Persian quickly repeated to Raoul.

Behind them, the wall had closed by completing its circular motion on a pivot. The two men stood still for a few moments, holding their breath. Unbroken silence reigned in the darkness.

Finally the Persian decided to make a movement. Raoul heard him sliding along on his knees, groping for something. Suddenly the darkness in front of Raoul was dimly lighted by the glow of a little shaded lantern. He instinctively stepped back, as though to escape the scrutiny of a secret enemy. But he quickly realized that the lantern belonged to the Persian, and he began following all his movements. The little red disk glided over the walls, ceiling, and floor. The wall on the right was made of masonry, the one on the left of boards.

Raoul told himself that Christine had come this way when she followed the voice of the Angel of Music. It must also have been the way Erik usually came when he went through the walls to take Christine's good faith by surprise and intrigue her innocence. And, remembering what the Persian had said, Raoul thought that this route had been mysteriously established by Erik himself. He was later to learn, however, that Erik had found an already prepared secret passage whose existence was for a long time unknown to anyone but him. That passage had been created in the days of the Paris Commune to enable jailers to take their prisoners directly to the cells that had been made in the cellars, for the insurgents had occupied the building immediately after the insurrection of March 18, 1871. They had made the lower part of it into a state prison, and the top into a departure point for the hot-air balloons that were to carry their inflammatory proclamations to areas beyond the city.

The Persian knelt and put his lantern down on the floor. For a time he seemed to be working rapidly at something in the floor, then suddenly he darkened his lantern. Raoul heard a faint click and saw a square of very dim light in the floor of the corridor. It was as if a window had just opened into the still lighted cellars of the Opera. He no longer saw the Persian but all at once he felt him beside him and heard his breathing.

"Follow me and do everything I do."

Raoul was guided toward the square of light. Then he saw the Persian kneel again, grip one edge of the opening and slip down into the cellar below, holding his pistol between his teeth.

Strangely, Raoul trusted the Persian completely. Even though he knew nothing about him and his words had only deepened the mystery of this adventure, he did not hesitate to believe that the Persian was with him against Erik at that decisive time. His emotion had seemed genuine when he spoke of the "monster," and the interest he had shown in Raoul had not seemed suspect. And finally, if he had had any sinister plans against Raoul, he would not have given him a pistol. Furthermore, Raoul had to reach Christine at any cost and he did not have a choice of means. If he had hesitated, even with doubts about the Persian's intentions, he would have regarded himself as a base coward.

He too knelt and hung from the edge of the trapdoor with both hands. "Let go!" he heard, and let himself fall. The Persian caught him, ordered him to lie down on the floor, closed the trapdoor above them by some means that Raoul could not see, and lay down beside him. Raoul wanted to ask for an explanation but the Persian's hand was clapped over his mouth and he immediately heard a voice he recognized as that of Mifroid, the police commissary who had questioned him.

Raoul and the Persian were behind a partition that hid them. Nearby, a narrow staircase led up to a little room in which Mifroid was evidently walking back and forth and asking questions, because they heard his footsteps as well as his voice.

The light around them was very dim, but having come out of the thick darkness in the corridor above, Raoul had no difficulty in making out the shapes of things. And he could not hold back a faint exclamation when he saw three bodies.

One of them lay on the narrow landing of the little staircase that led up to the door behind which Mifroid's voice could be heard; the two others had rolled to the bottom of the stairs and lay with their arms outspread. If he had been able to put his hand through the partition that hid him, Raoul could have touched one of them.

"Quiet!" whispered the Persian. He had also seen the bodies, and he said one word to explain everything: "He!"

Mifroid's voice then became louder. He demanded information about the lighting system, and the stage manager gave it to him. He was therefore in the pipe organ or one of the rooms next to it.

Contrary to what one might think, especially in connection with an opera house, the pipe organ was not for making music. At that time, electricity was used only for certain limited stage effects and for electric bells. The immense building and the stage itself were still lighted by gas; hydrogen was used to regulate and alter the lighting of a scene, by means of a special apparatus that was called the pipe organ because of its many pipes.

A recess beside the prompter's box was reserved for the lighting-crew chief. There he gave orders to his assistants and saw to it that they were carried out. Mauclair, the chief, was in that recess during every performance.

But now he was not in his recess and his assistants were not in their places.

"Mauclair! Mauclair!"

The stage manager's voice resounded in the cellars as though in a drum. But Mauclair did not answer.

We have said that a door opened into a little staircase that came up from the second cellar. Mifroid tried to open it but it resisted.

"What's the matter here?" he said to the stage manager. "This door seems to be blocked. Is it always so hard to open?"

The stage manager opened it by vigorously pushing on it with his shoulder. He saw that he was also pushing a human body and could not hold back an exclamation: he recognized that body.

"Mauclair!"

Everyone who had come with Mifroid on that visit to the pipe organ anxiously stepped forward.

"He's dead, poor man!" moaned the stage manager.

Mifroid, who was surprised by nothing, leaned over the tall body.

"No," he said, "he's dead drunk. It's not the same."

"If so, it's the first time," declared the stage manager.

"Then maybe he's been drugged. It's quite possible."

Mifroid straightened up, went down a few more steps, and cried out, "Look!"

Two other bodies lay at the foot of the stairs, in the glow of a little red lantern. The stage manager recognized Mauclair's assistants. Mifroid went down to them and put his ear to their chests.

"They're sound asleep," he said. "It's a strange business! It's obvious that some unknown person interfered with the lighting crew—and that person had to have been working for the abductor. But what an odd idea to abduct a singer on the stage! That's a case of doing something the hard way if ever there was one! Send for the Opera doctor." And he repeated, "Strange! It's a strange business!" He turned toward the little room and spoke to people whom Raoul and the Persian could not see from where they were. "What do you say to all this, gentlemen? You're the only ones who haven't said what you think, and you must have some opinion about it."

Raoul and the Persian saw the two managers' dismayed faces appear above the landing—only their faces could be seen there—and heard Moncharmin speak in a voice filled with emotion:

"Things are happening here that we can't explain."

"Thank you for that information," Mifroid said sardonically.

The stage manager, holding his chin in the hollow of his right hand, which is a clear indication of deep thought, said, "This isn't the first time Mauclair has fallen asleep in the Opera. I remember finding him one night, snoring in his little recess, beside his snuffbox."

"How long ago was that?" asked Mifroid, carefully wiping the lenses of his pince-nez, for he was nearsighted, something that can happen even to the most beautiful eyes in the world.

"Well, it wasn't very long ago. Let's see now. . . . It was the night . . . Yes, it was the night when Carlotta let out her famous croak! You remember that, don't you?"

"Really?" said Mifroid. "The night when Carlotta let out her famous croak?" Having put on his pince-nez again, he looked at the stage manager intently, as if he were trying to read his mind. "So Mauclair takes snuff?" he asked casually.

"Yes, he does. Look: there's his snuffbox on that shelf. Yes, he often takes snuff."

"So do I," said Mifroid, and he put the snuffbox in his pocket.

Raoul and the Persian, whose presence was still unsuspected, watched while stagehands carried the three bodies away. Mifroid left and the others all followed him up the stairs. Then their footsteps were heard for a few more moments on the stage above.

When they were alone, the Persian motioned Raoul to stand up. Raoul did so, but without again holding up his pistol in front of his eyes, ready to shoot, as the Persian did. The Persian told him to put his hand back in that position and keep it there, no matter what happened.

"But it tires my hand uselessly," said Raoul, "and if I have to shoot, I won't be able to do it accurately."

"Then hold your pistol in your other hand," the Persian conceded.

"I can't shoot with my left hand."

The Persian made this strange reply, which obviously did little to clarify the situation in Raoul's mind:

"It's not a question of shooting with your left hand or your right; what you have to do is to keep holding one of your hands as if you were about to fire a pistol, with your arm bent. As for the pistol itself, you can put it in your pocket if you want to. But do as I say, or I can't answer for anything! It's a matter of life and death! And now, silence, and follow me."

They were in the second cellar. By the dim light of a few scattered lamps, their flames motionless in their glass prisons, Raoul only glimpsed a minute part of the Opera cellars, that fantastic, sublime, and childish abyss, amusing as a puppet show and frightening as a bottomless pit.

Those cellars are awesome, and there are five of them. They reproduce the plan of the stage, with its trapdoors and slots for scenery, except that the cuts in the stage floor are replaced with rails. There are transverse frameworks under the trapdoors and slots. Posts resting on iron or stone supports, or on beams, form a series of rigid flats that can be used in producing stage effects.

They are given added stability, when needed, by connecting them to each other with iron hooks. Winches and counterweights are abundant in the cellars. They are used for maneuvering large pieces of scenery, producing transformation scenes, and bringing about the sudden disappearance of performers in scenes with spectacular stage effects. It is from the cellars, say X, Y, and Z in their interesting study of Garnier's work, that sickly old men are turned into handsome young gallants, and hideous witches into radiant fairies. Satan comes up from the cellars and goes back down into them. The fires of hell rise from them, and choruses of demons gather there.

And ghosts move through the cellars as if they owned them. . . .

Raoul followed the Persian, strictly obeying his instructions without trying to understand them, telling himself that he was his only hope. What would he have done without him in that bewildering labyrinth? He would have been stopped at every step by the prodigious jumble of beams and ropes. He would have been caught in that gigantic spider's web, unable to disentangle himself. And even if he had been able to pass through the network of ropes and counterweights that was constantly renewed in front of him, he would have run the risk of falling into one of the holes that occasionally appeared in the floor, plunging into what seemed to be endless darkness.

They went down and down. . . . They reached the third cellar, and their steps were still lighted by a few distant lamps.

The farther down they went, the more precautions the Persian seemed to take. He often turned back to Raoul and urged him to go on holding up his hand in the right way, showing him how he kept his own hand raised as if it were ready to shoot, though it no longer held a pistol.

Suddenly a loud voice made them stop. Above them, someone was shouting:

"All door-closers on the stage! The police commissary wants to see them."

Footsteps were heard, and shadows glided through the darkness. The Persian drew Raoul behind a flat. They saw figures moving past them and above them, old men bent by age and former burdens of opera scenery. Some of them could scarcely drag themselves along; others, out of habit, leaned forward with outstretched hands, trying to find doors to close.

For these were the door-closers, decrepit former stagehands to whom the management had charitably given the job of closing

doors in the cellars and the rest of the building.* They were
constantly coming and going above and below the stage to close
doors, and in those days (I believe they have all died since then)
they were also called "draft-stoppers." No matter where they
come from, drafts are very bad for the voice.

The Persian and Raoul were glad of this incident because it rid
them of unwelcome witnesses. Some of the door-closers, having
nothing more to do and being essentially homeless, stayed in the
Opera out of laziness or necessity, and spent the night there. The
two men might have stumbled over them, waking them up and
prompting them to ask for an explanation. For the moment,
Mifroid's investigation had saved them from such undesirable
encounters.

But they did not enjoy their solitude for long. Other men were
now coming down the stairs on which the door-closers had gone
up. Each of them carried a little lantern and moved it up and
down, examining everything around him, obviously in search of
something or someone.

"I don't know what they're looking for," the Persian whispered, "but they may very well find us if we stay here. Let's go!
Hurry! Keep your hand up, ready to shoot. Bend your arm more.
There. . . . Hold your hand in front of your eyes, as if you were
about to fight a duel and were waiting for the order to fire. Leave
your pistol in your pocket! Let's go down, quickly!" He led Raoul
into the fourth cellar. "Keep your hand in front of your eyes, it's a
matter of life and death! Here, this way, down those stairs." They
reached the fifth cellar. "Ah, what a duel, sir, what a duel!"

In the fifth cellar, the Persian caught his breath. He seemed to
be feeling safer than when they had stopped in the third cellar,
but he still kept his hand in the same position.

Though he said nothing more about it, because this was no
time for it, Raoul was once again surprised at the extraordinary
method of self-defense that consisted in leaving your pistol in
your pocket while your hand remained ready to fire it, as if you
were still holding it in front of your eyes—the position in which
duelists of that time waited for the order to fire. "I remember,"
he thought, "that he said to me, 'I've had these pistols a long
time and I know they're completely reliable.' " This led him to

---

*Pedro Gailhard told me himself that he created still more jobs as door-
closers for old stagehands whom he did not want to dismiss.

ask himself a question: "What good does it do him to have reliable pistols if he feels it would be futile to use them?"

But the Persian stopped him in his vague attempts at cogitation. He made a gesture telling him to stay where he was, climbed a few steps of the staircase they had just come down, then came back to him and said in an undertone, "How stupid of us not to realize it! We'll soon be rid of those men with lanterns: they're firemen making their rounds."*

The two men stood waiting, on their guard, for at least five long minutes. Then the Persian led Raoul back toward the stairs. But suddenly he motioned him to stop and stand still. Something was moving in the darkness before them.

"Get down!" whispered the Persian.

They lay down on the floor, not a moment too soon: a shadowy figure, carrying no lantern, only a shadow in the shadows, passed by so near to them that it almost touched them. They felt the warm breath of its cloak on their faces. For they could make it out distinctly enough to see that it wore a cloak that enveloped it from head to foot, and a soft felt hat.

It moved away, staying next to the walls and sometimes kicking them when it came to a corner.

The Persian heaved a sigh of relief and said, "That was a close call! That person knows me and has twice taken me to the managers' office."

"Is it someone from the Opera police?" asked Raoul.

"It's someone much worse!" the Persian replied without further explanation.†

*In those days, the firemen were still required to watch over the safety of the Opera even when no performance was taking place. That requirement has since been withdrawn. When I asked Pedro Gailhard why, he told me it was because there was fear that the firemen, having no experience with the cellars, might set fire to them.

†Like the Persian, the author will give no further explanation of that apparition. Though everything else in this historical account that sometimes seem abnormal, the author will not explicitly tell the reader what the Persian meant by "It's someone much worse!" (Much worse than the Opera police.) The reader will have to guess it, because the author has promised Pedro Gailhard, the former Opera manager, to maintain secrecy with regard to the extremely interesting and useful personality of the wandering cloaked figure who, while condemning himself to live in the cellars of the Opera, rendered such prodigious services to those who, on gala evenings, for example, dared to venture into the cellars. I am here speaking of state services and, on my word, I can say no more.

"It wasn't . . . *he*, was it?"

"He? If he doesn't come up behind us, we'll always see his golden eyes! That's our advantage in the darkness. But he may silently creep up behind us. If he does, we'll be dead unless we're still holding up a hand as if we were about to fire a pistol, in front of our eyes!"

The Persian had scarcely finished stating that line of conduct once again when a fantastic face appeared before the two men. A whole face, not just a pair of golden eyes. But it was a luminous face, a face of fire! Yes, a fiery face that came toward them at a man's height, *but without a body!* It gave off fire and, in the darkness, looked like a flame in the shape of a man's face.

"Oh!" the Persian exclaimed in a low voice. "This is the first time I've seen it. That fireman wasn't crazy! He really saw it! What's that flame? It's not *he*, but maybe he's sent it to us. Careful! Don't forget! Keep your hand in front of your eyes! In God's name, keep it in front of your eyes!"

The fiery face, which seemed a face from hell, a blazing demon, was still moving at a man's height, without a body, toward the two frightened men.

"Maybe he's sending that face toward us from the front," the Persian continued, "so he can better take us by surprise from behind, or from the side: with him, you never know. I know many of his tricks, but not this one. I don't know this one yet. . . . Let's run away from here—better safe than sorry! Come, and keep your hand in front of your eyes."

And they ran down the long underground passage that opened before them.

After a few seconds, which seemed to them long, long minutes, they stopped.

"Yet he seldom comes this way," said the Persian. "This side doesn't concern him. This side doesn't lead to the lake or the house by the lake. But maybe he knows we're on his trail, even though I promised to leave him alone and stay out of his affairs from now on."

He looked around and so did Raoul. They saw that the fiery face was behind them. It had followed them. And it must have run too, and perhaps faster than they, because it now seemed closer to them.

At the same time, they began to hear a sound whose nature they could not determine; they knew only that it seemed to come

earer with the flame in the shape of a man's face. It was a
squealing or grating sound, as if thousands of fingernails were
scratching on a blackboard, making the agonizingly unbearable
sound that it sometimes also produced when a piece of chalk
contains a small stone that scrapes against the blackboard.

They backed away from the fiery face but it went on moving
toward them, gaining on them. They could now see its features
clearly. The eyes were round and staring, the nose a little
crooked and the mouth large, with a drooping, semicircular
lower lip—a little like the eyes, nose, and mouth of the moon
when it is blood red.

How could that red moon glide through the darkness at a
man's height, with nothing to hold it up, without a body to
support it—apparently, at least? And how could it move so
fast, straight ahead, with its fixed, staring eyes? And what
was causing the grating, scratching, squealing sound that it
brought with it?

Finally the Persian and Raoul could back away no farther.
They flattened themselves against the wall, not knowing what
was going to happen to them because of that incomprehensible
fiery face and especially, now, because of that sound, which had
become louder, livelier, more "teeming," more "numerous,"
for it was clearly made up of hundreds of smaller sounds stirring
in the darkness, below the fiery face.

The fiery face kept coming toward them, with its noise, until
it was about to reach the place where they stood. Still flattened
against the wall, they felt their hair standing on end with horror,
because they now knew where the multiple sounds came from.
They moved in a throng, carried along in the darkness by
countless little hurried waves, faster than the waves that scurry
along the beach when the tide is rising; they were little night-
waves foaming under the moon, under the fiery-face moon.

The little waves passed between their feet and climbed up their
legs, irresistibly. Raoul and the Persian could no longer restrain
cries of horror, fear, and pain. Neither could they go on holding
one hand in front of their eyes, in the position taken by duelists
of that time as they waited for the order to fire. Their hands
moved down to their legs, to push away the gleaming little
waves that carried sharp little things, waves full of feet, claws,
and teeth.

Yes, Raoul and the Persian were on the verge of fainting, like Lieutenant Papin, the fireman. But the fiery face had turned toward them when they cried out, and now it spoke to them:

"Don't move! Don't move! And whatever you do, don't follow me! I'm the rat-killer. Let me pass with my rats."

The fiery face suddenly vanished into the shadows while the corridor ahead became lighter as a result of what the rat-killer had just done with his shaded lantern. Before, so as not to frighten the rats in front of him, he had kept the lantern turned toward himself, illuminating his own face; now, so that he could go faster, he was lighting the darkness ahead of him. He hurried forward, taking with him all the climbing, squeaking waves of rats, all the countless noises.

Released from their horror, Raoul and the Persian began breathing freely again, though they were still trembling.

"I should have remembered that Erik told me about the rat killer,"* said the Persian. "But he didn't say he looked like that, and it's strange that I never met him before." He sighed. "I thought it was another of the monster's tricks. But no, he never comes to this part of the cellars."

"Are we far away from the lake, then?" asked Raoul. "When will we get there? Let's go to the lake! To the lake! When we're there, we'll call Christine's name, we'll shake the walls, we'll shout! She'll hear us. And so will he. And since you know him, we'll talk to him."

---

*Pedro Gailhard, the former Opera manager, told me one day at Cap d'Ail, in the home of Madame Pierre Wolff, about the great underground damage that was caused by the ravages of rats until the management came to an agreement—at a rather high price—with a man who claimed he could put an end to that scourge by walking through the cellars every two weeks.

Since then, there have been no more rats in the Opera, except those admitted into the dancers' lounge. [In French slang, student dancers are called rats.—Translator's note.] Pedro Gailhard thought that the man had discovered a secret scent to which rats were attracted, just as fish are attracted to the lures that some fishermen put on their legs. He led the rats into an underground chamber where, intoxicated, they let themselves drown. We have seen the terror aroused in a fireman by the appearance of that man's head, a terror that, as Pedro Gailhard told me in one of our conversations, was so intense that it made the fireman faint. In my opinion, there can be no doubt that the head of fire encountered by the fireman was the same one that caused such painful apprehension in the Persian and Viscount de Chagny. (Reference: the Persian's papers.)

"You're talking like a child!" said the Persian. "If we go straight to the lake, we'll never get into the house by the lake."

"Why not?"

"Because that's where he's gathered all his defenses. I myself have never been able to reach the other shore, the one where the house is. First you have to cross the lake, and it's well guarded. I'm afraid that some of the people who have disappeared and never been seen again—former stagehands, old door-closers—simply tried to cross the lake. It's terrible. . . . I myself was nearly killed there. If the monster hadn't recognized me in time . . . Take my advice: Never go near the lake. And be sure to stop up your ears if you hear the underwater voice singing, the siren's voice."

"But then what are we doing here?" Raoul asked, seething with feverish impatience and rage. "If you can't do anything for Christine, at least let me die for her!"

The Persian tried to calm him.

"There's only one way we can save her, believe me, and it's to get into that house without the monster's knowing it."

"Can we hope to do that?"

"If I'd had no hope of it, I wouldn't have come for you!"

"And where can we get into the house by the lake without crossing the lake?"

"From the third cellar, from which we were so unfortunately driven away. We'll go back there now. I'll tell you the exact place," said the Persian, his voice faltering. "It's between a flat and a set piece from *Le Roi de Lahore*, exactly where Joseph Buquet died."

"The chief stagehand who was found hanged?"

"Yes; he was hanged and the rope was never found," the Persian said in a singular tone. "Come. Courage! Let's go, and raise your hand in front of your eyes again. But where are we?"

He had to open his shaded lantern again. He aimed its rays at two vast corridors that crossed each other at right angles. Their vaulted ceilings seemed to stretch out to infinity.

"We must be," he said, "in the part where the waterworks are located. I don't see any fire coming from the furnaces."

He walked in front of Raoul, seeking his way and stopping abruptly whenever he was afraid that one of the men from the waterworks might be passing. They had to avoid the glow of a kind of underground forge that was being extinguished. In front of it, Raoul recognized the demons that Christine had glimpsed during her first journey, at the time of her first captivity.

In this way they gradually came back under the prodigious cellars beneath the stage. They must then have been at the bottom of what was called the tub, and therefore at a great depth considering that the builders dug fifty feet below the level of the water that lay under that whole part of Paris; and they had to take out all that water. To form an idea of the amount they pumped out, one can imagine a body of water with the same area as the courtyard of the Louvre and a depth of one and a half times the height of the towers of Notre-Dame. Even so, they had to keep a lake.

The Persian tapped on a wall and said, "If I'm not mistaken, this wall may be part of the house by the lake."

He was tapping on a wall of the tub. And perhaps it will be useful for the reader to know how the bottom and the walls of the tub were constructed.

To prevent the water all around the building from being in direct contact with the walls supporting the whole installation of theatrical apparatus whose painted canvases and structures of wood and metal had to be protected from dampness, the architect had to build a double surrounding casing. The work of building it took a whole year.

It was on the wall of the first inner casing that the Persian tapped as he spoke to Raoul about the house by the lake. To anyone who knew the architecture of the building, the Persian's gesture would have seemed to indicate that Erik's mysterious house had been constructed inside the double casing, which was composed of a thick wall built as a caisson, then a brick wall, an enormous layer of cement, and another wall several yards thick.

At the Persian's words, Raoul threw himself against the wall and listened eagerly. But he heard nothing, nothing except distant footsteps on the floor in the upper part of the building.

The Persian again darkened his lantern.

"Careful!" he said. "Be sure to keep your hand up. And now, silence, because we're going to try to get into his house."

He led Raoul to the little staircase by which they had come down. They climbed it, stopping at each step, scrutinizing the darkness and silence, until they reached the third cellar.

The Persian motioned Raoul to kneel and then, walking on

their knees and one hand—with the other hand still in the required position—they reached the back wall.

Against this wall was a large abandoned backdrop from *Le Roi de Lahore*, and near this backdrop was a flat, and between them there was just enough space for a body. A body that had been found hanged one day—the body of Joseph Buquet.

Still on his knees, the Persian stopped and listened. For a moment he seemed to hesitate. He looked at Raoul, then up toward the second cellar, where the dim glow of a lantern could be seen through the crack between two boards. That glow obviously bothered the Persian. Finally he nodded and made up his mind.

He slipped between the flat and the set piece from *Le Roi de Lahore*, with Raoul close behind him. The Persian felt the wall with his free hand. Raoul saw him press strongly on it for a moment, as he had pressed on the wall in Christine's dressing room. And a stone tipped back. There was now a hole in the wall.

The Persian took his pistol from his pocket and signaled Raoul to do the same. He cocked the pistol. And resolutely, still on his knees, he crawled through the hole that the stone had left in the wall when it tipped back. Raoul, who had wanted to go first, had to be satisfied with following. The hole was very narrow.

The Persian stopped almost as soon as he had gone through it. Raoul heard him feeling the stones around him. Then he opened his lantern, leaned forward, examined something under him, and darkened the lantern.

"We have to drop down several yards without making any noise," he said. "Take off your shoes." He took off his own and handed them to Raoul. "Put them on the other side of the wall. We'll get them when we leave."*

The Persian moved forward a little, then turned all the way around, still on his knees, so that he was facing Raoul.

"I'm going to hang by my hands from the edge of the stone," he said, "and drop into his house. Then you'll do the same. Don't be afraid: I'll catch you."

---

*The two pairs of shoes were never found. According to the Persian's papers, they were placed between the flat and the set piece from *Le Roi de Lahore*, just where Joseph Buquet's hanged body had been found. They must have been taken by some stagehand or door-closer.

He did as he had said. Below him, Raoul heard the thud of the Persian's fall. He started, fearing that the sound might reveal their presence.

More than that sound, however, the absence of any other sound caused him terrible anxiety. According to the Persian, they were now within the walls of the house by the lake, yet they did not hear Christine! Not a cry! Not a call! Not a moan! Good God! Had they come too late?

He scraped his knees against the wall, clung to the stone with his sinewy hands, and let himself fall. A moment later he felt himself caught in the Persian's arms.

"It's I," said the Persian. "Silence!"

They stood still, listening. Never had the darkness around them seemed more opaque, or the silence heavier or more frightening. Raoul sank his fingernails into his lips to keep from shouting, "Christine! Here I am! Answer me if you're not dead, Christine!"

Finally the Persian began using his shaded lantern again. He shone its light above their heads, against the wall, looking for the hole through which they had come and not finding it.

"Oh!" he said. "The stone has closed by itself!"

And the rays of the lantern moved down the wall to the floor. He bent down and picked up something, a kind of cord. He examined it for a second and flung it away with horror.

"The Punjab lasso!" he murmured.

"What's what?" asked Raoul.

"It may be the hanged man's rope that was looked for so long," the Persian replied, shuddering.

Suddenly gripped by new anxiety, he moved the little red disk of his lantern over the walls. And, strangely, it illuminated the trunk of a tree that seemed to be still alive, with its leaves. Its branches rose along the wall and disappeared into the ceiling.

At first, because the disk of light was so small, it was hard for the two men to realize what was in front of them. They saw part of some branches, then a leaf, and another, and next to this they saw nothing at all, nothing but the beam of light that seemed to be reflected. Raoul ran his hand over that nothing at all, that reflection.

"Here's a surprise!" he said. "The wall is a mirror!"

"Yes, a mirror!" the Persian said in a tone of deep emotion. He passed his hand, the one holding the pistol, over his damp forehead. "We've fallen into the torture chamber!"

22

Interesting and Instructive Tribulations of a Persian in the Cellars of the Opera

THE PERSIAN HIMSELF wrote an account of how, until that night, he had vainly tried to enter the lakeside house by way of the lake; how he had discovered the entrance in the third cellar; and finally, how he and Viscount de Chagny found themselves pitted against the Opera ghost's infernal imagination in the torture chamber. I will here present the story he left us (in circumstances that will be described later). I have not changed one word of it. I will give it as it stands because I feel I must not pass over in silence the daroga's* personal adventures in connection with the lakeside house before he fell into it with Raoul. If that interesting beginning briefly appears to take us away from the torture chamber, it will only be to bring us back to it all the better, after explaining certain important things and some of the Persian's attitudes and ways of acting that may have seemed quite extraordinary.

*The Persian word *daroga* designates the commander of the government police.

THE PERSIAN'S STORY

It was the first time I had gone into the house by the lake. I had vainly begged the lover of trapdoors—that is what Erik was called, in Persian, in my country—to open its mysterious doors to me. He had always refused. I, who was paid to know many of his secrets and tricks, had tried unsuccessfully to get into the house by means of ruses. Since finding Erik in the Opera, where he seemed to have made his home, I had often spied on him, sometimes in the aboveground halls, sometimes in the underground ones, and sometimes on the shore of the lake when, believing he was alone, he got into his little boat and rowed to the wall on the opposite shore. But it was always so dark that I could not see exactly where he opened his door in the wall.

One day when I too believed I was alone, curiosity, and also an appalling thought that had come to me as I reflected on several things that the monster had said to me, drove me to get into the little boat and row toward the part of the wall where I had seen Erik disappear. That was when I discovered the siren who guarded the approach to that place, and whose charm was nearly fatal to me, in the following circumstances.

After I had left the shore, the silence in which I rowed was gradually disturbed by a kind of whispered singing that seemed to be all around me. It was both music and a sound of breathing; it rose gently from the water of the lake and enveloped me in some way that I could not discern. It followed me, moved with me, and was so sweet that it did not frighten me. On the contrary, wanting to approach the source of that soft, captivating harmony, I leaned over the side of the boat, toward the water, for I had no doubt that the singing came from the water itself. I was already in the middle of the lake and there was no one else in the boat. The voice—it was now distinctly a voice—was beside me, on the water. I leaned down, and leaned still farther. . . . The lake was perfectly calm. The moonbeam that shone on it, after coming through the ventilation opening on the Rue Scribe, showed me absolutely nothing on its smooth, jet-black surface. I shook my head a little to get rid of a possible ringing in my ears, but I had to recognize the obvious fact that no ringing in the ears could be as harmonious as the whispered singing that had been following me and now attracted me.

If my mind had been superstitious or receptive to fanciful tales, I would surely have thought I was dealing with some siren who had been placed there to confuse any traveler bold enough to venture onto the water of the house by the lake, but, thank God, I am from a country where people love the fantastic too much not to know it thoroughly, and I myself had studied it in great depth. With the simplest of tricks, any conjurer who knows his trade can make the poor human imagination work feverishly.

So I had no doubt that I was confronted by some new invention of Erik's, but once again the invention was so perfect that, in leaning over the side of the boat, I was impelled less by a desire to discover the artifice than to enjoy its charm.

I leaned farther and farther, until I was on the verge of capsizing the boat.

All at once two monstrous arms came out of the water, gripped me by the neck, and pulled me down with irresistible force. I would certainly have been lost if I had not had time to utter a cry by which Erik recognized me.

For it was Erik; and instead of drowning me as he had surely intended to do, he swam, pulled me to shore, and gently put me down there.

"That was rash of you," he said, standing in front of me with that infernal water streaming from his body. "Why were you trying to get into my house? I didn't invite you. I don't want you, or anyone else in the world! Did you save my life only to make it unbearable for me? No matter how great a service you did for him, Erik may finally forget it, and you know that nothing can hold Erik back, not even Erik himself."

He went on talking, but now my only desire was to know what I already called "the siren trick." He was willing to satisfy my curiosity, for though he is a real monster—that is how I judge him, having unfortunately had occasion to see him at work in Persia—in some ways he is a brash, conceited child, and after astonishing people, he loves nothing so much as proving the truly wondrous ingenuity of his mind.

He laughed and showed me a long reed.

"It's ridiculously simple," he said, "but it's very useful for breathing and singing underwater. It's a trick I learned from the

Tonkin pirates.* They use it to hide on the bottom of streams, sometimes for hours at a time.''

"It's a trick that nearly killed me," I said sternly, "and it may have been fatal to others!"

He stepped toward me with the look of childish menace that I had often seen him show. Refusing to let him intimidate me, I spoke to him sharply.

"You know what you promised me, Erik: no more murders!"

"Have I really committed murders?" he asked, taking on an amiable expression.

"Ah, you wretch!" I exclaimed. "Have you forgotten the Rosy Hours of Mazenderan?"

"Yes," he replied, suddenly sad, "I prefer to forget them, though I did make the little sultana laugh."

"All that is in the past," I said. "But there's still the present. And you're answerable to me for the present, since it wouldn't exist for you if I hadn't wanted it to. Remember, Erik: I saved your life!"

And I took advantage of the turn the conversation had taken to talk to him about something that had been on my mind for some time.

"Erik," I began, "swear to me . . ."

"Why?" he interrupted. "You know I never keep my oaths. Oaths are made for catching fools!"

"Tell me . . . You can tell me . . ."

"Tell you what?"

"Well, the chandelier . . . The chandelier, Erik . . ."

"What about it?"

"You know what I mean."

"Ah, yes, the chandelier," he said, laughing. "I can tell you. I didn't make that chandelier fall. It was badly worn."

When he laughed, Erik was even more frightening than usual. He leapt into the boat with such a sinister laugh that I could not help trembling.

"Very badly worn, my dear daroga," he went on. "The chandelier was very badly worn. It fell by itself, and hit with a big bang! And now, let me give you some advice: Go and dry

---

*An administrative report from Tonkin, which reached Paris in late July 1900, tells how the famous pirate leader De Tham and his men were pursued by French soldiers, and how they all escaped by using reeds in this way.

yourself if you don't want to catch a cold. Don't ever get into my boat again, and remember this especially: Don't try to get into my house. I'm not always there, daroga, and it would grieve me to dedicate my requiem mass to you!''

As he said this with his sinister laugh, he stood in the stern of his boat and began sculling it, swaying back and forth like an ape. Except for his golden eyes, he looked like the grim ferryman of the Styx. Soon I could see nothing of him but his eyes, and finally he vanished completely into the darkness of the lake.

From then on, I gave up all hope of getting into his house by crossing the lake. That entrance was obviously too well guarded, especially now that he knew I was aware of it. But I thought there had to be another one, for more than once I had seen him disappear in the third cellar while I was watching him, and I could not imagine how he had done it.

I cannot repeat too often that ever since I had found Erik living in the Opera I had been in constant terror of his horrible whims. I was not afraid for myself, but I felt he was capable of anything with regard to others.* Whenever there was an accident, some pernicious event of any kind, I said to myself, "Maybe it was Erik," as others around me said, "It was the ghost!" How often I heard those words spoken by smiling people! If those poor people had known that the ghost existed in flesh and blood and was much more to be feared than the imaginary shade they referred to, I can assure you that they would have stopped joking about him! If they had only known what Erik was capable of, especially in a field of action like the Opera! And if they had known about my appalling thoughts . . .

As for me, I was filled with anxiety. Even though Erik had solemnly informed me that he had changed and had become the most virtuous of men, now that he was loved for himself—those words had left me terribly perplexed—I could not help shuddering when I thought of him. His horrible, unique, and repulsive ugliness put him beyond the pale of humanity, and it had often

---

*At this point the Persian might have admitted that he was also interested in Erik's fate for his own personal reasons: He was aware that if the Teheran government learned that Erik was still alive, it would mean the end of the modest pension he drew as a former daroga. It is only fair, however, to add that the Persian had a noble and generous heart, and I have no doubt that he was greatly concerned with the catastrophes he dreaded for others, as was shown by his praiseworthy conduct in that whole affair.

been apparent to me that for this reason he no longer felt he had any obligations to the human race. The way he talked to me about his love affair—in a boastful tone with which I had become familiar—made me see it as a cause of new tragedies, worse than all the rest, and increased my fear still more. I knew how his sorrow could turn into sublime and disastrous despair, and the things he had told me, vaguely announcing the most horrible catastrophe, were constantly part of my appalling thoughts.

I had, moreover, discovered the strange relations that had been established between the monster and Christine Daaé. Hiding in the storeroom next to her dressing room, I had listened to admirable musical performances that obviously enraptured her, but I would not have thought that Erik's voice—which he could make loud as thunder or soft as an angel's voice, at will—could make her forget his ugliness. I understood when I learned that she had never seen him!

I had a chance to go into her dressing room. Remembering the lessons that Erik had given me in the past, I had no difficulty in finding the device by which the wall supporting the mirror could be made to pivot, and I saw the arrangement of hollow bricks, functioning as a speaking tube, by which he could make Christine hear him as if he were standing beside her. I also discovered the passage that led to the Communards' dungeon and the fountain, and also the trapdoor that must have enabled Erik to go directly into the cellars under the stage.

A few days later I was astounded to learn from my own eyes and ears that Erik and Christine Daaé were seeing each other, and to find him leaning over the weeping little fountain in the Communards' passage (at the far end, underground) and placing cool water on her forehead as she lay unconscious, evidently from having fainted. A white horse, the horse from *Le Prophète*, which had disappeared from the underground stable of the Opera, stood calmly beside them. I showed myself. It was terrible. I saw sparks fly from two golden eyes, and before I could say a word I was stunned by a blow on the forehead.

When I regained consciousness, Erik, Christine, and the white horse were gone. I had no doubt that the poor girl was now a prisoner in the house by the lake. Without hesitating, I resolved to go back to the lake despite the danger of doing so. For twenty-four hours, hiding near the dark shore, I waited for the monster to appear, for I thought he would have to come out to go

and get provisions. In this connection I must say that when he
went out into the city or dared to show himself in public, he
wore a papier-mâché nose with a mustache attached to it, to hide
his hideous nose-hole. Though this did not entirely take away his
macabre appearance, since people watched him pass and then
said such things as "He looks like death warmed over," it at
least made him almost—and I stress the word *almost*—bearable
to see.

As I watched for him on the shore of the lake—Lake Averne,
as he had called it several times, with a joyless laugh, in
speaking to me—I finally became tired from my long patience
and told myself that he must have left by way of another door,
the one in the third cellar. Then I heard a faint splashing sound
in the darkness and saw two golden eyes shining like beacons,
and soon the boat landed. Erik leapt out of it and came to me.

"You've been here for twenty-four hours," he said. "You're
bothering me, and I warn you that this is going to end badly.
And you'll have brought it on yourself, because I've been prodigiously patient with you. You think you've been following me,
you immense simpleton [*sic*], but *I've* been following *you,* and I
know everything you know about me here. I spared you yesterday, in my Communards' passage, but listen to me carefully:
Don't let me find you there again! You've been behaving very
recklessly and I wonder if you still know how to take a hint!"

He was so angry that for the moment I was careful not to
interrupt him. After snorting loudly, he expressed his horrible
thoughts, which corresponded to my appalling thoughts:

"You must learn once and for all—yes, once and for all—how
to take a hint! I'm telling you that with your recklessness—
you've already been stopped twice by the man in the felt hat; he
didn't know what you were doing in the cellars and took you to
the managers, and they believed you were only a whimsical
Persian interested in stage effects and fond of being backstage in
a theater (I was there, yes, I was there in the office; you know
I'm everywhere)—I'm telling you that with your recklessness,
people will finally wonder what you're looking for here, and
they'll find out that you're looking for Erik, and they'll begin
looking for Erik too, and they'll discover the house by the lake.
Then very bad things will happen, my friend! I won't answer for
anything!" He snorted again. "No, not for anything! If Erik's
secrets don't remain Erik's secrets, it will be too bad for many

members of the human race! That's all I have to say to you, and it ought to be enough, unless you're an immense simpleton [*sic*] and don't know how to take a hint.''

He sat down in the stern of his boat and began kicking his heels against it, waiting to hear what I would answer. I simply said, ''Erik isn't the one I've come here to look for.''

''Who is it, then?''

''You know very well: it's Christine Daaé.''

''I have a right to meet her in my house. I'm loved for myself.''

''That's not true,'' I said. ''You abducted her and now she's your prisoner!''

''Listen to me. Will you promise never to meddle in my affairs again if I prove to you that I'm loved for myself?''

''Yes, I promise,'' I answered without hesitation, because I was sure that such proof was impossible for such a monster.

''Well, then, it's quite simple. Christine will leave here as she pleases, and she'll come back! Yes, she'll come back, because she'll want to! She'll come back of her own accord, because she loves me for myself!''

''Oh, I doubt that she'll come back. . . . But it's your duty to let her leave.''

''My duty, you immense simpleton [*sic*], is my will, my will to let her leave, and she'll come back because she loves me! It will all end in a wedding—a wedding in the Madeleine church, you immense simpleton [*sic*]. Will you believe me when I tell you that my wedding mass is already written? When you hear the *Kyrie* . . .''

He again kicked his heels against the boat, this time in rhythmic accompaniment for himself as he sang softly: *''Kyrie, kyrie, kyrie eleison* . . . Just wait till you hear that mass!''

''Listen,'' I said, ''I'll believe you when I see Christine Daaé leave the house by the lake and go back to it of her own free will.''

''And you'll never meddle in my affairs again? Very well, you'll see it tonight. Come to the masked ball. Christine and I will be there for a time. Then you can hide in the storeroom. You'll see that Christine has gone to her dressing room and that she's perfectly willing to go along the Communards' passage again.''

''I'll be there.''

If I saw that, I would have to accept what Erik had said, because a beautiful woman always has a right to love the most horrible monster, especially when the monster has the enchantment of music in his favor, as this one did, and the beautiful woman happens to be a distinguished singer.

"Leave now," Erik said, "because I have to go and do some shopping."

And so I left. I was still worried about Christine Daaé, but I was especially preoccupied with my appalling thoughts, now that Erik had stirred them up so powerfully with what he had said about my recklessness.

I said to myself, "How is all this going to end?" And although I am rather fatalistic by temperament, I could not rid myself of a nagging anxiety because of the enormous responsibility I had taken one day by saving the life of a monster who now threatened "many members of the human race."

To my vast amazement, things happened as Erik had predicted. Several times I saw Christine Daaé leave the house by the lake and return to it with no sign of having been forced to do so. I then tried to put that amorous mystery out of my mind, but it was very hard—especially for me, because of my appalling thoughts—not to think about Erik. Resigned to extreme caution, however, I did not make the mistake of returning to the lake or the Communards' passage.

But since I was still haunted by the thought of the secret entrance in the third cellar, I repeatedly went there, knowing it was usually deserted during the day. I spent endless hours there, with nothing to do but twiddle my thumbs, hiding behind a set piece from *Le Roi de Lahore* that had been left there, I do not know why, since *Le Roi de Lahore* was not performed often.

All that patience had to be rewarded. One day I saw the monster coming toward me on his hands and knees. I was sure he did not see me. He passed between the set piece and a flat, went to the wall and, at a place whose location I mentally noted, pressed on a spring that made a stone swing back, opening a passage for him. He disappeared into that passage and the stone swung shut behind him. I knew the monster's secret; it would let me go to the house by the lake whenever I chose.

To make sure of this, I waited at least an hour and then pressed on the spring. The mechanism worked as it had done for

Erik. But, knowing he was at home, I did not go into the passage. Furthermore the idea that he might take me by surprise there suddenly reminded me of Joseph Buquet's death and, not wanting to risk losing the advantage of a discovery that might be beneficial to many people, to "many members of the human race," I left the cellars of the Opera after carefully putting the stone back in place, using an old Persian system.

As you can well imagine, I was still greatly interested in the relationship between Erik and Christine Daaé, not out of morbid curiosity, but because, as I have already said, of those appalling thoughts that never left me. "If Erik discovers that he's not loved for himself," I told myself, "we can expect anything."

I continued to wander—cautiously—in the Opera, and soon I learned the truth about the monster's sad love affair. He occupied Christine's mind by terror, but her heart belonged wholly to Raoul de Chagny. While, in the upper part of the Opera, they played at being an innocent engaged couple and avoided the monster, they were unaware that someone was watching over them. I was resolved to stop at nothing: I would kill the monster if necessary, and give explanations to the police afterward. He did not show himself, but I was not reassured by his absence.

I must tell you about my plan. I believed that the monster would eventually be driven out of his house by jealousy and that I would then be able to enter it safely, through the passage in the third cellar. It was important, for everyone's sake, that I know exactly what was in that house.

One day, tired of waiting for an opportunity, I made the stone open and I immediately heard powerful music: with all the doors in his house open, the monster was working on his *Don Juan Triumphant*. I knew it was the work of his life. I prudently stayed in my dark hole, careful not to move. He stopped playing for a time and paced back and forth in his house, like a madman. And he said aloud, in a resounding voice, "It must be finished *before!* Completely finished!" These words did not reassure me either. When he began playing again, I gently closed the stone. And even when it was closed I could still hear remote, indistinct singing coming from the depths of the earth, as I had heard the siren's song rising from the depths of the lake. I remembered something said by the stagehands who found Joseph Buquet's body, something at which people had smiled skeptically: They claimed that all around the body they had heard "a sound like the singing of the dead."

On the night of Christine Daae's abduction, I arrived at the Opera rather late, afraid of hearing bad news. I had spent a terrible day because, after reading in a morning newspaper that Christine and Viscount de Chagny were going to be married, I had constantly wondered if, after all, I should not denounce the monster. But reason finally returned to me and I realized that denouncing him might only precipitate a catastrophe.

When I got out of a cab in front of the Opera, I looked at the building as if I were surprised to see it still standing. But, like all good Easterners, I am something of a fatalist. I went inside, expecting anything.

Christine Daae's abduction during the prison act naturally surprised everyone else, but I was prepared for it. I had no doubt that Erik had made her vanish, like the king of prestidigitators that he was. And I thought that this time it was the end for her, and maybe for everyone.

For a moment I wondered if I should urge all those people lingering in the Opera to run away. But I was stopped by my certainty that they would think I was insane. And I knew that if I tried to make them leave by shouting "Fire!" for example, I might cause a catastrophe—people smothered or trampled to death in the rush, savage fights—even worse than the one I already dreaded.

I decided, however, that on an individual basis I would act without delay, especially since the time seemed propitious to me. It was quite likely that Erik was now thinking only of his captive. I had to take advantage of that to enter his house by way of the passage in the third cellar. I asked the desperate young Viscount Raoul de Chagny to help me and he consented immediately, with a confidence in me that touched me deeply. I sent Darius, my servant, for my pistols. He brought them to us in Christine's dressing room. I gave one of them to Raoul and advised him to be ready to shoot, as I was, for, after all, Erik might be waiting for us on the other side of the wall. We would have to go by way of the Communards' passage and through the trapdoor.

When he first saw my pistols, Raoul asked me if we were going to fight a duel. We certainly were! "And what a duel!" I said, but of course I did not have time to explain anything to him. He is brave, but he knew almost nothing about his adversary—which was all to the good!

What is a duel with the fiercest warrior compared to a combat with the most brilliant prestidigitator? I myself found it hard to accept the prospect of fighting against a man who was visible only when he wanted to be, and saw everything around him when everything was dark to others, a man whose strange knowledge, cunning, imagination, and skill enabled him to make use of all natural forces and combine them to produce illusions of sight and hearing that could lead his opponents to their doom. And he could now act in the cellars of the Opera—that is, in the land of phantasmagoria! Could anyone think of that without shuddering? Could anyone imagine what might happen to the eyes or ears of someone inside the Opera if, in its five cellars and twenty-five upper levels, there was a ferocious and playful Robert Houdin who sometimes joked and sometimes hated, who sometimes emptied pockets and sometimes killed? Think of fighting against the lover of trapdoors, who in our country made so many of those pivoting trapdoors that are the best kind, think of fighting against the lover of trapdoors in the land of trapdoors!

My hope was that he was still with Christine, who had no doubt fainted again, in the house by the lake where he must have taken her, and my terror was that he was already somewhere around us, preparing to use his Punjab lasso.

No one can throw the Punjab lasso better than he does, and he is the prince of stranglers as he is the king of prestidigitators. When he had finished making the little sultana laugh, in the time of the Rosy Hours of Mazenderan, she would ask him to amuse himself by making her shudder. And he had found no better way of doing it than to use his Punjab lasso. After a stay in India, he had come back with incredible skill in strangling. He would have himself enclosed in a courtyard to fight a warrior, usually a man condemned to death, armed with a long pike and a broadsword. Erik had only his lasso, and just when the warrior thought he was about to kill him with a mighty blow, the lasso would hiss through the air. With a deft movement of his wrist, Erik would tighten the slender lasso around his enemy's neck, and he would then drag him in front of the little sultana and her women as they watched from a window and applauded. The little sultana also learned to throw the Punjab lasso; with it she killed several of her women and even some of her visiting friends.

But I prefer to drop the terrible subject of the Rosy Hours of Mazenderan. I have spoken of it only because, having gone down into the cellars of the Opera with Viscount Raoul de Chagny, I had to put him on his guard against the constant threat of being strangled. Once we were in the cellars, of course, my pistols could no longer be of any use to us, for I was sure that since Erik had done nothing to prevent us from entering the Communards' passage, he would not show himself. But he might try to strangle us at any moment. I did not have time to explain all that to Raoul, and even if I had had more time I do not know if I would have used it to tell him that somewhere in the darkness a Punjab lasso was ready to fly toward him. It would have been useless to complicate the situation. I only told him to keep his hand at the level of his eyes, with his arm bent in the position of a duelist waiting for the order to fire. That position makes it impossible for you to be strangled by a Punjab lasso, no matter how skillfully it is thrown: It catches you around the arm or the hand, as well as the neck, and thus becomes harmless because you can easily remove it.

After avoiding the police commissary, several door-closers, and the firemen, then meeting the rat-killer for the first time and passing the man in the felt hat without being seen, Raoul and I arrived without difficulty in the third cellar, between the flat and the set piece from *Le Roi de Lahore*. I made the stone open and we leapt into the house that Erik had built in the double envelope of the Opera's foundation walls (which he did with no difficulty at all, since he was one of the foremost masonry contractors of Charles Garnier, the architect of the Opera, and continued working, secretly and alone, when construction work was officially suspended during the war, the siege of Paris, and the Commune).

I knew my Erik well enough to go on the assumption that I could eventually discover all the tricks he had been able to devise during all that time. I was uneasy when I jumped down into his house, however, because I knew what he had done with the Mazenderan palace. He had changed it from a perfectly honest building into a house of the devil where no one could say a word without having it overheard or reported by an echo. How many stormy family conflicts and bloody tragedies the monster had left behind him, with his trapdoors! Not to mention that in a palace he had "rearranged" you could never know exactly where you were. He had horrible inventions. Certainly the most horrible, curious, and dangerous of all was his torture chamber. Except for rare cases in which the little sultana amused herself by making some middle-class citizen suffer, only prisoners condemned to death were placed in it. To my mind, it was the most cruelly imagined part of the Rosy Hours of Mazenderan. When someone in the torture chamber had "had enough," he was always allowed to end his suffering with a Punjab lasso that was left at his disposal under the iron tree.

Imagine my consternation, as soon as Raoul and I were in the monster's house, when I saw that the room into which we had just leapt was an exact replica of the torture chamber of the Rosy Hours of Mazenderan!

At our feet I found the Punjab lasso that I had dreaded so much all evening. I was convinced that it had already been used for Joseph Buquet, the chief stagehand. Like me, he must have been watching one evening, unseen, when Erik made the stone move in the third cellar. Curious, he too had tried the passage before the stone closed; he had fallen into the torture chamber and come out if it only after he was hanged. I could easily imagine Erik, wanting to get rid of the body, dragging it to the set piece from *Le Roi de Lahore* and hanging it there as an example, or to increase the superstitious terror that would help him in guarding the approaches to his den. But, on thinking it over, he had come back to take away the Punjab lasso, which is very distinctively made of catgut and might have aroused the curiosity of an examining magistrate.

And now I saw the lasso at our feet, in the torture chamber! I am not cowardly, but cold sweat broke out on my face.

My lantern shook in my hand as I moved its little red disk over the walls of the infamous chamber.

Raoul noticed this and asked, "What's the matter?"

I vigorously motioned him to be silent, for I could still hope that the monster did not know we were in the torture chamber. Even if he did not, however, it would not guarantee our safety, because it seemed quite plausible to me that the torture chamber was intended to guard the house by the lake from the direction of the third cellar, and perhaps to do it automatically.

Yes, the tortures were perhaps about to begin *automatically*. Who could say what movements on our part would set them off?

I urged Raoul to remain absolutely motionless. An overwhelming silence weighed down on us. The red light of my lantern continued to glide around the torture chamber. I recognized it, I recognized it. . . .

23

In the Torture Chamber

(CONTINUATION OF THE PERSIAN'S STORY)

WE WERE IN the middle of a small hexagonal room. All six of its walls were covered with mirrors from top to bottom. Clearly visible in the corners were segments of mirrors attached to drums that could be rotated. Yes, I recognized them, and I also recognized the iron tree in one corner, the iron tree with its iron branch—for hangings.

I had gripped Raoul's arm. He was quivering, ready to shout to his fiancée that he had come to her rescue. I was afraid he might not be able to restrain himself.

Suddenly we heard a sound to our left. At first it was like the sound of a door opening and closing in the next room, and there was a dull moan. I gripped Raoul's arm more tightly. Finally we distinctly heard these words:

"Take it or leave it! A wedding march or a funeral march."

I recognized the monster's voice.

There was another moan, followed by a long silence.

I was now convinced that the monster was unaware of our presence in his house, for otherwise he would have seen to it that we did not hear him. He would only have had to close the invisible little window through which lovers of torture looked into the torture chamber. And I was sure that if he had known we were there, the tortures would have begun immediately.

225

We therefore had a big advantage over him: we were close to him and he did not know it. It was essential for us not to let him know it, and I dreaded Raoul's impulsiveness more than anything else. He was on the verge of trying to break through the walls that separated him from Christine Daae, whose moaning we thought we could hear at intervals.

"A funeral march isn't exactly cheerful," Erik's voice resumed, "whereas a wedding march . . . It's magnificent! You must make up your mind and know what you want! As for me, I can't go on living like this, underground, in a hole, like a mole! *Don Juan Triumphant* is finished, and now I want to live like everyone else. I want to have a wife like everyone else and go out walking with her on Sundays. I've invented a mask that makes me look like an ordinary man. People won't even turn to look at me. You'll be the happiest of women. And we'll sing for ourselves alone, we'll sing till we're ready to die from pleasure. . . . You're crying! You're afraid of me! But I'm not really a bad man. Love me and you'll see! To be good, all I ever needed was to be loved. If you loved me, I'd be gentle as a lamb and you could do whatever you pleased with me."

The moans that accompanied this litany of love soon became louder and louder. I have never heard anything more desperate. Raoul and I recognized that this frightful lamentation came from Erik himself. As for Christine, she must have been standing somewhere, perhaps on the other side of the wall in front of us, speechless from horror, no longer having the strength to cry out, with the monster at her knees.

Erik's lamentation was as loud as a roar and as mournful as the murmur of an ocean. Three times this wail burst from his throat:

"You don't love me! You don't love me! You don't love me!"

Then his voice became softer when he asked, "Why are you crying? You know you're hurting me."

A silence.

For us, each silence was a hope. We said to ourselves, "Maybe he's left Christine on the other side of the wall." And we thought only of how we might make her aware of our presence, unknown to the monster.

We could now leave the torture chamber only if Christine opened its door for us, and it was only on this condition that we could help her, for we did not even know where the door might be in the walls around us.

Suddenly the silence in the next room was broken by the sound of an electric bell. We heard Erik leap to his feet, and then his thunderous voice: "Someone's ringing! Please come in!" A sinister laugh. "Who's come to disturb us? Wait for me here while I go and tell the siren to open the door."

Footsteps moved away, a door closed. I had no time to think of the new horror that was about to take place, I forgot that the monster might be going out only to commit a new crime; I realized only one thing: Christine was alone in the next room!

Raoul was already calling her.

"Christine! Christine!"

Since we could hear what was said in the other room, he could surely be heard there. Yet he had to repeat his call several times. Finally a faint voice reached us.

"I'm dreaming. . . ."

"Christine! Christine! It's me, Raoul!" Silence. "Answer me, Christine! If you're alone, in heaven's name, answer me!"

Then Christine's voice murmured Raoul's name.

"Yes! Yes!" he cried. "It's me! It's not a dream! Trust me, Christine! We're here to save you. But be careful! As soon as you hear the monster, let us know."

"Raoul! Raoul!"

She made him tell her again and again that she was not dreaming and that he had been able to come to her with the guidance of a devoted companion who knew the secret of Erik's house.

But the too-quick joy we had brought her was soon succeeded by great terror. She wanted Raoul to go away immediately. She was afraid Erik would discover his hiding place, for he would then kill the young man without hesitation. She told us in a few hurried words that Erik had gone completely mad with love and had decided to kill everyone and himself if she did not consent to become his wife in the eyes of the civil authorities and before the priest of the Madeleine church. He had given her till eleven o'clock the following night to think it over. That was the final deadline. She would then have to choose, as he had put it, between a wedding march and a funeral march.

And Erik had said these words which Christine did not entirely understand: "Yes or no; if it's no, everyone is dead and buried."

But I understood them quite well, because they corresponded with terrible precision to my appalling thoughts.

"Can you tell us where Erik is?" I asked.

She answered that he must have left the house.

"Can you make sure of it?"

"No. I'm tied up. I can't move."

When we heard this, Raoul and I could not hold back a cry of rage. Our safety, for all three of us, depended on Christine's freedom of movement. We had to get to her and rescue her!

"But where are you?" she asked. "There are only two doors in my bedroom—the Louis-Philippe room I told you about, Raoul. Erik goes in and out through one of the doors, but he's never opened the other one in front of me and he's forbidden me ever to go through it because, he says, it's the most dangerous of all doors: the door to the torture chamber."

"Christine, we're on the other side of that door!"

"Then you're in the torture chamber?"

"Yes, but we don't see the door."

"Oh, if only I could drag myself to it! I'd knock on it and then you'd know where it is."

"Does it have a lock?" I asked.

"Yes."

I thought, "It opens on the other side with a key, like an ordinary door, but on our side it opens with a spring and a counterweight, and they won't be easy to find."

"Mademoiselle," I said, "it's absolutely essential for you to open that door."

"But how?" asked the young woman's tearful voice.

We heard her straining to free herself from her bonds.

"We can escape only by guile," I said. "We must have the key to that door."

"I know where it is," said Christine, who seemed exhausted from the effort she had just made. "But I'm tied very tightly. . . . Oh, the scoundrel!"

She sobbed.

"Where is the key?" I asked, after telling Raoul to say nothing and let me take charge, because we did not have a moment to lose.

"In the bedroom, near the organ, with another bronze key that he also ordered me not to touch. They're both in a little leather bag that he calls 'the little bag of life and death.' Raoul! Raoul!

You must get away! Everything here is mysterious and terrible, and Erik is about to lose his last shred of sanity. And you're in the torture chamber! Leave the way you came! There must be a reason the room is called by that name!''

"Christine," said Raoul, "we'll either leave here together or die together!''

"It depends on us whether we get out of here safe and sound," I said. "But we must keep cool. Why did he tie you up, mademoiselle? You can't run away from his house and he knows it.''

"I tried to kill myself. On the evening when he brought me here unconscious, half chloroformed, he went away and left me for a time. According to him, he was going to see his banker! When he came back, he found my face bloody—I'd tried to kill myself by pounding my head against the walls.''

"Christine!" Raoul moaned, and he too sobbed.

"So he tied me up. I'm not allowed to die till eleven o'clock tomorrow night.''

That whole conversation through the wall was much more cautious and fitful than I have been able to indicate in transcribing it here. We often stopped in the middle of a sentence because we thought we had heard a creaking floorboard, a footstep, some sort of stirring. And she would try to reassure us: "No, it's not Erik. He left. He's really gone. I heard him open and close the passage through the wall by the lake.''

"Mademoiselle," I said, "the monster tied you and he'll untie you. You can make him do it by putting on the right kind of act. Don't forget that he loves you.''

"Oh, if only I *could* forget it!''

"Remember to smile at him. Beg him, tell him your bonds are hurting you.''

But she said to us, "Sh! I hear something in the wall by the lake. It's Erik! Go away! Go away! Go away!''

"We couldn't go away even if we wanted to," I said emphatically, to impress my words on her. "We can't leave! And we're in the torture chamber!''

"Quiet!''

The three of us fell silent.

Heavy footsteps slowly approached the wall, then stopped, and again the floor creaked.

Then there was a formidable sigh, followed by a cry of horror from Christine, and we heard Erik's voice.

"Forgive me for showing you such a face! I'm in a fine state, as you can see! It's the other man's fault. Why did he ring? When people pass by, do I ask them the time? He'll never again ask what time it is. It's the siren's fault. . . ." Another sigh, deeper, more formidable, coming from the abyss of a soul. "Why did you cry out, Christine?"

"Because I'm in pain, Erik."

"I thought I'd frightened you."

"Please untie me. I'll still be your prisoner."

"You'll try to kill yourself again."

"You gave me till eleven o'clock tomorrow night, Erik."

The footsteps again moved slowly across the floor.

"After all, since we'll die together, and since I'm in as much of a hurry as you are . . . Yes, I've had enough of this life too, you understand? Wait, don't move, I'll untie you. . . . You have only to say a word, 'No,' and it will all be over immediately, *for everyone*. You're right, you're right! Why wait till eleven o'clock tomorrow night? Ah, yes, because it would be nobler. . . . I've always been obsessed with decorum, with the grandiose—it's childish! We should think only of ourselves in this life, of our own death. Everything else is insignificant. You're looking at me because I'm wet? Ah, my darling, I shouldn't have gone out. It's raining cats and dogs. You know, Christine, I think I have hallucinations. The man who rang at the siren's door just now—I doubt that he's ringing any bells at the bottom of the lake—well, he looked like . . . There, turn around. Are you satisfied? You're untied. . . . My God! Your wrists, Christine! I hurt them, didn't I? That alone is enough to make me deserve death. Speaking of death, I must sing his requiem mass."

Hearing these words, I had a terrible presentiment. I too had once rung at the monster's door, without knowing it, of course; I must have set some warning current in motion. And I remembered the two arms that had come out of the jet-black water. Who was the poor man who had strayed to that shore?

The thought of him almost prevented me from rejoicing in Christine's stratagem, even when Raoul whispered these magic words in my ear: "She's untied!" Who? Who was "the other man," the one for whom we now heard a requiem mass being sung?

Ah, what sublime and furious singing! It shook the whole house by the lake and made the bowels of the earth quiver. Raoul and I had each put an ear against the mirror-wall to hear Christine's wily deception better, the deception she was practicing for our deliverance, but now we heard only the requiem mass. It was more like a mass for the damned. There, deep underground, it evoked demons dancing in an infernal circle.

I remember that the *Dies Irae* that Erik sang enveloped us like a storm. Yes, we had thunder and lightning around us. I had heard him sing before, of course; he had even gone so far as to make my stone human-headed bulls sing, on the walls of the Mazenderan palace. But I had never heard him sing like this, never! He sang like the god of thunder.

Then the organ and the voice stopped with such startling abruptness that Raoul and I drew back from the wall. And the voice, suddenly changed, transformed, distinctly grated out these metallic syllables:

"What have you done with my bag?"

24

The Tortures Begin

"WHAT HAVE YOU done with my bag?" the voice repeated furiously, and Christine must not have trembled any more than we did. "So that's why you wanted me to untie you! So you could take my bag!"

We heard rapid footsteps as Christine hurried back into the Louis-Philippe bedroom, as though to take refuge in front of our wall.

"Why are you running away?" said the angry voice that had followed her. "Give me back my bag! Don't you know it's the bag of life and death?"

"Listen to me, Erik," Christine said with a sigh. "Since we're going to live together, what difference does it make to you if I took that bag? Everything that's yours belongs to me."

She said this in such a trembling way that I felt pity for her. The poor girl must have had to use all her remaining strength to overcome her terror. But the monster could not be taken in by such childishly deceptive words spoken between chattering teeth.

"You know very well that there are two keys in the bag," he said. "What do you want to do with them?"

"I'd like to see that room I've never seen," she answered, "the one you've always kept hidden from me. It's feminine curiosity!" she added in a tone she intended to be playful, though it rang so false that it must have succeeded only in increasing Erik's mistrust.

"I don't like curious women," he retorted. "You'd better remember the story of Bluebeard and watch your step. Come, give me back my bag. Give it back! Leave that key alone, you inquisitive little girl!"

And he laughed while Christine cried out in pain. He had just taken back his bag from her.

Her cry of pain was answered by a cry of helpless rage from Raoul, unable to control himself any longer. I tried to silence him by putting my hand over his mouth, but I succeeded only partially.

"What was that?" asked the monster. "Did you hear it, Christine?"

"No, no, I didn't hear anything."

"It seemed to me that someone shouted."

"Shouted? Are you losing your mind, Erik? Who could have shouted, down here in this house? I cried out just now, because you hurt me, but I heard nothing."

"You say that in such a way . . . You're trembling, you're all upset. You're lying! Someone shouted! I heard it! There's someone in the torture chamber. Ah, now I understand!"

"There's no one there, Erik!"

"I understand!"

"No one!"

"Maybe your fiancé!"

"But I have no fiancé! You know that!"

Another unpleasant laugh.

"It's easy to find out. My darling little Christine, my love, there's no need to open the door to see what's happening in the torture chamber. Would you like to see? Would you? Listen: If someone's really in the chamber, you'll see light from the invisible window, up there, near the ceiling. All I have to do is pull back the black curtain and put out the light here. . . . There, the curtain is back. Now let's put out the light. You're not afraid of the dark when you're with your loving sweetheart, are you?"

"Yes, I'm afraid!" Christine said in a voice that sounded as if she were dying. "I *am* afraid of the dark! I'm not interested in that room anymore, not at all! You were always frightening me, as though I were a child, with that torture chamber. I was curious, it's true, but now it doesn't interest me anymore, not the slightest bit!"

And what I had feared more than anything else began *automatically*. All at once we were flooded with light. It was as if everything on our side of the wall had burst into flame. Raoul, who had not been expecting it, was so surprised that he staggered. And the angry voice thundered in the next room.

"I told you someone was there! Now do you see the window, the lighted window? Up there! The man on the other side of the wall doesn't see it, but you're going to climb up on the stepladder. That's why it's there. You've often asked me what it was used for. Well, now you know! It's used for looking through the window of the torture chamber, you inquisitive little girl!"

"What tortures . . . what tortures are there in that room? Erik! Erik! Tell me you're only trying to frighten me! Tell me that, if you love me! There are no tortures, are there? That's only a story for little children!"

"Come to the little window and see, my darling."

I do not know if Raoul, beside me, had heard Christine's faltering voice, for he was absorbed in the incredible spectacle that had just appeared before his bewildered eyes. As for me, I had already seen that spectacle too often through the little window in the Mazenderan palace, and I focused my attention entirely on what was said in the next room, hoping it would give me a reason to act or a basis for making a decision.

"Come and see, come and see through the little window. You'll tell me . . . Afterward you'll tell me what his nose looks like."

I heard the ladder being pushed against the wall.

"Climb up," said Erik. "No, on second thought I'll do it myself, my darling."

"No, *I'll* go and see. Let me!"

"Ah, my little darling, my little darling, you're so sweet! It's very nice of you to spare me that effort, at my age. You'll tell me what his nose looks like. If people realized how lucky they are to have a nose, a nose of their own, they'd never wander into the torture chamber!"

A moment later we distinctly heard these words spoken from overhead:

"There's no one in the chamber, my dear Erik."

"No one? Are you sure?"

"Yes, quite sure. No one."

"Well, so much the better. . . . What's the matter, Christine? Come, come, you're not going to faint, are you? Since there's no one . . . But how do you like the landscape?"

"Oh, I like it very much!"

"Good. You're feeling better. You *are* feeling better, aren't you? So much the better, you're feeling better. You mustn't become overexcited. But isn't this a strange house, where you can see landscapes like that?"

"Yes, it's like the waxworks in the Grévin Museum! But tell me, Erik . . . There are no tortures in there! Do you know you really frightened me?"

"Why, since there's no one there?"

"Are you the one who made that room, Erik? It's really very beautiful! You're a great artist!"

"Yes, I'm a great artist, in my own way."

"But tell me why you call that room the torture chamber."

"It's quite simple. First, what have you seen?"

"A forest."

"And what's in that forest?"

"Trees!"

"And what's in a tree?"

"Birds."

"Have you seen any birds?"

"No, I haven't."

"Then what have you seen? Think! You saw branches. And what's on one of the branches? A gallows! That's why I call my forest the torture chamber. You see, it's only a figure of speech. It's all a joke. I never express myself like other people. I don't do anything like others. But I'm tired, very tired. . . . I've had enough, do you hear? Enough of having a forest in my house, and a torture chamber! Enough of being lodged like a mountebank in a double-bottomed box! I've had enough, enough! I want to have a quiet apartment, with ordinary doors and windows, and a good wife in it, like everyone else! You ought to understand that, Christine, and I shouldn't have to keep repeating it to you! A wife like everyone else . . . I'd love her, and take her out for a walk on Sunday, and amuse her all through the week. Ah, you wouldn't be bored with me! I have more than one trick up my sleeve, not counting card tricks. Tell me, would you like me to show you some card tricks? It will at least help us to pass a few minutes while we wait for eleven o'clock tomorrow night. My little Christine, my little Christine . . . Are you listening to me? You won't reject me anymore, will you? You love me! No, you don't love me. But it doesn't matter: you *will* love me. Before, you couldn't look at my mask because you knew what was behind it; now you don't mind looking at it and you forget what's behind it, and you won't reject me anymore! People can get used to anything when they want to, when they're willing to try. Many young couples don't love each other before they're married, and adore each other afterward! Oh, I don't know what I'm saying. . . . But you'd have fun with me! There's no one like me, I swear it before God, who will join us together in marriage if you're sensible, there's no one like me, for example, when it comes to ventriloquism. I'm the world's greatest ventriloquist! You laugh? You don't believe me? Listen!''

I realized that the monster (who really was the world's greatest ventriloquist) was trying to divert Christine's attention from the torture chamber by submerging her in a torrent of words. It was a foolish attempt because she was thinking of nothing but us.

She repeated several times, in the sweetest, most fervently imploring tone she could put into her voice, ''Put out the light in the little window. Please, Erik, put out the light in the little window.'' For after hearing the monster talk so ominously about the light that had suddenly appeared in the little window, she understood that there had to be a reason for it.

One thing must have calmed her anxiety, for the moment: She had seen us alive and well on the other side of the wall, standing in that magnificent blaze of light. But her mind would have been more at ease if the light had been put out.

Erik began demonstrating his ventriloquism.

''Look,'' he said, ''I'll raise my mask a little—just a little. You see my lips, such as they are? They're not moving. My mouth, what passes for my mouth, is closed, and yet you hear my voice. I'm talking with my belly. It's perfectly natural, and it's called ventriloquism. It's well-known. Listen to my voice. Where do you want it to go? In your left ear? In your right ear? In the table? In the little ebony boxes on the mantelpiece? Ah, that surprises you! My voice is in the little boxes on the mantelpiece! Do you want it to be far away? Close? Loud? Shrill? Nasal? My voice moves everywhere, everywhere! Listen, my darling. It's in the little box on the right. Listen to what it says: 'Shall I turn the scorpion?' And now, presto! Listen to what it says in the little box on the left: 'Shall I turn the grasshopper?' And now, presto! It's in the little leather bag. What does it say? 'I'm the little bag of life and death.' And now, presto! It's in Carlotta's throat, deep in Carlotta's golden, crystal throat! What does it say? It says, 'I'm Mr. Toad and I sing, "I feel without—croak!—alarm with its melody—croak!' '' And now, presto! It's in a chair in the ghost's box, and it says, 'The way she's singing tonight, she'll bring down the chandelier!' And now, presto! Ah, ah, ah, where is Erik's voice? Listen, Christine, my darling, listen. It's behind the door of the torture chamber! And what do I say? I say, 'Woe to those who are lucky enough to have a nose, a real nose of their own, and who wander into the torture chamber!' Ah, ah, ah!''

The formidable ventriloquist's cursed voice was everywhere, everywhere! It came in through the little invisible window, and through the walls. It ran around us, between us. Erik was there, talking to us! We made a move as though to rush at him, but, swifter and more elusive than the resounding voice of an echo, Erik's voice had already leapt back to the other side of the wall.

Soon we could hear nothing more, for here is what happened:

Christine's voice: "Erik! Erik! You're tiring me with your voice. Stop, Erik! Don't you think it's hot in here?''

"Oh, yes,'' replied Erik's voice, "the heat is becoming unbearable.''

And again Christine's voice, gasping with anxiety: "What's this? The wall is hot! The wall is burning hot!''

"I'll tell you, Christine, my darling: it's because of the forest next door.''

"What do you mean? The forest . . .''

"Didn't you see that it's a forest in the Congo?''

And the monster's terrible laughter was so powerful that it drowned out Christine's entreaties. Raoul shouted and pounded on the walls like a madman. I could not restrain him. But we heard only the monster's laughter, and the monster himself must have heard only his laughter. Then came sounds of a rapid struggle, of a body falling to the floor and being dragged away, and of a door slammed shut. After that, there was nothing, nothing more around us but the torrid silence of midday in the heart of an African jungle.

25

"Barrels! Barrels! Any Barrels to Sell?"

(CONTINUATION OF THE PERSIAN'S STORY)

AS I HAVE already said, the room in which Raoul and I found ourselves was regularly hexagonal and its walls were completely covered with mirrors. Since then, notably at exhibitions, there have been rooms made in the same way and called "houses of mirages" or "palaces of illusions." But the invention belongs entirely to Erik. He built the first room of that kind before my eyes, at the time of the Rosy Hours of Mazenderan. A decorative design, such as a column, for example, was placed in the corners and this instantly produced a palace with countless columns, for, by the effect of the mirrors, the real room was augmented with six hexagonal rooms, each multiplied indefinitely. To amuse the little sultana, Erik had first made a room that could become "an innumerable temple"; but the little sultana had soon tired of such a childish illusion and he had then transformed his invention into a torture chamber. He replaced the architectural designs in the corners with a perfectly lifelike iron tree that had painted leaves. Why was it made of iron? Because it had to be strong enough to withstand all the attacks of the victim confined in the torture chamber. We will see how the scene thus obtained was twice transformed into two other successive scenes by means of the automatic rotation of the drums in the corners. These drums were divided into thirds; they fitted into the angles of the mirrors, and each of them bore a decorative design that appeared in sequence with others.

The walls of the torture chamber gave the victim no grip or foothold because, aside from the thoroughly resistant decorative design, they were covered only with mirrors so thick that they had nothing to fear from the rage of the poor wretch who was thrown into the room barefoot and empty-handed.

No furniture. The ceiling was luminous. An ingenious system of electric heating, which has since been imitated, made it possible to increase the temperature of the walls, and therefore of the air in the room, at will.

I have given the specific details of that natural invention that, with a few painted branches, produced the supernatural illusion of an equatorial forest under a blazing midday sun, so that no one can cast doubt on my present mental equilibrium or feel justified in saying, "That man has gone mad," or "That man is lying," or "That man takes us for fools."*

If I had simply written, "Having gone down into a cellar, we found ourselves in an equatorial forest under a blazing midday sun," I would have obtained a foolish effect of surprise, but I am not trying to obtain any effect; my purpose in writing these lines is to tell exactly what happened to Viscount Raoul de Chagny and me in the course of a terrible experience with which the French legal system was concerned for a time.

I will now resume my narrative where I left it.

When the ceiling and the forest around us became illuminated, Raoul was utterly dumbfounded. The appearance of that impenetrable forest, whose countless trunks and branches seemed to extend infinitely in all directions, plunged him into frightful consternation. He passed his hands over his forehead as though to drive away a nightmarish vision, and his eyes blinked as if he had just awakened and were having difficulty in returning to reality. For a moment he even forgot to listen!

As I have said, the appearance of the forest did not surprise me, so I listened for both of us to what was taking place in the next room. Finally my attention was especially attracted less by

*It is understandable that, at the time when the Persian was writing, he took so many precautions against incredulity, but they would be unnecessary nowadays, when everyone has been able to see such rooms.

the forest scene, on which my mind was not focused, than by the mirrors that produced it. Those mirrors were broken and scratched in places; despite their solidity, someone had been able to make star-shaped cracks in them. This proved to me beyond doubt that the torture chamber had been used before we came into it.

Some poor wretch, less barefoot and empty-handed than the condemned prisoners of the Rosy Hours of Mazenderan, must have fallen into that "deadly illusion" and furiously attacked those mirrors, which continued to reflect his death struggle in spite of their slight injuries. And the tree branch on which he had ended his torment was placed in such a way that, as he was about to die, he had had the final consolation of seeing a multitude of hanged men kicking convulsively with him.

Yes, Joseph Buquet had been there!

Were we going to die as he had done? I did not think so, because I knew that we still had a few hours left and that I could spend them more usefully than Joseph Buquet had been able to do. I had a thorough knowledge of most of Erik's "tricks," and if ever there had been a time to use it, it was now.

First, I gave up all thought of going back by way of the passage that had brought us into that cursed room or moving the inside stone that closed the passage. The reason was simple: I had no means of doing so. We had dropped into the torture chamber from too great a height; there was no furniture to help us reach the passage, the branch of the iron tree was useless to us, and it would have done no good for one of us to stand on the other's shoulders.

There was only one way out: the door that opened into the Louis-Philippe bedroom where Erik and Christine were. But while it was an ordinary door on Christine's side, it was absolutely invisible to us. We therefore had to try to open it without even knowing where it was, which was no ordinary task.

When I was quite sure there was no longer any hope for us from Christine's side, when I had heard the monster drag her out of the Louis-Philippe bedroom so that she would not interfere with our torment, I decided to begin looking for a way to open the door without delay.

But first I had to calm Raoul, who was already walking around in the illusory clearing like a madman, uttering inarticulate cries. The scraps of conversation between Christine and the monster that he had overheard in spite of his agitation had done much to drive him to distraction; if to that you add the magic forest and the heat that was beginning to make sweat stream down his temples, you will easily understand that he was becoming a bit overwrought.

Despite my urging, he had abandoned all caution. He paced aimlessly back and forth, sometimes rushing toward a nonexistent space, thinking he was going to enter a lane that would take him to the horizon, and then, after a few steps, banging his forehead against the reflection of the illusory forest. He would then shout, "Christine! Christine!" brandish his pistol, and call out to the monster at the top of his lungs, challenging the Angel of Music to a duel to the death and railing against his forest.

The torture was beginning to have its effect on a mind unprepared for it. I tried to combat it as much as possible by calmly reasoning with poor Raoul. I had him touch the mirrors, the iron tree, and the branches on the drums; I explained, according to the laws of optics, the luminous imagery that enveloped us, and I told him that we could not fall victim to it like ordinary ignorant people.

"We're in a room, a small room: that's what you must keep telling yourself. We'll get out of this room when we find its door, so let's look for it!"

And I promised him that if he let me act without distracting me with his shouts and frantic pacing, I would discover the secret of the door within an hour. He lay down on the floor, as if he were resting under the trees, and said he would wait till I found the door of the forest, since he had nothing better to do. And he added that he had a "magnificent view" from where he was lying. The torture was acting on him in spite of everything I had said.

Forgetting the forest, I began feeling all over a mirror panel, trying to find a weak point on which to press in order to make the door turn in accordance with Erik's system of pivoting doors and trapdoors. In some cases the weak point was a pea-sized spot on the mirror, behind which was the spring that needed to be released. I kept searching. I felt as high as my hands could reach. Erik's height was about the same as mine and I thought he must not have placed the spring beyond his own reach; that was merely a hypothesis, but it was my only hope. I had decided to examine all six mirror panels minutely and resolutely, then examine the floor with equal attention.

While I carefully felt the panels I tried not to waste a single minute because the heat was affecting me more and more and we were literally baking in that fiery forest.

I had been working in that way for half an hour, and had already finished with three panels, when, as bad luck would have it, I turned around on hearing an exclamation from Raoul.

"I'm stifling!" he said. "All those mirrors reflect the infernal heat back and forth! Will you find your spring soon? If you take much longer, we'll be roasted here!"

I was not sorry to hear him talk like that. He had not said a word about the forest and I hoped that his reason could hold out against the torture for quite a while longer. But he added:

"What consoles me is that the monster gave Christine till eleven o'clock tomorrow night: If we can't get out of here and save her, at least we'll have died for her! Erik's requiem mass can be for all of us!"

And he took a deep breath of hot air that nearly made him faint.

Since I did not have the same desperate reasons for accepting death as he did, I turned back to my panel after giving him a few words of encouragement, but while I was talking I had made the mistake of taking several steps, with the result that, in the confusing tangle of the illusory forest, I could not be sure I had come back to the same panel. I would have to choose a panel at random; I could not help showing my dismay and Raoul realized that I had to start over. This gave him another blow.

"We'll never get out of this forest!" he moaned.

His despair grew stronger, and the stronger it grew, the more it made him forget that he was dealing with mirrors, and he became increasingly convinced that he was in a real forest.

As for me, I resumed my groping search. I too was becoming feverish, because I found nothing, absolutely nothing. There was still the same silence in the next room. We were lost in the forest, with no way out, without a compass or a guide, without anything. I knew what lay in store for us if no one came to our rescue, or if I did not find the spring. But I searched for it in vain; I found only branches, beautiful branches that rose straight up in front of me or curved gracefully above my head. But they gave no shade! That was only natural, however, since we were in an equatorial forest with the sun directly overhead, a forest in the Congo. . . .

Several times, Raoul and I had taken off our coats and put them back on, feeling sometimes that they made us hotter and sometimes that they protected us from the heat.

My mind was still resisting, but his was completely "gone." He claimed he had been walking three days and nights in that forest without stopping, in search of Christine. Now and then he thought he saw her behind a tree trunk, or slipping through the branches, and he would call out to her in a beseeching tone that brought tears to my eyes.

"Christine! Christine! Why do you run away from me? Don't you love me? Aren't we engaged? Christine, stop! You can see how exhausted I am! Christine, take pity on me! I'm going to die in the forest, away from you. . . ."

Finally he said deliriously, "Oh, I'm so thirsty!"

I was thirsty too. My throat was burning. But, now squatting on the floor, I went on searching and searching for the spring of the invisible door, especially since our stay in the forest was becoming dangerous as evening approached. Shades of night were already beginning to envelop us. It had happened very quickly, as darkness falls in tropical lands, suddenly, with almost no twilight.

Night in an equatorial forest is always dangerous, especially when, like us, one has no way of making a fire to ward off ferocious animals. For a few moments I had interrupted my search for the spring and tried to break off some branches, intending to light them with my shaded lantern, but I too had bumped into a mirror, and that had reminded me in time that I was seeing only images of branches.

The heat had not subsided as daylight faded; on the contrary, it was now even hotter in the blue glow of the moon. I told Raoul to keep our pistols ready to fire and not to wander away from our camp, while I went on looking for my spring.

All at once we heard a lion roar from only a few paces away. The sound was almost deafening.

"He's not far," Raoul said softly. "Don't you see him? There, through the trees, in that thicket. . . . If he roars again, I'll shoot!"

The roaring came again, even louder than before. Raoul shot, but I do not think he hit the lion; he broke a mirror, as I saw next morning at dawn. We had evidently covered a good distance during the night, because we suddenly found ourselves at the

edge of a desert, a vast desert of sand and stones. It was really
not worth the trouble, coming out of the forest only to reach a
desert. I gave up and lay down beside Raoul, tired of looking for
springs that I could not find.

I told him I was greatly surprised that we had not had any
more unpleasant encounters during the night. After the lion,
there was usually the leopard, and sometimes the buzzing of
tsetse flies. Those effects were easily produced. While we were
resting before crossing the desert, I explained to Raoul that Erik
imitated the roar of a lion by means of a long, narrow drum with
one end open and the other covered by a taut piece of donkey
skin. Over that skin was a tightly stretched catgut string attached
at its center to another string of the same kind that passed through
the drum from top to bottom. Erik had only to rub that string
with a rosin-coated glove, and, depending on the way he rubbed,
he could perfectly imitate the voice of the lion or the leopard, or
even the buzzing of the tsetse fly.

The thought that Erik might be in the next room with his
ingenious devices made me decide to try to negotiate with him,
for we obviously had to give up the idea of taking him by
surprise. And by now he surely knew who was in the torture
chamber. I called him.

"Erik! Erik!"

I shouted as loudly as I could across the desert, but there was
no answer. All around us were the silence and the bare immen-
sity of the stony desert. What was going to become of us in that
terrible solitude?

We were actually beginning to die of heat, hunger, and thirst,
especially thirst. Finally I saw Raoul raise himself on one elbow
and point to the horizon. He had just discovered the oasis.

Yes, out there the desert gave way to the oasis, an oasis with
water, water as clear as a mirror, water that reflected the iron
tree. . . . Ah! It was the mirage scene, I recognized it immediately; it was the worst of all. No one had ever been able to resist
it, no one. I tried to cling to my reason and not expect water,
because I knew that if a victim of the torture chamber expected
water, the water in which the iron tree was reflected, and that if,
after expecting water, he came up against a mirror, there was
only one thing for him to do: hang himself from the iron tree.

"It's a mirage!" I said to Raoul. "Nothing but a mirage!

Don't think the water is real! It's only another trick with the mirrors!''

He angrily told me to leave him alone, with my mirror tricks, my springs, my pivoting doors, and my palace of mirages. I was either blind or crazy, he said, to think that the water flowing over there, among all those beautiful trees, was not real! And the desert was real! And so was the forest! There was no use trying to take him in: he had traveled all over the world.

He dragged himself along, saying, "Water! Water!"

His mouth was open as if he were drinking. And I too had my mouth open as if I were drinking, for we not only saw the water, we also heard it. We heard it flowing and splashing. Do you understand the word *splash?* It is a word that is heard with the tongue. The tongue comes out of the mouth to hear it better.

Then came the most unbearable torment: we heard rain and it was not raining. It was a diabolical invention. Yet I knew how Erik produced that effect too. He filled with little stones a very long and very narrow box partially obstructed on the inside by flat pieces of wood and metal placed at intervals all along its length. As they fell, the little stones collided with the obstructions and bounded from one to another, and the result was a sound exactly like the patter of a heavy rain.

You should have seen us with our tongues hanging out as we crawled toward the water splashing against the riverbank. Our eyes and ears were full of water, but our tongues were dry as dust.

When we reached the mirror, Raoul licked it and so did I. It was hot!

We rolled on the floor with a hoarse cry of despair. Raoul took the only pistol that was still loaded and aimed it at the side of his head. I looked at the Punjab lasso at my feet.

I knew why the iron tree had reappeared in that third scene. It was waiting for me! But as I looked at the Punjab lasso I saw something that made me start so violently that Raoul, who was already murmuring, "Good-bye, Christine," was stopped before he could kill himself.

I grabbed his arm and took the pistol away from him, then I crawled on my hands and knees to what I had seen.

Beside the Punjab lasso, in a groove in the floor, I had just discovered a black-headed nail whose use I knew.

At last I had found the spring! The spring that was going to open the door, and free us, and put Erik in our hands!

I touched the nail and turned to Raoul with a broad smile. The black-headed nail yielded to my pressure. And then . . . And then it was not a door that opened in the wall, but a trapdoor that opened in the floor.

Cool air immediately came to us from the opening. We leaned over that square of darkness as if it were a clear spring. With our chins in the cool shade, we drank it in.

And we bent lower and lower over the trapdoor. What could be in that hole, in that cellar whose door had just opened mysteriously in the floor? Maybe there was water in it, water to drink. . . .

I put my arm into the shadows and felt a stone, then another: a staircase, a dark staircase leading down into the cellar. Raoul was ready to plunge into the hole. Even if we found no water down there, we could at least escape from the radiant embrace of those abominable mirrors. But I stopped him because I feared another of the monster's tricks. With my shaded lantern open, I went down first.

The winding staircase took me into deeper darkness. How wonderfully cool were the stairs and the darkness! That coolness must have come less from the ventilation system that Erik had necessarily built than from the coolness of the earth itself, which was no doubt saturated with water at the level we had reached. And the lake was probably not far away.

We soon came to the bottom of the stairs. Our eyes were beginning to adjust to the darkness and distinguish shapes around us. Round shapes. I shone the light of my lantern on them.

Barrels! We were evidently in the cellar where Erik kept his wine, and maybe his drinking water! I knew he was very fond of good wine. Ah, there was plenty to drink here!

Raoul caressed the round shapes and repeated tirelessly, "Barrels! Barrels! So many barrels!"

There were indeed quite a number of them, lined up in two equal rows. We were between the rows. They were small barrels and I assumed that Erik had chosen them in that size to make them easier to carry into the house by the lake.

We examined them one after another, looking to see if one of them might have been tapped. But they were all tightly closed.

After half raising one to make sure it was full, we knelt, and with the blade of the little knife I had on me, I set about removing the stopper.

Just then I heard a kind of monotonous chant, seeming to come from far away, whose rhythm I knew well because I had often heard it in the streets of Paris:

"Barrels! Barrels! Any barrels to sell?"

My hand was immobilized on the stopper. Raoul had also heard the chant.

"That's odd!" he said. "It's as if the barrel were chanting!"

The chant resumed, fainter this time.

"Oh!" Raoul exclaimed. "I could swear the chant was moving away *inside* the barrel!"

We stood up and went to look behind the barrel.

"It *is* inside!" said Raoul. "It's inside!"

But we heard nothing more. We were reduced to supposing that we had been deluded by the bad condition of our senses.

We went back to the task of opening the barrel. Raoul put his clasped hands under it and, with one last effort, I pried out the stopper.

"What's this?" cried Raoul. "It's not water!"

He put his two full hands close to my lantern. I leaned over them and immediately threw the lantern away from us so violently that it broke and went out—and was lost to us.

What I had just seen in Raoul's hands was gunpowder!

26

The Scorpion or the Grasshopper?

AND SO, IN going down into Erik's cellar, I had reached the darkest depths of my appalling thoughts. He had not been bluffing with his vague threats against "many members of the human race"! Feeling cut off from other human beings, he had built himself an underground lair and he was determined to blow up everything, including himself, if aboveground people came to hunt him down in the retreat to which he had withdrawn with his monstrous ugliness.

Our discovery threw us into a state of agitation that made us forget our past suffering and present distress. Even though we had been on the verge of suicide a short time before, only now did we know the full, terrifying truth about our situation. Now we understood what Erik had said to Christine, and what he had meant by these abominable words: "Yes or no; if it's no, everyone is dead and buried." Yes, buried under the wreckage of the great Paris Opera! A more frightful crime could not have been imagined by someone who wanted to make his exit from the world in a climax of horror.

He had made preparations for the catastrophe in the tranquillity of his retreat. It would serve to avenge the amorous frustrations of the most heinous monster who ever walked the earth. He had told Christine she must decide by eleven o'clock the following night, and he had chosen his time well. There would be many people, "many members of the human race," at the festive gathering in the resplendent upper part of the Opera. What finer assembly could he desire for the occasion of his death? He would go down into his grave with the loveliest and most lavishly bejeweled shoulders in the world. Eleven o'clock tomorrow night! We would all be blown up in the middle of the performance if Christine said no. Eleven o'clock tomorrow night! And how could she fail to say no? Surely she would rather be married to death itself than to that living corpse, and she could not know that her refusal would bring instant annihilation to "many members of the human race." Eleven o'clock tomorrow night!

And as we groped through the darkness, fleeing from the gunpowder and trying to find the stone stairs—for, above us, the trapdoor opening into the torture chamber had also become dark—we repeated to ourselves, "Eleven o'clock tomorrow night!"

Finally I found the staircase, but suddenly I stopped on the first step because a terrible thought had just set my brain afire: *"What time is it?"*

Ah, what time was it? What time? Maybe eleven o'clock tomorrow night was now, or in only a few moments! Who could tell us the time? It seemed to me that we had been imprisoned in that hell for days and days, for years, since the beginning of the world. . . . Maybe everything was about to blow up at any second! Ah, a noise, a cracking sound!

"Did you hear that?" I asked Raoul. "There, over there in that corner! My God! It sounds like some sort of mechanism! There it is again! If only we had a light! Maybe it's the mechanism that's going to make everything blow up. Don't you hear that cracking sound? Are you deaf?"

Raoul and I began shouting like madmen. Spurred by fear, we ran up the stairs, stumbling as we went. Maybe the trapdoor above us was closed, maybe that was why it was so dark where we were. We were frantic to get out of that darkness, even if it meant going back to the deadly light of the torture chamber.

When we reached the top of the stairs we found that the trapdoor was not closed, but it was now as dark in the torture chamber as in Erik's cellar. We came up through the trapdoor and crawled on the floor of the torture chamber, the floor that separated us from that powder magazine. What time was it? We shouted, we called. Raoul cried out with all his reviving strength, "Christine! Christine!" And I called Erik, I reminded him that I had saved his life. But nothing answered either of us, nothing but our own despair and madness.

What time was it? "Eleven o'clock tomorrow night!" We discussed the time, we tried to decide how long we had been there, but we were incapable of reasoning. If only we could see a watch with moving hands! My watch had long since stopped, but Raoul's was still running. He told me that he had wound it while he was dressing for the evening, before coming to the Opera. From that we tried to draw a conclusion that would let us hope that we had not yet reached the fateful minute.

I had vainly tried to close the trapdoor. The slightest sound that came through its opening threw us into painful anxiety. What time was it? Neither of us had a match. But we had to know. . . . Raoul had the idea of breaking the glass of his watch and feeling its hands. There was a silence while he questioned the hands with his fingertips, after using the ring of the watch to determine where the top of its dial was. From the position of its hands he judged that it might be exactly eleven o'clock.

But maybe it was not the eleven o'clock that we feared. Maybe we still had twelve hours ahead of us.

"Quiet!" I said.

It seemed to me that I had heard footsteps in the next room.

I was not mistaken. I heard a sound of doors, followed by rapid footsteps. Someone tapped on the wall. Christine's voice:

"Raoul! Raoul!"

All three of us began talking through the wall. Christine sobbed. She had not known if she would ever find Raoul alive. The monster had been terrible, it seemed. He had raved constantly while he waited for her to say yes and she refused to say it. She promised to say it, however, if he would take her into the torture chamber. But he had stubbornly refused, making dire threats against all members of the human race. Finally, after hours and hours of that hell, he had just gone out, leaving her alone to think over her decision one last time.

Hours and hours? What time was it?

"What time is it, Christine?"

"Eleven o'clock, or rather five minutes to eleven."

"But which eleven o'clock?"

"The eleven o'clock that will decide life or death," Christine said in a voice hoarse with emotion. "He told me that again when he left. He's terrifying! He talked like a maniac, and he took off his mask, and fire came from his golden eyes! And he kept laughing. He was laughing like a drunk demon when he said to me, 'Five minutes! I'll leave you alone because of your well-known modesty. I don't want to make you blush in front of me, like a shy bride, when you say yes. That's not something a gentleman would do!' Yes, he was like a drunk demon! He reached into the little bag of life and death and said, 'Here's the little bronze key that opens the ebony boxes on the mantelpiece of the Louis-Philippe bedroom. You'll find a scorpion in one box and a grasshopper in the other, both very well imitated in Japanese bronze. They're animals that say yes and no. If you turn the scorpion on its pivot, to make it face in the opposite direction, I'll know that your answer is yes when I come back into the Louis-Philippe room, the engagement room. If you turn the grasshopper, I'll know that your answer is no when I come back into the Louis-Philippe room, the room of death!' And again he laughed like a drunk demon. I begged him on my knees to give me the key to the torture chamber and promised that if he did, I'd be his wife forever. But he said that key would never be needed again, and he was going to throw it into the lake! Then, still laughing like a drunk demon, he left me after saying he would let me be alone for five minutes because a gentleman knew how to spare a woman's modesty. Oh, yes, he also said, 'The grasshopper! Be careful of the grasshopper! Grasshoppers jump, and they jump *very high!*' "

I have here used coherent sentences in trying to reproduce the meaning of Christine's broken, almost delirious speech. She, too, during those twenty-four hours, must have reached the extremes of human suffering, and perhaps she had suffered even more than we had. She kept interrupting herself and us to cry out, "Raoul! Are you in pain?" And she felt the wall, which was now cold, and asked why it had been so hot.

The five minutes were passing, and the scorpion and the grasshopper were scratching my poor, exhausted brain. But I still had enough lucidity to realize that if the grasshopper was turned it would jump—that is, it would blow up the Opera and all the "members of the human race" inside it. I had no doubt that the grasshopper controlled an electric current that could set off the powder magazine.

Now that he had heard Christine's voice again, Raoul's mind seemed to have regained all its strength and clarity. He quickly told her about the danger threatening us and the whole Opera. She had to turn the scorpion immediately. Since it corresponded to the "yes" that Erik wanted so fervently, turning it would surely prevent the catastrophe from happening.

"Go, my darling, go," said Raoul.

There was a silence.

"Christine," I called out, "where are you?"

"In front of the scorpion."

"Don't touch it!"

It had occurred to me, for I knew my Erik, that he might have deceived Christine again: maybe it was the scorpion that would blow up the Opera. For why was he not there? The five minutes had long since passed, and he had still not come back. Probably he had gone to a safe place and was now waiting for the mighty explosion. He had nothing more to wait for, since he could not really hope that Christine would ever consent to be his voluntary prey. Why had he not come back?

"Don't touch the scorpion!"

"He's coming!" cried Christine. "I hear him!"

He was indeed coming. We heard his footsteps approach the Louis-Philippe bedroom, then stop. He had rejoined Christine, without saying anything.

"Erik!" I said loudly. "It's me! Do you recognize me?"

"You two didn't die in there?" he answered in an extraordinarily peaceful tone. "Well, then, try not to cause any trouble."

At this point I tried to interrupt him, but he said so coldly that I stood frozen behind my wall, "Not a word, daroga, or I'll blow everything up." And he continued, "The honor goes to Mademoiselle Daae. She didn't touch the scorpion"—how calmly he spoke!—"and she didn't touch the grasshopper"—with such frightening composure!—"but it's not yet too late. Here, I'll open the little ebony boxes, without a key, because I'm the lover of trapdoors and I open and close anything I want, as I please. Look into the little ebony boxes, mademoiselle, and see the pretty little animals. They're realistically made, aren't they? And they seem so harmless! But you can't judge a book by its cover." All this was said in a steady, toneless voice. "If you turn the grasshopper, mademoiselle, we'll all be blown up. Under us is enough gunpowder to destroy a whole Paris neighborhood. If you turn the scorpion, all that powder will be flooded. In honor of our wedding, mademoiselle, you're going to give a fine present to the several hundred Parisians who are now applauding a poor masterpiece by Meyerbeer. You're going to give them the gift of life, because, with your pretty hands"—how weary his voice was!—"you're going to turn the scorpion. And the wedding bells will ring for us!" A silence, then: "If in two minutes you haven't turned the scorpion—I have a watch that runs very well—I will turn the grasshopper. And remember that grasshoppers jump *very high!*"

The silence resumed, more alarming than all the other alarming silences. I knew that when Erik spoke in that calm, peaceful, weary voice it meant he was at the end of his rope, capable of either the most titanic crime or the most ardent devotion, and that if a single word displeased him, it could set off a storm.

Having realized that there was nothing left to do but pray, Raoul was on his knees, praying. As for me, my heart was pounding so violently that I put my hand over it, afraid it might burst. We were both horribly aware of what was taking place in Christine's panic-stricken mind during those final seconds; we understood why she hesitated to turn the scorpion. What if it were the scorpion that would make everything blow up? What if Erik had decided to make us all die with him?

Finally we heard his voice, now angelically soft:

"The two minutes have passed. Good-bye, mademoiselle. Jump, grasshopper!"

"Erik!" cried Christine, who must have seized his hand. "Will you swear to me, you monster, will you swear by your infernal love that the scorpion is the one to turn?"

"Yes, it's the one that will send us to heaven."

"Oh! You mean it will kill us?"

"Of course not, innocent child! I mean it will send us to the heaven of our marriage. The scorpion opens the ball. . . .

Enough! You don't want the scorpion? Then I'll turn the grasshopper.''

"Erik!"

"Enough!''

I had joined my cries to Christine's. Raoul, still on his knees, continued to pray.

"Erik, I've turned the scorpion!''

What a second we went through! Waiting! Waiting to be blown to bits in the midst of thunder and ruins! We felt things cracking in the abyss beneath our feet, things that might be the beginning of a climax of horror. Through the trapdoor open in the darkness, a black maw in the black night, we heard a disquieting hiss, like the first sound of a fuse, faint at first, then a little louder, then very loud.

But listen, listen! And hold both hands over your pounding heart, ready to be blown up with many members of the human race!

It was not the hiss of fire. More like rushing water. . . .

To the trapdoor! Listen! Listen!

It was now a gurgling sound.

To the trapdoor! To the trapdoor! What coolness! Cool water! Cool water!

Our thirst, which had left when terror came, returned stronger than ever with the sound of water.

Water! Water! Rising water!

It was rising in Erik's cellar, above the barrels, all the barrels of gunpowder. (Barrels! Barrels! Any barrels to sell?) Water! We went down to meet it with our throats ablaze. It came up to our chins, to our mouths. And we drank in the cellar, from the cellar, as from a glass.

We came back up the stairs in the black night, step by step; we had gone down to meet the water and now we were coming up with it.

All that gunpowder wasted, drowned! A job well done! There was no stinting on water in the house by the lake! If it went on like that, the whole lake would come into the cellar.

We did not know where it would stop. We were out of the cellar and the water was still rising.

And it came out of the cellar, and began spreading over the floor. If it went on like that, the whole house by the lake would be flooded. The floor of the torture chamber was itself a little lake in which our feet splashed. There was already more than enough water! Erik would have to turn it off.

"Erik! Erik! There's enough water for the gunpowder! Turn it off! Turn the scorpion!"

But Erik did not answer. We heard nothing but the rising water. It was already up to the middle of our calves.

"Christine! Christine!" Raoul shouted. "The water is rising! It's up to our knees!"

But Christine did not answer. We heard nothing but the rising water.

Nothing, nothing from the next room! No one! No one to turn off the water! No one to turn the scorpion!

We were alone in the dark, with the dark water gripping us, climbing, chilling us. Erik! Erik! Christine! Christine!

We lost our footing and the water carried us with it in its powerful swirling motion. We were thrown against the dark mirrors and they seemed to shove us away, and our throats wailed above the churning water.

Were we going to die there, drowned in the torture chamber? I had never seen that happen to anyone. Erik had never shown such a thing to me through the little invisible window in the time of the Rosy Hours of Mazenderan.

"Erik! Erik! I saved your life! Remember! You were doomed! You were going to die! I opened the gates of life to you! Erik!"

We were whirling in the water like pieces of wreckage.

Suddenly my wildly groping hands seized the trunk of the iron tree. I called to Raoul and soon we were both clinging to the branch of the iron tree.

The water was still rising.

Try to remember! How much space is there between the branch of the iron tree and the domed ceiling of the torture chamber? Try to remember! After all, maybe the water will stop. It has to find its own level. Yes, I think it is stopping. . . . No! No! It's horrible! We have to swim! Swim!

Our arms became entangled as we swam. We choked, we struggled in the dark water, it was hard for us to breathe the dark air above the dark water. The air rushed away from us, we could hear it escaping through some sort of ventilation system. We had to go on whirling till we could find the air vent and press our mouths against it. But my strength was abandoning me. I clutched at the walls, the glass walls, and my desperate fingers slipped across them. We were still whirling, but now we were beginning to sink. One last effort! One last cry!

"Erik! Christine!"

A gurgling sound in our ears. Beneath the surface of the dark water, a gurgling in our ears. And just before I lost consciousness it seemed to me that I heard, through the gurgling, "Barrels! Barrels! Any barrels to sell?"

27

End of the Ghost's Love Story

WE HAVE NOW come to the end of the written account that the Persian gave me.

Despite the horror of a situation in which death seemed certain, Raoul de Chagny and his companion were saved by Christine Daaé's sublime devotion. The rest of the story was told to me by the Persian himself.

When I went to see him, he was still living in his little apartment on the Rue de Rivoli, opposite the Tuileries. He was very sick and it took nothing less than all my ardor as a reporter-historian in the service of truth to make him consent to relive his incredible experience with me. His faithful old servant Darius was still with him, and it was he who led me to him. The Persian received me beside a window overlooking the Tuileries gardens. He sat in a big armchair, and as he tried to hold himself erect I could see that he had once been a handsome, well-built man. He still had his magnificent eyes, but his poor face looked very tired. His head, usually covered with an astrakhan hat, had been shaved. He wore a loose, simple coat and unconsciously amused himself by twiddling his thumbs inside its sleeves. But his mind had remained quite clear.

He could not recall the horrors of the past without being gripped by a certain agitation, and I had to extract the end of that strange story from him in bits and pieces. Sometimes I had to plead with him a long time before he would answer my questions, and sometimes, stimulated by his memories, he would spontaneously evoke, with striking vividness, the hideous image

257

of Erik, and the terrible hours that he and Raoul de Chagny had gone through in the house by the lake. I can still see the way he quivered when he described his awakening in the disquieting shadows of the Louis-Philippe bedroom after losing consciousness in the water.

And here is the end of that terrible story, as he told it to me to complete the written account he had been kind enough to give me.

When he opened his eyes, he found himself lying on a bed. Raoul lay on a sofa beside the mirror wardrobe. An angel and a demon were watching over them.

After the mirages and illusions of the torture chamber, the precise, middle-class details of that quiet little room seemed to have been invented for the purpose of bewildering anyone rash enough to have ventured into Erik's domain of waking nightmares. The curved bed, the waxed mahogany chairs, the dresser with brass fittings, the little crocheted antimacassars carefully placed on the backs of the armchairs, the clock, the harmless-looking little boxes on either end of the mantelpiece, the shelves displaying seashells, red pincushions, mother-of-pearl boats, and an enormous ostrich egg, the shaded lamp that stood on a pedestal table, discreetly lighting the whole scene—all those furnishings, with their touchingly homey ugliness, so peaceful and reasonable, at the bottom of the Opera cellars, disconcerted the mind more than all the fantastic events that had just taken place.

And in that tidy, cozy, old-fashioned setting, the figure of the masked man seemed all the more formidable. He leaned down to the Persian's ear and said softly, "Are you feeling better, daroga? You're looking at my furniture? It's all I have left from my poor, miserable mother."

He said other things that the Persian did not recall, but he remembered clearly—and this seemed strange to him—that during all the time he spent in the antiquated Louis-Philippe room, Christine did not say a word. She moved noiselessly, like a nun who had taken a vow of silence, and occasionally brought a cup of hot tonic or tea, which Erik would take from her and give to the Persian. Raoul, meanwhile, still slept.

As he poured a little rum into the Persian's cup and nodded toward Raoul on the sofa, Erik said, "He regained consciousness long before we knew if you were going to live, daroga. He's asleep now. We mustn't wake him."

When Erik left the room for a short time, the Persian raised himself on one elbow, looked around, and saw Christine's white figure seated beside the fireplace. He called her name and spoke to her but, still very weak, he fell back onto the pillow. She came to him and put her hand on his forehead, then walked away. And he remembered that as she walked away she did not even glance at Raoul, who, it is true, was sleeping peacefully. She went back and sat down beside the fireplace, still as silent as a nun who had taken a vow of silence.

Erik returned with some little bottles that he put on the mantelpiece. After sitting down at the Persian's bedside and feeling his pulse, he said to him, softly again, so as not to wake Raoul, "You're both safe now, and I'll soon take you aboveground, to please my wife."

He then stood up and left again without any further explanation.

The Persian looked at Christine's calm profile in the lamplight. She was reading a little gilt-edged book of a format often used for religious works; *The Imitation of Christ*, for example, appears in such editions. The Persian could still hear the natural tone in which Erik had said, "to please my wife."

He gently called Christine again, but evidently she was deeply engrossed in her book, because she did not hear him.

Erik came back and gave the Persian a potion to drink, after advising him to say nothing more to "his wife" or anyone else, because it could be very dangerous to everyone's health.

After that, the Persian remembered seeing Erik's black figure and Christine's white one gliding silently across the room and leaning over him and Raoul. He was still very weak, and the slightest sound—the door of the mirror wardrobe squeaking when it opened, for example—gave him a headache. Finally he slept, like Raoul.

This time he awoke in his own bedroom, tended by his faithful Darius, who told him that he had been found the night before outside the door of his apartment, where he had been brought by someone who rang the doorbell before going away.

As soon as he had regained his strength and lucidity, he sent Darius to ask about Raoul at the home of his brother, Count Philippe. He learned that Raoul had not been seen and that Philippe was dead. His body had been found on the shore of the lake under the Opera, in the direction of the Rue Scribe. The

Persian recalled the requiem mass he had heard through the wall of the torture chamber, and he had no doubt about the murder and the murderer. Knowing Erik as he did, he could all too easily reconstruct the tragedy. Believing that his brother had eloped with Christine, Philippe had gone off in pursuit of them on the road to Brussels, where he knew that everything had been prepared for the elopement. After failing to find them, he had come back to the Opera, recalled the strange things his brother had told him about his fantastic rival, and learned that Raoul had tried to go into the cellars of the Opera and then disappeared, leaving his hat in Christine's dressing room, beside a pistol box. Convinced that Raoul had gone mad, Philippe had also plunged into that infernal underground labyrinth. To the Persian, this was enough to explain why Philippe's corpse had been found on the shore of the lake, where the song of the siren, Erik's siren, the custodian of the Lake of the Dead, kept watch.

And so the Persian did not hesitate. Appalled by that new crime and distressed at not knowing what had happened to Raoul and Christine, he decided to tell everything to the police.

An examining magistrate named Faure had been placed in charge of the investigation. The Persian went to see him. It is easy to imagine how his testimony was received by a man like Faure, who had a shallow, skeptical, pedestrian mind (I write what I think) and was not at all prepared to hear such things. The Persian was treated like a lunatic.

Having no hope of ever being able to obtain a hearing, he began to write. Since the judicial system wanted no part of his testimony, maybe the press would take it up. One evening, when he had just finished writing the last line of the account that I have faithfully presented here, his servant Darius announced a visitor who would not give his name or show his face, and had said that he would not leave until he had spoken to the daroga.

Immediately guessing the identity of that singular visitor, the Persian told Darius to show him in without delay.

He was not mistaken. It was the ghost. It was Erik.

He seemed extremely weak and leaned against the wall as if he were afraid of falling. He took off his hat, revealing a forehead pale as a sheet. The rest of his face was hidden by his mask.

The Persian stood in front of him.

"After murdering Count Philippe de Chagny, what did you do with his brother and Christine Daae?"

At the terrible accusation contained in this question, Erik staggered, went to an armchair in silence, and sank into it with a deep sigh. Then he spoke in small clusters of words, gasping for breath.

"Daroga, don't talk to me . . . about Count Philippe. He was . . . already dead when I . . . left my house. He was . . . already dead when the siren sang. It was . . . an accident, a . . . sad, pitifully sad, accident. He'd . . . fallen clumsily . . . and simply and naturally . . . into the lake."

"You're lying!" cried the Persian.

Erik bowed his head and said, "I didn't come here to . . . talk about Count Philippe . . . but to tell you that . . . I'm about to die."

"Where are Raoul de Chagny and Christine Daae?"

"I'm about to die."

"Raoul de Chagny and Christine Daae?"

"I'm about to die . . . of love, daroga . . . of love. That's how it is. I . . . I loved her so much! And I still love her, daroga, since I'm dying of it . . . as I said. If you knew how beautiful she was when she let me kiss her *alive*, because she'd sworn on her eternal salvation . . . It was the first time—you hear, daroga, the first time!—that I'd ever kissed a woman. Yes, alive, I kissed her alive, and she was as beautiful as a dead woman!"

Standing close to Erik, the Persian dared to take hold of his arm and shake it.

"Tell me if she's dead or alive!"

"Why are you shaking me like that?" Erik said with an effort. "I'm telling you that I'm the one who's about to die. . . . Yes, I kissed her alive."

"And now she's dead?"

"Yes, I kissed her on the forehead, and she didn't move her forehead away from my lips! Ah, she's an honorable girl! As for being dead, I don't think so, though it no longer concerns me. . . . No, no, she's not dead! And I'd better not hear that anyone has touched a single hair on her head! She's a good and honorable girl, and she saved your life, daroga, at a time when your chance of surviving seemed very close to zero. Actually, no one was paying any attention to you. Why were you there with that young man? You were going to die just because you hap-

pened to be with him. She begged me to save her young man,
but I told her that because she'd turned the scorpion I was now
her fiancé, by her own choice, and that she didn't need two
fiancés, which was quite true. As for you, you no longer existed;
you were going to die because you were with the other fiancé, as
I've already said.

"But—listen closely, daroga—while the two of you were
yelling like maniacs because of the water, Christine came to me
with her big blue eyes wide open and swore to me, on her eternal
salvation, that she consented to be *my living wife!* Till then, in
the depths of her eyes, I'd always seen her as my dead wife; this
was the first time I'd ever seen her as my living wife. She meant
what she said, since she'd sworn it on her eternal salvation. She
wouldn't kill herself. We made our bargain. Half a minute later,
all the water had flowed back into the lake and I was surprised to
find you still alive, because I'd thought you were done for! And
so . . . Well, the agreement called for me to take you both
aboveground. When I'd cleared the Louis-Philippe room of you,
I came back to it, alone."

"What have you done with Raoul de Chagny?" asked the
Persian.

"Well, you see . . . I didn't want to take him aboveground
immediately. He was a hostage. But I couldn't keep him in the
house by the lake, because of Christine, so I locked him up
comfortably, properly chained (the Mazenderan perfume had
made him limp as a rag), in the Communards' dungeon, which is
in the most remote and deserted part of the Opera, below the
fifth cellar, where no one ever goes and a prisoner can never
make himself heard. My mind was at ease and I went back to
Christine. She was waiting for me."

It seems that at this point in his story Erik stood up so gravely
that the Persian, who had sat down in his armchair, had to stand
up also, as though obeying the same impulse as Erik, feeling that
it was impossible to remain seated at such a solemn moment, and
he even took off his astrakhan hat (as he told me himself) in spite
of his close-cropped hair.

"Yes, she was waiting for me," Erik went on, trembling like
a leaf from fervent emotion, "she was waiting, standing erect,
alive, like a real, living fiancée, and she'd sworn on her eternal
salvation. . . . And when I came toward her, shyer than a little
child, she didn't turn away. No, no, she stayed . . . she waited

for me. . . . And I even believe, daroga, that she moved her forehead toward me a little—not much, but a little, like a living fiancée. And . . . and I . . . kissed her! *I* kissed her, *I!* And she didn't die! And after I'd kissed her like that, on the forehead, she went on standing there, close to me, as if it were perfectly natural. . . . Oh, daroga, it's so good to kiss someone! You can't know how I felt, but I . . . I . . . My mother, my poor, miserable mother would never let me kiss her. She would throw my mask to me and run away. . . . And no woman . . . ever . . . Oh, I . . . I was so happy . . . so happy that I cried. I fell at her feet, still crying. I kissed her feet . . . her little feet . . . crying. You're crying too, daroga, and so was she. . . . The angel cried!''

As he told of these things, Erik sobbed, and the Persian could not hold back his tears before that masked man who, with his shoulders shaking and his hands on his chest, moaned sometimes with sorrow and sometimes with a tenderness that seemed to melt his heart.

"Oh, daroga, I felt her tears dropping onto my forehead—*my* forehead! They were warm, they were sweet, they flowed everywhere under my mask. *Her* tears! They mingled with my own tears in my eyes, they even flowed into my mouth. . . . Ah, her tears, on me! Listen, daroga, listen to what I did. . . . I took off my mask to keep from losing any of her tears, and she didn't run away! She didn't die! She stayed alive, crying . . . over me . . . with me. . . . We cried together! God in heaven, you gave me all the happiness in the world!"

And Erik collapsed, moaning, into his armchair.

"Oh, I'm not going to die yet, not at this moment," he said to the Persian. "But let me cry!"

And a short time later he continued:

"Listen, daroga, listen to this. . . . While I was at her feet, I heard her say, 'Poor, unhappy Erik!' *and she took my hand!* From then on . . . You understand . . . I was only a poor dog ready to die for her, believe me, daroga!

"I had a ring in my hand, a gold ring that I'd given her; she'd lost it and I'd found it. It was . . . a wedding ring. I slipped it into her little hand and said, 'Here, take this, take it for yourself . . . and him. . . . It will be my wedding gift, a gift from "poor, unhappy Erik." I know you love your young man. . . . You don't have to cry anymore.' She gently asked me what I meant. I told her—and she immediately knew I'd become a poor dog ready to die for her—that she could marry her young man whenever she pleased, because she'd cried with me. . . . Ah, daroga, you can imagine . . . When I told her that, it was as if I were calmly cutting my heart to pieces. . . . But she'd cried with me, and she'd said, 'Poor, unhappy Erik!' ''

Erik's emotion was so strong that he had to warn the Persian not to look at him because he was choking and had to take off his mask. The Persian told me that he then went to the window and opened it, with his heart full of pity, but that he was careful to look at the tops of the trees in the Tuileries to avoid seeing the monster's face.

"I went to the young man and freed him," Erik continued, "and told him to follow me to Christine. They kissed in front of me, in the Louis-Philippe bedroom. . . . Christine had my ring. . . . I made her swear that when I was dead she would come one night, by way of the lake in the direction of the Rue Scribe, and bury me in secret with the gold ring she'd worn till then. I told her how she could find my body and what she should do with it. Then *she* kissed *me* for the first time, here, on the forehead—don't look, daroga—on *my* forehead! Don't look, daroga. And they left together. . . . Christine wasn't crying anymore, only I was crying. . . . Ah, daroga, daroga, if she keeps her promise, she'll come back soon!''

And Erik fell silent. The Persian asked him no questions. He was completely reassured about the fate of Raoul and Christine; after hearing the weeping Erik that night, no member of the human race could have doubted his word.

He put on his mask again and summoned up his strength to leave the Persian. He told him that, to thank him for the kindness he had once shown him, when he felt death approaching he would send him what was dearest to him in the world: all the papers that Christine had written at various times in the course of the events I have described (she had written them for Raoul and left them with Erik) and a few objects that had belonged to her: two handkerchiefs, a pair of gloves, and a shoe ribbon. In answer to a question from the Persian, Erik told him that as soon as the two young people had found themselves free, they had decided to go and find a priest to marry them in some solitary place where they could hide their happiness, and that they had "taken a northbound train" to go there. And finally Erik told the Persian that he was counting on him to announce his death to the two young people as soon as he received the promised relics and papers. To do so, he was to place a notice in the obituary section of the newspaper *L'Epoque*.

And that was all.

The Persian showed Erik to the door of his apartment and Darius accompanied him to the sidewalk, supporting him as he walked. A cab was waiting. Erik got into it. The Persian, standing at the window, heard him say to the driver, "To the Opera."

The cab drove off into the night. The Persian had seen poor, unhappy Erik for the last time.

Three weeks later, *L'Epoque* published this obituary notice: "Erik is dead."

Epilogue

SUCH IS THE true story of the Opera ghost. As I stated at the beginning of this work, there can no longer be any doubt that Erik actually lived. So much evidence of his existence is now available that anyone can *rationally* follow his actions through the drama of the Chagnys.

There is no need for another description of the excitement that affair stirred up in Paris. The singer's abduction, Count de Chagny's death in such extraordinary circumstances, his brother's disappearance, the three members of the lighting crew found unconscious . . . What tragedies, passions, and crimes had surrounded the idyll between Raoul and the sweet and charming Christine!

What had become of that sublime, mysterious singer of whom the world was never to hear again? She was said to have been a victim of rivalry between the two brothers, and no one imagined what had really happened; no one realized that Raoul and Christine had disappeared because they had withdrawn from the world to enjoy a happiness that they would not have wanted to be made public, after Count Philippe's unexplained death. One day they had "taken a northbound train." Some day I too may take that train, to go and look around your lakes, O Norway, O silent Scandinavia, for the perhaps still living traces of Raoul and Christine, and also of Mama Valerius, who disappeared at the same time. And perhaps some day I will hear the solitary echoes of the Northland repeat the singing of the woman who knew the Angel of Music.

For a long time after the case was abandoned, unsolved, thanks to the unintelligent efforts of Monsieur Faure, the examining magistrate, the press still tried now and then to clear up the mystery, and continued wondering what monstrous criminal was responsible for Count de Chagny's murder and the disappearance of his brother and Christine Daae. A newspaper familiar with all backstage gossip was the only one that wrote, "Those crimes were committed by the Opera ghost." And even that was written in the context of the paper's usual irony.

The police had refused to listen to the Persian and, after Erik's visit, he made no further efforts to be heard. Yet he alone knew the whole truth, and he had the main proofs of it: they had come to him with the pious relics promised by Erik.

It rested with me to complete those proofs, with the help of the Persian himself. I kept him informed of my investigation day by day, and he guided it. He had not been back to the Opera for years and years, but he still had very precise memories of the building and I could not have had a better guide to help me discover its most secret parts. He also gave me sources of information and told me which people I should question. It was he who urged me to go and see Monsieur Poligny at a time when the poor man was almost on his deathbed. I had not known that his condition was so desperate. I will never forget the effect my questions about the ghost had on him. He looked at me as if he were seeing the devil. He answered only in brief, disconnected sentences, but they were enough to show—and this was the main thing—how much O. G. had perturbed his already agitated life (Poligny was what is called a pleasure seeker).

When I told the Persian about the meager results of my visit to Poligny, he smiled vaguely and said, "Poligny has never realized how much he was taken in by that incredibly vile Erik." (The Persian sometimes spoke of Erik as a god, and sometimes as a base scoundrel.) "Poligny was superstitious and Erik knew it. Erik also knew many things about the public and private affairs of the Opera."

When Poligny heard a mysterious voice tell him, in Box Five, about the use he had made of his time and his colleague's confidence, he did not question it. At first he was thunderstruck, as if he had heard a voice from heaven, and he thought he was damned; then, when the voice asked him for money, he finally realized that he and Debienne were victims of a blackmailer. Already tired of being managers for various reasons, they both left without trying to learn any more about that strange O. G. who had given them such a singular book of instructions. They passed on the whole mystery to the next managers, heaving a big sigh of relief and glad to be rid of a situation that had intrigued them without ever amusing them.

That was what the Persian told me about Debienne and Poligny. I then spoke of their successors and expressed surprise that in the first part of his *Memoirs of a Manager* Moncharmin gave such a complete account of O. G.'s doings, but said almost nothing about them in the second part. The Persian, who knew those memoirs as well as if he had written them himself, told me that I would find the explanation of the whole affair if I thought carefully about the few lines that Moncharmin did devote to the ghost in the second part. Those lines are also of special interest because they describe the simple way in which the business of the monthly twenty thousand francs came to an end. Here is the passage in question:

Concerning O. G., some of whose odd whims I have described at the beginning of these memoirs, I will say only one thing here, namely, that with one noble act he made up for all the trouble he had caused for my colleague and, I must admit, for me. He must have decided that there were limits to any practical joke, especially when it had cost so much money and when the police commissary had been brought into it, for just when we had made an appointment with Monsieur Mifroid in our office to tell him everything, a few days after Christine Daae's disappearance, we found on Richard's desk an envelope bearing the words "From O. G." in red ink and containing all of the rather large sum of money that he had succeeded in temporarily and playfully extracting from the managerial treasury. Richard immediately expressed the opinion that we should be satisfied with getting the money back and not pursue the matter any further. I consented to share his opinion. And all's well that ends well. Don't you agree, my dear O. G.?

Moncharmin continued, of course, especially after the money was returned, to believe that for a time he had been the victim of Richard's farcical sense of humor, and Richard never stopped believing that Moncharmin had amused himself by concocting the whole O. G. affair to get even for several practical jokes that had been played on him.

I asked the Persian what trick the ghost had used to make twenty thousand francs vanish from Richard's pocket in spite of the safety pin. He answered that he had not gone into that little detail, but that if I wanted to go and "work" at the scene of the incident myself, I would surely find the key to the mystery in the managerial office, bearing in mind that Erik had not been called "the lover of trapdoors" for nothing. I promised the Persian I would investigate the scene as soon as I had time, and I will now tell the reader that the results of my investigation were perfectly satisfactory. I had not expected to find so much undeniable evidence that the acts attributed to the ghost really took place.

The Persian's papers, those of Christine Daae, statements made to me by former collaborators of Richard and Moncharmin, by little Meg herself (the good Madame Giry has unfortunately passed away), and by La Sorelli, who now lives in retirement at Louveciennes—all these constitute documentary evidence of the ghost's existence. I am going to place them in the archives of the Opera and I would like it to be known that they are corroborated by several important discoveries in which I can justly take a certain pride.

While I was unable to find the house by the lake because Erik had blocked all its secret entrances (even so, I am sure that it could easily be found if the lake were drained, as I have several times asked the Fine Arts Administration to do*), I did at least

---

*I discussed that subject with Monsieur Dujardin-Beaumetz, our charming Undersecretary of the Fine Arts Administration, only two days before the publication of this book. He gave me some hope and I told him that it was the duty of the government to put an end to the legend of the ghost and establish the story of Erik on a solid foundation. To do so, it is necessary— and this would be the consummation of my own efforts—to find the house by the lake, in which there may still be musical treasures. There can no longer be any doubt that Erik was an incomparable artist. Who can say whether we may find the famous score of his *Don Juan Triumphant* in the house by the lake?

discover the Communards' secret passage, whose wooden wall
is falling to pieces in some places, and I also found the
trapdoor through which the Persian and Raoul went down into
the cellars of the Opera. In the Communards' dungeon I saw
many initials inscribed on its walls by some of the poor people
who were imprisoned there, and among those initials was
this pair: R. C. Is that not significant? Raoul de Chagny!
The letters are still perfectly visible today. I did not stop
there, of course. In the first and third cellars, I opened and
closed two trapdoors that work by a pivoting system unknown
to the Opera stagehands, who use only horizontally sliding
trapdoors.

Finally, I can say to the reader, with full justification, "Visit
the Opera some day, ask permission to roam through the building without a stupid guide, go into Box Five, and knock on the
enormous pillar separating that box from the stage box; knock
on it with your cane or your fist and listen up to the height
of your head: you will find that the pillar sounds hollow! And
after that, do not be surprised at the idea that the ghost's
voice could have come from there, for the pillar has enough
room for two men inside it. If you are surprised that no one
turned to it during the happenings in Box Five, remember that it
appears to be made of solid marble and that the voice inside it
seemed to be coming from the opposite direction, because Erik,
being a ventriloquist, could make his voice come from wherever
he chose."

The pillar is decorated with intricate carvings. I have hope of
some day discovering the piece of sculpture that could be raised
and lowered to enable the ghost to carry on his mysterious
correspondence with Madame Giry and give her his generous
gifts.

All this, which I have seen and touched, is nothing in compar-
ison with what a prodigious, fantastic man like Erik must have
created in the mystery of a building like the Opera, but I would
trade all those discoveries for the one I was able to make in
front of the administrator himself, in the managerial office,
a few inches from the armchair: a trapdoor as wide as a floorboard and no longer than a forearm, a trapdoor that can be
moved up and down like the lid of a box, and conceals an
opening through which I can easily imagine a hand coming

out to reach dexterously into the lower pocket of a swallow-tailed coat touching the floor. . . . That is the opening through which the forty thousand francs left and, with the aid of an intermediary, returned.

When I spoke about this to the Persian, with understandable emotion, I asked him, "Since the forty thousand francs came back, was Erik only joking when he gave the managers that book of instructions?"

"Not at all!" he answered. "Erik needed money. Feeling that he was outside the human race, he wasn't hindered by any scruples and he used his extraordinary gifts of dexterity and imagination, which nature had given him as a compensation for his ghastly ugliness, to exploit human beings in ways that were sometimes very artistic and often very lucrative. He returned the forty thousand francs to Richard and Moncharmin because he didn't need it at that time. He had given up his plan to marry Christine Daae. He had given up everything aboveground."

According to the Persian, Erik was born in a little town near Rouen and was the son of a masonry contractor. At an early age he ran away from his parents' house, where his ugliness made them regard him with horror and fear. For a time he exhibited himself at fairs, with a showman who presented him as a "living corpse." He must have crossed Europe from fair to fair and completed his training as an artist and a magician at the well-spring of art and magic: among the Gypsies.

A whole period of his life remained rather obscure. He was seen at the Nizhni Novgorod fair, performing in all his hideous glory. He was already singing as no one else in the world has ever sung; he showed his skill in ventriloquism and did amazing magic tricks that were talked about in caravans all the way back to Asia. That was how his reputation reached the Mazenderan palace, where the little sultana, the shah's favorite, was suffering from boredom. A fur merchant, on his way to Samarkand from Nizhni Novgorod, described the wonders he had seen in Erik's tent. The merchant was brought to the palace and questioned by the daroga of Mazenderan. Then the daroga was ordered to go off in search of Erik. He brought him to Persia, where for several months he had great power.

He was guilty of quite a few horrors during that time, for he seemed not to know the difference between right and wrong. He calmly took part in a number of political assassinations and used his diabolical inventions against the Emir of Afghanistan, who was at war with the empire. The shah took a liking to him. This was the time of the Rosy Hours of Mazenderan, which we have glimpsed in the Persian's story. Since Erik had highly original ideas in architecture and conceived of a palace as a prestidigitator might conceive of a "magic box," the shah ordered him to build a palace of that kind. He did so, and the result, it seems, was so ingenious that His Majesty could go anywhere in his palace without being seen, and disappear in ways impossible to discover.

When the shah found himself in possession of this gem, he followed the example of a certain czar's behavior toward the brilliant architect of a church on Red Square in Moscow: he ordered that Erik's golden eyes be put out. But then he reflected that, even blind, Erik could still build an equally extraordinary edifice for another sovereign, and that as long as Erik was alive, someone knew the secrets of the wondrous palace. He decided to have Erik killed, along with all the men who had worked under his orders.

The daroga of Mazenderan was charged with carrying out that abominable decision. Erik had done him a few favors and often made him laugh. The daroga saved him by giving him the means to escape. But he nearly paid for that generous weakness with his own life. Luckily for him, a corpse that was found on the shore of the Caspian Sea, half-eaten by seabirds, was successfully passed off as Erik's after friends of the daroga had dressed it in clothes that had belonged to Erik. The daroga escaped execution but was punished by exile and the loss of all his property. Since he was a member of the royal family, however, he was given a small income in monthly payments from the Persian treasury. He went to live in Paris.

As for Erik, he went to Asia Minor and then to Constantinople, where he was employed by the sultan. To give an idea of the services he could render to a sovereign haunted by all sorts of terrors, I need only say that it was Erik who built all the famous trapdoors, secret chambers, and mysterious strongboxes that were found in the Yildiz Kiosk palace after the last Turkish revolution. It was also he* who made automata, dressed like the sultan and exactly resembling him, that made people believe he was awake in one place when he was actually asleep in another.

He naturally had to leave the sultan for the same reason he had had to flee from Persia: he knew too many things. Then, tired of his adventurous, formidable, and monstrous life, he wanted to become someone "like everyone else." He became a contractor, like an ordinary contractor who built ordinary houses with ordinary bricks. He successfully bid on a contract for certain work on the foundations of the Opera. When he found himself in the cellars of that vast theater, his artistic, whimsical, and *magical* nature came to the fore. He was still as ugly as ever, and he dreamed of creating for himself a home unknown to the rest of the world, a home that would hide him forever from human eyes.

The reader knows most of what followed, and can guess the rest; it is implicit in this whole incredible yet true story. Poor, unhappy Erik! Should we pity him? Should we curse him? He asked only to be someone like everyone else. But he was too ugly. He had either to hide his genius or play tricks with it, when, with an ordinary face, he would have been one of the noblest members of the human race. He had a heart great enough to hold the empire of the world, and in the end he had to be content with a cellar. Clearly, then, we must pity the Opera ghost.

In spite of his crimes, I prayed over his remains and asked God to have mercy on him. Why did God make a man as ugly as that?

I am sure, quite sure, that I prayed over his remains the other day when they were taken from the ground at the place where phonograph records were being buried. His corpse had been reduced to a skeleton. I recognized him not by the ugliness of his head, for all men are ugly when they have been dead a long time, but by the gold ring he wore. Christine Daae had undoubtedly come and slipped it onto his finger before burying him, as she had promised.

---

*See the interview that Mohammed Ali Bey gave to the special correspondent of *Le Matin* on the day after troops from Salonika entered Constantinople.

The skeleton lay near the little fountain, where the Angel of Music first held the unconscious Christine Daae in his trembling arms after taking her into the cellars of the Opera.

And now, what is going to be done with that skeleton? Surely it will not be buried in a pauper's grave! I maintain that the skeleton of the Opera ghost belongs in the archives of the National Academy of Music; it is no ordinary skeleton.

BANTAM CLASSICS ✪ BANTAM CLASSICS ✪ BANTAM CLASSICS

Don't miss these classic tales of high adventure from master storytellers